Perfumed Dragons

The Adventures of John Grey
Book Eight

Perfumed Dragons

The Adventures of John Grey
Book Eight

Frederick A. Read

A *Guaranteed* Book

First Published in 2011 by
Guaranteed Books

an imprint of The Guaranteed Partnership
Po Box 12, Maesteg, Mid Glamorgan, South Wales, CF34 0XG, UK

Copyright © 1998, 2011 by Frederick A Read
Cover Illustration Copyright © 2011 by Jason Schndra

This Edition Copyright © 2011 by
The Guaranteed Partnership

All Rights Reserved, in Accordance with the
Copyright, Designs & Patents Act 1988

No part of this publication shall be reproduced in *any form*
without the *express written consent* of the publisher.

Frederick A Read asserts his moral right to be identified
as the owner of this work.

ISBN 978 1 906864 18 7

Typeset by Christopher Teague

Printed and bound in Great Britain by
CPI Antony Rowe, Chippenham and Eastbourne

www.theguaranteedpartnership.com

Chapters

I	Whereabouts Unknown	1
II	Predictions	15
III	Hard Pressed	27
IV	Beggars	40
V	Fiendishly Clever	54
VI	Water Falls	63
VII	Good Company	71
VIII	Taking a Ride	80
IX	Reporting for Duty	87
X	Orders	94
XI	An Old Custom	102
XII	Whistles	114
XIII	Tried and Tested	123
XIV	Incompetence	130
XV	No Excuse	139
XVI	Oops a Daisy	151
XVII	Fu Ming	162
XVIII	Dung	180
XIX	Lashed Up	197
XX	Junks	214
XXI	Hairy Moments	228
XXII	Questions	239
XXIII	Fathoms	250
XXIV	Surprise Packages	259
XXV	Nelson's Blood	273
XXVI	A Deal	277
XXVII	Decisions	287
XXVIII	Another Berth	296

Dedication

This is in two parts:

<u>One</u>

To the memory of a special Artillery Battery who fought and helped win the debacle at Peking during the 'Boxer Rebellion' known as 'The Dragon Battery', the only Artillery Battery ever to wear the Chinese 'Dragon motif on their uniforms. This Battery was stationed out in Hong Kong between 1957 and 1960, based at Sek Kong in the New Territories of Hong Kong. This Battery was the 127 Independent Field Battery and the senior Battery of the 49th Field Regiment Royal Artillery.

This was where I lived and attended the combined forces school called St Georges, where I had enjoyed several months with the Pupils of the school and where we, from the Sek Kong village, gave 4 performances of the pantomime 'Cinderella'. Alas since then, when each of us left to return back to the UK, we all went our separate ways never to meet up again.

So if there were any reader out there who lived in Sek Kong during 1959-1960 who took part in the pantomime then I would dearly love to hear from them again:
"Oh no he won't!"
"Oh yes he will!"

<u>Two</u>

My dedication in this part, is not only to the memory of all my 'shipmates' whom I served with in ships and submarines during my service in the Royal Navy out in the Far East, based at Singapore from 1962 to 1969, but also my frequent visits to Hong Kong and other exotic places around the Pacific several times during that time.

My memory dictates that from all that I experienced, underlines what I had been missing to be able to appreciate it during my time in Hong Kong as a youth. Oh to be a 'cherry boy' again!

Foreword

On nearly reaching the pinnacle of his career, John's euphoria has been tinged with sadness and a feeling of loneliness, at the prospect of having reached the parting of the ways between him and his two almost constant companions who had been together now for over 15 years.

Maybe their joint successes on the promotion ladders, and their close friendships were already destined from their first meeting on the fog-shrouded docks of Belfast.

Maybe it's the facts of life and the nature of being 3 very good friends, which sailors normally collect over their years sailing on the same ship, each prepared to give their lives for the others.

But fate has finally caught up with them, and stepped in to make its mark in all 3 of them

His experiences and those of his 2 special Huckleberry friends manifested itself when they were out in the mystical Orient, proving to be the main turning point between them and the individual paths holding their future lives they must now tread.

This was also John's wake up time for him to realise he is but one person in the relay of life within the many souls who share the same call of the sea, especially close friends on the same ship, no matter what trade he earns his salt by.

CHAPTER I

Whereabouts Unknown

"Here are your travel documents, tickets and the like. You will catch the next ferry over to the mainland and contact our office in the Victoria air terminal in London. Before you go, collect the green nylon mailbag from the doorman." the agent stated gruffly, thrusting a small brown paper bag into John's hands.

"What's all this in aid of?" John responded with equal abruptness.

"You lot are all the same! Swanning all over the world, only coming back as and when you feel like it. I wish I was able to have a few days off like you lot seem to get."

John looked at the man more closely recognising him as the one he had forgotten to have a word with, until this very moment.

John did not say anything, but went out into the foyer and dragged the nylon bag into the agent's office, then picking it up threw it at him with all his might.

"Here! Catch this you bastard! If you want a bloody holiday, then you can take this yourself. I've got all I need thank you!" John roared, as the surprised agent was knocked backward, out of his chair.

"In case you haven't read your instructions properly you ignorant bastard, I only came home to bury my father, and now on my way back to join my ship again." John shouted at the terrified looking agent.

"But! But!" the agent stammered.

"You must take this back with you. It says so in my book!" he managed to say in a querulous voice.

"Does it now! So why don't you take it! You've obviously nothing else better to do than insult us hardworking mariners. I'm off to catch my ferry, so unless you want, or are inclined to call a bloody strike then I suggest you get some other sucker to take it." John concluded angrily, as he left the office with a bitter taste in his mouth.

He didn't get as far as the front door of the building again before he heard whistles, shouting and two men ordering everybody out of the building.

"STRIKE! Everybody out! C'mon brothers, we're on strike! STRIKE! STRIKE!" the men shouted as they ushered John along with several other men out of the building.

"What's happened?" John asked the two burly men in total surprise.

"It's a STRIKE! STRIKE! Somebody has just called for a STRIKE, brother! Now I suggest you get yourself down to the picket line with the others unless you want to be tarred and feathered as a scab!" was the gruff reply from one of them as he shouted and emphasised the word 'strike'.

John allowed himself to be propelled out of the building along with several other seamen, but carried on walking past the rapidly forming strikers picket line and away from the scene.

'Bloody hell! Here's us working our balls and everything else off 'to keep the sea-lanes open' as Andy and Bruce would say, yet all the men back here are too busy striking at the drop of a bloody hat. Reminds me of the old days with the Lea line. Must tell the lads about this. Maybe they'll be warned not to come home until the so-called 'brethren' have stopped their nonsense. Still, maybe when that bastard of an agent realises that it was he who caused this upset, he'll not take the blame but find some excuse to fob the sack onto some other poor sod. Anyway, I'm an Engineer running engines of all sorts, not running a bloody pony express mail service.' John muttered angrily to himself, as he walked over the passengers' gangway and onto the ferry.

John arrived at the terminal and managed to locate his next contact, who was carrying a large card above his head with John's name on it.

"I'm Engineer Grey!" John stated as he tapped the shoulder of the tall, well-dressed, middle-aged man.

"Oh hello Grey! I'm Captain Karl Hopkins!" he said breezily.

"Had a good trip over from Belfast? Come into the office and meet the other crewmen who will make the flight with you." Hopkins chatted, leading John to a sparsely filled office at the back of the large Hughes, which was full of other would-be travellers.

"Yes thanks! I managed to leave the Belfast office in time before some strike or other was being organised. Haven't a clue what caused it, but here I am." John replied.

"Not another strike! Something must be done about all this striking nonsense. I blame it all on the Labour Union movement. One wrong word said somewhere and they're out on strike before you know it." Hopkins moaned.

"Tell me about it." John agreed, before he was introduced to six other men.

Hopkins gave a swift introduction between them, then stated as he was part of the management team but was to join a ship in Singapore, he would act as transit co-ordinator.

"Good for you, er Karl! I did that a while ago, going right across the States by train we were. Took us a good a week, it did." John remarked with a frown on his face.

"That's good John! Then you know all about the need to stick close. So listen up the rest of you." Hopkins replied, before he explained briefly what their travel plans were, and that each man was to ensure he had his passport and medical documents on him at all times.

He issued each man with an envelope that contained ready cash as spending money, but told them their wages or larger amounts of monies would be available for them when they arrived onto their respective ships.

John looked into his envelope and noted the several different currencies of different denominations, mostly of high values. But on seeing one of the other men's contents, he realised he got more, putting it down to the fact he was an officer and others weren't. He didn't say anything but made a mental note of it as unfair, until he had a quiet moment with Hopkins.

The eight men left the agency office and settled down with a duty free drink waiting until they were called to board the coach which would take them to the airport.

"This is my first flight John, and by the way you can call me Hoppy. I understand you've done a fair bit of air travel yourself, so what can I expect?" Hopkins whispered into John's ear, as he was sitting next to him.

"Nothing to it, er, Hoppy. Just take the piece of nutty the pretty air stewardess offers you, and suck it slowly until the little red sign above your head gets switched off. But I suggest you sit on the outside and let me have the window seat, in case you get some sort of a panic attack for you to want to jump off. Parachutes are not standard issue on these airlines, you know." John whispered back hiding a big grin with his hand.

Hopkins was quick to oblige before the stewardess came around with a tray full of candy she was giving out.

John looked out of the window watching the wings of the plane flap gently under the aerodynamic stresses and strains, almost as if the plane had to flap its wings to take off just like a bird does. He noticed the two very large propellers on the wing his side of the plane, had created a wind vortex, which seemed to create a wisp of smoke from each of them, likening it to the wake of a ship. The very large buildings he saw on the ground were just like dolls' houses now, and all the people coming in or out of it were almost ant like.

John looked around at Hopkins, who was crunching on his sweet nervously whilst keeping his eyes shut. He leant over and in a moment of devilment said in a loud voice

"Boo! This is angel Gabriel calling Karl Hopkins!"

Hopkins choked and nearly swallowed his sweet in surprise, but managed to open his eyes to see John grinning at him. He started to call John all the names under the sun he could think of, including several expletives, just to add to the flavour of his annoyance.

Nobody heard much of what was said as the engines were still making a loud noise before settling down to their rhythmic throbbing noise and for the passengers to get used to it.

"That'll cost you a very large whiskey Grey!" Hopkins snorted, managing to recover from his shock.

"Certainly Hoppy. In fact here comes the drinks trolley now." John replied with a smile, and ordered two very large whiskeys for them. The stewardess, who had seen and heard what happened between them, offered Hopkins an extra splosh of soda into his drink.

"Drink this down now sir, and I'll refresh your glass. Now you're no longer a virgin of flying, congratulations!" she purred, as she offered Hopkins his second drink.

"I don't mind if I do! Anyway, he's paying for it." Hopkins answered, receiving his second drink.

"No sir, it's free and gratis, as are all your meals and refreshments whilst on this flight."

Hopkins looked round at John, who pretended to look out the window at the carpet of clouds below them.

"Well fancy that! No doubt the rest of my party will warm to your hospitality. Thank you all the same." Hopkins said affably, as the stewardess moved down the aisle serving the rest of the passengers.

"You sir, are a reprobate! What are you?" Hopkins asked with a grin, turning to John who was acting the innocent, who also wore a large grin on his face.

"See I told you I'd get you a drink. In fact, you got two to my one." John chuckled.

"I can see we're going to have a long flight John Grey, now I'm no longer a virgin as that pretty damsel had put it. Come to think of it, I can't remember when I was a virgin last, can you? These air firms must be giving virgins away for free these days. Glad to be a sailor, what do you say?"

"Same here. Too long at sea to remember! Maybe we can get one of them duty free next time the trolley comes around." John responded with a grin.

This bit of banter finally broke the ice between the two men as they started to discuss various subjects, mostly nautical, while the plane droned its way over the lands and waters of the world.

The plane stopped several times to discharge some of the passengers or to take on fuel and more supplies. During which time, everybody flying to further destinations were required to disembark to wait in the transit lounges with free refreshments to enjoy whilst this was taking place. John managed to purchase some small trinket as a souvenir or send off a postcard, thus marking off the list of stops on the way.

Zurich, Rome, Istanbul, Karachi, Delhi, Rangoon, Kuala Lumpur, Singapore, before they go on to Hong Kong. Out of the eight men, two left at Istanbul, three were earmarked for Singapore, with the remainder going up to Hong Kong.

"Fasten your seat belts. We shall be arriving at Singapore airport in 20 minutes. All passengers leaving at Singapore are requested to ensure they take all hand luggage with you, and have your passports, visas, including your medical documents ready for inspection by Customs. We hope you enjoyed your flight and travel with us again. Thank you!" the Captains cultured voice announced over the intercom.

"This is where you get off Hoppy, but you didn't say which ship you were joining." John remarked.

"I should be joining the tanker *Castle Peak Bay*. But she's been delayed at Calcutta, so I'll have a few days ashore to kick my heels until then. What about you?"

"Mine is the tanker *Repulse Bay*, which should be arriving at Hong Kong in the next few days if my calculations are correct. I too will be able to have a chance to look around before joining her."

"Been out here before John?"

"Not up this far, but I've been around the Polynesian Islands and Australia. I understand the Orient is a magical place to visit, so I'm looking for some quality time before I swim back to Blighty again."

"I've been around the Far East for years now, from Karachi to Kobe. If there is one piece of advice I can impart to you, it is that you do not treat the locals with disrespect. Instead, try to learn their language, erm, mostly Cantonese Chinese, Malay or even Hindu, as you'll probably find it will come in mighty handy in some sort of a crisis when there's nobody around except yourself who is able to speak English. We're both fortunate in that respect as we're entering a part of the British Empire, which has English as the official language. As I'm able to speak those languages I've mentioned anyway, it doesn't matter much to me. Maybe that's why I keep being sent out here by the top management."

John reflected on what Hopkins had told him for a moment then suddenly remembered what Whateley had said in the Balmoral Hotel in Belfast.*

"Is it true that the company is trying to set up a Maritime college for Merchant Navy officers, here in Singapore and Hong Kong?"

"Now that you've mentioned it, yes. The lines' Board of Governors has already put my name down for the Hong Kong College, as it will be taking Deck Officers. The one in Singapore will be the Engineering side of it. I expect it's because there's a large ship building complex there in the making, which is part of the company assets, although they've got a smaller one in Hong Kong too. Mind you, if Singapore does its sums right, it will have the biggest shipbuilding yards this side of the world to rival those of the British shipyards of the Clyde, Tyneside, and even Belfast, let alone the Yank shipyards."

"Oh well! At least it explains what my shipmate friends and I were told a while ago. I'll be able to tell them when we meet up again, as it sounds an exciting prospect." John enthused, as they felt the plane touch down onto the warm soil of Singapore.

---

* See *Ice Mountains*.

"Here we are John. It will be pandemonium when we disembark. So in case I don't get the chance to meet you again, take care. See you around, if not in Hong Kong!" Hopkins said pleasantly as he shook John's hand in farewell.

"And you Hoppy!" John responded, as everybody got ready to leave the aircraft.

John arrived into the transit lounge to join up with the other passengers who were going on to Hong Kong, waving to Hopkins as he left the adjacent arrival lounge.

"Engineer Grey?" a voice asked from behind him.

John turned around to see a young man dressed in a light coloured suit with a gaily-coloured shirt opened at the neck to display a chunky gold chain.

"I am he. Who are you? State your business with me!"

"Never mind who I am. You will accompany me if you please. Your luggage will be taken care of. Just follow me out to the waiting car." the young man insisted.

"Sorry and all that mate, but I've got a plane to catch to meet my ship in Hong Kong. Tell your friends whomever they are, I'll take the day off meeting them." John said sternly.

"This is exactly why I have been sent to bring you to the company's HQ here in Singapore." the young man countered as he ushered John out of the transit lounge and through the customs area.

John walked out of the cool transit lounge into the humid heat of the tropics before he climbed into the relatively cooler vehicle, by virtue of the fact the windows were wide open to take advantage of the blast of air coming through them.

The ride through the dusty crowded streets was a short one, before John got out only to be ushered into a tall whitewashed building with palm trees around it as if to shade the building.

"You will wait here please." the man stated pleasantly, before disappearing seemingly into nowhere, leaving John standing in the middle of a domed hallway which had several electrical fans turning slowly around to keep the place cool from the ravages of the baking sun outside.

His wait was not long, before he saw a bearded man dressed in long flowing white garments, and a large towel wrapped around his head, which John took to be called a turban, who approached to offer him a large frosted glass of liquid.

He nodded his thanks and drank it down to quench his thirst.

The bearded man took the empty glass then disappeared into nowhere just like his courier.

Before long John heard two men coming towards him, talking as if they were on some afternoon stroll.

"Engineer Grey! Pleased to meet you! I'm Mr Stafford the senior manager for the company here, this is Mr Parfitt my director of operations." Stafford greeted cheerfully in a plummy voice, as they all shook hands in greeting.

"Pleased to meet you both I'm sure. But why have I been virtually abducted now waylaid thus stopping me from my company duties? I should have been on a plane bound for Hong Kong, so I can rejoin my ship the *Repulse Bay*." John responded civilly but feeling a bit miffed at this sudden course of events.

"Ah yes, the *Repulse Bay*! That's why we've brought you here. Sorry you feel as if you've been, shall we say, 'Shanghaied', but needs must in the given circumstances." Parfitt responded quietly, as he saw John's uncertainty and unease.

"What of the ship? Tell me now if you don't mind!" John snapped.

Stafford and Parfitt exchanged glances before Stafford spoke.

"You obviously have not been informed, so if you will accompany us to my office we can talk about it there." he started to say but was cut short by John.

"Cut the crap Stafford. Tell me what's wrong! I want to know now right this minute." John snapped, taking the other two by surprise.

Stafford looked at Parfitt again, who nodded as if in a silent agreement.

"It's like this Grey! The *Repulse Bay* no longer exists except for a pile of scrap. We have all the details for you if you care to come to my office." Stafford insisted in a hushed manner.

John looked dumbfounded at the two men, feeling a sense of foreboding.

"I think you'd better take me to your office. This had better be bloody good Stafford." John snarled, swiftly following the two retreating men.

They arrived into a well-appointed office obviously befitting a senior member of the management board.

"Kindly take a seat Grey! Dave, get the articles from the safe would you. Oh! Better get the steward to bring in Mr Dimple if you please." Stafford ordered as John sat down on a rattan ware chair next to its complimentary table.

"Before you start Stafford. First off! If your intonations and implications given to me are correct, I am to believe something has happened to her crew. If so, I am obviously concerned as I have two very close friends and others on that ship, and I want to know if they're okay.

Secondly how did a fine ship get reduced to a pile of scrap all of a sudden? Last by no means least, what happens now?" John said angrily.

Stafford seeing that John was obviously in a state of shock and agitation, tried to calm him down, as Parfitt arrived with a large brown envelope and a waiter close behind with a drink-laden tray.

John took the large glass of whiskey and soda then sat down next to the table, as Parfitt unrolled a large drawing of the ship, also had a list of the names of the crew on board.

"Now then, who are the friends you are concerned about?" Stafford asked soothingly.

"Marconi Radio officer Bruce Larter from Liverpool, and 3rd mate Andrew Sinclair from Fraserburgh." John replied woodenly. Stafford scanned through the list and identified them, then looked at another list before replying.

"This first list is the ships' enrolment of officers and crew which states your two friends were indeed part of the ships company. The second list is those who perished, but as they are not on it, then you can rest easy they are okay."

John stood up, grabbed hold of the two lists, looked first at the first one then looked at the second list to make sure, before he handed back the lists and grabbed the whiskey bottle from the table and took a large swig from it. He had that strange glowing feeling inside him and knew all would be fine. Neither of the other two men stopped him. Merely making sure John sat down safely again.

"That is one long list of victims, over half of the crew in fact, the others must be dockyard workers. I noticed Chief Engineer Alan Hodgson is on the second list. He was a good engineer, and I got on well with him. Captain Denton may be a loss to his family, perhaps even to the company as are the rest of the poor sods, but I care nought for them. But it seems there's one name missing from both lists, that of 3rd engineer Clarke. He too was a special friend of mine. So what has happened to him, considering was part of the crew for the so-called Islands run?" Stafford looked through some other sheets of papers for a moment before finding what he was looking for.

"It says here 3rd Engineer Clarke had been discharged from the ship on return to Brisbane, whereabouts unknown. Maybe he went back to his former company and is still in Brisbane."

John sat quietly for a long while as his memory recall was playing back all what happened and what was said between Clarke and him. Rapidly followed by his two close friends Larter and Sinclair, and finally about Chief Hodgson. Parfitt and Stafford waited patiently until John was able to absorb the implications of what had happened. Whilst they did so, they saw to it John had a fresh glass of whiskey and a cigarette to draw from whilst he tried to make sense of the tragedy.

"Okay then Stafford. I've sorted things out in my mind as far as my friends are concerned. Now tell me how all this happened if you please." John said quietly, after he had a few minutes to gather his thoughts.

Stafford briefly explained about an explosion in one of the empty fuel tanks, creating a fireball which spread quickly to other parts of the ship. It took several fireboats to get the flames under control before an ocean going tug came and towing it down into the bay, beached it so it would burn itself out without affecting or endangering anybody else.

"Did they mention the tug's name? Was it the *Mackenzie* by any chance?" John asked swiftly, listening intently while the drama was being told.

Stafford checked the reports then nodded his head.

"The *Mackenzie* it is! How do you know ?" Stafford asked with surprise.

"I'm glad it was, because Clarke was the Engineer on that vessel. Which is how you would have found where my friend Clarke was at the time, to take him into account. That means he is safe and well. Good for him!" John said, as he looked into his ever-full glass,

'Well done Aussie. Thanks for looking after our good friends Andy and Bruce.' He thought, feeling the warm glow slip away from his body.

"What is going to happen to the survivors now we have no ship? Do they get brought up here for onward flight back to Blighty and me along with them to be classed as DBS or have you got another assignment for us?" John asked with uncertainty.

"As it happens Grey, your two friends Larter and Sinclair will be stopping here and join you for a couple of days before they get another assignment. Sinclair should be joining the tanker *Castle Peak Bay*, and Larter to join the tanker *Deep Water Bay* for a while before he starts up a radio station here on the island. You'll be joining the freighter SS *Tsun Wan*, which is alongside in the naval base at Sembawang. The military gave us the contract to ferry stores, military hardware and the like for them, between here and Hong Kong." Parfitt stated, showing John the lines' ship movements all around the orient.

"With respect to you both, but we come in threes' not singly, if you get my drift. Larter, Sinclair and I have been together on the same ships for the best part of 14 years or more, and we don't intend getting split up even if we've got to join another line. In fact that is just what we did the last time we were threatened to be sent to all parts of the compass." John asserted, feeling better now from his shock news.

Stafford went over to his large filing cabinet, flicking through some folders before he picked out three of them.

"Here we are. What you see are the personnel files for Engineer Grey, Radio Officer Larter, and Deck Officer Sinclair. Now let us see just what's so special about you." he announced, offering Parfitt one to read.

Both men muttered and commented on and were suitably impressed by what they read, swapping files over to read them all.

"It appears that all three of you have been specially selected to join the company and your profiles are of superior quality. That you are all earmarked for our college project which is still in the process of being set up. It also states that you are to be utilised for the benefit of the company and independently from each other until this project is under way.

Which ultimately means, you will each join your separate ships as mentioned earlier. In the meantime, when your two friends arrive, you will be temporarily accommodated and in style, at our temporary repair base which the Navy lets us use as part of our contract with them." Parfitt concluded.

John nodded his acceptance of this, but asked about Hopkins whom he travelled with to come out here.

"You've met our Captain Hopkins, that's good. Then you'd best tell your friend, erm, Deck Officer Sinclair, that Hopkins will be his Captain on the *Castle Peak Bay* then hopefully in a few months, his senior instructor in the new college currently being built up in Hong Kong.

Unless you have any further questions for us, we have some other equally important details to see to, and for you to get yourself settled into your new quarters. You will have a trusted manservant who will see to your daily needs. By the way, this person is one of our ship's stewards temporarily off ship just like you.

If you need to go sightseeing then he is to go with you just in case you get lost. Come and see us tomorrow morning about 1100." Stafford said pleasantly, escorting John to the office door.

"Thanks for sharing my shock with me Stafford, and you Parfitt. It is much appreciated." John said in earnest, as Parfitt then Stafford smiled shaking John's hand farewell.

"That's okay Grey! That's what we're here for. Now have a good nosh up and get turned in, this heat takes a lot of getting used to. See you tomorrow." Stafford concluded, as John was ushered back out into the foyer where he saw his luggage waiting for him.

CHAPTER II

Predictions

SINGAPORE! The 'Lion City' of the Far East, is in fact, an island on the tip off the Malay Peninsula and is some 240 square miles of real estate, which Sir Stamford Raffles managed to lease from the neighbouring Sultan of Johore in the early 1800's. Almost a decade later it became a British Colony under the guise of the British East India Company, to be known as the Singapore Straits Settlements. It lies on the equatorial tropics which means it is always of a hot and humid place to live in, and prone to the heavy monsoons or the typhoons causing havoc all around that area of the globe.

It has many attributes, including a large natural harbour, which is amongst one of the busiest harbours in the world, with at least 400 ships per day paying their visits there.

The astuteness of Stamford Raffles was he could see that Singapore was destined to become a major business centre at the crossroads of Asia. Perhaps it was the reason why he managed to secure the island for his company and for the good of the British Empire.

It has a teeming population, mostly of Malay, Chinese, Indian and British European, governed by a British High Commissioner, but shortly to become a self ruled Parliament.

In the early 1920's and 30's the island was turned into what should have been an impregnable fortress, containing the largest Far East British Naval base and other military installations.

Yet it was the place that became the most ignoble and terrible debacle that was to be the biggest setback in the annals of British Military history including Dunkirk. For Malaya and Singapore had over 58,000 British or allied troops there, yet in this so-called impregnable fortress they surrendered to the invasion of a mere 15,000 invasion force of the Imperial Japanese troops in the early 1940's. Out of those 58,000 that surrendered, less than 5 percent survived to tell the tale, add to that, the deaths of millions of local and Chinese people at the hands of those murdering butchers of a so-called Japanese Imperial Army.

At the time of John's visit, there is a new vision of self rule being carved out by one single person and his followers, which will eventually, change the entire face of the island and its people. It is a place whereby shipbuilding, copper, rubber, tin, fruit, textiles or other products will make its people among the highest earners per head of population, in the entire world.

But for now, it is the new home for John and all those he will meet during his stay here, for the story of his life and times to recommence.

John stepped out of the taxi and entered a three-storey building, to be met by the same young man who had brought him to meet Stafford.

"Welcome to the Sembawang Harbour hotel, engineer Grey. I'm your steward both here and on board ship." he greeted pleasantly.

"That's fine by me, but what is your name?"

"Kim Soon. I'm my Father's number 2 son. I am the Chief steward, normally living on board with the rest of the crew. But the ship is undergoing certain modifications for its next trip, so I've been put here to help run the hotel." Soon explained.

"Maybe it shows you're a versatile young man Kim Soon. Now which cabin do I get to stay in?"

"You're up on the third floor on the east wing. Come I show you!" Soon replied as he grabbed hold of John's suitcase.

Soon opened the door to the room and went over to open the wooden shutters covering the windows.

John looked out of the window to see a panoramic view of the entire naval base, which was seemingly spread out just for his approval.

"My, what a grand view steward!" John declared as he scanned around the various buildings.

Soon stood next to him pointing out the various features, before he identified their ship.

John was taken aback when he saw the state of her.

"Bloody hell! It looks as if it came straight out of the history books. I mean, she's got a stovepipe of a funnel which looks as if it's about to capsize by the slant of it. Judging by the amount of canvas she has covering the decks, she must use them as secondary propulsion when the coal has run out no doubt. Unless I'm mistaken, she's got an open bridge in front of her extended wooden superstructure. She's even got bamboo derricks by the looks of her. When was she built, the 1880's or what? How do you manage to live in that relic?" John asked quickly in astonishment.

Soon looked angrily at John before he replied.

"She was built by my Uncles at their yard in Shanghai in 1929. She is only 285 feet long, a draught of only 8 feet as she was built to sail up and down the Yangtze River. Just to confuse you, she is high sided to at least 25 feet because she can be loaded up to the river mark of 2 feet from the deck. As her trading posts were always in the deeper parts of the river, she could always get away with it. Having said that, during the summer months when the river was low, she was restricted to the 15feet mark. But since the communists took over China we lost our trade, so we were forced to sail around the South China Seas looking for work, mostly on big rivers such as the Mekong. That was until we got the contract from this shipping company and the British Navy to freight for them. She might not look much to you but it is my home. My father was her Captain, my mother the ships purser, with the rest of the family sharing other duties on board,. I was born on her as were the rest of my brothers and sisters, although I'm the only one left on board for about four years now.

She can do a good 8 knots for at least ten days before refuelling. We can take several different types of cargo in one shipment including up to 20 full time passengers." he explained.

"Maybe a conducted tour around her might put things into

perspective steward. When is she due to sail?" John responded in a softer tone of voice.

"I would be delighted to show you around as I'm probably the only one left of the original crew who knows the ship well enough to do so. As for sailing her again will depend on how soon the ship can be refitted and loaded up. Maybe six to ten months, I don't know."

"Sounds great! Maybe I can get a few decent runs ashore and see the sights before I face another long swim across the extremely wet and lumpy stuff we earn our living from. By the way, I have a couple of very close friends arriving soon from Australia. Radio Officer Larter and 3rd Mate Sinclair by name. I would appreciate it if you'd see that they arrive at this address instead of elsewhere, and let me know when they're here."

"This can be arranged for you. Now in the meantime, as it's nearly dinnertime the dining room will be open soon but the bar is open all the time. On the wall there are the 'House' rules for you to observe. Here is the room phone just in case you need anything." Soon advised, as he showed John around the room and the facilities that were available to him.

John thanked him for his small tour and gave the steward his choice of evening meal, before the steward left him to his own devices.

'A coal ship getting modifications indeed, probably from steam coal to anthracite no doubt. Can't see any coal yards around the place though. Probably the Navy is giving it wood to burn, judging by the pile of logs next to her. Can't wait until I get on board to see her engines, even though they may be steam recips. Now that really would be going back to the classroom basics.' John mused as he stared out over the dockyard to his next ship assignment.

"Morning Engineer Grey! It's 0600. Breakfast is ready to be served. You have an appointment with Mr Stafford in his office at 1000, so I'll arrange for your transport for 0900. Here's your fresh laundry." Soon announced from the other side of John's room door.

"Morning Soon! Come in, the door's not locked." John called as he finished his wash and shave.

Soon breezed in and commenced to remove John's mosquito nets and generally tidy the room up.

"The shower wasn't working, so I've given myself a good wash down instead." John stated.

"Oh yes, sorry to tell you. We have water rationing during the night from midnight until about now. Suggest you have one after breakfast." Soon replied, handing John a spotless white shirt and shorts.

"Here's your official uniform whilst staying ashore. Try your shoes on, in case they need changing. You won't need your cap until you go on board, but you'll be issued with overalls by then." John thanked him as he got dressed, stating that the shoes were just fine.

"Where is the office of Stafford if it takes a good hour to get there?"

"The HQ is in the city along the Orchard Road. It's taking that long today because of the detour around the Simbang to Nee Soon area due to the new roads being built. You'll probably go through the naval base to join up with the other highway called the Bukit Timah road, but it's almost the same either way. I shall be with you anyway, so not to worry. Incidentally, we finish work at 1300, as Stafford has a special meeting later he will not keep you long."

"Sounds a busy day Soon. See you later then!" John said amiably as he walked out of his room and made his way to the dining room.

John's taxi arrived promptly at the very ostentatious facade of the shipping HQ which seemed to vie for the most prestigious façade on the whole of the most vibrant road Singapore had to offer the worlds leading entrepreneurs. It could be comparable to the same streets of London that has the Bank of England and the Stock Exchange as cheek by jowl neighbours.

"There you are Grey! Come in and sit awhile. The steward will supply your refreshment needs." Stafford invited, rising up to shake hands with John.

"Glad you're on time, as I'm expecting a visit by the Navy's dockyard Chief Superintendent any moment now. The reason why I've asked you to attend this meeting will be relevant when you meet him, and from what I understand, will put a lot of pieces into the jigsaw I have been trying to fit together for some time now. Perhaps all may be revealed to me, but I would request that you enlighten me on it all afterwards." Stafford informed in a civil tone, yet his face portrayed the look of a worried man.

John looked at Stafford's worried face, feeling and felt as if he was being put into a very difficult spot that perhaps he would not able to get out of, mentally listing several incidents which befell him earlier.

"I shall do my best not to let the side down Stafford, but it all depends on just who you are meeting." John replied, taking a large glass of fruit juice from the steward's tray.

John had only just sat down when he heard a very familiar voice then saw the familiar face of a man to whom he had written on several occasions since they last met.

John stood up to see the large figure of Fergus McPhee coming through the portals of the ornately decorated office.

"Fergus McPhee! My it's glad to see you!" John greeted in unison of McPhee's greeting.

"Hello John Grey! My you certainly know how to keep a man on his toes! Did you get my last letter? How are you dear boy? Understand you had a narrow escape on the *Repulse Bay*, glad you and your pals escaped." McPhee said rapturously, as both shook hands energetically in fond greetings.

Parfitt with a couple of others from the company who had also arrived and joined by Stafford, were mere bystanders as they stood in amazement to witness the mutual greetings these two men were sharing.

Stafford gave a gentle but discreet cough to draw to the attention of these two friends, others were present who needed to be included as part of the accepted gathering of the moment.

McPhee looked over to the inquisitive faces of Stafford and his colleagues, explaining to them he and John were old friends, and of how they met. He explained how John is looked upon as a future light in the annals of the Institute of Naval Architecture. Of how Stafford along with his shipping company would be able to benefit from John's uncanny insight to the problems of the shipping world of today. John just stood there letting McPhee extol his virtues, although he personally would have much preferred it to keep it all under his hat, such was the upbringing from his parents.

"So, Engineer Grey. It appears your company profile is a little, shall we say, understated. Let's hope the two shipmates you spoke about will be of the same calibre." Stafford said with a magnanimous smile, which betrayed the real inference that his voice was telling the listener.

John told McPhee about Larter and Sinclair's imminent arrival from Brisbane, of their different assignments, also of his own immediate future.

McPhee nodded or grunted when he accepted the facts as told and confirmed by Stafford, before he made his own predictions. Which in shipping parlance, meant that unless Stafford and his staff were prepared to make the appropriate changes to accommodate these 3 special friends, then the shipping company would lose a lot more than just the one ship.

"Not as bad as that surely, Superintendent?" Parfitt asked timidly

"The *Tsun Wan* is an old ship is in need of radical modifications, but you much prefer to spend your money on her rather than get a brand new one off the slips. Engineer Grey here would, and no doubt about it, perhaps save you several thousands not only on these modifications, but by getting that ship out at sea, earning her keep, long before your lot can deliver the paperwork." McPhee declared, as he helped himself to a large glass of whiskey taking the time to splash some soda into it.

"Not so fast Fergus! I've not had the chance to board her yet, but it could all be possible once that has been done." John admitted quietly, as he too helped himself to a glass of the golden whiskey.

McPhee looked at the uncertainty and felt the hesitancy Stafford and his staff was showing, before he rammed home his slight advantage of the situation.

"Come now gentlemen. I know of the *Tsun Wan,* her makers and her past history. At present she is a total liability and because of her reputation as a Jonah ship, nobody from the Oriental mariners fraternity would want to sail in her again. All of which means you will be hard pressed to get a crew on board to sail her around the oceans, let alone around the islands. It is up to you to make your company decisions, but as the current Naval Dockyard Manager, you will be well advised to listen to my advice if you ever want the *Tsun Wan* to make its money after her current expensive refit." He advised with sincerity.

John was sitting quietly at a large table laden with charts and maps of the entire area of the countries sharing the same coastline of the largest sea in the world, the infamous South China Sea. He noticed symbols which appeared to dot all over the map and deduced that they were in fact, the ships of the company. One such symbol had a red box around it with a special marking to differentiate it from all the rest, and on closer inspection, it gave the name *Tsun Wan*. He didn't say anything to comment about his discovery, but noted what McPhee had said about getting a crew together.

John suddenly sensed there was an uncomfortable pregnant pause, before Stafford managed to break the silence.

"No doubt you have infinite knowledge of the ship and background knowledge of engineer Grey. But as we own both, it would be polite of you to bow to our policy and judgement making powers of perception of the problems in hand. However,

McPhee, your comments are duly noted." Stafford responded diplomatically, but was clearly annoyed with the boldness of McPhee to try to insert his own authority onto the matters that were of the shipping lines, nobody else's.

"Indeed Mr Stafford! My apologies for pointing out certain matters that might otherwise have been missed." McPhee replied, with a nod of his head.

"Now to the matter in hand. What is it we are about to do for you Mr Stafford?" McPhee asked in a more conciliatory tone of voice.

Stafford along with his other colleagues poured over the several diagrams and ships drawings, mentioning all the things which needed to be done, how and when. John sat there watching them quite unconcerned as to what was taking place, but listening intently to what was being said.

'A lot of hot air and still they can't grasp the simple solution to the problem. If it were me.' John muttered to himself, forcing himself against getting involved with what was becoming a heated debate.

"Excuse me gentlemen! If you're finished with me I'd like to leave you to your obvious differences of opinion on what seems to me a very simple matter." John said aloud during a lull in the debate.

McPhee turned round to see John about to leave them and called him back.

"It seems gentlemen, we forgot one of our visitors. It appears that as he's listened to us squabbling amongst ourselves, he has managed to formulate a simple solution to the problem. I vote we give him a chance to speak up to see just where we place our arguments." McPhee announced, as he beckoned John back to the table.

"Come John! What have you concluded that would put an end to the problems?" McPhee asked in a soothing tone of voice.

John sighed then pushed his way into the circle of men crowding the large technical drawings of what he managed to recognise as the layout of the *Tsun Wan*.

Taking a pencil from the hand of Parfitt he drew lines across the drawings, whilst offering an explanation to each mark he made. When he had finished, the original plans were almost obliterated by his pencil marks, so he grabbed hold of a clean sheet of paper and re-drew the entire area of the discussion, before throwing it back onto the table for the rest of them to look at.

McPhee and one of the other men looked closely at the drawings, comparing them with what they had offered, before McPhee spoke out.

"It seems as if John has created a special asbestos lined bulkhead that annexes the coal bunker from the boilers. These coalbunkers to be converted to hold FFO (Furnace fuel Oil) with the supporting pipes installed to feed the boilers like a normal oil burner would have. He has not altered the engines only the boilers, and even then merely to ensure special inlet and discharge pipes to accommodate the flow of liquids both in and out of them, including the modified condenser. The cold water would then be returned to the evaps for re-use, thus to cut down the need for polluted seawater from the intake valves. His formulae for the cubic capacity of the engine is rough considering he has not seen the engines for real, but they could be adapted to suit nevertheless." McPhee crowed, as he explained John's workings.

John was looking at a large detailed map of the Orient, and of the large clusters of the island he had sailed around only a few weeks ago, yet seemed such a lifetime away. His eyes focused on Taraniti, which made him almost see the place and the people. TeLani, King Phatt, Joe Tomlinson, Aussie Clarke and a confusion of other such memories that were flooding into his brain, before he was brought back to reality, by the voice of McPhee.

"C'mon John Grey, don't be shy! Expand your theory on these doodles of yours!" McPhee said triumphantly, in harmony with all the others.

John went over to the table again and picking up one of his doodles, looked at them closely, before he threw it back onto the table.

* * *

"I'm but a 2nd Engineer, and that's all I can tell you until I've had a good look at the exact problem facing you on board. In other words, I cannot offer any more until then. You would perhaps take only a few months to complete what's on those drawings, but what's the point of all this expense, especially when it would take you forever to get a crew together to man the ship." John stated flatly.

"Just a few months Grey?" Parfitt asked quickly.

"Something like that, unless you happen to have strike-happy dockyard mateys working here, or you've got a half day working period as well." John sneered.

"We don't have strikes out here John, too many local men looking for a days work preventing it.. They work as long as we want them to, providing we're there with them just so they don't disappear into the heat of the day." McPhee said abruptly, but with a grin on his face.

"Besides, all we do is make sure they have an extra bowl of rice and they put all their tools back into the lockers again to ensure they don't rob us blind. No tools no work is their motto." McPhee added.

"Whatever Fergus! I'm already assigned to the ship so it really doesn't matter to me one-way or the other. Just as long as I have a decent bunch of stokers to rely upon then the work gets done." John riposted as he stood up, starting to leave again.

"Quite right Grey!" Stafford agreed civilly, moving over to accompany John to the door.

"You will go on board the ship in the morning to take over from the Dockyard Engineer. Some of the other senior engineers from the dockyard and I will come to see you around 1100 so you can put into reality what your drawings seem to imply. Have a good run ashore and keep out of trouble. Don't want one of our engineers missing on his first day on board now do we. Mind you take Kim Soon with you." he added with a smile.

"Yes John! See you 1100. Don't forget the customary hospitality when I arrive." McPhee said with a large grin and a glint in his eye.

John smiled at McPhee and nodded.

"Maybe we'll have more than the usual hospitality if my two friends arrive today, Fergus. See you then Stafford." John concluded then walked down the cool corridor towards the foyer of the building.

CHAPTER III

Hard Pressed

"**Morning** Engineer Grey! Breakfast will be served in fifteen minutes. Here's your clean laundry. I shall meet you in the foyer to take you down to the ship." Soon announced quietly, as he entered John's room.

John woke up with a start and started to climb out from behind his mosquito net, getting tangled up in it in the process.

"Morning Soon! Can't seem to get the hang of these bloody things. I'd rather do without them if it's all the same to you." he grunted, as Soon came to extricate him from the netting.

"I think that is a wise decision, as it's a lot less fuss for me every time I wake you up in the mornings." Soon said with a smile.

John noticed the smile, but said nothing, save for thanking him for helping out.

"We certainly had a good night in the Navy's dockyard NAAFI club, those king prawn and mayo banjos were superb. Better than the stuck up sods at the Officers mess with their tuna and cucumber sarnies, what do you say steward?"[*]

"My Cousin How Ling is the head barman there, who took kindly to your fellowship with me. It is a good omen for you which you must build upon when you get onto the ship." Soon replied enigmatically.

"Well I don't know about your life steward, except what you've allowed me to know, but as I keep saying, I'm only here to do a job as best I can, and I'm leaving the building to others."

"No man is an island 2nd. You will be joining my ship as the engineer, but you will need friends or close allies to be able to conduct your business on board it, especially at sea. I am your manservant granted, but I will not always be around when

---

[*] Banjos are baguettes filled with whatever filling you wanted.

something happens on board. That is why precious few, if any of you English officers are prepared to sail on it."

John looked at Soon's face for a moment, hoping to gain some sign from it, but found nothing.

"I do not take kindly to implied or real threats towards me steward. If just one person so much as interferes with my work then he or she will find themselves in deep shit right up to their eyeballs and beyond. I need dedicated engineers who are competent and capable of understanding what their job requires off them. From this place be they Chinese, Indian or even European, any one of them not filling the bill will be put ashore, that is a promise. As for the rest of the crew, that is up to the Captain to deal with. And that dear steward, is not a threat but a promise." John replied coldly, then added offhandedly.

"On the other hand, if it's your ship and it's all down to you who gets to sail on her as crew, that's fine by me. But tell all those whom you choose as the crew what I've just said, and I won't take any rice bowls off them providing they do their job as per my instructions."

"I cannot guarantee a problem free voyage 2nd, I can only do my best." Soon admitted.

John finally saw some recognition of what he told Soon, by using his relaxed body language decided to conclude this very awkward situation.

"Good! That is all we English Officers ever require. Any funny stuff and they're over the side without a sampan and their chopsticks shoved right up their arses. One last thing before I go. I think you and me have just had an understanding which should see us both happy. It is now up to you to keep it that way. Oh and by the way! For your information, I happen to be Irish, not English." he said quietly as he nodded his head to accentuate his meaning, then left the steward to his duties.

John strolled out of the dining room to the foyer and bought a local paper from the receptionist, to read during a quiet moment.

He sat in one of the rattan chairs under one of the large rotating fans which kept the place cool, and spotted a blue and white bus with the bold letters of RN on the side, arrive outside the building. He never gave it a thought save to remember that he was in a naval base after all, started to read his paper whilst enjoying a good after breakfast cigarette.

"If there's one thing that we can't stand it's a long haired engineer. Get yer 'air cut laddie!"

"Yes, especially one lounging around like a stuffed dummy!" two loud voices called out from behind him.

John dropped his paper as he stood up, then turned to answer the very familiar voices of his two friends.

"Bruce! Andy! I really am glad to meet you two reprobates again." John said happily, embracing them both in turn.

"Now now then John! What would the neighbours think!" Sinclair said softly, as he shook John's hand energetically, as did Larter.

All three were obviously delighted to see one another again, as their own special brand of banter started to flow once more, with John leading them to the dining room to have something to eat.

Whilst the two arrivals ate their breakfast, John told them what the company had in store for them, but they had a few days grace before anything happened.

They sat talking for quite a while until Soon came to take John to his ship.

"This is our Chief steward Mr Kim Soon. He is what I might call, Mr Fix It, who will arrange all your cabins, dhobying and such like, won't you erm Kim! Anyway must go now. I'll see you here in the bar at about 1300." John explained as he left with his friends waving him off.

"They are my two friends I told you about. We have sailed on many a ship, through many a storm and tsunami. Been in the deserts of Africa together and even on the *Ice Mountains* from the white continent of Antarctica. Yet as soon as we all arrive at the exotic and mysterious Orient, we get spilt up and put onto different ships. So you see, it does not pay to build things up when it is not you who controls your own destiny." John explained, as the two men walked through the bustling dockyard.

"If it is of any consequences to you 2nd, but I happen to know that so far, you're the first officer to be assigned to the ship. My sources tell me no other officer has volunteered to join her due to her reputation as what you people call a 'Jinxed' ship. In fact, I too am hard pressed to recruit suitable crew members." Soon admitted with a worried look.

"It seems we have now got a common purpose which will perhaps suit both our needs, steward.

I'll get the officers if you get the crew. Between you and me, we will have a good ship to be proud of once again. You wait and see!" John replied confidently, as the two men stepped into a launch that would take them across the river to the creek to where the ship was berthed.

No sooner had the launch pushed off from the jetty when John heard a string of curses and some rattling from the stern of the launch, so went back to see what the problem was.

"Stokes, I thought you fixed the bloody gear. The chain's come apart again, and we're about to stand into the way of the *Antares* which is due out of the KG5 dock any minute now." the coxswain cursed.

John looked at the offending chain, and at the gear to see what could be done.

"Bosun, erm Coxswain, whatever you call yourself. I'm an Engineer officer. Have you got a lanyard of some sort I can use?" he enquired.

"Yes sir! But this is an Admiralty launch, with standard Kitchener gear steering fitted. You'd need galvanised chains to operate it through the ratchets." came the offhanded reply.

"Unless you are prepared to be run down by the bloody great heavy cruiser coming straight for us, then issue us all with lifejackets and you can just bloody well fix it yourselves." John snarled as he turned his back on them, starting to return to his place in the launch.

The hapless stoker came after him and told him he had some chains attached to a small davit for stores handling, but it might be of a different size to what's fitted.

"Right, stokes! Get it stripped off then bring it to me in the stern. Be quick about it." John ordered, going to the stern of the launch to see to the broken gears.

He took off some of the unaffected chain to thread it through the ratchet, then with the much thicker chain the stoker gave him, he attached it to the buckets that was part of the Kitchener gears. Once he tied the lanyards around the two ends of the chains he told the coxswain to turn the gear handle slowly one way then the other, before he was happy all would be well.

"Right then coxswain. You can now proceed forward, but take it very slowly when your reverse the buckets to stop the launch. The ratchet chain is fine, but the lanyard attached to the other end will only last a few times before it snaps." John explained.

The passengers in the launch were getting quite agitated, some even jumping overboard trying to get out of the way of the skyscraper sized lump of warship that was rapidly bearing down on them.

The launch managed to get clear in time before the mighty bows of the heavy cruiser swept into the very space they had occupied only a few seconds ago.

Everyone in the launch held their breaths and watched in awe as the grey mountain of steel passed only feet away from them, were more than relieved the launch had reached the safety of the landing jetty where they all got off feeling quite shaky from their ordeal.

"I say there! Well done that man. Would you mind awfully if you gave me your name." a posh English voice asked as John stepped ashore.

John looked around to see a Royal Naval officer coming towards him.

"Why? Haven't you got one of your own?" John asked sarcastically.

"I'm Commander Hughes, Doug to my friends.. That was my ship you managed to get out of the way of. May I ask who you are, to make a very timely intervention on our behalf?" the man persisted.

John sighed, looking at Soon before he turned to Hughes.

"I'm 2nd Engineer Grey. That is my new ship you see over there." John replied wearily, as he pointed out to the rusty and decrepit looking *Tsun Wan*.

Hughes looked to where John pointed to and sneered in disgust at the sight of it, but turned to John giving him a big smile.

"It appears that your ship is in need of a good Engineer, Grey. Hope it works out for you. The thing is, in appreciation for your swift action which saved all on the launch from a ducking, I would take it kindly if you would come aboard my ship some time this evening for a round of cocktails. Say around 1700. The *Antares* will be astern of the two cruisers *Herald* and *Valour* down at the No 2 basin, so come aboard and ask for me. Bring a couple of your friends if you wish to, the more the merrier." Hughes said breezily.

"That is kind of you Hughes, I will. I shall be bringing two other officers and my steward here with me, if that is okay with you."

Hughes looked down his nose at Soon starting to make some objections.

"If Mr Kim Soon, the erstwhile owner of the S.S. *Tsun Wan* cannot come then so be it. Otherwise it's good day." John said sharply, and left Hughes with a distinctly red face.

Soon had listened to all that was said but walked silently alongside John until they reached the steeply sloped Med ladder which they had to climb up to get onto the ship.

"Here we are 2nd. Welcome to my home, even though it might not look much to you." Soon announced, leading the way up the ladder.

They arrived on deck for John to see most of the decking had been removed, there was lots of equipment strewn across the place, making it difficult to walk over.

As John picked his way over the deck he noticed a large hole in the back of the superstructure, so went over to look down into it.

Soon came back to escort him safely into the superstructure and into the main accommodation area which had the dining room, saloon, and cabin area.

"This is where I choose to start your tour of the ship 2nd. I'll be back with a nice cool drink each." Soon said politely, then left John to look around him.

Soon arrived back carrying a tray with some large frosted glasses full of beer.

"Here we are 2nd. Just what Dr Woo ordered." Soon declared, handing John a glass, then took one for himself.

"I can see why you were proud of your ship. She must have been one lovely ship in her day. Still, not to worry. If my plans work out, then the dockyard will make her better again and be much faster than before. But first she must have her sanitation arrangements sorted out and some sort of temporary living quarters if we're to stay and work on board full time"

"What do you mean 2nd?"

"This is a Chinese ship with an Asian sanitation system, which needs to be adapted for European use. That is to say, from Asian 'squat down' toilets to European pedestal toilets. If we're to have a split European Asian crew on board then the toilets aft will be fine for the Asian crew, but the bridge superstructure for British crew. " John said amiably as he took a large slurp from his glass.

"Yes, I see what you mean. As it happens the ship does have a western type of toilet in the passengers lounge, but was always locked up. It's the only one on board in fact, maybe we'll use that for now."

"How long has the ship been alongside?"

"In this creek for nearly a year now, but before that she was down next to the breakers yard for another two years."

"Hmmm! Then our first priority is to have the entire ship cleaned and disinfected before we do anything else. I'll get onto Mr McPhee about that" John said, as he accepted yet another drink.

"We're expecting Stafford and Parfitt plus a few from the Shipwrights workshop around 1100. Time enough for us to enjoy this treat and a quick look around before then."

When they had finished their beer, Soon took John up to the bridge to show him the for'ard part of the ship, before taking him along the lifeboat deck and down to the stern of the ship.

He was surprised to find that she still had an emergency steering wheel on the poop deck, complete with a set of engine telegraphs and binnacle.

But when he finally got down into the engine room to see the dirty state of the place, even though he made allowances for the coal hoppers, he was furious..

"No wonder nobody wants to sail in this ship. It would take a month of Sundays just to scrape away the muck and filth. Are you sure there's steel decking below my feet Soon? Judging by the coal dust and the large hole in the deck-head, I'd say she had an explosion of some sort. This is exactly what I said earlier about getting the ship safe and in a hygienic working set up." John raged.

Soon nodded his head, but steered John towards the large steam engine with its two boilers that were almost gleaming compared with the rest of the compartment.

John gave a quick inspection of them, making mental notes of the features that were earmarked for scrap or modified for new usage.

"I've seen enough Kim Soon. Better get back up to the saloon to meet the others." John shouted, as they climbed out of the seemingly black hole at the centre of the ship.

When they got back, Stafford, his gang and McPhee who was the first to speak on their behalf, met them.

"Morning John! Judging by the soot on your clobber you've

already been down the engine room, to see if your drawings would match up with what you saw on the ships diagrams." McPhee said affably.

"Morning gentlemen. Yes Fergus, something like that. Mr Soon here was kind enough to give me a sneak preview before we got down to business. Although I have to admit I was not expecting such a poor set up all the same. There's still a lot of coal dust around the hoppers causing me to worry a bit. This ship needs a thorough clean throughout before I or anybody else occupies it." John responded.

"In that case, make that our first job on the list. Now gather round everybody, let's get down to business." McPhee announced, as he unrolled a large sheaf of ships drawings onto a dusty table.

They went through the modifications, with John stating what needed to be done if certain other fitments were also to be augmented and McPhee or his deputy were agreeing with what he said.

During one of the refreshment breaks, John explained to Soon that he was due to meet up with his two friends, but asked him if he would fetch them over to the ship, seeing as he would be quite some time.

Soon agreed, leaving to do his errand, returned shortly with Larter and Sinclair, who, on looking around the ship, were amazed by the state of the ship.

When they arrived they were introduced to the other senior dockyard officers who would be involved with the ship, but were recognised by McPhee.

"Glad you two made your remarkable recovery gentlemen, the BMH certainly has some lovely caring nurses to look after you, especially if it was a tasty nurse Sandra Hodgson I think her name tally said. No doubt you two are here to see just what beast you have to tame and get back into harness again." he said affably, causing Stafford and Parfitt to frown at his statement.

"We don't know about that McPhee, but judging from what we've seen, compared with this ship, the *Repulse Bay* is in a better state even though it was a total burnt out wreck." Larter opined.

"No, these two are earmarked for other duties. Only Grey here has been assigned so far." Parfitt said quickly, adding his tuppence worth into the conversation.

"As a matter of fact Parfitt, I happen to know this ship will be hard pressed to get even a ships' cat to sail on her. I mean, just look at the filthy stinking state she is in. Would you fancy staying on board her for more that two hours at a time? These three officers are good friends would sail anything that floats including a ruddy big iceberg, just as long as it doesn't sink under them. So if these three officers were to volunteer to become part of your Officer compliment on board then not only have you halved your crew of officers manning problems in one go, but have gained three out of the four needed to sail this or in fact any vessel. Mr Soon is still the official owner of this vessel even though he no longer has a crew, but no doubt he can get some men together to man her when she sails. In the meantime, we've got a mountain of work to do on her before that happens, starting with the decontamination of the ship.. I can provide a full time, 24 hour working gang to get her seaworthy with perhaps a new coat of paint to make you proud you've decided to take this ship back under your company payroll." McPhee stated authoritatively.

Soon nodded his head and advised them of his ongoing selection but needed the company officers approval.

Sinclair squared off his shoulders telling them he would relish the challenge of getting the ship turned round and back to sea again, quoting several warships he had served on that had been severely damaged during the war but were quickly repaired and back in action again.

"I cannot do it alone mind you, so I'd need the office of Mr Springle here to sort out the, shall we say, all the little details etcetera!" Sinclair opined with a nod to Springle, who merely responded with own nod of approval.

Larter stated he could use the ship as his floating Radio station, adding that he would rather use this ship with his friends on than any shack ashore.

"I state this, providing the support from your Electronics supervisor, er, Mr Westwood, can give a hand. He'll sort out your nav aids, main transmitter installations etc."

"This can be arranged Mr Larter, but let me sort out a suitable work schedule for it first though." Westwood said with a smile.

Stafford and Parfitt looked disdainfully at each other, sensing this was some sort of mutiny or a plot being set up by the three friends, and told them in no uncertain terms what they felt.

One of the dockyard Engineer supervisors sighed, turned to McPhee to give an angry announcement.

"Chief! I am here to discuss possible dockyard assistance in getting this vessel out of the naval dockyard and back to wherever it came from, not to become embroiled in a political argument between officers of a shipping line. Now unless we have progress on this singular subject then my department will withdraw its support, which means this ship will be forcibly towed away and scrapped for us to reclaim some of the already sky high cost it has incurred already."

"Indeed Mr Bishop! Seeing as your team will be responsible for installing the boilers etc." McPhee said with a slow nod of head adding his own comment, and even offered a workable solution for Stafford and Parfitt to agree upon.

Both Stafford and Parfitt withdrew from the gathering talking animatedly between themselves for several minutes before they came back to offer their deliberations.

"We agree to the terms of all three officers being allocated to this ship, with the proviso for them to be in attendance on board during all important works or improvements being carried out. More to the point, for them to live and remain on board during this refit period.

As for the innovations or other modifications conducted on board, we have no objections to them being carried out, with your guarantees written on paper that everything is under warranty and that the ship can sail with full Maritime Safety and

Registry requirements in place. We will need this ship to be ready for sailing within 14 weeks as of today, if not then financial penalties will be imposed upon the dockyard management as stipulated by our main HQ." Stafford stated pompously.

It was McPhee's turn to remind them quite bluntly as to who decided what work schedules were being operated. He reinforced his own criteria that the ship would not sail until he was satisfied with it and that the shipping company signed the ship Acceptance Form when the trials were duly completed.

The heat of the debate was almost as fierce as the afternoon tropical sun, Soon brought in some iced drinks for them all to cool down and have a breather. This was also the time for everybody to take stock of the horse-trading with various agreements made during the several hours they were on board.

The proceedings eventually reached a happy conclusion as everybody felt they had something out of it all, including McPhee.

"John, come over to my office in the morning for us to sort out some suitable equipment for you. I'll get a couple of donkey boilers set up for you to have your hot water system going at least. You're already connected up to the dockyard electrical supply, the fresh water and salt water system for the ship's sanitation system etcetera. There's an old frigate laid up for disposal in the nearby creek, maybe we can salvage some furnace plumbing and the like from it. Make it about 1000, but confirm your arrival with my deputy here as he's usually in around 0700. Mr Stafford, you have got 3 very good officers to see that your ship will be completed on time.

You will however need to support them in whatever way possible, and I mean support them to the hilt including getting your crew together.

Mr Parfitt, I suggest you start getting a contract together for when the ship sails. See the army Brigadier wallah, erm Thomas I think his name is. He is in need of a lift to bring some of his heavy armour and guns from here up to the north of Malaya around Kota Bahru, I think.

The Admiral Crawford is the top military brass around here, but can't spare any of his own ships right now, so it looks as if this one will do nicely thank you very much. By the way, I shall be in close contact with this ship, as I too need it to be shifted so that I can build a new Submarine Depot and their Support Unit." McPhee concluded, as everybody started to leave the ship.

John nodded his agreement to McPhee, then thanked everybody for turning up, before he too left the ship with his two friends.

"We've been invited on board that heavy cruiser down there. Got to be there for 1700, with the time now being 1530. Let's get to the hotel, and clean ourselves up and attend, we can always make our official boarding of the *Tsun Wan* in the morning." John announced.

"Hob nobbing with the Pusser again are we?" Sinclair teased.

"Just how did you manage that, is what I want to know?" Larter asked, as he scratched his head.

Soon briefly explained what happened on the launch, the verbal exchange between John and Crawford, for him to be included in the invitation despite Crawford's reluctance to accept the idea.

"We'll go and show him just how we civvy sailors conduct ourselves, you included steward, or should we say Mr Kim Soon." Sinclair responded with bravado.

Soon looked at the three friends for a moment realising that these were in fact three very good men who he needed to get his ship back into commercial trading again. Thanking them, he led them off the ship then back to the hotel where he got them all organised and ready for their visit.

CHAPTER IV

Beggars

"**M**orning 2nd, time we had breakfast and left for the ship. I've been given a report for you off the Sanitation Department." Soon greeted breezily, as he opened the curtains to let in the early morning sunlight.

John sat up slowly stretching himself before he got out of bed and made his way to the showers.

"Yes Mr Soon. 'Fraid you're right. Today's our first official day, lets hope the other two are up and about as well." John replied sleepily, taking the neatly typed report off Soon and read its contents before went and stood under the cold spray of the shower and bathed himself.

"They've been seen to by the other stewards, but I'll get all your things packed whilst you're at breakfast. I have a 'tilly' arranged to take us to the jetty and a small launch to take us across."*

"Well let's hope this one can go directly across instead of trying to dodge ruddy great lumps of floating metal in the middle of the harbour. Which reminds me, kindly contact McPhee's deputy for me and tell him I might be slightly late, due to my transfer over to the ship. And thank him for his swift work on the sanitation plumbing and tanks."

"I shall do so, and have his launch pick you up from the ship to take you McPhee's office.

As I have been given my status as ships purser back from the company, it means that I shall be signing all three of your articles at the same time when we arrive on board."

"Purser! Congratulations Mr Soon! But what of your stewards job that you're doing now?"

---

* The real name is a Utilicon van, but called a 'Tilley' and was a Bedford van with side windows and sliding doors that can be adapted to carry either up to 8 passengers plus their luggage, or half a tonne of stores.

"For now, I am that too. In fact, I shall be coming on board as well to look after you three until the end of the refit. That is my choice and so it shall be."

"In that case I thank you for your loyalty Mr Soon. By the end of the refit you will perhaps change your mind about some of us English officers, although some of us are of Scottish, Irish or even Welsh descent. Anyway, let's hope we have a successful refit and are able to show the company management that we're not just a name and number in their books."

Soon bowed slightly in acknowledgement of John's candid statement, as he handed him his clean laundry.

"Can't tell the difference, as you all look the same to me, 2nd! But you can now call me Kim, so you can tell the difference between me and all the others" he said with a cheeky grin.

John and his friends stepped onto the *Tsun Wan* with optimistic fervour and willing to turn the pile of ships debris and wreckage back into something looking more like a ship.

"Mr Soon. As this ship is under engineering control, I shall assume command of the vessel during its refit. Does anybody have any objections to this?" John asked diplomatically.

"That's okay by me John!" Sinclair responded quickly, which was unanimously agreed by the other two.

"Thank you gentlemen. We each have a mountain of work to do even before we start the real work, so we'll make today our settling in period, and start the ship's programme tomorrow.

Mr Soon! The first thing we've got to do is get our cabins and the saloon back into their former glory so that at least we can have some sort of order around us. We might as well make ourselves comfortable whilst we're at it. Maybe if you can find a couple of friendly workers to do that and a decent chef to get the galley cleaned up and back into service again, it just might tempt other men to come and join us. When I get back from my visit I shall take a look at the air conditioning and other services. Bruce, Andy, I feel sure that you both have a million and one things to do, but I need you both to give the ship a good recce, excluding the engineering department, then sit down and write out a planned work schedule.

I shall be asking for some dockyard supervisors to visit us some time this afternoon to go through the schedule. We have to show them that we mean business so they will offer us the workforce we shall be needing." John explained, as they stood in the shambles of the dining room.

After a few minutes discussion, Soon advised John that his launch was arriving alongside, and for him to make his way.

"Here is the ship's dockyard telephone number, in case you might need it to contact us." Soon said, handing John a piece of paper.

"Can't remember seeing a phone on board Kim, where is it found?"

"I had it installed in the saloon yesterday."

"Good thinking Kim. I'll see you around 1300." John concluded as he stepped onto the waiting motor launch, which roared away from the ship in a great rate of knots.

John stood in the stern sheets of the launch; looking at the various warships he passed, and noticed how busy the base was. *'Like the fair ground dodgems, with all the craft dashing around the place.'* he mused, as the launch passed the mass of a warship looming like a grey cliff above him.

"Let's hope Hughes keeps his word and send us the stores he promised. They live like lords whilst we live from hand to mouth. No wonder Andy and Bruce kept rubbing it into them about the peacetime navy and their wartime one. If it weren't for that engineer who did war service agreeing with them, Hughes would not have offered his services. Still, beggars can't be choosers as the saying goes, and at the moment we're definitely beggars if the Tsun Wan is anything to go by. But we'll show them, just wait and see." John muttered annoyingly, as the launch finally reached the pontoon stage where John was to get off.

"Mr Grey?" a slim beanpole of a man asked, as he approached John.

"Yes, I am he? Who are you and state your business!"

"Morning! I'm Chief Engineer Keith Ellis and with Engineer Supervisor Cross we're both McPhee's Deputies. I've come to escort you to his office." the man replied civilly. He invited John to walk the short distance from the pontoon to the large imposing office block set back from the rest of the dockyard and separated by a bank of earth full of gaily coloured tropical plants and magnolia trees.

John looked at the ornate sign that was prominent above the portals of the building:

'HM Dockyard Sembawang. Commodore & Chief Superintendent Offices'.

"Looks like I've come to the right place, judging by all the posh sounding offices that are here." John opined, as Ellis opened McPhee's office door for him.

"Don't hold your breath Grey as there's a purge on expenditure and budgets at the moment. Make do and mend is the catch phrase around here, so be careful who you approach and what you'd be looking to beg borrow or steal from." Ellis advised.

John looked around at the array of model ships and photographs that adorned the modest yet spacious office.

"Morning John, come in and sit yourself down! This is perhaps the first time you've come into my world of desk engineering, let alone the politics that surround each nut and bolt I have at my disposal." McPhee said amicably, as he swept his hand around the room.

"Hello Fergus, nice of you to see me. Your office seems quite befitting for a man of your stature." John replied with equal affability.

They spoke of past encounters, and of the work that John had submitted to McPhee over the years, until there was a short lull in their conversation when a young Asian woman came into the office bearing a tray of tea and sandwiches.

"Now then John! There's a big change of plan from what we

discussed yesterday." McPhee started, as he explained at length, using various drawings and technical maps to help John understand what was going on. It took them two hours to wade through the proposals and make a temporary work schedule to go by before they were satisfied they had got on top of it all.

A knock on the door interrupted them as Soon came in with the work schedule that John had asked him to supply.

John introduced them as a courtesy, but as they already knew each other, the conversation started to flow again, with Soon being included.

"This is our own work schedule on board as you can see Fergus. If we're going into dry dock as you say, then we'd be able to combine the dockyard routine and maintenance with our own. We were hoping you'd supply around 10 men per each work section, leaving Mr Soon free to gather a crew together. Hopefully Kim is quick about it as it means that they will be able to make a cohesive ships company, before we undock." John stated, as he went through the details.

McPhee summoned Cross to attend this part of the meeting, and delegated him to assist John and his officers. He in turn offered some ideas of his own which were adopted by them, especially Soon, who managed to expand on some of the ideas put forward, which turned out to be acceptable to them all.

McPhee concluded the meeting with a flourish, stating that he would take a personal interest in the affairs of the ship, but with Ellis acting as John's go between and Cross' secretary to help Soon.

"Right then gentlemen. I've got a meeting with the Flag Officer 2nd in Command and his cohorts on the *Antares*. He's got a few engine problems of his own to sort out before he lets his battle group loose in the South China Sea. Keep in touch John, and let me have any drawings you come up with, if only to keep my own technical library and records straight. Don't forget any problems contact Keith Ellis or my secretary. But in emergency contact me direct. See you immediately the ship gets docked down." McPhee announced, as he politely dismissed them

Ellis escorted John and Soon out of the building and saw that they caught their launch back to the ship again.

"I'll send a few shipwrights and labourers and some stores over for you Grey. They'll be with you in about an hour from now. You will have a relief shift sent over around 1700 and will remain on board until 0800. We may have to delay your cold move for a couple of days whilst we wait for an empty floating dock. The normal plan is to send a couple of tugs around the 0900 so be on the ball when they arrive. Incidentally my supervisors are British, but most of the local shipwrights speak fairly good English. No doubt Mr Soon will act as your interpreter if required at any other time. Here is a short reminder of what I've just said in case your timing catches up with whatever you'll be doing." Ellis concluded, handing John a neatly typed piece of paper.

"Thanks Ellis. See you sometime." John said and waved as the launch sped away from the pontoon.

"Looks as if we're in business Kim. Look, we've got shipwrights, welders, carpenters, and a couple of electricians coming to see us." John said gladly as he showed Soon the long list of dockyard personnel, which Soon glanced over and expressed his satisfaction.

The launch arrived alongside the silent hulk of the *Tsun Wan*, and deposited the two passengers who climbed swiftly up the steep wooden ladders, to be met by Sinclair.

"Good afternoon gentlemen. Sorry the cruise has been cancelled, but if you care to grab a broom to help sweep up then it's extra beer in your rations." Sinclair greeted with a big grin.

"Hello Andy! What's the big cheesy grin for? If I know you, you're up to something dastardly." John responded, but whispered aside to Soon.

"Watch him, he's the number one crazy man around here!" he said with a nod and serious look on his face.

Soon looked po faced at Sinclair saying nothing, but the look of alarm on his face told John that Soon was a quick one to be wound up, but put it down to his oriental way of life.

When they arrived into the saloon, both John and Soon were quick to respond to the surprise.

"That Doug Hughes certainly kept his word Kim. Look at the pile of uniforms he's given us to wear. We've got some decent tableware and a couple of electric fans to keep us cool until the fridge system is fixed. We've been given a complete set of bedding for our cabins. On top of that, he's given us a hamper full of food, a couple bottles of whiskey and a couple of crates of beer to sup. His note says that he's sorry he can't spare the steward or chef to provide for you, but hopes what has been sent is of some use." Larter said, as he handed John the note accompanying the supplies. John read it then handed it to Soon.

"Here you are Kim. How would you like to reply to it and thank him for his generosity? Tell him, once we've got Bristol fashion again he will be more than welcome to visit us."

Soon read the letter and the list of contents, nodding his head in appreciation.

"It is a good gesture from Hughes. Maybe we can build on it with what Ellis or Cross can offer us. Perhaps it will supplement what the line will be sending us." he replied, and putting the letter into his pocket, added.

"I shall get us a meal organised now, providing that we've got a hot plate in the galley to use."

"What a good idea, I'll come with you and check it out. We've got shore side electrics, so if Bruce can get the fans on the go, at least we can have the saloon cooled down to hot instead of boiling. From what I see, you've been clearing and cleaning the saloon for us Andy. Perhaps if you could finish it off and set a table for us, we'll have our lunch before the dockyard personnel arrive." John stated, as he followed Soon down to the galley.

He checked the electrics, the fresh water systems also the hot water pipes, before declaring the galley was usable, although needed cleaning up before use.

He went to the ships large fridge space and checking up on its state, decided it needed work done to it before any further stores were brought on board again.

"Right Kim. The galley can be used on a reduced capacity as it needs cleaning and fumigating including the fridge, which is out of action. Have we got any coolers or small locker fridges on board we can use in the meantime?" John asked, as he returned to the galley to where Soon was cleaning and scrubbing an area for him to work in.

"Yes. There's one in the Captains' cabin that I've been using."

"I'll get it set up in the saloon. After that, how soon can we eat?"

"Soon! Very soon! But not me! We'll have sandwiches and tea instead. I think its Grey." was the impish reply from Soon, smiling at his play on words.

John laughed, shaking his head in appreciation.

"We'll get along just fine. See you later then." John replied then left the galley to go up to the Captain's cabin.

He returned to the saloon again just in time for Soon to bring their lunch.

"We'll get this fridge working after lunch and make this place our HQ. We'll leave the cabins until they're fumigated and back into use again. We'll lock all the main deck doors and only use the one that leads into the cabin space. That way the saloon will become a cool room for us sooner." John advised, which the others accepted eagerly.

After their lunch and a quiet smoke, Soon cleared away the table and had them washed before the launch full of dockyard workers arrived.

The friends stood on the gangway meeting the British supervisors and their foremen as they came aboard. John advised them the saloon area was out of bounds for everybody, also for the crews mess aft to be used for any breaks or meetings.

This was met with dismay from some of the supervisors, but John emphatically stated that the saloon was, after all, their communal cabin, therefore their private quarters until such times as the ship was fully manned again.

Ellis, present as the senior engineer spoke up for the others.

"We fully understand, Grey. The workers can use the crews mess, but we would prefer to use the Captain's cabin if possible, because it will give us more seclusion to discuss our schedules and the like." He asked politely.

John looked at Soon quickly, who gave a nod in approval, as did the other two.

"It seems a unanimous decision and a diplomatic one Ellis. So be it. Mr Soon will show you the way. In the meantime I would ask your foremen to get their men organised into teams to carry out immediate, shall we say, cleaning or repairs duties. Your first task is to make the ship safe from explosions. There's a large quantity of fine coal dust in the boiler room and stoke holds which needs to be got rid of. Just one spark from a welder's torch could blow the ship and everybody on it sky-high. Suggest your Fire watch Officer, er Ted Lewis, according to this (who's who) list, provides a very fine spray nozzle onto the fire hoses to hose down the entire area. He's also an ex stoker I understand, so get him to have the ballast pump working to have the water removed and be dried off with a few large heaters suitably placed to dry the compartment out. The rest of the ship needs fumigated with DDT or whatever, you've got about 3 days to complete these tasks before we even start on the rest. On top of that, I have prepared a list of areas that need immediate attention, which we will be discussing in the Captains cabin." John advised, which resulted in the group of men being split up their working parties.

"Here we have the main drawings of the ship. For the main part, it will only be cleaned, repaired, and items replaced as required. The two major factors for me to keep a close eye on, are the cargo holds, and of course the major alterations to the engine and boiler rooms." John commenced as the Supervisors and Foremen looked on intently.

During the meeting, Soon suggested they all adjourned to the open bridge where it was much cooler under canvas as opposed to a hot metal box. They were all glad to do so and were made comfortable as Soon ensured that everybody had a cool drink to hold onto.

When the meeting finally came to an end. Ellis thanked John and his friends for their help in what he considered to be a tall order fraught with problems or possible setbacks.

"I understand present austere financial measures are in force hence the need to make do and mend. Most of our engine room plumbing including a host of other hardware needed will be salvaged from the scrapped frigate and the redundant Auxiliary freighter. We have ways to make this ship worthy again in more ways than one, so let's commit ourselves to this cause. Who knows, it could be one big feather in our caps if we succeed. It may be the start of a new trend in which each of us will be a founder member, to look back on and count ourselves part of it. Promotions all round if we succeed, but recriminations if we don't. My fellow officers and I are fully committed to this venture, with or without your involvement. At the end of the day, this vessel must sail sooner rather than later. But then, it's all down to you gentlemen, as to which road you will march on." John responded enthusiastically.

Ellis and the others nodded their heads in recognition in what John had said, voicing their approval in one unanimous cheer, which seemed to conclude the meeting.

"Now that we know what is required Grey, we will ensure you will have a trouble free refit. We are leaving now to complete our own ends of this ship's refit, but we shall be keeping in close contact with every facet of your ships' make over, if you like. Don't forget you've got a night shift of workers coming on board soon. In view of the fact your galley is still out of commission, we'll send over hot makan, erm that's Malay for food, for you and the workers, around 1800. The local workers also will need feeding around 2200, 0200 and again at 0600, so I'll send more makan over for them accordingly. Must go now Grey, but one word of advice. Let the workers do their jobs as we've trained them.

If you've got specific problems with the work in hand, then let us know via our Foremen. Failing that, speak to Cross, whom you've already met. I really must go now, I've got a round of golf with my Malay counterpart over in Johore Bahru in a couple of hours. Toodle pip!" Ellis said as his parting words, as the supervisors left the ship and boarded the launch to take them back to the dockyard.

'Lucky bastard! I haven't had a round of golf for years now, let alone tested my new fishing tackle and all the lures I've made. Mind you though my new matching twin bore shotguns work a treat.' John muttered as he saw the launch disappear behind a long line of destroyers moored midstream between them and the dockyard.

"Right then Kim, you heard the man. Supper at 1800 and breakfast at 0600 for us officers, but make sure the workers have their food too. I have a machinery inspection to conduct now, and no doubt my two friends have a myriad of things to do until then. Keep yourself available in the saloon in case we have some problems with the language or whatever." John ordered diplomatically, to which Soon nodded in acquiescence to his orders.

"By the way Kim, two things that I would appreciate you sort out for overnight arrangements. One, we have been given a launch to use for our own convenience, so make sure you have a reliable crew to man it. Secondly, and to make things a little more pleasant than they currently seem at the outset, is to make sure the workers know after 2200, and unless there're some work problems to overcome, if any of the married men wish to sneak ashore to see their families then they may do so. But under the strict understanding they're all back by 0600. The rest of them will secure at that time but remain in the crew's quarters aft. Lay on a couple of crates of Tiger Beer or whatever the local ale is, for them to quench their thirst when they have their food. They can also have their girlfriends on board to keep them company if they so wish, but only until 0600, when they must be off the ship. The thing is Kim, I want a good team of men who will work long and hard for me. Unless they have some incentive such as I've just stated, then I will not achieve their loyalty nor get all this work done. I want workers not shirkers. So if you have anything else to suggest to keep them sweet, then I am open to reasonable ideas."

Soon thought for a moment but said that what John proposed was generous enough, given that most of them would have somehow vanished in the night anyway.

"Fine Kim. We shall see if our ploy works, in the meantime I'll see you soon, erm, later that is." John said with a smile as he left Soon to his own tasks.

The call for supper was a relief for John and his friends, as the heat of the day had been replaced by the cool darkness of the evening.

John had got the passengers communal bathroom plumbing systems fixed up so that they could have a shower and ablutions. He also had a temporary air-conditioning unit (a.c.u) and the small fridge to help them feel more at home instead of in a permanent sauna which was the norm for that part of the world.
Larter fixed up a radio for them to listen to, and somehow managed to purloin several crates of bottled Tiger Beer. Sinclair had the saloon rigged into two separate areas with bunks made up in the one, and easy chairs to sit in and a set of table and chairs to use as their dining area in the other.

Soon put Venetian blinds over the windows to provide privacy, and had the donated tableware laid out for them to dine with, even down to a galvanised bucket full of ice, which contained a magnum bottle of champagne.

"Evening dinner is served gentlemen!" Soon announced, entering the saloon with a large tray of traditional British fare.

"Good old British fish and chips!" Sinclair quipped as he gazed down at his very full plate of food.

Soon joined them shortly bringing in his own tray of food, which were little dishes of this, that and the other, along with a large bowl of rice that had two enormous chopsticks poking out of it.

"Glad you could join us Kim. Here, have a drop of this champers that Hughes gave us." John said amicably, handing over a full glass of it to him.

All four men ate heartily making small talk whilst they did so, until all was consumed with the magnum bottle now empty.

Sinclair gave a loud burp, which earned him a light clip around the ear with a serviette by Larter.

"Now then Bosun, remember your manners. There's officers present you know!" Larter said in mock horror.

"Sorry B'wana. Me forgot um manners!" Sinclair quipped, as he held his hands as if in prayer.

Soon laughed at this small show of banter between them, then gave a belch just as loud as Sinclair, saying.

"Sorry boss! Me also forgot!"

Soon received the same treatment with a serviette byLarter, so as not to make any distinction between east and western manners.

"It seems that we've got two little pigs waiting to go to market, John! What shall we do with them?" Larter asked piously, looking at John.

"It's just as well we know these two reprobates dear Bruce. Heavens knows what the natives would think otherwise." John chuckled, and they all joined in laughing at the banter.

This was the moment when all four men realised it was time now to relax and let the workers get on with the myriad of things they had to oversee during the past several hours.

They had earned it, and the ambience created by them was very conducive of a well-being factor.

Soon started to open up by revealing some of his life to John and his friends, then kept on talking as if a dam had been burst, keeping the others enthralled by what he had to say.

In the spirit of things, John and his friends spoke of their voyages together, which in turn, had Soon enthralled with their own dits and anecdotal narration of their adventures together.

Little by little, all four men felt that this night was the formation of a bond between them that would strengthen during their voyages on the *Tsun Wan*. Perhaps even to have a much wider impact and maybe become similar to what they shared with Aussie Clarke, Tansey Lee, Crabbe and others. Such is the fellowship that can be made and felt between seafarers from different parts of the world and their associated cultures.

CHAPTER V

Fiendishly Clever

John and his two friends along with Soon stood on the open bridge watching the tugs get themselves ready to heave the ship away from her isolated wooden jetty, that seemed almost ostracised by the rest of the naval base.

"Morning John! I'm coming with you during your cold move. I need to monitor the floating dock's performance, as it is about to handle a larger and heavier vessel than normally gets lifted by it. These type aren't a patch on the SFD's you took down to the Falklands.

If it performs okay, then we've got a lucrative contract lined up with Mr Ting and Ling's shipping company. The thing is John, although Singapore is in the process of providing a good ship building empire, there's no facility for ship repairs except what this naval base can offer. Maybe you will get to learn a few things in the process." McPhee announced as he came up onto the bridge where John and the other three officers were gathered.

"Morning Fergus! You're welcome anytime. The tugs are on time, and I've still got the dockyard workers on board. They can be dispensed with until such times as we complete the docking." John responded cheerfully.

"Yes I'd noticed you'd still got them, and agree to them being sent ashore. How did your overnight work schedule go?"

"Very well actually. We managed to get quite a lot done in the for'ard cargo hold and are ready for my layout as on the *Inverlaggan*. Thanks to Mr Ted Lewis, the engine and boiler rooms have been scrubbed from the keel bilges up to the engine room deck-head, are looking like brand new pins, all ready for the transfer and modifications. One thing though, its thanks to Mr Soon's work, I have discovered the reason why this ship is so sturdy. Fancy my great mentor and patron not discovering it beforehand. Maybe he can tell me what I've discovered." John said, handing McPhee a square foot of ships material.

McPhee gave John a blank look, then began to scrutinise it.

"Unless we're here to play charades John, which I do not have the time for at the moment, then I ask you to enlighten me." McPhee replied offhandedly.

"It's quite simple dear Fergus. This ship has very few transverse ribs because the hull is made of cold rolled steel exactly one and three quarters of an inch thick, that is custom built for its design and riveted right up and onto the main deck, presumably to withstand any underwater knocks or grounding. But the superstructure and internal bulkheads are only half inch thick, and is dressed in half inch thick of tongue and grooved timber, especially from the main weather deck right up to the lifeboat deck. In other words Fergus, it solves my problem as to how come a ship so flimsy above the water line could cope with the heavy deck cargo etc, which it has been doing since her launch way back when. It means that all the weight is where it should be, below the water line so to speak, instead of making her top heavy and prone to capsizing. Centre of gravity etc springs to mind."

"What was her normal trading route for this to come about?"

"Up and down the major Chinese rivers such as the Yangtze. Her engine only needed to combat the strong Yangtze river current going up stream plus a few extra knots to give it some credence to carry out her commercial existence. The engines and the boilers maybe of a hybrid type since she was built, and as such its efficiency somewhat suspect, but at least the man who designed and had built the ship knew what he was doing. However, his apparent lack of being able to get hold of European propulsion technology has kept the ship's performance well below its full potential, which is where we step in and rescue this fine ship from the breakers yard.

My theory of adapting the coal burning boilers into fuel oil should stand correct. And again, in theory it should increase the ship's speed let alone its longer range of voyages before having to refuel. In fact, if all goes well Fergus, the shipping company will eventually be glad to offload the ship into Admiralty hands, for them to gain an absolute bargain in a ready-made ammunition ship." John explained.

McPhee took a closer look at what was given him then took a further look around the bridge comparing from what he saw to what was on the ships technical drawings.

"Hmm! I see what you mean John, and your comments are well noted. Fiendishly clever these Chinese people are too!" McPhee admitted candidly.

"I also have the measure of the man who last had the pleasure of designing the engine room. Here are some of the original plans as per builder. Then here's the new design, which the ship can sustain without major upheaval or heavy lifting of machinery. All we've got to do is adapt her accordingly and get on our way, not only with a refurbished ships system but also with a more powerful propulsion. When we have the piston rods to take into account the 'missing quantity' we can then calculate its new piston loads and inertia forces etc. The engine will have to be re-balanced especially when we convert the differences between a coal-powered engine to that of an oil powered one. Incidentally, we need a different prop shaft and different propeller to give the ship the advantage of its new power source, but then who am I to teach his Granny to suck eggs Fergus." John added.

McPhee nodded his head in agreement, telling John what he said was on a similar plane to which he once had advocated some decades ago. All of which helped him to where the job he is doing and enjoying today, but even more importantly, as a prominent member of the ISDM.

The ship was about to cast off from the jetty when McPhee called down to Cross, who was sitting on a bollard watching the work going on all around him.

"These men can be taken off now. Get a new set of workers detailed off to continue when this ship had completed her docking down." he commanded.

The men, with almost indecent haste, abandoned the work they were doing, made their way quickly down onto the now departing launch.

"Bloody hell Fergus. It was as if they didn't have a thought for the work they were doing. Local habits, maybe local unionism to blame or what?" John opined

"We might be the owners of a naval base which provides work for several thousands of the local work force, but it's the local 'band of brothers' who control the workforce. Unionism is alive and well in this part of the world, let alone the influence of the local communist Mafia gangs which our security forces are trying, as yet unsuccessfully, to finally stamp out. Maybe the new voice of reason from the brand new local political party who is making a name for itself will intervene, and perhaps get the world to rights so we can live in peaceful harmony again.

Anyway, that is by the by. In the meantime, what you must understand, is that as of today, this ship becomes the property of the Royal Navy. To you, it means that your Captain could be from the Royal Navy or their Auxiliary fleet, but the rest of you officers will be Merchant Navy. The crew will be almost half-and-half, between local and company sailors and stokers. The reason is because this ship is about to be equipped to carry ammunition and other hazardous cargo which the normal run of the mill cargo vessel would not be equipped nor be prepared to carry." McPhee explained at length.

Soon, who was standing nearby heard this conversation, came over and posed a few questions that had a direct influence of his standing on board.

McPhee gave Soon the simple explanation that the ship was to be part of the Royal Navy's civilian side of operations called the Royal Fleet Auxiliary service. He explained that Soon would be expected to serve on the ship as a 'Special Duties Officer', which encompassed the role of his present duties as the ship's purser. McPhee explained that it was the decision of the shipping company to allow this to happen, providing that the Royal Navy paid for their personnel who were on board. He emphasised this point that as such, their monthly salary would be almost double the current going rate to maintain their pay differentials. Also the need to keep the status quo between the different maritime agencies, even though the job involvement was performed in the same manner within their own navy.

"At last McPhee, we're getting onto the same mind wave length. For I was beginning to wonder where I was to fit into all this, especially as I represent the ownership of the vessel, and not the shipping company from which she seems to have passed into the Royal Navy's hands.

But I wish to know how long will this, shall we say, special charter between the shipping line and that of the Royal Navy last?"

"As far as I'm concerned Mr Soon, at least until the Admiralty builds one of their own to replace it. As your type of vessel is unique, they would need to obtain the necessary permission to build a ship in the same likeness to it. Ship designs and copyrights and all that stuff.

Think of it this way Mr Soon, at least you're on board your own vessel, more importantly, you're being paid not from your own pocket but that of the British Admiralty."

Soon agreed with the statement and thanking McPhee for his honesty, left the bridge to do his next round of chores.

"It seems that Mr Soon is in a cleft stick Fergus. I mean, it's one thing for us merchantmen to move between one shipping company and another, but for him it is a whole different ball game. His problem is that his ship has been taken over without his specific say so. It's the present shipping line's unilateral decision to sign the ship over to the Royal Navy for its own purposes, and they had no business to do so in the first place. To me they have robbed Soon of his rights of ownership and prevented him from vetoing any such adverse decisions concerning his ship." John stated in defence of Soon.

"I really don't see the problem John. The ship is being

virtually rebuilt, and about to be given a new lease of life rather than be stuck up some mangrove swamp to rot away. At least the ship will be earning its keep, as will its owners, Soon amongst them. You would be best advised to stay out of the politics of these things John, believe you me, because you really don't want to know. Just concentrate on what you do best and get yourself into that college we talked about in Belfast." McPhee countered softly.

"I hear what you're saying Fergus, and I appreciate your advice. It's just that it's only now that I've discovered the devious and underhand tricks each shipping company tries on each other. At the moment, it seems that Belverley and his cronies are small boys compared with Whateley's lot. For me and my friends it's like jumping out of the frying pan and into the bloody fire." John exclaimed.

"That's where you're wrong John. You made the right decision to join Whateley's company, as did your two friends. The thing you must appreciate is, that you have to move on and experience at least one shipping company to be able to make comparisons when it comes to your own field of expertise. Yours is being able to solve marine engineering problems; to be able to create new and innovative ideas and improve on existing criteria found at the time. For that, you've been recognised and duly acclaimed as such. You have one further hurdle to overcome before we give our final judgement on your suitability to be able to join the elite students currently in our ISDM College in Southampton. You will kindly note that as I am your mentor in those things, I ask you not to speak of these things again, nor will you rock any boats in the meantime. Just do your job John and all will be well. Do we have a gentleman's agreement on that?"

John looked at the concern written on McPhee's face and decided that he was right on all accounts, so held out his hand in friendship.

"I'll shake your hand as our agreement Fergus, and thank you for your 'guardian angel' attitude towards me, although heavens know why I deserve it." John replied with a smile.

McPhee grunted his approval and shook John's hand, which signalled the end of the quiet but meaningful discussion they just had between them.

Cross arrived onto the bridge and advised that he was going ashore in the fast launch to get things organised on the floating dock, and that he would organise a full shift pattern set up for when the ship finally docks down.

McPhee nodded his head and gave a string of other reminders to Cross, before Cross left the bridge to be seen speeding away.
Once the ship was lined up for her to sit nicely onto the special dock bottom cradle, the floating dock started to raise itself out of the water. All the time, stout timbers were being wedged into place to keep the ship steady and in position, until the dock bottom finally rose out from the water and the ship finally settled on its little cradle.

The gangway was lowered onto the ship so that access could be made, but it meant a long steep climb down almost vertical steel ladders to get to the bottom and get off the dock onto dry land.

"There you are John, all safe and sound. You can consider yourself relieved of command for a few days until we start getting the spares and other requirements shipped. Then you and your friends will be required to just oversee what's being done to the ship until we're satisfied that all that can be done has been done. You will be required to submit reports to and be visited upon by Stafford and his gang down in Singapore City. As for me, I'm quite happy to come on board and see you as and when. Don't forget! If you've got an engineering problem, or you see something that is needed to correct one, make out a preliminary report before you contact Ellis or even Cross. Just give me a bell on your ship's phone. Your new ship's Captain will be visiting you some time Monday morning, so have a good time until then.

Must go now John, so see you whenever. Oh! and by the way, I nearly forgot. Here's an authorisation note for you to procure any stores etc for your personal use. Also see the Transport manager to get yourself a vehicle for your private usage during your stay. Self drive I'm afraid though." McPhee said magnanimously, as he nodded to John and left the bridge to go over the seemingly slender gangway.

John called his friends to accompany him to the saloon where they met up with Soon.
"We have to stay on board during this docking period, which will be sheer purgatory at the outset, but for now we have a few days off duty until Monday morning. The saloon will remain our little citadel from the outside world, so it will remain shut at all times that we're away from it. We will do our own fumigation of the place so as not to have strange bodies come into our little home. Kim, be kind enough to arrange the security arrangements for this place, issue us with a key if necessary.

We have been given the loan of a vehicle for our private usage although it's self-drive. So gentlemen, we're now relieved from our duties until 0800 Monday morning, but I'm expecting a visit from Stafford and his cronies at some point. Still, he's got our phone number to phone us beforehand. That means Kim, the phone is now out of order unless we decide to use it. Outgoing calls only if you prefer it. One thing more, we've got our new Captain coming on board some time on Monday, but don't ask me who it is, sufficient to say it's going to be one from the Royal Navy, just to cheer you all up."

Soon nodded eagerly at the suggestion, clapped his hands and declared that he was going to make them all a good lunch before going ashore to visit the wide world again.

Larter and Sinclair muttered about Hughes and his ilk were of today's Pussers Navy, and not the real McCoy ones they had during their days through the war.

"As long as Trewarthy hasn't joined them to come out here

and haunt us then I don't give a hoot. Anyway, I'm off to take a good shower, before Kim brings our, erm, makan." John concluded, which the other two heartily agreed with.

"Yes, I'll lock up the radio shack in case some bugger takes a fancy to the new fangled radio Mr Westwood and I've just constructed and finally got working." Larter quipped, leaving the saloon.

"It looks as if I'm mother hen again. A skivvy's work is never done." Sinclair added in mock horror, as he started to lay the table for dinner.

CHAPTER VI

Water Falls

"The dockyard mateys have buggered off for some sort of holiday by the looks of it, Kim. So much for that 24hour shift work pattern. What say we get ourselves organised, and maybe take a trip up country for a bit of sight seeing, but be back in time for the undocking. It will give the fumigation chemicals a chance to do its work." John observed, as he watched the workers leave in their droves.

"Yes Soon! If we get the supplies loaded into the land rover, how about you taking us up country for a banyan?" Sinclair suggested.*

"Hey, that sounds like a good idea. No doubt there would be a few willing bar girls that would accompany us. Just for the fun you understand." Larter added enthusiastically, yet with a big grin.

"Why not! We deserve a break anyway. I know of a nice secluded spot that we can use. I'll contact my family who will give us the supplies. I have a couple of friends in Sembawang village who would supply you with female company, but first you'd have to pay them around 35 Singapore dollars each." Soon agreed with a smile.

"What $35 for the day or what? What if we decide to stay overnight Kim? $35 is a lot to hand over without sampling the merchandise, so to speak. Er lets see, you said it's $8.50c to the pound, so it mean that's a good £4 in sterling." Sinclair asked swiftly, as Soon started to make his phone arrangements.

"These are good girls, very pretty and clean too. If you were to give $85, they'll stay with us for the whole time."

"That's £10 each. Well wherever you intend taking us, it can't be very far if they can find their way home again. Then again, if the communist insurgents are still active around here, the girls would want to stay with us anyway until we do come back." Larter reasoned.

---

* Banyan is the Malay term for having a picnic.

"We will agree on the $85 Kim, and you can take it from the petty cash that's set aside for us. Get provisions for the entire time we're away and set it against our daily ration allowances, but we'll see to the petrol and the like. As it's your mystery trip Kim, you get to do the driving." John advised, with Soon nodding his head in agreement.

"Yes, I'll go and get the girls and bring them here." he replied with a big grin and left.

"We'll cross the causeway and go through the town of Johore Bahru before heading up country. It should not take us very long, so we might as well take our time." Soon said, as the land rover was stopped at the gates of the naval base.

"Going up country in company of some pretty girls are we gentlemen? Not far I hope?" a smartly dressed police officer asked politely.

"Yes officer. Why, is there a problem?" Sinclair responded with his own question.

"The army is flushing out some of the communist insurgents that have come down here to create mayhem. You will see the army on patrol along the main roadways, so if you fall into difficulty, contact them immediately. Where is it you will be going, just in case we've got to send somebody after you?"

"We're going up to the Kota Tingghi waterfalls. I have friends living near there that will look after us if needs be." Soon replied.

"That's okay then, but make sure you meet up with the other two groups of people who passed through about two hours ago. Have a good time!" the officer stated and waved them through the checkpoint.

"We'll keep an eye out in case we meet unexpected guests coming to bother us, so you just concentrate on the driving Kim." Larter advised.

It took them two hours before they arrived at a small clearing in the jungle near an outcrop of boulders, which perched precariously on the side of a steep slope. Once they had decided on where they were going to park the vehicle, they off loaded the jeep and carried their stuff through some bushes to another clearing.

John and his friends stopped to take in the beauty of a waterfall which filled a natural pool that had been built up by man to catch the water before it cascaded down to another but smaller one only to disappear into the jungle again.

There were several people sitting around the pool with children standing under the waterfall and generally playing around.

"This is it. Kota Tingghi water falls." John stated as he read out the details of the place from a tourist style notice board.

'A sloping fall of some 95 feet high and 50 feet wide, with a splash pool that feeds the smaller one of only 10 feet high. The water is at a constant temperature and is part of a permanent watercourse. Bathing is only allowed in the main pool. A hut as marked has been provided as your lavatory. The whole area is cordoned off to protect against wild animals, but keep a lookout for snakes. You will only light a fire in the areas marked on this map. All rubbish is to be taken away.'

"This will do us very nicely Kim. Maybe if you and the girls get our banyan area organised, we'll get the vehicle seen to. We won't want it nicked by some black enamelled thieving bastard now do we." Sinclair suggested.

"We forgot to bring the radio." Soon called out, as John and his two friends left to see to the vehicle.

"Being up jungle brings back quite a few memories. Still, at least the natives seem friendly." John quipped, as they were camouflaging the vehicle from view.

"It looks as if the others are here just for the day, judging by the way they've left their vehicles. Any bugger could come along and pinch them at will, and they would not know until they came back because of the noise from the waterfall." Larter agreed.

"Which reminds me! Once they've gone, we can move our site to a more secure spot for the night, just in case we have undesirable guests calling in on us." Sinclair insisted.

They finished their task and returned to the waterfall to find that Soon and the girls had arranged their food for them.

"Just in time for makan gentlemen. The beer bottles are in the water keeping cool, help yourselves." Soon announced as he handed out the barbecued steaks and rolls.

"This is more like a picnic. Couldn't get used to the banquets our friend Phatty gave us. I mean we didn't know which end of the table to start with." Sinclair mumbled as he munched his ham and egg salad banjo.

After the food was eaten and the campsite cleaned up, the girls who had already paired themselves up with John and his friends and started to cavort around and generally enjoy the fresh mountain waters.

The water was cool, but the fun and games were full of warmth and happiness. Even Soon somehow managed to discard his aloof manner, and joined in the 'silly games'.

They happily wrapped themselves into their own little cocoon and hardly noticed that all the others were leaving to go back home again.

It was starting to get dark when Sinclair noticed that they were now all on their own.

"It seems we have the campsite to ourselves now, so we'd better get ourselves into a safer spot for the night. If what was said back at the security gate is right, then there may be some mighty desperate men roaming around the place. Since we can't wait for the cavalry to turn up and rescue us, we must protect ourselves as best we can." he announced, then pointed to a clear area in between some boulders.

"We'll move over there inside that circle of rocks. It's big enough for all of us, and the rocks will shelter us from intruders. Kim! If you and the girls get our stuff moved over, we'll get our campsite protected. John, you start collecting firewood and fill the water bottles up. We don't want to start foraging after dark. Bruce, let's check on the vehicle and provide a perimeter picket line.

Just like we did in Africa, only this time we don't have dick-heads to help us."

They all carried out their allotted tasks, with Larter and Sinclair arriving back some time later.

"I've left the other fire to burn out, but it will keep that part of the area lit until it does. We can start our new fire in between those rocks over there, Kim. That way, the glow will be shielded from any outside onlookers. All they will see is the smoke, which would only look like yet another fire that was not put out, just like the one we left over there." Sinclair explained.

"We have built a security screen around us, so nobody is to leave this little compound. We'll put the tarpaulin over us in case it rains. John, get a hole dug, we'll use it for our overnight toilet." Larter stated, as he started to drape the tarpaulin over the top of them to form a tent.

Sinclair left the small compound and came back some minutes later.

"We are virtually invisible. We have bushes to hide our entrance and on the top to disguise our makeshift roof, and that's it. From now on, nobody is to speak except in a whisper. Everybody is to keep still and quiet if they hear any sudden noises. No coughing, sneezing, snoring or whatever you get up to during the night, we need complete silence. Remember, we have the place secure from intruders, but it also means that we can't leave here either, so settle down now everybody and let the fire burn itself out." he advised.

"Bruce, give me a hand to dig a pit at the entrance." he asked softly.

Larter and Sinclair dug a deep hole for Sinclair to place a hand-made barrier of bamboo spikes into it, before covering the hole over with vegetation to disguise it.

"Now you understand why I said that we can't leave the campsite." Sinclair whispered, as John and the others looked on.

"That's good enough for me Andy. I'll take the first watch until midnight." John whispered.

"Better take this then." Larter whispered, as he handed John a revolver.

"Where the bloody hell did you get this Bruce?" John asked in surprise.

"It's part of the jeep's equipment, as is the radio. But don't switch it on in case it gives off any noises. The revolver is fully loaded with a few spare bullets in its holster. Suggest you sit behind this rock at the side of the entrance. Anything that manages to cross over the entrance, or starts to come through the tarpaulin, just stab it with this spear. We'll keep the gun in reserve just in case there's more than three of them. First sign of intruders get Andy and me up immediately, but quietly. I shall be your relief at midnight." Larter explained as he handed John a vicious looking spear that had a serrated tip finished off by a very sharp point.

Sinclair whispered the same instructions to Soon, who volunteered to take the watch after John, but was told that he was to take over after Andy, and that it was his job to look after the girls if something bad should befall them.

The girls were oblivious as to what was going on, as they simply got themselves comfortable and settled down for the night, awaiting their partner to join them.

The darkness of the night was silently transformed into a silver glow as the moon showed its face from behind a blanket of cloud. As if it was the natural signal, the noises of the night began to fill air as the nocturnal animals came out of hiding to play in their world of moonbeams.

John was sitting quite still with his new-found girlfriend, listening to the different sounds that came from all around them. Fortunately for them all, they got used to the noise of the cascading waterfalls, as it somehow seemed to blend in with the rest of the night, so John was able to distinguish one sound from another.

They watched the night sky being illuminated by falling stars, with the occasional flicker of a lightning storm adding to the natural display of lights.

"It is kind of you to stay and keep me company." John whispered.

"You and your friends have been good to me and my friends. Each one of you have been a good gentleman, unlike the kind of men we normally get to meet. None of you have asked us to do what we are paid to do; yet you seem quite happy to be with us. Is it because you find us unattractive, or maybe you are all, what we call Kai Tais? Maybe you call them He-She's, or even, how you say, poofters, and queers?" she whispered back to him, as she undid his shorts to expose his genitals before she started to gently fondle them.

"No, we are not what you say. It's just that we have had a very heavy time on a distant island which has made us empty for a while. It is a long story, but for now I need to be wide awake to keep guard over us. Besides, I would have thought that you and your friends would welcome a break, just to enjoy yourselves and not think about pleasing others."

"Yes, it is true. We came here to relax and please ourselves in what we do. Maybe you will ask us again next time you have time off. We girls are fed up seeing to at least eight men a day or night, without ever having this luxury that you and your friends have shown us." she whispered back, then started to perform oral sex on him.

John gently stopped her and raising her up from her knees, sat her gently down next to him.

"You really don't have to do this to me, if you don't want to. Just keeping me company during the night will be fine." John insisted, which made the girl give him a strange look.

"Just sit by me and I will tell you why I am not ready to help you please me." John demanded. When he saw that she was relaxed and listening, he told her about their experiences on Taraniti, and of his Kiria Ma'ana ceremony.[*]

When he had finished, she took hold of his face in her hands and gave him a tender kiss.

"You have experienced what we girls have to do every day and

---

[*] See *The Repulse Bay*.

night to earn our keep. It is expected from us as a normal day, so your lover was lucky as she had just the one time. We have but two days a week to rest with a further five days rest each month, and have to see the doctor to make sure that we are clean for our clients. If we're not clean, then our clients will beat us up, and we'd lose our wages for the time it takes for us to get better again. Maybe my friends have not been told about all this, but I will make sure that they do know."

"So you see, we're not Kai Tai's or whatever you think. Maybe next time we get together it might be different. At least we've enjoyed your company today, which perhaps makes it all the more special. All you need to remember and for you to tell your friends is, we've enjoyed your company without you feeling that you need to, shall I say, earn your money." John concluded.

The girl kissed John again and thanked him for his kindness before she went over to the strip of rush matting where they were going to sleep together.

It wasn't long before John was relieved on watch by Larter, before he slipped under the terry towelling covers that were his blankets, and snuggled up to his sleeping partner.

The night wore on getting colder, for John and his sleeping partner to start clinging together for warmth, as indeed did the other sleepers. As if it was a mutual agreement, they all huddled up close but in pairs, until their collective warmth began to take effect, finally for each pair to settle into each other's little world.

John was extremely tired as no doubt were the others, but in his tiredness, he felt the soft curves of his partner crush upon his almost naked body. Maybe it was the yearning for Telani that tormented his memory or just the almost naked body next to him, but nature started to take its course, where they both shared in each other's body making the natural heat for them to sleep like babies.

CHAPTER VII

Good Company

John felt somebody shaking him roughly and whispering his name. He sat bolt upright in an automatic reaction, before he looked around and down at his sleeping partner to see that she was still sleeping.

"John, better get up and dressed. We've got company." Sinclair whispered.

"What time is it Andy? What's the score then? The others up too?" John whispered back, in quick succession.

"It's 5o'clock and Kim's just heard some voices coming from the other side of the clearing. Quickly, get dressed and grab your spear. We're about to be joined by intruders, but as soon as the sun comes up and they see our little hideaway, they'll be coming for us. We've got about one hour's darkness until then, so we've got to make some sort of plan. Wake your girl and tell her to listen to Kim's instructions" Sinclair advised.

"On my way Andy." John responded, as he gently woke his partner up and whispered to her what was happening.

Soon they were all dressed and organised to meet their so far unseen threat.

"I count 9 of them coming along the pathway." Larter stated, as he re-appeared under their camouflaged roof.

"The one in front is a guide, but there's one hanging back as their tail end Charlie. If they see this place has been well used, with a good supply of fresh water, they'll probably stay for a few hours, before moving off to whatever they're up to." Larter informed them.

"By their language, they're Chinese and communists at that." Soon whispered.

"If you can understand what they're saying Kim, for God sake tell us. We need to know why they are here and for how long. If they decide to make camp here then we're in for trouble in a big way." Sinclair demanded anxiously.

Soon whispered each word he heard to them and when the intruders started to enter the beauty spot, he pointed out the person he deduced was their leader.

Two of the intruders came right up to the entrance of their little hideout, dumping several weapons and some boxes onto the ground, before they went off to join the others who were arriving.

"It seems they have abducted two women from the local village, which means they will be raped and murdered before the men leave. It also appears this is a raiding party intent on blowing up an armament train loaded with tanks and the like, only a couple of miles from here.

They have decided to take some time to relax and have some food before they make their move. The train is due in 4 hours, but because of the British patrol not far from them, they have to keep low with the hope that they pass this area." Soon whispered, translating what they had heard.

"Can you make out what the writing is on the side of those boxes Kim?" Larter asked.

Soon slithered towards the small pile of boxes and silently taking one without being noticed, brought it into their hideout, but was careful enough not to fall into the man trap they had placed at the entrance.

Sinclair examined it and discovered it was several pounds of explosives with its detonator connected to a timer not set for usage just yet.

"Dismantle it and keep the explosives and the detonators separate, we can use them later. Fill the package up with our rubbish, then put it back. We'll do the same with the other boxes so as not to make things look suspicious. See if you can reach the machine gun and bring it inside as well." Sinclair whispered, as he started to dismantle the explosive device.

The girls helped to refill the explosive sacks as Larter started to make smaller explosive devices with what he found.

The two captive women started to plead for their lives, sobbing pitifully as their clothing was heard being ripped from their bodies.

"Do something for them, please! Don't let them suffer. Make those beasts leave them alone." the girls asked in unison, as the pleas of the captured women got louder.

Soon grabbed a machete, starting to leave the hideout before Sinclair grabbed hold of him.

"We have somebody on the rocks above us. One step outside and we'll all get it. Let's form a plan of attack." he whispered.

"Right then Kim, we'll start off with you." Sinclair said as he led Soon to the back of the hideout.

Sinclair peeled away some of the tarpaulin to show Soon one of the insurgents who was standing almost right on top of them.

"I'll grab his legs and pull him down. You put his shirt and jacket on then get back up there pretending you're him. Our entrance is slightly concealed from them because we're on the other side of the pool almost facing the other way. We'll sneak out and grab a few of them who are just standing back waiting their turn with the women. Once we start throwing dynamite around, you keep a lookout and protect our backs just in case there might be more of these men coming along. Here's the pistol, use it wisely as there's only a few spare bullets with it. When you're up there, tell us where the others are located." he whispered.

Soon nodded his head in agreement, getting ready to pounce on the unsuspecting man above them.

The man was dragged through the hole and killed without giving a sound, such was his surprise to the swiftness of his demise.

Soon climbed back up onto the rocks whispering his instructions, which prepared Sinclair, Larter and John to proceed with their side of the plans.

"Once we've dealt with the men, you girls see to those poor women. Bring them up here and start a fire going. But don't come out until Kim tells you to." Larter instructed, as the three friends left their hideout then proceeded to creep up to the unsuspecting men who were only interested in their so-called fun with the 2 women.

Sinclair garrotted the first man as Larter grabbed hold of the second one to snap his neck like a twig. John used his spear like a bayonet as he stabbed the one in front of him. One of the others must have turned round to see the three friends approaching, raising the alarm. He died instantly as Larter shot him between the eyes, starting up a vicious firefight between John's machine gun and the men's rifles. Sinclair began to lob the small sticks of dynamite at them, which induced them to stand up and raise their hands in surrender.

By the time John and his friends had stopped firing there were only 3 of the men left alive.

Larter tied them up in such a way that if they moved, the little sticks of dynamite he attached to their genitals would explode making instant eunuchs of them. In terror they simply did as they were told, not daring to move, not even an eyebrow.

It was during the time when the girls untied the 2 captured women and started to tend to them, that they heard a commotion coming from their little hideout.

Sinclair and John rushed up the slope to see what it was, to find Soon was in the middle of sorting out 3 more men who had tried to sneak up on them.

They watched enthralled as Soon kicked, karate chopped, poked and thumped the men until they were lying flat out on the ground.

Sinclair clapped his hands and congratulated Soon on his show of Kung Fu fighting.

Soon smiled, bowing his head slightly then kicked the chin of one of the men who was starting to come around. The sickening crack of the neck being broken brought a satisfied smile to Soon.

"My pleasure gentlemen." he sighed, then calmly put his canvas shoes back onto his feet.

"Glad you're on our side Kim. Didn't know a man could fight like that. Oriental style of fighting is it?" John asked in amazement.

"Kim appears to be a martial arts Master, which very few non Orientals can match." Sinclair nodded, returning Soon's smile.

Larter had arrived in time to start tying up the victims of Soon's punishment when they heard voices coming from the bushes.

"Bloody 'ell Sarge! The shooting came from over 'ere! Careful as there's some sort of cliff and by the sound of it, some waterfall or other." a cockney voice came from just a few yards away.

"Over here gentlemen. Just follow the small pathway down." Larter called out, which was answered by the ricochet of a bullet bouncing off the rocks where the friends were standing.

"Hey cut that out you miserable English Sassenach!" Sinclair shouted.

"Bloody 'ell, they're even speaking ruddy Jock! Must have captured some of our boys! Right men, fan out and approach those rocks very carefully." came a gruff voice.

"Come out, come out wherever you are before we start throwing dynamite at you. Look we're the good guys around here." John shouted, as he lit up a torch that flared with the gunpowder he put onto it.

The flaring torch showed the soldiers were only a few yards away from the friends, but facing the other way, almost as if they were going the wrong way.

"Good morning gentlemen. We heard a spot of shooting a while back and decided to find out what it was. There's a platoon of insurgents in the area we're after, have you seen them?" a posh English voice asked, as a young officer came striding towards them, stowing his pistol at the same time.

When he came up to the friends he introduced himself and his sergeant as his men started to come out from wherever they were hiding.

"Morning Lt. We're a party of 4 Merchant Navy officers with our escorts. Yes we've seen them. In fact we've got them all nicely packaged ready for posting home if you like." Larter stated as he swept his hands over the area to where the dead and captured insurgents were being held.

"But what the blazes are you doing out in the jungle. You could get killed, worse than that get bitten on the goolies by the 'orrible creepy crawlies." the sergeant asked in amazement.

"Just an overnight bivouac in good company sergeant. Nothing to write home about." Sinclair quipped, as the officer issued a string of orders to his men.

The soldiers had the dead men put into sacks then got the surviving insurgents to carry them.

The officer picked up one of the explosive sacks to examine it. "Whoever their quartermaster is has had them fooled. Look, only rubbish and stones." he said in amazement as he showed the sullen prisoners what the sack contained.

One of the prisoners, flabbergasted at the find, started to babble away in his native tongue. He got his second shock when the officer shouted at him in his own language. Soon laughed at the shocked expression of the man then told him that he and his friends who raped the women should be returned to their village for punishment, as a British bullet was too good for them.

The other captives started to plead for mercy but the officer shook his head and told them to face their punishment like true soldiers, not like the cowards they were.

"It appears Kim, we've got guests for breakfast, have we enough victuals to supply them?" John asked politely.

The officer was swift to offer his apologies saying that he would provide their breakfast instead, as soon as the insurgents were taken care of. This was accepted by all for the girls to start make a big fire to warm everybody up in the very cool of the early dawn.

The officer left with his men some hours before the days crop of trippers came along to fill the silence with their carefree, happy voices.

"Here we are again, happy as can be." John started to hum, as he and his friends simply relaxed or slept under the shade of their tarpaulin.

"Just another day of fun for them. If only they knew." Soon said with a yawn, settling down to enjoy the advances of his partner.

They kept a loose but drawn out conversation going, as they discussed the fates of the men when they were handed over to the elders of the village. Of how Soon showed his prowess in martial arts, of what they were going to eat for their next meal, of the girls and how well they coped in the situation.

Apart from emerging to use the toilet facilities, they were in a little world of their own as none of the other day trippers seemed to be inclined to bother with, and even keeping their children away for fear of disturbing them.

The morning had slipped into the afternoon before the friends began to waken up and take notice of their surroundings, but it was a loud rumbling noise that brought them back to reality.

John felt a warm glow engulfing his body yet it seemed as if it was coming from nowhere. He somehow knew it must have been a visitation from Helena and Telani to tell him something was about to happen.

"I have a nasty feeling something is about to happen, so we'd better get from here as of five minutes ago!" John shouted over the noise to the others.

Within moments they saw a man approaching their little hideout who called out to them.

"Hello in there. The waterfall is starting to look very dangerous so you'd better get away before you get washed away." he shouted in alarm.

John was first to arrive outside their hideout to discover a torrential tropical downpour had the day-trippers trying to shelter under the meagre sun umbrellas they had all brought with them. He looked over to the waterfall to see that instead of a benign gentle flow of crystal clear water down the fall, there was now a thick brown cascade of angry water swamping the paddling pool.

The water was rising rapidly for him to estimate it would take only a few minutes or so before they were flooded.

John told the others what he saw and what was happening as they decided it was time to decamp and make their way back to the ship.

The girls packed up all their belongings, whilst John and his friends sorted out their jeep and got it loaded up again.

As the jeep roared back into life again, making its slippery way along the muddy jungle roadway, there was an almighty crack and a rumble. Stopping the jeep they looked round to see what it was, to discover that their little hideout was being destroyed by a mini avalanche of the boulders which were above and behind them.

John's warm feeling had now left him, letting him somehow make light of the imminent danger they had all been faced with.

"Kim! Remind me to complain to the water board about excessive water pressure." John shouted over the noise. His friends merely laughed at the wisecrack but the girls looked a bit distraught at the sight.

"Got out in the nick of time then. Maybe next time we come, we'll make us a new den to be cosy in." Larter said, trying to comfort the girls.

'Thank you for keeping watch over me both of you, my dear loved ones.' John whispered to himself, as he thought of Helena and Telani.

The rain lashed down upon them as the rumbles of thunder got louder while the flashes of lightning became more frequent and brighter.

"Better get onto the main road Kim. Make sure we're under some trees, not out here in the open." Sinclair advised, as Soon drove slowly and almost blindly by the heavy downpour.

"Can't see a thing. I'm on the road I think, but we must be in some dip in the road as the water is getting higher." Soon replied.

"Remember old Catchpole and his convoy trick?" Sinclair asked.*

---

* See *The Lost Legion*.

"Although we're only just the one vehicle, we can form a human convoy to lead us to safety. Get a line hitched up onto the for'ard bumper and two of us will lead, one behind the other. If the first one is in difficulty then the man behind can haul him back again. If both get into difficulty then the vehicle will take the strain." he added as he handed out some rope.

"I'll take the lead on account that I'm the smallest and lightest of us." John volunteered, which was unanimously agreed upon.

"Right then Kim, when I give you the word, you will drive forward as slow as possible. I will guide you along, but be alert in case I ask you to reverse a while. Bruce and John will try to lead us to the relative safety of higher ground." Sinclair shouted over the rumble of thunder.

CHAPTER VIII

Taking a Ride

The rain was heavy but warm, as was the muddy water that swirled around John's legs.

There were small trees and vegetation starting to flow past him which he took notice of, especially when he spotted a small barrier was being formed in front of him. When he reached the increasing barrier of logs he realised the water had reached a high point in the road, therefore offered a temporary 'island' for them to get onto and out of the flash flooding.

Larter had almost bumped into John who he found clearing a path for the vehicle to pass through.

He helped John as quickly as he could before the vehicle finally arrived next to them.

"We can stop here for a while on what appears to be a hill in the roadway." John shouted to Sinclair, who shouted to Soon to stop the vehicle. John walked a few yards further on to see they were in fact on the lower slope of the hill, so they could move up higher onto it.

Soon drove the vehicle slowly up the slope until he could see the 3 friends standing in front of him.

"That will do us for a while Kim!" Sinclair shouted, as the rain started to ease off until it finally stopped.

The noise of rumbling thunder with the hiss of the downpour of rain was soon overtaken over by the sounds of the jungle as if silence, just like a vacuum, was not allowed on the planet.

John looked at the ever-increasing dam below, forming where they had just come from, decided that although it was creeping higher up the slope towards them, they were in no immediate danger.

"We're safe for now John. Once the water has subsided and drained off, we can get going again." Sinclair conceded as he too looked at the activity of nature at the bottom of their little hill.

"Time for a brew up, erm a cuppa, perhaps Kim?" Larter asked, as he started to take off his wet clothing wringing them out before draping them over the bonnet of the vehicle.

John and Sinclair joined him, as did Soon followed closely by the girls.

Soon they were all quite naked and had a makeshift clothes line rigged up to dry off their clothes, whilst they sat drinking their tea quietly chatting amongst themselves, without any regard to their nudity.

Larter managed to get the little transceiver working once it was dried off, so he could make contact with any local military radio station.

John dried the engine off and running normally again, whilst Sinclair sorted out the equipment to work out just where they were.

They all got dressed again with Soon and the girls preparing a little camp in the middle of the road just in case they had to stay put overnight.

"They say the Marines have several landing craft operating in this area, rescuing people who got stranded. The road north from Johore Bahru has been washed away and there's a large tree dam just above us, which might give way to take our part of the road away too. They suggest that we try to get off the road and to higher ground. Never mind the vehicle, just get away from the danger area. They say the falling rocks that had been washed away have drowned or killed several of the day-trippers at the waterfall. Including a village near them, which is probably where your friends are Kim! I've told them who we are, where to find us, but we're fine for the moment." Larter reported, as he finished his transmissions.

"The way I see it, is if we make ourselves a raft that will take the vehicle as well, we can float across that section of water there, and drive up that solid looking earthen ramp. It looks a good 100 feet higher than we are, but at least we can be above that dam whatever." John suggested, as he pointed towards where he was looking.

"Yes, but we don't know how long we've got or if in fact that dam will burst and send its water our way." Soon responded, pointing to a deep gully down the side of another hill close to them on the other side of the road.

"Well there's plenty of material creeping towards us already Kim. Otherwise its one good shove and it's all over for us." Larter offered.

The girls raced towards the slowly advancing pile of logs, starting to drag some of them back to the vehicle.

"It looks as if the girls are leading the way on this one gentlemen." Soon opined, as he too raced away bringing back some large branches.

"John, if you construct the raft, we'll get it all lashed together." Sinclair said quickly, as he and Larter went to fetch some logs too.

Soon drove the vehicle to the waters edge for John to construct their raft. They worked frantically as John finally put the last piece of his handiwork in place for Sinclair to lash up tightly.

"We will need the engine running just to keep any water out of the exhaust, for when we reach the slope. Once we do, we'll strip off the raft then use the logs to help the vehicle get a grip on it in case the land is soggy or unstable." John advised.

They managed to paddle their way over the swirling lake of muddy water to reach the slope, they stripped the heavy raft from the vehicle before it started to lurch its way up the steep slope.

"Keep her going Kim!" Sinclair advised, as he threw yet another log under the wheels to help it grip the sodden earth.

John and Larter had the towrope wrapped around a stout tree further up the slope, taking up the slack every time the vehicle moved upwards, thus preventing it from sliding backwards again. The girls were climbing up the slope with the equipment, taken off to lighten the vehicle.

It took a good hour for them to get the vehicle up the slope onto a flatter piece of ground, where they placed the logs in such a way as to prevent the vehicle from sliding back down the slope again.

All of them were exhausted and caked in mud by the time they finally got themselves organised with a small campsite.

"We've got plenty of timber for fire wood, with plenty of water even though we've got to boil it. How about the provisions Kim?" Sinclair asked breathlessly.

Soon told of their meagre food store, but declared they were still all right for a cuppa.

"Looks like Malayan bush tucker, then Kim!" Sinclair grinned, as he drew his sharp looking machete from its scabbard.

"We must wash and clean up first." One of the girls piped up.

"Okay then! John and I will go hunting for food whilst it's still light. Bruce, you get the water organised, with luck get the radio on the go. Kim you and the girls get plenty of firewood first before you get yourselves cleaned up. We'll need a few stones to make our cooking fire mind you." Sinclair suggested, which everybody agreed to.

"Shades of the Namib Andy!" John said almost absentmindedly as he followed Sinclair down to the waters edge with the revolver in his hand.[*]

"All we've got to do John, is to shoot any animal taking a ride on one of these tree trunks passing by. Be careful of the water snakes though." Sinclair advised, as they sat waiting for just such an event.

It wasn't long before they spotted a wild pig standing precariously in the middle of a large tree trunk, shrieking and grunting almost incessantly.

"I'll lasso the tree trunk to pull it over to us. You get ready to shoot it as it tries to jump off, but make sure you shoot the animal, not me." Sinclair said quickly as he threw the line over the water, successfully snagging the log.

---

[*] See *Fresh Water*.

John took careful aim and with one shot, killed the animal.

The pistol shot echoed over the densely wooded slopes, which was a signal to the others in the camp they would eat today after all.

"C'mon John. Roast pork and biscuit stuffing for supper. Maybe some bacon for breakfast in the morning, we'll sort the eggs out then if we're still here." Sinclair grinned, as he lifted the large dead animal over his shoulder and started to climb the hill again.

"Welcome the hunters! We gatherers are ruddy starving!" Larter quipped, as John and Sinclair arrived back into camp.

Soon along with two of the girls commenced to prepare the animal for cooking, whilst John and Sinclair were stripped naked, to be washed from head to toe by their partners.

"You are two naughty boys. You must have a good wash before you eat!" they chided as they gave their partners dangly bits extra special washing, generally teasing them playfully.

John and Sinclair just stood in the large warm pool of water letting the girls help themselves, whilst they were enjoying the attentions of their partners.

"That'll take you back a little while, John!" Larter chuckled as he threw a bucket of cold water over him, which splashed over his partner.

"Now look what you've done! Now I've got to get out of these wet clothes again, you silly boy." Larter's partner cried and started to strip off.

"I'm all in favour of that, maybe we'll join you." Larter responded, pretending to strip off too, but got a clip around his ear from his own partner, who said he was to behave.

Soon shook his head slowly, muttering something in Chinese to the effect that all Englishmen were crackers, off their heads and loopy, which one of the girls translated for them, having them all laughing in the end.

The sun was about to go and lie down for its own rest, when John finished eating his meal. He decided to enjoy a well-earned cigarette, which he was sharing with his partner when they all heard a rumbling noise that was getting louder by the second.

"Bloody hell! Where's that coming from?" Larter asked quickly.

They got up and went in separate directions trying to find out where it was coming from.

John managed to see some trees starting to fall down, only some yards away from him, shouting to the others to come and see what he had found.

"It appears the dam must have broken down and the water is coming our way. There's a natural gully over there, so if we're lucky it will all funnel down it, not for it to wash over to us." Larter suggested, as the girls started to get anxious and panicky.

"That sounds about right Bruce, because the ground beneath us is dry and still. Otherwise, we'd have been flooded long before now." Sinclair stated, as he felt the ground all around where they were standing.

"If I remember rightly, flash floods only last a few hours, or until all the water has flowed away over from the broken dams. It's always like that on the Yangtze River." Soon offered.

"We can count ourselves lucky this time around, given that it could have burst whilst we were on the road below us." John added philosophically.

They scouted around their little campsite anxiously, waiting and watching for the noise of the raging floodwater to subside for them to feel safe.

"It appears we're okay now. Perhaps we can settle down now and get some sleep, as it's been one hell of a day." Sinclair offered, as they all crept along in the dark towards the warmth of their campfire again.

"Okay then everybody. The camp is camouflaged and secured for the night. Kim! You and your partner will keep the first watch. My partner and me will be your relief. Let the fire die down but keep the tinder dry in case it starts to rain during the night again." Sinclair directed, as he gave them their times for watch.

Soon the weary so-called weekend trippers were fast asleep in their little cocoon in the jungle, to await their turn to be rescued.

CHAPTER IX

Reporting for Duty

The distinct noise of a helicopter approaching their little camp on the side of a high hill sparked a mini stampede towards open ground, where they waved their arms or any piece of clothing coming to hand.

Larter tore off one of the vehicles wing mirrors then started to flash at the whirlybird until it finally saw them to begin to make its approach.

The down draught of the rotor blades created a mini tornado onto them but they didn't care, as the helicopter finally touched down near their vehicle.

A man jumped out of the helicopter wearing a flying suit complete with helmet, and walked towards the happy people.

"Good morning gentlemen. Flight Lt Roy Ward Royal Navy, at your service. How many are there of you? Are there any casualties or fatalities among you?" he asked politely as he met up with John.

"Good morning! I'm 2nd Engineer Grey. We are a party of 8, all of whom you see around you.

We were originally camped at the Kota Tingghi waterfall up to mid-day yesterday, trying to make it back. As you can see we're all safe and well as can be expected."

"That's fine Grey. We can lift you all up but you'll have to leave your vehicle behind. Judging by your campsite, you have been extremely lucky, as the hill just a few yards away from you on both sides has been completely washed away. You are in fact on a single promontory with no visible means of getting off it other than by air. If you're ready to leave then we'll go. We've still got stranded survivors further up country from you to rescue." Parsons stated.

"I'm Radio Officer Larter. It was me who contacted an army radio station. They mentioned there were marines in the area."

Larter said as he carried his radio and other personal belongings with him.

"The army is west of here helping to sort out the roads. The marines are engaged with insurgent activities further to the north. Now better step lively, as we're running out of fuel. Duck your heads when approaching the aircraft." he advised.

With a roar of engines, the helicopter lifted off the ground gracefully, before spinning around and heading its way over the green canopy of the Malayan jungle and to safety.

They had managed to get a quick glimpse of where they had camped, and were astounded at what they had seen. Parsons had understated their predicament, as there would have been no way they could have even climbed down from their lofty perch. All the land and trees around them had been stripped bare, leaving an ugly scar on the natural tapestry of the land below them.

"What caused all this damage Ward?" Sinclair asked.

"The indiscriminate logging of the rain forest. Each large tree needs several hundred gallons of water a year to survive. But once they're cut down, the earth gets dry and easily washed away when the monsoon rains come along. That causes flash flooding and natural damming of the waters. Once those get breached it's like another bigger flood of almost tidal wave proportions. You have seen the consequences for yourself and you are extremely lucky to survive it."

"It will take more than a flash flood to do us in, Ward. Believe you me." Sinclair replied with a nod.

The helicopter finally landed at its airfield where an ambulance was waiting to take them for a brief medical check up.

The medical attendant and orderly were gentle and considerate towards them all, especially towards the girls.

"We need to contact our shipping agent, and the girls their own people. Any chance of a few phone calls?" John asked the orderly.

"Certainly. But not until Matron has seen you all first." the orderly replied, before he disappeared behind a maze of screens.

"The ship should have undocked some hours ago, unless they're waiting until we get back! Maybe the company will penalise us for being absent on such an occasion." Soon surmised.

"No! Fergus will just carry on with what was agreed until we show up again. But no doubt Stafford and co will be worried sick about us not being there for the move." John replied.

"We can't do much on board until the dockyard has finished anyway, Kim. So stop worrying yourself into an early grave." Sinclair assured.

"Yes, what we must be concerned about is the girls and what their pimp will do to them for not turning up for their shifts." Larter said, as he added to the conversation.

The girls had been taken away for a while and were returned to the group, each wearing a smile.

"We have been given a free check up and we are all well. We also managed to contact our boss who said that he was happy we are alive and well, and that we can have the day off." One of them said happily.

"That's good! Just as long as the merchandise has been returned in good order. Maybe we can borrow you lot again sometime." Larter quipped as he gently hugged his partner, which was copied in turn by the other 3 friends.

"Now then you lot! This is a hospital not a bordello! You have been found fit to return to your units and you women back to your homes wherever they may be. There is a tilley to take you back to the naval base, so be off with you." a very large bosomy woman dressed in over starched white uniform, stated crossly.

"Oh Matron! Many thanks matron, I'm sure." John responded with a nod of his head, and ushered out his troupe.

The tilley stopped long enough for the girls to get out and for John and his friends to arrange a future meeting before it sped away into the sprawling grounds of the naval base until it passed through the large wrought iron gates of the dockyard.

After a brief security check they were allowed to enter the main dockyard and the tilley finally arrived alongside the smartly painted floating dock which was slowly coming out of the water, complete with a scruffy little merchant ship cradled inside it.

"Look there's Fergus on the dock side. Let's go and cheer him up! But leave the talking to me." John said quickly as they baled out of the tilley with their belongings, and walked swiftly to arrive next to the small crowd of observers.

"Hello Fergus! Lovely day for a move what?" John asked softly and casually.

McPhee turned sharply to see John and his friends smiling at him, looking pleased with themselves.

"Bloody hell John! What the hell are you playing at? Where the hell have you lot been these last couple of days. I've been searching everywhere for you. We've had to re dock the ship to a bigger one as you can see." McPhee said crossly.

"Yes, it needed one that size anyway. Sorry for our absence Fergus, but I'm not responsible for the monsoon weather that held us up. The fact of the matter is, we were caught in the flash floods up jungle at the Kota Tingghi waterfalls where we went for a short camping trip. We were rescued by naval helicopter only a couple of hours ago and have just come back from the BMH. The transport we were given is still up country, and unless there's a heavy lift helicopter to rescue it as well then you'll have to write it off. We brought all the equipment that we could including the radio, of course." John replied nonchalantly.

McPhee looked at the others then back to John before he responded.

"If I didn't know you better Engineer Grey, I'd say that you're definitely taking the piss, and it's all a pack of lies. Still! Now that you're here, perhaps when the ship is secured, you can take over from my deputy who was forced to stand in for you. Believe you me he has certainly lived up to his name over it, too." McPhee sighed.

"Actually it will be a pleasure Fergus. It's no fun being bitten on the goolies by unseen teeth you know, especially from the creepy crawly types." John said breezily, making McPhee scowl even more.

"Anyway, be that as it may. Oh! by the by, your man Parfitt was looking for you lot yesterday, something to do with your new Captain. I'm expecting Stafford sometime today, so try and get on board before he sees that you're shore side, or he'll have a fit, because, if I can remember rightly, you were told to remain on board at all times."

"Thanks for the tip Fergus, but we really were caught up in the big floods up country and there's nothing he could say about it. Sufficient to say that the shipping company still has 4 officers ready and reporting for duty and not 4 more ready to be buried." John responded, as McPhee took his leave from them.

John told the others what McPhee had said and that it was possible that they would be on the carpet, for going ashore instead of obeying their direct instruction of remaining on board.

"That was one instruction we could not have been carried out. Nobody would have expected us to stay on board a virtual hulk without proper accommodation and provisions." Soon scoffed.

"Yes, you're right there Kim. Anyway, once we get back on board it will be all systems go." John agreed.

The ship had now rested comfortably in her little cradle, held up by a mini forest of trees propping her up to prevent it from tipping over.

The friends tramped up the steep steel steps to the top of the floating dock, and crossed the narrow gangplank to arrive on board where one very irate person was waiting for them.

"Visitors are not allowed on this vessel!" Cross shouted over to them, until he recognised John and is friends.

"Just where the hell were you lot that I had to come and do your move? I have better things to do with my time than to play nursemaid to you bunch of layabouts. You're supposed to be professional officers, so far you're nothing but a bunch of wasters!" Cross replied angrily, and in a sarcastic manner.

"Oi Cross! Watch your lip mate before I give you a knuckle sarnie!" Sinclair shouted as he tried to lunge past John to get to the offensive man.

"There is no need to be cross with us Cross! Just think of it this way, if it hadn't been for our good fortune up country where the big flood was, you'd still be here for the rest of the refit. Now bugger off and let some real officers take charge." John countered angrily.

Cross looked at each of the friend's faces for a moment before he stormed across the gangway with his parting words.

"You have exactly ten days now to get your scrap of metal off my floating dock. Until then, I need a daily report from each of you." he shouted as he left.

"Not unless you can provide a full secretarial team and technical drawing staff to do so Cross!" John shouted back, but only got a muttered string of abuse and expletives in reply.

"It appears McPhee was right after all. Cross really was cross!" John chuckled, as the friends made their way into their little inner sanctum of the saloon.

"Right then you lot! We'll have some grub before we start our planned schedules. Kim, kindly see to that, and see if you can arrange an itinerary for our daily runs ashore that will include our lady friends. We might as well work hard during the day and live it up in the night. The proviso being that we will have a roster drawn up for the purpose of having an evening 'Duty Officer'. That is to say, we will take it in turns to be Captain of the ship and see to any problems that might arise after hours. Bruce, you will kindly see to that item.

Andy, I need you to ensure that we don't have stowaways on board. By that I mean, make sure that all dockyard mateys who are not required for work, will be sent ashore. That way, we can keep a check on those using the crews quarters aft overnight." John directed, to which the others responded with a nod in acceptance of John's orders.

"One thing though! We're supposed to be getting a Royal Naval Captain to take over the ship, but don't know who or when. Until then we're on our own to show these people that we're just as professional as them." John added.

"Just as long as it's not Hughes. Why he couldn't sail a wee boat in a bath tub, let alone a bloody great cruiser." Sinclair drawled, which made the others laugh at his old chestnut of a saying.

CHAPTER X

Orders

Over the next ten days, John and his friends played the key roles in transforming a ship looking doomed to the scrap yard, into one, which looked almost ready, to take on anything man let alone the sea could throw at it. The local dockyard mateys worked a full 24hour shift during those days, with a procession of their various departmental Supervisors coming or going to make sure all was well.

John had his modified engine room and his version of the special cargo holds. Soon had his modernised accommodation area and crew's quarters, new fridges and even two complete sets of crockery, cutlery, linen, bedding plus all the trimmings, including a new set of furniture to grace the dining saloon. Sinclair had his new rigging, capstans, lifeboats, or any other deck fitments his men would be deemed to use during a voyage. Larter, with the superhuman efforts by his dockyard supervisor Westwood and his men, managed to update his communications and radar equipment, even obtaining a full set of Admiralty charts along with other vital bridge equipment the Captain would deem the prerequisites for him.

In fact, John and his friends worked so hard, that although demanding the best out of the workforce they managed to gain the esteem of the dockyard's British personnel, who treated the 4 officers with respect, even vying to have the privilege to be able to work alongside them. Soon was quick to pickup on that, and was able to get a full list of very willing volunteers to man the ship when it finally sailed away.

During their off time duties they were shown the sights of Singapore by the same four girls who had shared their weekend venture. Now close friends, they were regular visitors staying overnight instead of working all hours in the bar, which was their so-called home.

It was visits to 'Change Alley' where you could swap various countries' currency at bargain prices and even pick up a 'genuine' designer product for less than an 'nth price of the real thing. The girls even took them to enjoy the spectacle of seeing young men who had grown breasts and bended their gender's to make themselves even more lovelier than the 'real girls'. They would be universally known as Kai-Tai's' or even 'He-She's'. It was a time of stopping at a nearby cart to buy a bowl of bird's nest soup followed by a portion of 'king plawns and 'flied lice' coming from a flaming, smoking wok a local man was cooking their meal in. All for a few dollars and be washed down by the ever present bottle of ice cold Tiger Beer. The friends enjoyed themselves to the full, with no strings attached by their partners, and such was their idyll, it was becoming a trendsetter amongst the rest of the unattached British sailors inhabiting the massive naval base.

The ship had a new coat of paint inside and out, and was waiting for it to dry in the baking sun of the tropics, when their new Captain finally showed up, to be met by Soon.

"Good morning! I'm Commander Farquhar joining as the new Captain of this vessel. Kindly take me to meet the officers on board, will you. Here, you may take my luggage whilst you're at it, there's a good chap!" Farquhar stated offhandedly, throwing his bag over to Soon.

"My name is Mr Soon. I am the Purser of this ship and one of its officers. You are now on a merchant ship, which means you will carry your own luggage like the rest of us. Follow me if you please." Soon asserted, but with a slight now of his head.

Farquhar was taken aback by this unexpected response, but managed to browbeat a passing worker into carrying his baggage for him as he followed Soon into the saloon.

Once there, Soon nodded to the worker that he was done, who dumped the baggage unceremoniously onto the deck and sauntered away cursing the man in his own language.

Farquhar turned round making his own response in the same

language, which astounded not only Soon, but also the hapless worker.

John and the others were already in the saloon having one of their daily 'end of day' briefings, when Soon entered the saloon and introduced Farquhar to them all before he offered some refreshments as befitting the occasion.

Farquhar was of medium height but a stocky build, with ginger hair and a twinkle in his blue eyes, that seem to light up his slightly freckled face.

"We are in the middle of our daily de-briefing Captain. We will not be long, so please be seated and join in if you are inclined to do so." John informed him politely.

"Yes, do carry on! I like to see my officers in action, especially to find out what they've been up to." Farquhar replied civilly, sitting down heavily to enjoy a cool soft drink offered by Soon.

Once the debriefing was over, Farquhar stood up giving a brief reprise on what he had heard, which was agreed to by John and the others.

"So gentlemen, I have heard all what I want to hear. Maybe my Captaincy on this ship will be a much easier one, once you realise that I'm the new Captain not just a bystander. Now I must find my cabin to get myself in an appropriate dress. Mr Soon, will you be good enough to bring me the ships log and other records so that I may install myself as your new Captain as of this day. I need a conducted tour of the ship from each department later on, so kindly be on hand gentlemen." Farquhar said bumptiously, then leaving the saloon, followed Soon to the Captains day cabin, where he re-emerged some half hour later to rejoin John and the others.

"Right then gentlemen. Ships' drawings and the like are one thing, but I prefer to see the ship as she really is. I want to see her from stem to stern; from mast to keel, and all points in between. So lets all take a stroll down memory lane if only for my sake." Farquhar ordered, as he breezed into the saloon wearing civilian clothing but with his Captain's cap stuck on his head at a rakish angle.

Sinclair who led the way out of the saloon showed Farquhar all the new upper deck equipment to see how everything worked. Soon showed him the accommodation area including the newly refurbished passenger's cabins, the new type of fridges that John had designed, then the revamped crews quarters aft, all in his own traditional Chinese style dubbed by John and the others as 'Fung Shoey'.

Larter showed him the communications, navigational equipment and other items that would make life easier for the Captain on the bridge. John showed him the cargo hold layout he had designed on a previous ship, before Farquhar was taken down into the spotlessly clean and shiny engine room, which only a few weeks ago resembled a 'slag heap' now housing newly installed motor generator, and other such vital equipment the Captain would be using to sail his ship through any stormy waters.

When they arrived back into the saloon, Farquhar thanked them for the tour, stating the fact that even though he was not altogether too impressed by what he had seen; the ship had at least been reprieved from the certainty of being scrapped forthwith.

McPhee entered the saloon along with Cross, just as John was enjoying a solitary cup of coffee.

"Morning Fergus! Come to review the situation? We have our new Captain on board, by the name of Commander Farquhar. He's ashore at the moment if you wanted to see him." John informed.

"Morning John! I'm meeting him here shortly, but it's you I came to see." McPhee replied, as he unrolled a sheaf of drawings onto a table and proceeded to go through some points with him. Once he had his questions and problems satisfactorily answered or explained by John, he rolled up the sheaf then put his had on top of it as if to indicate that he was now 'off duty'.

"Care for light refreshments Fergus, or maybe a visit by Mr Dimple?" John asked cheerfully.

"Just a white coffee for now John. I need to keep my brain focussed on those drawing amendments. Farquhar should be here any time now, so best I kept sober." McPhee responded with a sigh, then chatted for a while and drinking his coffee until Farquhar came marching into the saloon

"Chief McPhee! Glad you made it. This ship is half Chinese and half British, which seems to work and therefore okay with me but throws up a couple of problems that I need you to sort for me." he announced and with a magnanimous wave of his hand told John to dismiss himself from the room.

McPhee saw the signal, telling John to remain where he was, when quite by co-incidence they were joined by the other 3 officers.

"Whatever problems you've got Farquhar, you'd had better start to change your tack if you wish to survive on this vessel. This is no way to treat your officers. You have 4 very good officers who will form the backbone of your command. So start thinking Merchant as opposed to Royal, and climb down off your high horse. These men have worked like Trojans to see this refit came to a proper and early conclusion, so accord them the same respect you wish to receive." McPhee chided, then took a breath before he gave them news of pending acceptance trials, which were going to be held shortly.

Whilst McPhee was instructing John and his friends, Farquhar was sitting at a separate table paying, almost sulkily, little heed to what was being said. Soon handed out cold glasses of soft drinks to each of them during this impromptu meeting, until McPhee concluded his oration.

"Captain! You will have the privilege of taking the ship down creek to the Singapore Roads for the speed trials, then over to the degaussing ranges, as of two days time. Senior dockyard officers such as myself plus certain shipping company officers will be on board during all the trials. This will be your chance to iron out any problems, but most importantly, for you to get to know your ship, which is after all something quite different you've discovered from the last one you were on.

You undock first thing tomorrow morning, so don't you lot go astray again as I can't put up with Cross's whinging again. One last thing Captain! Just you keep reminding yourself this is a merchant vessel with a civilian crew, just like the Torpedo and Mine Recovery Vessel you commanded some time ago as a young Lieutenant. If you can't remember that far back, I certainly can." McPhee concluded and left the saloon with his arm full of drawings.

John escorted McPhee to the gangway promising to see him later on.

"Why did we get Farquhar, Fergus? Why not one of our own Captains or at least one of their Auxiliary officers?"

"Farquhar might seem an oddball, but he's a bloody good Deck Officer who knows how to handle ships especially around these waters. He is also an expert on explosives, which is a must on this type of vessel. He was to take over the job from Hughes whom you met on the *Antares*, who was the Gunnery and Weapons Officer. He does speak Cantonese and Hindu, also Dutch and French. I suggest that you will have to humour him now and again even though he is a bit of a stuffed shirt on times. Just you keep the faith John for all to be well. Oh and by the way, we had to put a different propeller on, that will hopefully give you a few extra knots. I mention this because you'll need to know when working out your fuel figures." McPhee chuckled, as he left the ship.

Farquhar stood on the open bridge with his binoculars watching the proceedings of the undocking, in company with John, Larter and a few dockyard supervisors.

"Here come the tugs now, 3rd mate." he shouted down to Sinclair who was on the foc'sle.

"Sparks, tell them that we're ready. Engineer Grey, make a swift survey to make sure that we haven't inherited some leak or other." Farquhar ordered quietly, sending his officers to do his bidding.

It took a couple of hours to undock and for the ship to be pushed and secured alongside her allocated berth.

"All compartments dry and secure!" John reported promptly as he arrived back onto the bridge.

Larter told Farquhar that the tugs had now finished and were returning to other duties. Sinclair came onto the bridge informing him that all was well and that the extra fenders were in place.

The senior dockyard supervisor turned to Farquhar telling him all seemed to be well, and that the dockside trials for accepting cargo would commence early the following morning.

The gangway was already in position for the scores of dockyard workers to stream off and for others to come aboard to finish off their work tasks.

Cross came over the gangway making his way up to the bridge, then spoke to Farquhar and his now gathered officers.

"You will have a supply truck arriving soon with your provisions for 7days. You are advised that due to the ratio of LEP's is 3 to 1 British crewmen, your stores will be catered mainly for them   In other words you'll just have to get used shark fin soup, sweet and sours or other curries, whatever.. A lighter will be alongside later today for you take on fuel. You will flash up your boilers and be on 2 hours notice as at 0400 in the morning.   The shore supply umbilical cord will be connected soon for you to have electricity, water etcetera, but by 0800 tomorrow it will be disconnected so you must get your own supplies up and running by then. I understand that the intentions are for you to do a couple of days sea trials and suchlike. Let us know of your E.T.A. each day so we can reconnect your umbilical cord again. If all goes well gentlemen, you will be sailing out of here for the last time about 5 days from now. Mr McPhee along with other personnel will be with you in the morning prior to your first venture down creek, so I would suggest you get a crew organised as we'll be lending you the extra crew during the trials only." he stated in a perfunctory manner.[*]

Farquhar nodded his head accepting the verbal orders but demanded a written statement to the same effect, just in case

---

[*] LEP's mean Local Entry Personnel.

there was some sort of misunderstanding or change to them.

"Here are those orders and agenda of intent." Cross said indignantly, as he thrust the thick ream of papers into Farquhar's hands.

"Thank you Cross! A written word is a much better medium to interpret than the spoken one. Accents and dialects let alone native tongue can distract from the true orders you know." Farquhar insisted as he took the papers and threw them onto the chart table behind him.

Cross left the bridge along with the other British dockyard workers, for Farquhar to turn to his officers.

"Right then gentlemen. You heard the man, lets get this ship under control before anybody leaps ashore. Incidentally, and as of now, no officer will leave the ship without my express permission unless on ships business is that clear! I'm expecting the arrival of a few more officers to swell our ranks, so you will stay on board and be here to meet and greet them. Mr Soon, be kind enough to make sure you do the appropriate paperwork for all personnel who are boarding between now and then. Engineer Grey, I need your comment on the current state of my engines, so you will come and see me in my cabin in about 1 hour from now." Farquhar ordered pompously, before he left the bridge to the astonished John and his friends.

"Bloody hell, talk about Trewarthy!" Sinclair stated with concern.

"Cresswell, even 'Spanners' Jones were much worse than him, so take no heed Andy." John opined, and left the bridge to his friends.

CHAPTER XI

An Old Custom

The ship received the rest of its volunteer crew, which was a mix of British and Asian.

Soon managed to see that the senior deck hands and engineers had a good command of English before he allocated them their jobs according to qualifications and the like. The junior officers and deck hands, although a mix between Malay and Chinese, also had to have some basic knowledge of the English language before they were accepted on board. Just as long as they were capable and willing to do their duty on board, was the maxim John and Sinclair had issued to Soon.

That evening, Farquhar with Stafford, Parfitt and McPhee, gathered the ships officers together in the saloon for a pep talk concerning the role the *Tsun Wan* was to undertake, which he underlined in no uncertain manner.

He paused to answer any questions before concluding the meeting with some good news, which was something of a surprise to them.

"The 4 officers who stood by the ship and saw all the work undertaken was to the highest standard, had changed this virtual hulk of scrap into a living breathing ship with a future, will stand up. Namely Engineer Grey, Deck officer Sinclair, Radio Officer Larter and Mr Soon, acting Purser." Farquhar commanded, which prompted the 4 officers to stand as ordered.

Farquhar then nodded to Stafford and the other officials to take over.

"We of the shipping line have the privilege to promote 2nd Engineer Grey to Acting Chief engineer. That Deck officer Sinclair be promoted to the exalted heights of First Mate. Mr Soon will become one of our management team as our Chief recruiter, but meanwhile he will remain on board as our administrator and ships purser. Radio Officer Larter has almost reached the pinnacle in his hierarchy as decreed by Marconi, but we will promote him to Deputy Chief Radio officer. They will remain on this ship for the duration of and the completion to the building of our proposed new Marine Colleges both here and Hong Kong. With Cape Town, Vancouver and Halifax N.S already coming on stream, if you pardon the pun." Stafford announced then turned to McPhee and the other senior officials.

"That is unless there is an objection or dissent from you gentlemen? And from those recipients of these promotions?" he added.

McPhee, Parfitt and even Farquhar cheered and clapped to show their pleasure and agreement to the sudden promotions.

John and his friends looked at each other in surprise but were quick to nod their heads stating they would honour the accolades accordingly, before realising what the promotions had meant for them. Their own cheers and jubilation were like a volcano exploding, as they stood up and congratulated each other with handshakes and lots of backslapping.

"You certainly deserve them, gentlemen. For you also managed to reduce the budget by at least one third, which HM government will be pleased to hear." McPhee said with equal elation as he came over shaking John's and his friend's hands in congratulations.

Once the euphoria died down and some of the other dockyard officials had given their say, the meeting broke up with the prospect of conducting various trials starting the following morning.

John escorted McPhee again to the gangway thanking him on behalf of his friends for his kindness.

"Just keep the faith dear boy! Or shall I start calling you Chief, now! Congratulations John, you're now on your way to fulfilling the promise you made me in Belfast. Anyway I'll see you in the morning once you've had time to reflect on your well earned promotion." McPhee whispered as he left the ship once more.

* * *

John was down in the engine room keeping an eye on the pressure gauge, only one amongst the several items to make up the important parts of the ships propulsion, so that when the ship slipped her berth, the Captain would have immediate control over its performance.

He had the entire engine room staff down there taking notice of what was going on, using the occasion as a dress rehearsal prior to them settling down into a proper engine room watch at sea.

"Right then gentlemen, you all know what is expected from you. Chief stoker Hurley! Make sure you have a stoker in each watch who understands English and can write properly, using Stoker Fat Soh as an example. He will man the telegraphs and answer the telephone just like the bridge messenger does. He will also be required to log each telegraph order coming down from the bridge, then relay them to the officer of the watch in case that person who may have his eyes elsewhere or not heard the telegraph warning alarm. I want this engine room kept clean at all times, and each man will dress in standard overalls when working in these compartments." John ordered, then went on to explain his rules and regulations which would eventually be promulgated to become the criteria on board the ship, as a permanent reminder to them all what's expected from them and how to conduct their watches. The meeting lasted for half an hour before he dismissed them, leaving the engine room to the care of the duty officer.

"I shall be in my cabin if you need me 2nd. Ask the outside engineer to come and see me in half an hour. We sail at 0800, so make certain the Captain is informed of the '1 hour readiness'. These Naval wallahs are a stickler for correct procedures so let's not have him on our backs before we start this show." John said calmly, as he climbed the statutory ladder up from the bowels of the ship.

"You sent for me Chief?" the 3rd Engineer asked as he first knocked then entered Johns cabin.

"Ah yes! Do come in, erm what's your name." John invited, and was promptly reminded of whom the man was.

"Yes, sorry for not remembering you Dave Ottley. Only you've joined the ship without seeing me first." John apologised before he told the 3rd exactly why he was sent for.

"That's fine by me Chief. I'm used to planned machine maintenance as it's practised in the Royal Fleet Auxiliary Service (RFA), anyway. If you want a double round each day but just one report per day, and even then only on what went wrong for me to fix, then that too is fine by me. At least we both can have a bit of breathing space to get on with something of more importance." Ottley said earnestly, handing John his task and logbooks for him to read.

John scanned through them noticing the concise way everything was described and in normal engineering parlance before giving them back.

"You appear to keep excellent records Ottley, maybe you and I will get on just fine. But in future, you will organise any extra training with the 2nd Engineer as appropriate. From now on, I will only see you for your reports at 1200 each day, but if anything untoward should happen to the engineering side of things on this ship, for God sake let me know first. You may get turned in now as we're in for a heck of a first day at sea. All manner of things could, and sods law states will happen all at the same time for us poor engineers." John concluded.

"Right then Chief, see you at breakfast." Ottley responded cheerfully, leaving the cabin to John, who stood staring at the spot to where Ottley had been standing.

'I wonder if I was like that. All cocky and full of myself?' he mused, sighed and sat down heavily onto his bunk with a large tome of an engineering manual to read.

'Oh to be a 3rd once more. No care or thought for anybody but yourself and your machinery. Sod this book! I know virtually each word that has been written. Maybe now I've nearly become top of the pile, I can start relaxing and enjoy the rest of my career. I've had some very good role models and teachers to get

me this far, including the despot Cresswell. May God save his black heart. It will be up to me to keep their standards as they helped me to maintain mine. Like passing the baton onto the next person in a relay race. Yes, that's it.' he muttered and promptly fell asleep fully clothed on his bunk.

"Morning Chief! It's 0600, here's an early morning cuppa. Breakfast is at 0630. The Captain wishes to see you on the bridge at 0745." the steward announced quietly, as he shook John roughly to waken him up.

John rose up slowly then sat on the edge of his bunk and looked towards the pile of engineering manuals, ships diagrams, and reams of paper that somehow seemed to breed amongst themselves whilst he was asleep. He took the cup of hot liquid and drank it down to feel it take effect on his cold body, before handing the empty cup back.

"Cheers steward, whatever your name is. Make sure I've got a clean set of white overalls lined up for later. I shall be wearing my white tropicals for now. Oh and by the way, make sure my uniform reflects my new rank. You know what our Captain is like for dress code and all that crap." John whispered hoarsely, as he started to undress to prepare for his early morning ablutions.

"As it happens, one of the stewards is a bit of a tailor on the quiet, for he's already done the favours to your uniform already. He says you can put it on your mess bill for him to collect later. You've been given a new set of clobber and footwear, so when you've finished with all your old clothing, we can hand them in as replaced 'new for old', as I've been told by the purser. And for future reference I'm the Chief steward on board, and my name is Thompson, but apart from calling me all the names under the sun, I'll respond to 'Tommo!" the steward chirped as he went about tidying up and cleaning around the cabin.

"That's fair enough erm, Tommo! Leave me for a moment whilst I get organised."

John had his shower and shave then got dressed into his well-starched white tropicals.

"Bloody hell! Somebody's heavy handed with the starch. I could cut myself on these creases." John observed.

"Yes our dhoby* wallah, mistook the starch for the dhoby dust° yesterday. Still, he'll soon get used to the routine. Mind you, he's a dab hand on the ironing board. He'd definitely make a fortune in the dhoby trade back home. Incidentally, for your info Chief, all facilities like your dhobying, ironing, and the like, will be added to your mess bill, to be paid up monthly."

"Monthly? Why is that when we only get paid at the end of each voyage?"

"Actually, we will be paid monthly as of this month, and for a special reason. Now lets see.

The tailor is called 'Sew Sew', the cobbler is called 'Shoe Shoe, the barber is called 'Snip Snip'. The dhoby wallah is So Hi, and his brother is called So Lo due to the fact that they're from both ends of the measuring tape. The shop manager and some of the crew, are all local men who live on board earning their living from us. We call it "earning their rice bowl" just like we do with the shipping company. This is an old custom brought down from Hong Kong and works a treat, just as long as you pay them their dues. They work damn hard for what they earn, so pay up on time to keep them happy."

"Sounds like a pretty good little enterprise then Tommo. What about the cooks and the other stewards? Are they company owned or free lance too?"

"All the British, or white men are 'company property' by virtue of being recruited and paid by the company. But these itinerants and other locals get taken on board at the discretion of and solely by permission from the purser of each ship, Mr Soon in our case. If they prove themselves to be loyal to the company and to the ship, then they get to stay for as long as they want to. Those who do earn that privilege get to bring their wives and

---

* Laundry.
° Washing Powder.

family with them, but are limited in numbers. They, the families that is, look after the crew's quarters aft, and generally help out in the galley. In all Chief! A good set up with plenty of benefits for them and the ship." Thompson explained at length.

"That explains what Kim, erm Mr Soon, mentioned when I first arrived. Mind you, some of the locals who volunteered to join us are bloody good workers and seem to know their stuff. In fact some of them are probably better at their job than some of the British crew I've had the misfortune to come across."

"Yes, I've found that out too. They seem to know who amongst us British people are genuine and hard workers, for they will do anything for us, the others are given short shrift. Mind you, it is the proverbial two way street, in that they expect you to reciprocate in kind and perhaps reward them for their efforts."

"Thanks for the info and an interesting topic of conversation Tommo! I'm off for breakfast now, what's on the menu?" John asked, as he picked up his cap and put it under his arm.

"You and the Captain will probably get a choice of fruit juice, bacon and eggs, toast and marmalade then either tea or coffee. The rest of the officers will only get fruit juice, a boiled egg or baked fish, rolls and a cuppa."

"Sounds good. But tell the chef to make my breakfast with thick slices of bacon in between fresh hot buttered rolls and a large mug of tea. But what about you and the rest of the crew?"

"Right, I've noted your request and will see the Chief chef accordingly. However, we stewards get what the other officers get, call it perks of the trade if you like, but what you've just ordered sounds so delicious I'll ask for it as well. The lads will probably get braised kidney on toast, commonly known as 'Shit on a raft' or yellow peril with a poached egg, toast and tea. Our local friends aft will have their usual "flied lice" and "chicken cully". Smells delicious but probably tastes fowl!" Thompson responded, chuckling at his own pun.

John smiled at this friendly steward and left him to continue cleaning the cabin, as he made his way to the dining room.

***

"Morning Andy! Or is it First Mate now?" John greeted affably, as he sat down opposite Sinclair.

"Hello Engines!" Sinclair replied with a broad grin.

"Just like you dear Andy, not quite there yet. Seen anything of Bruce?"

"Yes, he's just left. Says to say hello to the new Chief! Maybe he could pay a visit some time."

"I should be so lucky, Andy. At least not until we're out at sea on our first voyage, something to do with it going with the territory when you've got the gold rings on your shoulders." John responded ruefully.

"Would you listen to her! Now that you've almost achieved your ultimate goal of being Mr Engines, unless you've been having Bruce and me on all these years since we first met up in Belfast waiting on the old '*Brook*', what's with the change of mind all of a sudden?" Sinclair rebuked gently.

"It was something which happened this morning and what was said that has suddenly woken me up to the reality of life around me. Maybe I'm not ready to play pass the parcel, or be part of the baton relay team just yet. Maybe its not sunk in yet that I could just sit back a bit now to let others do the donkey work, I don't know. It's as if something has changed as if overnight, and I feel as if becoming Chief Engineer is a bit of a let down, a kind of an anticlimax if you like."

"Nonsense, John! We all know, which also includes the management team, you, out of the four of us deserve your promotion. I mean, look at all the engineering adapting or modifications that you personally created to see them come to fruition. The rest of us merely tagged along, but I personally will enjoy my new rank as it now gives me the platform I need to strike out for a full Captaincy before I finally retire shore side. If it wasn't for you I would still be with the Triple Crown line as a bloody Bosun. Bruce feels the same, and as for Kim, he's working on getting his ship back into his ownership again. He's already promised me I could be his first Captain. So don't sound ungrateful and throw all your toys out of the pram." Sinclair insisted, as the steward arrived and laid John's breakfast down in front of him.

John saw the surprised look on Sinclair's face when he looked at John's food.

"You see! You even dine better these days. All I got was a scabby slice of toast with a few crumbs of scrambled egg on it, which was in fact the bloody powdered stuff and not the real McCoy. Maybe you'll feel better after your breakfast." Sinclair added, making John give a little smile that was noticed by Sinclair. "There you go Chief! Not exactly like the hot buttered farls and an enamel mug of scalding tea on a foggy morning, is it?" Sinclair asked his young yet old friend, in a soothing manner.

John nodded his head and ate his breakfast with gusto as Sinclair sat quietly smoking away.

When he finished his tea Sinclair offered him a cigarette, which he smoked slowly and in a relaxed manner.

"To quote a well known phrase, 'I feel a bit more civilised now'. Thanks for cheering me up Andy. Maybe when we get back alongside, we can have a run ashore to celebrate our fortunes. I'll get the steward to contact Kim and ask him to set up the venue for then. Must go now and see what the Captain wants off me. New experiences for us all no doubt. See you later!" John confided, as he rose to leave the table.

"Yes, I must go too. I've got a few loose ends to sort out before we cast off. From what I've been told by the new 2nd Mate, er, Alan Spencer, Farquhar is a bit of a wall banger. He likes to bang the ship against the dockyard wall before he leaves, and calls it his 'calling card'. If McPhee is on board he'll go absolutely bananas if the ship gets damaged before it actually gets out into mid-stream. Anyway, see you on the bridge. You'll probably bump into Bruce on the bridge as well." Sinclair said with a grin, as both men parted company and went their own separate ways

"Erm, excuse me Chief, but I've got a problem with one of the for'ard a.c.u's." Ottley stated, as he tackled John on his way onto the bridge.

"What is the problem 3rd? Maybe overloaded and needs de-icing, or maybe on the wrong ring main circuit?" John responded.

"No! The unit is totally knackered. I had to replace the saloon's a.c.u. with a new one, then have the old one installed in the for'ard hold due to lack of a further replacement for that machine. In other words, I need a new one as a total replacement." Ottley stated confidently.

John raised his eyebrows and looking at this young engineer, realised that he had also walked down the very same avenue. Whereas he had McPhee to turn to this young engineer only had John. This gave him a feeling of goose bumps rising along his tropically heated arms and neck, making him shiver slightly at the thought.

"Okay then 3rd! We will get you a spare a.c.u. but keep it to one side, as all you'll need is a single axial fan for each of the cargo holds. This ship will be carrying inert cargo such as steel and possible live explosives, all of which only need dry and cool conditions as opposed to a refrigerated cargo such as fruit and animal carcasses." John directed, to which Ottley nodded in acceptance of the word from his Chief.

"Thanks Chief! But there's one other problem with our after cargo hold!" Ottley continued, and swiftly outlined the problem.

Yet again John was surprised at the knowledge shown by the young engineer, and within moments decided he would take Ottley under his wing, just as his old engineer friends Happy Day, Tansey Lee, and others did for him. His thoughts immediately turned to the *Inverlaggan* and his own set of exactly the same problems, as he gave his advice, thus passing on his own knowledge and experiences.

"Okay! They call you Dai Ottley, maybe from a Welsh connection yes?" he asked gently.

"Why yes Chief! How did you know? But my pals call me Dave but take your pick." Ottley asked in total astonishment.

"Okay then Dave it shall be! I am already impressed by your attitude, and your apparent appreciation of the varied nature of the different machinery on board, as it says a lot about your fastidiousness to duty. If it was me, your next move would be to get someone shore side to fix you up with another single extractor fan and use it to replace that a.c.u. Having said that, make sure you keep the duff unit in case you need some of it for spare parts elsewhere."

Ottley's face beamed at the advice he was given and thanked John for it, as he left to carry on with his passage onto the bridge. *'Maybe this is around the time and place I came into the business. Ottley seems a likely candidate for this baton relay team. But then I suppose I did for Aussie Clarke, Ken Morris, and all the others I've met over the years. Maybe time will tell and if Fergus is still around, who knows!"* John mused, as he arrived onto the bridge to be met by a posse of dockyard officials who surrounded Farquhar, his Captain.

"Morning Chief! What a good morning for a sail down the creek! I trust all is well below?" Farquhar greeted breezily, saluting John as he appeared onto the bridge.

"Good morning Captain! Yes, we're ready at full steam and standing by to obey telegraphs." John responded civilly, as he gave Farquhar the customary salute between Captain and Chief engineer.

"Thank you Chief! Pilot, I'm in your hands now!" Farquhar announced to the officer standing by the Bosun at the ships wheel.

"Chief! You are advised that once we've cleared the jetty, you will only get slow or half-ahead orders, until such time we clear the creek and reach the roads. That is unless we start knocking against immovable objects, in which case we'll order emergency full astern, of course. Suggest that you make a note of our telegraph or rev speeds during that time for future use." the pilot warned in a friendly manner.

"I thank you for your advice pilot, but that is one precaution I have already anticipated, and have a man ready to take your orders. For yourself, just remember we have an old engine, which may take some time to respond to your speed or helm orders, so kindly take these matters into concern. That will apply especially to the full astern command " John answered knowingly, to which the pilot nodded in recognition of what he had said.

"Right then Captain! Cast off and lets get this ship down stream." the pilot ordered, which was the signal for John to leave the bridge.

"Good luck John!" Sinclair whispered, as John stepped off the bridge.

"Cheers Andy! Same to you!" John replied hastily and disappeared into the bowels of the ship.

CHAPTER XII

Whistles

For three days the ship transited up and down the twisting and turning creek, which separated the island of Singapore and the mainland of Malaya. It was the time for it to carry out various acceptance trials so the ship could be accorded its full Ministry of Transport and Lloyd's Insurance papers to enable her to ply her trade in deep waters between nations.

John was at full stretch during those few days, as the engine and its accompanying parts, needed to be monitored closely to make sure it performed as well as it should. A constant change of speeds and the occasional 'Full Astern' orders thrown in, as rung on the telegraphs were taken during the transit down the 20 mile creek before entering into the 'roads' which offered a straight course again for a while and the engine settled into a steady rhythm. By the time the trials had finished, John and his engine room crew had shaped themselves into a good team with everybody knowing what they had to do and when to do it.

The usual clang as the ship thumped against the harbour wall told them they had arrived and that the engine could be put to sleep for the next time.

With the ship secured alongside the harbour wall after its final trial, much jubilation was felt between the dockyard masters, the ship owners and the officers of the ship's company.

John was on the bridge to find out the verdict on his department and of the rest of the ship's performance before the dockyard masters left for good.

"Thank you Captain! Your papers will be made up and delivered to you by the weekend. Before I leave I need a word with your Chief Engineer." McPhee informed Farquhar, as he beckoned John over to speak to him.

"You may have the usual problems from time to time with ship borne auxiliary machinery, but I think your engines have been re-born to steam another half a million miles. The 'White' engine layout is a good set up for this ship. Your only real fly in the proverbial ointment might be the steam steering gear. Maybe when you get up to Hong Kong, they will give you one that is somewhat more modern than the existing one. By the by, I suggest you sort out the written language on your machinery. This is a British ship for the next few years, so have everything written in English, with the appropriate colour coding used on all pipes and valves. You can't afford to have an interpreter to explain your commands."

"Actually, we're getting on pretty well as a team and they know what to do on a given signal. But what I really need is a 'wrong way round' alarm system set up a.s.a.p. Maybe your boys can sort something out for us before we take our first paying voyage?"

"Glad you mentioned it, as it's one of the 'must have' alarms on board. Better leave it with me to sort out. Now as to the verdict on the show so far John, it was a bit hairy at the beginning considering most of the engine and boiler room seem to be a Heath Robinson affair.

So, on that basis I congratulate you on the smooth running of your department, even though your 2nd Engineer seems a bit dodgy around the edges. However, you and your friends certainly have moulded this ship into shape adding at least a decade of life to her. Your new cargo handling array will impress them even more, you watch." McPhee said proudly, as he shook John's hand first, before Farquhar's.

"It will give me great pleasure to offer a special party on board tomorrow evening, to celebrate this day, Chief Superintendent. I shall fly the pink gin pennant at 1700 tomorrow, for you and your management team to be welcomed aboard." Farquhar announced with a big smile.

"Yes Captain! That sounds a good gesture on our behalf. We shall provide the necessaries. Ladies are welcome too don't forget, McPhee!" Stafford stated magnanimously

"In fact, as a bonus, the ship will not be required until Monday. So we can stand down the officers over the weekend, as our appreciation to their hard work in making all this seemingly impossible project such a success story." Parfitt admitted, adding weight to the high-powered decisions being made in moment of triumph.

McPhee turned to John and spoke aside to him.

"You see the rewards of a job well done John. See you tomorrow evening at the cock and arse party. Sandy Farquhar isn't a bad skipper, he's inclined to be a bit toffee nosed at times, and apt to forget his humble beginnings. Keep your feet on the ground and be like you've always been John and don't let success go to your head like he did." McPhee said, with a knowing wink of his eye, and a nod of his head.

"Thank you for being here Fergus. At least you've witnessed my latest triumph rather than me having to explain it in written form and in triplicate. See you tomorrow evening!" John responded candidly, as McPhee and the entourage trooped off the bridge with Farquhar escorting them off the ship.

"First Mate! Kindly send for the purser to attend us in the saloon in 10 minutes if you please!" John ordered, but with a big smile on his face.

"My pleasure Chief! Must stand my men down first though." Sinclair replied with a touch to his cap, then turning to the Bosun commencing to give him a long list of orders with pointers as to what he needed done.

"We've seen Bugis Street by night, visited some of our friends on board ship in Keppel harbour. Had a race in a trishaw, swam in the Britannia Club pool, had cocktails at Raffles, been to the Tiger Beer brewery, hobnobbed with the rich down Orchard Road, and so on. Including tea with McPhee's pal 'Peanuts' Dry cleaners who really was a 'Dockyard job!' All brilliant stuff Kim but you must be running out of places to go. Apart from us visiting the famous Nee Soon virgins that is, which our girls would definitely not take kindly to. They say that most of the soldier boys in the Nee Soon Barracks there are always visiting the famous 'Rose Cottage to have their knobs syringed out from the pox they picked up. Also according to them, several have even contracted oral diseases such as Tonsillitis, Mumps, and the odd case of Elephantitus. No wonder their missus's are leaving them and going back to Blighty in their droves. So where are you taking us today?" John asked politely as their taxi sped through the now deserted dockyard.

"Pasir Panjang! Lo Sing is a friend of mine who works there, will show us around the place in case we get lost, but we'll pick up the girls first." Kim replied with a smile.

"We'll be needing two taxis then." Larter observed, so they ordered another from the taxi rank, which was situated only a few yards away from the main gate.

Meeting the girls the taxis whisked them all away to the exotic location of Singapore's Tiger Balm Gardens. Which in fact is part of a large villa owned by a very rich man who invented the very popular mentholated ointment called 'Tiger Balm'.

They arrived at one of the ornate gates which looked like part of a pagoda, with a large statue of a tiger over the entrance, which is the symbol / logo of the ointment.

"Here we are, we can have a stroll around for a while before we get some king prawns down our neck!" Sinclair said, as they climbed out of the taxi.

Kim met his friend who greeted them cordially and gave a running commentary, during their walk around.

The girls provided a perfect escort for the friends that added to the magic of the day, and after their evening feast at a roadside café, they decided that it was time for some good old horizontal exercises.

"C'mon, let's catch the bus back, it's much cheaper, and besides it's a nice evening" one of the girls suggested, which was agreed by all the others.

They were sitting at the back of the bus talking amongst

themselves, when 3 young men boarded wielding sharp machetes, with one holding a gun to the bus driver's head. They shouted and threatened the passengers whilst demanding they handed over their valuables. When they approached the friends, they were perhaps careless and feeling quite brave after taking the valuables from all the others.

"You British pigs! Give us your wallets and your watches now, before my friend split you open!" the one with the gun snarled in Pidgin English.

Sinclair sighed and stood up pretending to do as he was told, but in fact, grabbing hold of the gun-wielding robber, literally threw him right out of the nearest open window. At the same time, Larter and Soon dispatched the other two in similar fashion, whilst John calmed the girls down.

The friends raced out of the bus to where the robbers were still lying where they had landed, and immediately stripped them of their ill-gotten gains. John took the plunder asking the other passengers to reclaim theirs, as he held onto his and his friends' belongings.

Soon started to strip the robbers and having done so, tied their hands up behind their backs before tying them all together in one string.

"What have we got here then!" a booming voice came from behind John.

He turned round to see 4 naval patrolmen climbing out of a jeep coming towards them.

"Just in time! We've apprehended 3 would be robbers who tried to rob everybody on the bus. My friend has ways of making sure they don't escape, and especially without their clothes." John advised.

"What ship are you men off, and why are you in civvies? You know it's against Service regulations to go ashore in civvies? Show us your pay books right now!" one of the burly patrolmen asked gruffly.

"As it happens, we are Merchant Navy officers from a ship currently undergoing a refit in the naval dockyard." Larter said authoritatively.

"Yes, we're on our way back with our escorts before returning to the ship. Which one of you is in charge?" Sinclair asked sharply.

The smaller of the patrolmen came forward and told him that as he was the Petty Officer of the patrol it was he who was to ask the questions and nobody else.

"Well suit yourselves, but these men should be handed over to the civil police, unless of course you think they are part of some communist insurgent cell operating under your noses. As for us, you have no jurisdiction over us as we're civilians just like the rest of the passengers on the bus." John responded angrily, telling his friends to board the bus and the driver to go.

"Not so bloody fast, pal! You're under the charge of a Naval Patrol. How do we know you've not just picked on these men!" the Petty officer shouted.

Soon called over to the rest of the passengers asking them to tell the patrolmen what happened, which they did excitedly and in their own language.

The patrolmen looked totally bewildered by this verbal onslaught, before the Petty officer relented.

"Okay okay! So they really are robbers. Get back on the bus and bugger off! Don't let me see you lot again tonight!" he shouted over the noise.

Without any further prompting, John and his friends joined the rest of the grateful passengers, for the bus to speed away into the evening moonlight.

As each group of passengers got off they smiled and waved to John and his friends as the bus departed. When they too got off, the bus driver shook their hands thankfully as they left him.

"Let's hope the bar is quiet tonight, as I've had too much excitement for one day." Larter said quietly as they walked into the well lit bar reeking of tobacco and booze.

The girls left them for a while before they returned wearing their hostess 'uniforms', comprising of loose flimsy blouses and gaily coloured sarongs secured to their waist with a slim silver buckled belt.

The owner of the bar nodded his thanks to the friends and gave them a large bottle of whiskey to drink, for looking after his best girls. This however was noticed by a couple of sailors who started to pester the girls, and become rather a nuisance to the friends.

Whilst the girls were obliged to pander to the sailors, as was their job, they were becoming alarmed at the antics of these men. Soon went to get up to speak to them but John stopped him, telling him Sinclair and Larter would sort them out, and besides it would only start a riot among the locals.

Sinclair went over and spoke to the unruly, troublesome sailors, and more or less threatened them with the naval patrol if they did not stop their nonsense

"Just who the fuck are you pal? Some sort of fucking dockyard ponse judging by your clobber." a Geordie drawled, standing up belligerently.

Sinclair gave him an uppercut, knocking the man out cold, sending him flying over the table, scattering glasses and beer everywhere.

"Hoi mush! That was my beer you've spilt!" a cockney shouted, as two more men got up to remonstrate with Sinclair.

Larter then arrived and between them they laid out the sailors almost without drawing breath.

The other sailors in the bar took umbrage at their shipmates being manhandled like that, and started to round on them.

"Let's see now, it's 4 to 1 against. Maybe its time we need to lend a hand or two, Kim. But first, tell the girls to get out of the way then get the owner to phone the patrol." John whispered as he grabbed a chair and started to swipe his way through the bodies of the sailors, leaving them strewn all over the floor. Soon joined the friends, and between them they were thumping or throwing sailors here there and everywhere, as the entire pub got involved in a free for all.

Just as the friends got into their swing of things, they heard the loud shrill of whistles as several naval patrol men came wading into the crowd, hitting bodies in their way with the helves (large pick axe handles) they wielded.

When the patrolmen got to the centre of the scrum, instead of telling the friends to stop fighting, they made the mistake of trying to subdue them also, with their sticks. So they too ended up on the pile of other unconscious sailors, except for the one in charge who was none other than the one the friends had met earlier.

"You 4 men are in big trouble now especially as you've assaulted one of my men." he growled and commenced to blow his whistle. But Soon kicked the Petty officer's hand so hard against his face that he nearly swallowed his own whistle which rendered the man temporarily out of action.

Every time the patrolman breathed out there was a shrill sound coming from the whistle lodged in his throat.

John started to take 'donations' from the unconscious sailors, whilst Sinclair and Larter began to tidy things up again. When John had collected enough money he handed it over to the barman explaining it was to pay for the damages.

The bar man was almost beside himself with anguish and moaning about the damage, but seemed to be much better when he grabbed the money off John, stuffing it swiftly into his till.

The girls came back into the bar when they found it was all quiet and safe for them. Quiet that is, if you discount the moaning or curses from the hapless sailors.

"We must be getting back to the ship now, girls. Come and visit us tomorrow afternoon about 4pm. Ask the taxi to take you to the Stores basin, you'll see us at the No 4 berth. See you all then!" John advised, as the friends walked out of the bar and hailed a taxi to take them into the dockyard.

The taxi had just moved off when two patrol wagons arrived loaded with several helve wielding sailors, who rushed into the bar looking for the troublemakers.

"Just like old times Bruce! I haven't had a decent knuckle dust-up for ages, or at least not since the last time! The patrolmen were all off the *Valour*, so she must be guard ship. There'll be a few men under punishment by the morning, I'll warrant." Sinclair opined.

"Yes Andy! Mind you, I don't suppose the Navy will take kindly to us civilians cramping their style ashore. We'd better stay low and remain on board tomorrow, as some of those sailors might just take it into their heads to start looking for us."

"They started it all! And besides, none of them would ever own up to have been beaten by a few local dockyard mateys." John insisted, which drew nods of agreement from the others.

"Kim! Wish you'd show me that karate combination move of yours. Looks quite handy so it does, but I'm getting too old for all this caper now, anyway." Sinclair grinned sheepishly, as the taxi finally arrived at their ship.

"And me!" John added swiftly.

"Perhaps I show you sometime, old man!" Soon replied with a grin at John, but nodded to Sinclair.

"Maybe we'll have time for a quick drink before we turn in, I'm feeling quite thirsty again for yet another old man. How about it Kim?" Larter asked.

Soon looked amazed at these 3 friends but nodded his head

"Okay then just the one this time, as we're still on limited rations until tomorrow." Soon agreed.

CHAPTER XIII

Tried and Tested

"**D**ave! See me on the for'ard cargo deck in 5 minutes." John ordered, as Ottley passed him going into the dining room.

"I've just completed my morning rounds Chief, and am about to have my breakfast." Ottley replied apologetically.

"Fair enough! See me in 20 minutes then, as I need to instruct you on the imminent loading of our cargo."

"Thanks Chief! See you then." Ottley answered cheerfully.

John walked onto the for'ard cargo hold deck to have a leisurely cigarette whilst he waited for Ottley to arrive.

"Morning John, what a lovely morning for a quick trip up the coast." Sinclair chirped as he arrived next to John, who offered him a cigarette, inviting Sinclair to join him.

"We've had a brilliant weekend thanks to the girls, but I fancy that will be our last piece of horizontal action for some time if our schedule is correct and according to Bruce. I mean, the last time we took the army anywhere the voyage ended in disaster." Sinclair opined.

John stared out into the empty creek casting his mind back to their voyage on the *Inverlaggan*.

"No chance Andy! We're in a different part of the world, which guarantees our survival even if we live off coconuts and local bush tucker. The only sand we'll see would be on a decent beach not a ruddy desert." John replied almost absentmindedly as their life and death struggle on the sands of the Namib desert came flooding into his head.

"You're right there! Anyway, according to Bruce, we're away for a good 6 weeks helping out the army, although given the distance it should only take us 3. Unless of course the army boys have a hidden agenda for us, that is. Perhaps Farquhar might enlighten us before we sail."

"He won't tell us sod all, as he's Royal, and doesn't have pre-voyage briefings like us. Maybe Kim will tell us, but either way, I'm not particularly fussed. Pressure of work and all that Andy." Sinclair nodded in agreement then told John of his own somehow added workload.

"Perhaps we should put it down to being part of the territory as our new rank dictates then." Sinclair said stoically, before he left John to attend to his business.

"Right then Chief, am at your command!" Ottley announced cheerfully as he arrived next to John.

"Okay then 3rd. As the outside Engineer, it is your responsibility to see the cargo gets loaded in a fairly good balance. The cargo holds on this ship have been specially designed by me so you can utilise maximum stowage space, and at the same time ensure the safe transportation of it." John stated, then went into the basic rudiments of what he meant, with several drawings to show graphically what was what, so for Ottley would understand what was required.

"Here they come Dave!" John stated, pointing to a column of lorries towing field guns and their respective limbers.

"That looks like a battery of seven 25pounder field guns, the type a Brother-in-law of mine has in his Regiment. As it appears to be an independent battery, they bring all their own men and equipment wherever they go, so you'd be talking of about 200 men. The overall length from truck to gun barrel is around 25 feet, but can be reduced to about 20, with a combined weight of around the 10ton mark. As you can see, they also have an assortment of supply vehicles and all probably loaded up. All of which I reckon will be around the 300 tons mark, plus of course a special consignment of ammo coming alongside by barge, and again around the 200-ton mark I believe. Although it doesn't sound much, in fact it will take all our cargo capacity. As it happens we've got a decent sized for'ard hold for you to put all ammo, the entire gun units, supply trucks, into three columns of five vehicles to use up the three deck layers. The men and their personal equipment plus the jeeps with their trailers can go into the after hold. The fuel has to be siphoned off all the vehicles to be put into 45gallon drums. They can be put with the full petrol bowser and the ammo truck, to be stowed on the after deck as deck cargo. Here's the diagram of the new layout for the after cargo hold which will accommodate the men. Note the ventilation system required, which means you'll be required to flash up the spare a.c.u. Their officers and senior NCOs will probably be put into the spare cabins. Incidentally, make sure you've got a double axial fan in their accommodation area to back up the a.c.u." John explained at length.

Ottley took notes and made a few comments during John's oration, before he was satisfied with his task, even though he seemed uncertain of the wisdom of such a crammed environment for the soldiers.

"Take it from me Dave, it is a tried and tested system. I know, because it was me who invented it during such a similar situation, some years ago." John confided.

"Well Chief, if it was good enough for you it certainly is for me. Having said that, would it not have been better to just crate them all up and stack them on top of one another, sealed units if you like?"

"Yes that is the general idea. But in view of the army needing rapid use of their hardware when they arrive, they don't have the time to, shall we say, unwrap the presents. Anything else you wish to know?"

"It will do for now and thanks for the info, as I'll be writing it up in my report."

"That's the ticket. Mind you though, keep a good eye out during the assembly of the holds, as each prefabricated section must lock into each other solidly, otherwise you'll have a floating spar somewhere, which will snap under the load. Also make sure you have a good welder to spot-weld the false deck plates over each layer. Watch for gas and the like as our Captain doesn't want his ship blown to pieces just yet."

"Will get right onto it Chief! Thanks for your instructions!" Ottley beamed, as he scurried off.

'He's going to be a good one. Lets hope he's got a good imagination and the where-with-all to back up his decent attitude and job application. He mentioned crating the cargo up, which sounds good. I've had the same notion in my head for a while now, so maybe I can pursue the idea further. Perhaps I can devise a ship to carry just such a cargo." John mused, as he watched at Ottley performing his duties for a little while, before he made his way down into the bowels of the ship.*

Everybody on board heard and felt the dull clang as the ship thumped the stone jetty before it got free to manoeuvre in less restricted waters.

John kept his eye on the telegraph repeaters as if not trusting the new system, which had been installed over the weekend. The 'wrong way' alarm system was crucial for the engineer who would be sending the ship on the reciprocal course, thus instead of going full astern the ship would in fact still be steaming full ahead. If the ship came to grief over it, then it would be the fault of the engineer and not the Captain whose orders it came from.

The situation did crop up three times during their transit down the creek, and John took the appropriate action, preventing the ship from ending up in grief.

'It appears that Farquhar still hasn't appreciated we're only a small merchant vessel, without an abundance of crew like a warship has. As long as we're switched on to him, then we engineers will prove to him that we're worthy of our salt.' John shouted aloud over the noise of the engine, but to nobody in particular.

"Amen to that Chief!" Ottley said with a grin, as he somehow appeared next to John without him knowing.

John turned round to see this young engineer had obviously not come down to the engine room to look at the scenery.

"What can I do for you, Dave?" John asked nonchalantly.

---

* See *Future Homes*.

"I stowed the army just as you've instructed. My problem is with their food stores. Our own fridge is already topped up, along with the dry stores locker." Ottley stated.

John thought about the problem and was weighing an answer in his mind, when there was an enormous thump and a scraping sound which was not only heard, but also felt right throughout the ship.

He looked to the telegraphs to anticipate the next order, which as far as he was concerned, was full astern. The telegraphs did ring to full astern, but was changed immediately to register full ahead.

'What is the man playing at? Maybe his days with explosives has blown what brains he has left.' John sighed, as he nurtured the engine to the required order.

The ship seemed to shudder from stem to stern, before a screeching and scratching sound invaded all the noises that reverberating through the entire ship, for several minutes. John looked at the steam pressure gauge, which governed the engine's speed, then at the rev-counter of the prop shaft.

They felt a sudden surge forward, which meant that the ship had broken free of its bonds, and the sound of the propeller took on a more recognised rhythm.

"We must have struck a sand-bar. Now all I can pray for is the mud box is not all fouled up. If it is then we're in trouble with taking water on board for the engines." John stated with concern.

"What would the remedy be then ?" Ottley asked eagerly, looking around the engine room and at the frantic efforts of the slaving stokers.

"Okay, seeing as you've asked. I'm hoping that a swift back pass from the ballast pumps will blow and clear the mud boxes. The boilers have a ready use storage tank of water to siphon off for about 2 hours. If the problem has not been solved by then, then you have my permission to get a 5th Engineer and a couple of off duty stokers to help you, as I will need you to provide a couple of porto pumps rigged up onto the after cargo deck. These hoses are needed to supply the intake tanks, and of course to help the evaporators." John explained.

"I'll get them ready anyway, as I'm hoping to provide a portable swimming pool for our passengers. Must keep them happy whatever, that's my motto." Ottley breezed.

"If you do, then you must drain the pool, to have it cleared away after supper time each night, then re-erect it the following morning. That however, is providing all is well on board and we're not about to enter into the teeth of a typhoon or anything else."

"Whatever, at least you'll have your porto pumps on standby." Ottley responded, as he conceded to John's superior and infinite wisdom, and started to leave.

"Before you go Dave! You will sit down and work out a solution to the army's provision problems, then give me a preliminary report by 0800-tomorrow morning. Suggest you speak to the Chief chef, and enlist the help of one of the so-called 'Fridge engineers' to come up with something feasible. This is only a suggestion mind you, but I need something to work on by then, if only to save the proverbial bacon."

"Thanks, but I'm already into such an item, as it helps me to keep me up to speed with my other ship borne problems." Ottley offered.

"You've got other problems Dave? Such as? More to the point, why haven't you informed me?" John chided.

"It's complicated enough for me let alone trying to explain it in engineering fashion to you Chief. Sufficient to say, that once I've sorted things out and put it down in writing, then I'll certainly let you know."

"I commend you for your endeavour Dave. But what you must understand is that I need to know immediately about anything that affects my department. I shall expect a good report from you on this, whatever it is. But this is the last time you take on things without letting me know first. And just in case you think I'm getting on your back, you're right. The reason being is that you might just trespass into the realms of something, which would not only be detrimental to your well-being on board, but also to all the rest of us who sail with you. If you get my drift on this then we need not speak of it again. Just for the so-called record, I will give you as much encouragement as you want, but you really must beware of stepping outside your remit as a 3rd engineer, unless you have full understanding and co-operation from your Chief. Have I made myself clear on that?"

"Yes Chief! I would not expect anything less from you, as you would expect nothing less than my best." Ottley mumbled in reply.

"In that case 3rd, what are you standing around like a spare prick in a wedding for? Off you go and see to your duties." John quipped, as he dismissed Ottley with a sweep of his arm.

CHAPTER XIV

Incompetence

The ship cleared the twisting and turning creek before entering on a straight course again for a decent period of time, and the engine settled down into a steady rhythm.

"Right then 2nd! We're full away now, so you have the watch. Any problems then see me in my cabin." John directed, as he signed the engine room logbook. He climbed wearily up the shiny steel ladder, through the air lock and stepped into the cool of the open deck, only to be met by Ottley.

"I was on my way to see you with a written solution to the problem which I spoke to you about earlier." Ottley said cheerfully, as he handed John a small roll of paper.

"Right then Dave! I'll look at it after I've had my supper. Come and see me at 2100 to discuss it." John ordered wearily. Ottley seeing that John was tired, offered to see him in the morning after they both had time to rest up.

"Suits me Dave! 0900 tomorrow in my cabin it is." John replied with a nod.

"By the way, how did you manage with the double axial fan for the soldiers? Everything as I predicted?" he asked swiftly.

"Works a treat Chief! I've even managed to get a temporary sanitary system down there for them, which saves them from stampeding to the crew's quarters to use the heads. You will find the appropriate tracings in my notes. That by the way, was one of my big problems which I had to sort out first before offering it to you."

"Good for you Dave! I'll look out for it. In the meanwhile, make sure that the vehicle ventilation system is working correctly, else we'll get a build up of petrol fumes, and you know the implications of that I'm sure. Anyway, see you in the morning." John concluded, to which Ottley nodded his head in recognising he was being dismissed.

"0900 it is!" he responded, then left John to continue his journey to his cabin.

"Hello Andy! All settled in for a few days laze in the sunshine?" John greeted, as he entered the saloon to join the other off watch officers.

"Not quite John, but I dare say that once we've got the heavy duty canvas awnings rigged over the decks again, we can all cool down for a while. These army boys sure are keen to help out, and I've managed to get a couple of them to help out with helmsman duties. A bit like you had with those engineers on the *Inverlaggan*. Just as well, because Farquhar is giving me advanced navigational studies, such as sun and star sights and the like. I need the knowledge if I'm to become skipper." Sinclair replied jovially.

"Sounds a decent set up then. Where are we bound for Andy?"

"We're on our way to the delights of Hong Kong. Should only take us about 4 days, but judging by the speed you're giving us, it'll be more like double that. The expression 'a slow boat to China' springs to mind."

"Well, at least we'll get there. Although the Bosun couldn't sail a wee boat in a bathtub, is the expression I seem to be hearing." John responded with a grin, as he offered Sinclair a cigarette, before sitting down next to him.

"See anything of Bruce? Only I was hoping to get the latest weather report from him."

"No Andy! Been stuck down the engine room since we got 'full away' (steaming under full power). Why are you asking?"

"This type of vessel is great for sailing up and down rivers, and does not require a freeboard over 3 feet. Now that we're in deep water, I would have preferred a lot more space between our decks and the water level. Our freeboard is only about 9feet, which means that any lump of water taller than will wash our decks good and proper. I mean, we are in the South China Sea after all."

"You're obviously speaking from experience, but this is a good and sturdy ship Andy! If Neptune decides to send his troops to bother us, we'll just sail right through them, even at this speed." John stated.

"Let's hope you're right John, I don't fancy being washed out of my bunk during the wee hours of the morning."

"Come now Andy! Surely you're not starting to get nervous at sailing into the wild blue yonder, at your time of life? You being be a hairy-arsed, roughie-toughie?" John asked mildly surprised at his friend's edginess.

"No John! It's just that this part of the ocean has a very bad habit of turning nasty, at the drop of a hat."

"Well make sure you don't drop yours then Andy!" John teased, getting a beer mat thrown at him in response.

Larter arrived into the saloon to sit next to his two friends, and Sinclair asked about the weather.

Larter told of what he knew which eased Sinclair's concern, with John telling him not to be so silly.

Soon all three were lost in each other's company, and whiled away the evening, before it was time for the saloon to shut for everyone to get either on watch or to their cabins.

John returned to his cabin and worked his way through the roll of papers Ottley had given him, before he too finally got turned in.

"Chief! The Captain wants to see you on the bridge." Thompson whispered loudly into John's ear, to waken him up. John woke with a start, climbed out of his bunk, got dressed and started to leave the cabin, all in robotic fashion, but stopping short as if to wake up properly, asked the steward what time it was, and why did the Captain want him.

"It's 0230 Chief, but I don't know what it is. He's on the bridge at the moment, and has been there since 2330s."

"Thanks Tommo! Must be something bothering him to be up there all that time." John replied, as he made his way up to the bridge.

"You sent for me Captain?" John asked civilly, struggling to get his eyes accustomed to the bright lights of the bridge.

"Morning Chief! We're about to enter a very large low trough area, which in a mariners' parlance means, we're about to go into a large storm right in our path. What I need to do is to try and skirt around it, or at least head for these islands here and shelter before it hits us." Farquhar advised, as he pointed to a group of islands marked on the sea chart.

"We're on an economical cruising speed as per orders from the shipping board Captain. If you want me to increase the speed for any length of time, then it might mean we'll run out of fuel before we actually get to our next port of call." John replied diplomatically, knowing full well the ship wasn't fully fuelled to take on such a long voyage to provide extra speed above economic consumption.

"According to the rules as laid down by the Minister for Transport and shipping, each vessel going deep sea, must have enough fuel on board for 10 days. Our voyage is scheduled to last only 6 days, so that should give me a good 4 days leeway. In theory I can increase my speed by half for 2 days before we start worrying about it." Farquhar replied abruptly.

"Have we got the required fuel supply on board for me to do so, or not?" Farquhar asked quickly.

"We only took on what was given us. That is to say, we're 30tons of fuel and 10tons of oil light, or in your terms, about 3 days steaming, and therefore short of the regulation tonnage."

"What did you say? Do you mean to tell me you let me sail knowing full well we were short of fuel?" Farquhar demanded sharply.

John sighed and shrugged his shoulders.

"I took all that there was Captain. If the lighter was short of fuel then blame the person who sent it, not me. As far as I was concerned, we were only going up the coast for a few hundred miles, not across the ocean to some destination 1600 miles away. Unless you tell me of your change of plans, for me to appropriate the correct amount of fuel, don't start blaming me.

Merchant Navy Captains always hold a pre-voyage briefing so all departments have the necessaries on board for the voyage. As you deemed it unnecessary to inform me then I suggest you blame nobody else but yourself Farquhar. Just one more thing before I leave the bridge, this ship is a merchant ship not a warship for you to charge around the ocean willy-nilly. You can have 8hours full power and that's all I can spare. To you, it means you can have a burst of full speed giving you up to 16 knots for those 8 hours only. And even then Captain, it will depend on how this old engine can support those 8 hours. So don't go ordering emergency full ahead whilst my back is turned." John hissed, as he left the bridge under a barrage of abusive language from Farquhar.

'Maybe if he's luck we'll find whatever islands they are, have a fuel dump. Other than that, we're in for a longer swim up to Hong Kong. Maybe he's used to charging around the oceans at over 25knots or more, but perhaps this ship will bring him down a peg or two, the bumptious twit' John muttered, as he got back to his cabin to try and get some much needed sleep.

He climbed into his still warm bunk and was about to switch off his overhead bunk light when he heard a loud insistent knock on his cabin door.

"Who the bloody hell is it this time?" John shouted peevishly.

"Me, Chief Stoker Ho Ping to see you Chief!" came the hesitant reply.

"Well don't just stand there Ho Ping come in, but it better be good." John demanded

The Chinese man came swiftly into the cabin with his head bowed and his cap gripped tightly in his hands.

"There's trouble in engine room. I know the problem and how to fix it but the 2nd Engineer, he ordered me to get you." Ho Ping stated in reasonable English, even though he couldn't pronounce his 'R's.

"Okay then Ho Ping! You can tell me what the problem is on the way down. Now lets get there double quick" John said quietly, as he climbed down from his bunk and donned his overalls.

During the short time it took them to get down to the engine room, Ho Ping explained the basic problem and as to how he himself would have tackled it. He even suggested other actions that would need to be taken.

When they arrived, John found that the engine room was engulfed in steam, and literally bumped into the 2nd engineer.

"What the bloody hell are you doing to my engine room Rowlands? Just what the blazes is happening? It better be good for you to get me down here!" John shouted over the hissing and other noises of the compartment.

Rowlands told him exactly what had happened and what he thought was wrong but was not able to offer a solution to the problem, having exhausted his own theories.

John listened intently to what he said, before asking a few pertinent questions to ascertain exactly what had been done and how much this 2nd engineer was supposed to know to prevent this mishap.

"Rowlands! You have the privilege to go and tell the Captain exactly what has happened, and we don't know how long it will take to get 'full away' again." John snapped, before turning to the rest of the engine room crew who were looking anxiously at him for direction.

He rattled off a series of orders before commencing his own series of important tasks, but making certain that Ho Ping was in the forefront of taking charge of the remedial repairs.

"Chief! What the hell is happening to my ship? I can't seem to get any straight answers from your 2nd. Maybe you can enlighten me!" Farquhar screamed into John's ear, as he worked furiously to get the engine working again.

John turned round sharply, almost gouged Farquhar's face with his wheel spanner, who leapt back out of danger.

"What the bloody hell happened here?" Farquhar insisted.

"It seems Captain, that you decided to play at beating Campbell and his water speed record. I told you earlier this engine needs a steady pace to run. Your demand for extra speed over its limitations was its last straw. Not only do we have a problem with the condenser, which meant the engine had to be shut down so we could fix the offending part. But the H.P cylinder unit got destroyed, which means, once I've carried out the repair using the only spares we managed to carry and converted the engine to a compound, you'll be automatically reduced to about 80% of full power. Had the 2nd known what to do on the first item he might have been able to prevent the second one. I can give you emergency lighting, and power to all on board machinery but I'll have to guess on the time of our delay. Say about 1 hour. But remember, the fact we've only got 80% power until we reach Hong Kong. That is the best I can do Captain." John advised.

"Very well Chief! We're not far from shelter, so get all your men onto it and let me know when you're back to power again." Farquhar said calmly as he watched the repairs being carried out.

"You know where to find me Chief! And by the way, I suggest that you get a new 2nd engineer, or at least somebody who knows their job on board. I will not have any incompetent crew on my ship, for they are a danger not only to themselves, but also to every man jack of us on board, women and children included. I shall need a full report from you as soon as you can." Farquhar concluded, as he climbed lithely up the ladder and out of the engine room.

John had Ho Ping standing next to him to do what John told him to do, like teacher to pupil, when Rowlands finally arrived back into the engine room.

"2nd Engineer Rowlands! Come over here! What the bloody hell did you tell the Captain? Why couldn't you answer his questions, as any fully qualified 2nd Engineer should have? In fact, where the bloody hell have you been until now?" John exploded.

Rowlands sauntered over to where John was standing, and started to explain his words and his absence, but John was having none of it.

"I've heard just about enough! Now you've arrived, you can take over. All you've got to do is start the engines up again, if you're capable enough of doing so." John shouted sarcastically.

Rowlands seemed to pale at this remark, trying once more to explain himself, but found a deaf ear from John.

"Chief Stoker Ho Ping! You know what to do. Take the throttle and get this ship under way again!" John commanded, shoving Rowlands away from the controls of the engine.

Ho Ping made a thorough job of getting the engine up and running as per telegraph orders before he turned to John thanking him for that unique privilege. Rowlands was trying to look nonchalant and unconcerned during the procedure, was goggle eyed when Ho Ping succeeded in doing what he should have done himself.

"There you are Rowlands! Even a Chinese Chief Stoker can do your rotten job. If you'd have listened to him in the first place then all this could have been avoided." he taunted, as he slapped Ho Ping on the shoulder in praise.

"Chief Stoker Ho Ping, you will report to me in my cabin at 1200 tomorrow, whether you're on watch or not. You can carry on with your duties for now." he ordered

"As for you Rowlands! If there's one thing the Captain and I have in common, its that we just can't stand incompetence, and especially from a 2nd officer and sadly in your case, an Engineer officer. Even he pointed out that fact, and coming from a non-engineer, that is a total condemnation on your skills. I want a full report of your actions and activities during your watch: Of how this incident occurred: Of how you solved the problem, or at least deduced what the remedial action would have been when I, as the Chief had to do in your place. In other word, I demand a full engineering explanation complete with drawings and other supporting material to back your actions. It will be your guts for garters the Captain will be getting not mine. But remember this when you make your report, I was only a 2nd engineer just like you, when I joined this ship. Also whereas you had 3 days to sort things out, I only had 1 day and a set of ships' drawings to produce this ships engine and boiler room, which I personally had converted from coal to oil. Now get yourself on watch and give me your report by 1200. Oh! And by the way, don't be adrift either, Rowlands!" John raved scornfully, before leaving the engine room as if nothing had ever happened.

'I bet he'll claim his lack of knowledge is due to only being on board for a couple of days, to hide his down right incompetence. It only took me one look at the ship, its drawings and the pile of metal, which was to be taken out of those hulks. Let's hope I don't turn out to be a Chief like Cresswell or even Spanners Jones, as I fancy I'd be more like Happy Day, or even Tansey Lee. Mind you though, Ho Ping was one of the original engineers Kim managed to locate and bring back on board again. He's a fast learner and certainly deserves promotion. Maybe he and Ottley will be in my voyage recommendations when we eventually arrive in Hong Kong!' John mused as he reached his cabin for the third time of the night. Shutting the door of his cabin he wearily climbed into his bunk once more, burying his head under his pillow to try get some sleep from the remains of the night.

CHAPTER XV

No Excuse

It was the in-built knowledge of a seafarer that woke John up. Even when fast asleep, he knew the feelings and signs telling him his ship was either in calm waters, or the seas were throwing the ship from one alarming degree to one side or the other. Adding to that was a feeling as if they were in a lift, which was out of control, by going one way up one second then rapidly falling the other way in the next.

Climbing out of his bunk he went straight to the porthole to look out at the world, and was surprised at what he saw.

'*So you finally made the Islands then, Farquhar. If you speak nicely to the Admiralty, they'll let you have a quick suck off their tanker only a few chains away.*' he observed. He also noticed a whole array of ships and fishing vessels almost cheek by jowl as they huddled into the small sheltered bay of the island.

'*Looks like several takers to shelter from the storm*' he muttered, giving a large yawn before he got himself prepared for the day, as the steward arrived into his cabin with his usual early cuppa.

"Morning Chief! You're up bright and early. Can't remember shaking you though." the steward commented, as he set the tray of tea and toast onto a small table.

"Just what doctor Woo ordered, thanks steward!" John said gratefully as he pounced on his early morning refreshment.

"I've had a rough night what with one thing and another, so I was awake anyway." John lied.

The steward nodded his head in agreement with what John said, before he turned and left the cabin.

"Before you go, just where the hell are we?" John asked swiftly, but got no answer as the steward had already gone out of earshot.

'*Must go and see Bruce. He'll tell me, no problem.*' John muttered, as he dressed for the day.

John managed to get through the bridge and out onto the deck where Larter's radio shack was located, without being waylaid by Farquhar or some inquisitive deck officer on the bridge.

"Morning Bruce! Have we arrived yet or is it some sort of mirage?" John breezed, as he entered the warm radio office.

Larter was busy talking to some unknown voice on the other end to him, but the 2nd radio officer replied.

"I take it you're Bruce's oppo, John Grey from the engine room! I'm Scouser's 2nd Radio Officer. My name is John Penn, but everybody calls me Inky, for obvious reasons." Penn spoke civilly, as he held out his hand to shake John's.

"Hello, er, Inky, pleased to meet you. I came here to find out exactly where the bloody hell we are, and for me to find out, unofficially that is, to see exactly how much salt water we've got to swim in before we run out of fuel." John replied amiably

Penn went over to the large sea chart, which was pinned onto the bulkhead, and pointed out the places of interest to John, culminating on the exact spot where they were now.

John did some mental arithmetic before he examined the sea charts measurement scale.

"Yes it should be about there." John agreed, then went on to tell Penn about the shortage of fuel to get to Hong Kong.

"As a matter of fact, Bruce is talking to the naval tanker almost alongside of us. He's arranging a fuel transfer and some supplies for us. Just as well the *Antares* is around to sanction it though, else we'd be rowing our way up there." Penn informed politely.

John merely nodded his head as if he understood the implications, rather than show his ignorance of the significance of such a ship. It was only moments later when he analysed what was said did he realise these facts, but kept them to himself.

Another Radio Operator entered the cosy office, shutting the door heavily as if to keep out the typhoon that was breaking over them.

"Bloody hell Inky! Just as well we're anchored inshore of these rocks to the starboard of us, cause I've just seen a small merchantman get smashed onto them." the man gasped, starting to strip off his foul weather gear.

"We'd better get the 500kc distress log going then, even though the *Herald* is the nearest ship to it, thus in doing the honours for her." Penn said swiftly, as he reached over and tuned the receiver into the international distress frequency for shipping.

John could not differentiate between the dashes and dots coming from the radio as it sounded like one big noise, but he did understand the dramatic and dreaded symbols of S.O.S even a schoolboy knew all about.

Larter had finished his voice transmission and went straight over to the DF radio equipment to find out exactly where this ear shattering S.O.S. was coming from. After a few moments of turning his dials and checking the bearings, he switched the set off with a sigh.

"Stupid bugger! There's no need to clutter up the frequency as he's surrounded by vessels that will help him. What we must listen out for, are those several hours steaming from here." He stated quietly, before saying hello to John.

"So you've finally made it! State visit and all that John, or just passing?" Larter asked jokingly.

"Hello Bruce! Just coming to see where the hell we are. I understand from Inky here, that we've got an RFA tanker loaded with juice? If so then we'll need at least 50 tons of the stuff plus 20 tons of oil."

"Yes John, that was my message to them. They will do the transfer once the typhoon has cleared the area, and before they sail with the *Antares* task force."

"The sooner they bugger off the better too!" Penn rejoined.

"But we're the Red Duster mob not White Ensign. I know we've got what you call 'ships side grey', but we've got the '*Tsun Wan's* Chinese title embossed on her bows and painted black and her stern. Or what's left of the paint after the waves had finished with her Surely they can't dictate our Captain's voyage plans and such like?" John asked in idle curiosity.

"Don't you believe it John, they're the boss around here. If they say we can't sling our hook and bugger off then we can't, and must wait until they decide when we can. Something to do with the British Naval protection, in that when they're around all British ships must adhere to their orders. Most foreign ships don't take any notice since the Japanese war, as they feel British gunboat policy and deterrent no longer applies. Farquhar knows the score as he's RN anyway, but then if he wasn't we wouldn't have the extra fuel we're about to get from them." Larter explained.

"A sort of poisoned chalice then Bruce. Perhaps in our case, as we've got British troops and weapons on board, they would be more protective towards us than say an ordinary steam packet."

"Something like that John. Anyway, as to your visit! No doubt Inky has filled you in, but here's where we are, the Anambas Islands, and here's our transit out from Singapore to Hong Kong, marked in red. The blue arrows are alternative routes should we meet up with more than one typhoon during our transit." Larter explained, pointing to the bulkhead-mounted chart.

"You will know that this particular typhoon over us is typhoon Gloria, but by the time we get to King Kong, we'll be in the grips of say, typhoon Iris. The reason being is it's the typhoon peak period around these parts, just like the Yanks have their hurricanes off their Florida coast. In short, our planned transit will take us a good 3 to 4 days extra. The Admiralty and the Army have allowed for this, so it means we get extra pay for our troubles. If I had a tot of rum right now, I'd give those boys a toast in good old Nelson style." he concluded.

"I'll drink to that!" Penn cheered, as he held up his cup of kye[*] and drank its muddy brown contents down.

John nodded in appreciation to what was said, before he thanked Larter for his info.

---

[*] Cocoa.

"Must go and see El Capitano to find out if he can tell me when we're going to get that refuelling. 3rd Engineer Ottley will have that task, but I must make sure he's okay. Thanks everybody." John stated as he made his exit from the warm radio shack and back into the now very draughty upper deck.

He scurried through to the bridge to make his internal progress down to his cabin but met up with Sinclair, who was looking through his binoculars to the outside world.

"Hello John! How's Bruce and his gang getting on?" Sinclair asked breezily, as he scanned the immediate vicinity of the ship.

"Hello Andy! Oh he's just his usual self. And you?"

"I'm all right, and loving every moment. Being First Mate really makes a difference, John! You really must try it some time. We could always swap duties for a shift if you want to, it's that easy. Having said that, I've just had a few scary moments down on deck with the stupid 2nd mate. See the liner ahead of us? That's a 25,000tonne Bibby Line troopship, the *Nevasa*. If I wasn't on the ball, then we'd be dining in their saloon tonight instead of our own." Sinclair stated, pointing out a large ship right in front of them and so close you'd swear that it was an extension to their own.

"I wondered about the frantic telegraph orders too, and now I know. How come we missed it then Andy?"

"I had the 3rd Mate to drop the kedge anchor, erm the stern anchor to you. That managed to stop us short of only a few chains of hitting her. Although it will be a different story when we've got to bring it back on board again."

"What about the tanker over there? I understand she is going to give us some juice, would we have to move from here to suckle from her?"

"Yes. But when we're full away again. It's a good sight to watch, so be on deck when we do. It's called a R.A.S. In your case it stands for refuelling at sea. She drops her refuelling derricks down to stream the fuel lines into the water. All we've got to do is pick them up and connect them to our fuelling system and away you go." Sinclair informed, pointing to the several crane like jibs with hoses dangling from them.

"I've been on one of them before, but I'd like to see it done on the move Andy. Have you ever seen it done before?"

"Yes, several times. Our boffins invented that type of refuelling at sea way back in the 1920's. The Yanks tried to copy us as did the Krauts, but they still haven't mastered it like us. Anyway, we're now at anchor for at least the next 12 hours or so, so let's get below and get some rest. Once I've sorted out the anchor watch, I'll see you in the saloon."

"Sounds about right Andy. I've got some arses to kick down in the engine room, so perhaps I'll see you soon. Speaking of which, how is Kim doing, only I haven't seen him since we sailed?"

"Neither have I John. But no doubt we shall, during the next day or so when we're pinned down under the lee of these islands. Incidentally, this reminds me of those islands off Scotland when we sheltered from that storm on the *Maple Leaf.*"

"Yes Andy, her and a couple of others not to mention the top hat of them all, the *Inverlogie.*" John responded, with a faraway look in his eyes[*].

"Well never mind them as it really doesn't pay to dwell on the past, John. We're in the here and now with yet another one to contend with which is what counts. See you later!" Sinclair answered soothingly, as John finally left the bridge.

The *Tsun Wan* was among a host of ships of different makes, sizes and nationality, huddling together in the small bay to take shelter from the fierce typhoon raging all around them. Although the waters in the bay were a bit choppy, it paled into insignificance to the almost sky scraper sized waves outside it, which were trying to do mischief to the raft of men and their flimsy man made vessels.

---

[*] See *Beach Party*.

The typhoon roared and raged for almost two days before there was a lull of a few precious hours so the ships could get any damage repaired before the tail end of the typhoon struck them again.

It was during that time John managed to sort out the aftermath of the engine room saga, and get his department back into shape again.

"You asked me to report to you Chief!" Ho Ping stated, as he first knocked John's cabin door before entering, and handed his report over.

"Morning Chief Stoker. Yes, come in and stand by my desk. I'm expecting Rowlands as well, so I'll read your report whilst we wait." John said civilly, which put Ho Ping at his ease.

John read the report and had time to comment on it before a loud knocking on his cabin door heralded the arrival of the 2nd Engineer.

"You're adrift 2nd! I told you 1200, it's now quarter past. I hope for your sake, you've made a proper report which I also demanded off you." John said angrily, as he took the offered piece of paper from Rowlands.

"Now stand by the other side of my desk from the Chief stoker, whilst I review your report. No talking and no smoking." he commanded roughly.

John sat down at his desk taking his time to read Rowland's notes very carefully, re-reading the Chief stokers for good measure before he stood up and donned his cap.

"I have read your report Rowlands! The fact that you've been on board for a short time is no excuse, besides that only applies to 3rd Engineers and below. How are you able to instruct the Captain let alone junior engineers to the realms of steam engines, when you yourself haven't a bloody clue?" John demanded angrily, as he threw the report onto his table.

Rowlands mumbled his reply, which John was at pains understanding what he said. After listening to the man, John sighed, slamming his own copy of the Engineers' Bible onto the table, gave him a thorough dressing down. John pulled no punches, nor did he spare the 2nds feelings especially when the man was not able to answer what John thought were elementary and basic questions which even a 5th Engineer should have answered.

"It appears, that you're either part of the funny handshake brigade or you like touching your toes now and again, for you to get to the dizzy heights of 2nd. As far as I'm concerned, you have been found wanting. Which means, until we get to Hong Kong, you will confine yourself to engine room watch keeping duties only. Therefore you will stop any further instructional duties, as I have suspended it until we reach port. When we do finally reach Hong Kong, I personally and certainly the Captain, will be seeking your replacement. But whilst you are still on board, you will make it your personal duty to show me just how you became a 2nd engineer in the first place. This ship is a very special ship carrying special cargoes, which means we can't have duff crewmembers on board. Every man has his duties allocated to him, and every man should be able to conduct those duties, with the exception of the junior engineers and junior deck officers who are under training. In short, you have placed yourself in a position on board whereby you do not comply with standard regulations regarding a 2nd engineer. It is incumbent upon me to place you under my scrutiny, for me to see you fit the requirements of such a lofty position, and I shall be giving you ample opportunity for you to prove me wrong. Do I make myself clear Rowlands?" John bellowed, but stopped to give him time to reply.

Rowlands just stood there looking numb and rendered temporarily speechless, before he started to protest at John's punishment.

"You can't do this to me, you have no rights to do so. I'm a qualified 2nd Engineer as taken on by the management board in Singapore, and only they can undermine my authority on board any ship where I sail as the 2nd Engineer." he blurted out, full of rage.

"It is not me who has damned you, nor caused your downfall, but your own report in your own hand writing. My report, let alone chief Stoker Ho Ping's both state exactly what happened, who did what, who said what and how the incident was resolved. Your report does not describe the scene as I have done, including the special log I had put into place in the engine room. Here, it tells exactly what had happened, what orders were given to whom, who did what, even down to my chat with the Captain. On top of that, Chief stoker Ho Ping submitted a far better report than yours, and although he is still not quite au fait with the English language, never-the-less it makes yours almost worthless. Let the records speak for themselves, and not whomever or whatever you're hiding behind." John hissed, as he threw the engine room log at him.

Rowlands caught hold of it, thumbed through the smudged pages to where the incident was recorded and read it quickly. When he finished he threw the book back at John.

"Pah! So what! I'm a fully qualified 2^{nd,} whereas you're only a paper Chief who probably wouldn't recognise a proper engine even if it fell on you. I shall be doing my normal duties as my articles state, nor will I answer any of your cock-a-mamie questions. As far as your log is concerned, you can stick it right up your arse." he shouted angrily.

"Can I take it that is your final word Rowlands?"

"Yes you can! I care nought for your opinion nor do I recognise your authority!" Rowlands sneered and spat at both John and Ho Ping.

"If that is the case 2nd Engineer Rowlands, you leave me no alternative but to issue you with this order, as witnessed by Chief Stoker Ho Ping, here. But before I do you had better listen very carefully.

As it happens Rowlands, Chief stoker Ho Ping was this ship's original Chief Engineer before the ship was laid up a fair while ago. He was the one whom I used as my helper to get the ship back to sea again. He assisted me in most of the refurbishment projects done on this ship during its dockyard conversion, and I have every confidence in this man. His input has been noted by the management team and by the dockyard Superintendent." John declared with anger written on his face, then turned to Ho Ping.

"Chief Stoker Ho Ping! I am promoting you to acting 2nd Engineer and for you to take over those duties, but excluding junior engineer instructions just for the moment. The Captain will be informed of this change, which no doubt he will be pleased to see, also Mr Soon, who will see to your pay and conditions. You will have the assistance of 3rd Engineer Ottley if you ever need it. As for you Rowlands! You will take over the duties as performed by 3rd Engineer Ottley. These are my order and made under my remit as Chief Engineer of this ship. You will understand Rowlands, that I have a duty of care and attention for my entire engine room department, from myself right down to the most junior stoker. You will retain your rank and pay for now, as your, shall we say, certain expertise is needed elsewhere on the ship. You will see Ottley who will give you his hand over notes, and I expect you to maintain that standard."

"You can't do this to me! I was allocated as the ships' 2nd. You just haven't got a clue who I am for you to demote me to a 3rds duties!" Rowlands bellowed.

"As it happens! I have every right to demand your demotion to whatever level I choose, given my authority as the Chief Engineer of this ship. What you don't seem to realise is that you may happen to be the precocious lad of your family who always pander to your every whim. Unfortunately for you, the Lloyds Insurance, the Admiralty, and even the Ministry for Shipping will demand a thorough investigation as to why and how you managed to get to such a responsible position on board any ship let alone this one. And whilst I'm at it you are an impostor to your rank and a total danger to everybody on board whichever ship you sail on. We are in the middle of the South China Sea, with a typhoon raging around us and we've got several hundred tons of ammunition on board. I don't suppose your relatives would survive the shame if this ship perishes, and found out that it was all due to your personal mistakes and mishandling of your remit.

For make no bones about it Rowlands, they will be made bankrupt not only by the Ministry for Shipping and Lloyds insurers, but also by the relatives of those who perished at your hands. I've seen it happen a couple of times so don't ever threaten or even attempt to blackmail me ever again. Just keep yourself confined to the new duties I have allocated you, and make certain you give your best, for you are now under probation, as is Ho Ping here in his new duties." John responded with disgust.

Rowlands turned on his heels and stormed out of the cabin slamming the door hard.

John looked at the door which was still rattling in its housing and looked at Ho Ping.

"Remind me to get that door fixed 2nd! Off you go now and get yourself prepared for your new role on board. Kindly ask 3rd Engineer Ottley to attend my cabin if you will." John said evenly, but with a slight grin on his face.

Ho Ping was euphoric in his manner as he shook John's hand, thanking him for his promotion.

"I was told by Kim Soon who you were, that's why I made certain I kept you for myself during the refit. You have earned your reward Ho Ping, which perhaps might go a long way in getting you back into your status as a fully qualified marine engineer again. But you really must get a better command of the English language, and on the finer points of engineering mathematics. Maybe your increase in pay will subsidise a course on them." John answered with a smile as he concluded their meeting.

Talk about a meteoric rise up the promotion ladder, Ho Ping certainly has done that. I'd sooner trust Ho Ping and Dave Ottley in the engine room than that stupid 2nd. You might be able to flannel your way up the ladder *but you need the expertise and the knowledge to go with it, which was his downfall in the end. My conscience is clear on those decisions, as my report will indicate. Glad I learned a bit of diplomacy from Fergus and Happy Day.'* John muttered to himself, as he concluded his own report and subsequent orders, in time for Ottley to appear.

"You sent for me Chief?" Ottley asked cheerfully.

"Come in Dave! I've got a change of duties for you, which you will probably curse me for if I know your ways." John commenced, then told Ottley exactly what it was.

"Bloody hell Chief! You know I like my duties as outside engineer." Ottley complained.

"Put it this way Dave! Due to certain, shall we say, diplomatic manoeuvres which go way above even my head, I need your energy and capabilities where they are best for this ship, namely down in the engine room. I have entered your name for promotion to a full 3rd engineer, so you'll get your new pay scale as of today. Before you change over, you will give Rowlands a conducted tour of the ship whilst we're still at anchor. He doesn't know, nor is aware of the changes you and I have made to the ship, which are unique to this ship and effectively non-standard. So if he starts to get uppity and prevents you from handing your department over to him, let me know immediately.

Also if it is apparent that he's totally ignorant of certain machinery then I must know sooner than later. At the end of the day, Dave, let his imposition be a lesson to all of you, as there's no substitute to good old fashioned know how, be it learned from text books or by practical efforts."

"As you say Chief, I learned from the latter! Here's my last report for you then, and thanks for my promotion. I'll not let you down, you have my word." Ottley averred as he handed over his report.

"I don't need your word Dave, just your best effort at all times. Now off you go and enjoy the next few days at sea." John said with a smile as he ushered Ottley out of his office.

CHAPTER XVI

Oops a Daisy

It took nearly 2 more days for the typhoon to clear the islands and for ships to extricate themselves from the huddled shelter of the bay, and go on their own separate ways again. All except for the *Tsun Wan* and the tanker that dwarfed her, for they had business to attend to which needed privacy from the prying eyes of the departing ships.

"Rowlands! Have we got a special tank valve adapter to take their fuel line?" John asked civilly.

"No Chief! But according to Sparks, they're sending one over by cutter, which I'm waiting for right now. Besides which, we have twin tanks each side of the engine room with no cross feed connection. That means we need to open both sides for fuelling instead of the one, but only be able to take singly due to just the one coupler." he declared.

"Yes, you're spot on there. Maybe if we get a standpipe attachment from the fire equipment locker and use a universal coupler on the one end with a tundish, we could make one as a temporary measure. Might be a bit messy though, so get a couple of stokers with the detergent sprayer to hose the decks down just in case, extra to the fire fighters that is. How much are you taking on?"

"We only need 30 tons each side, and 15tons of lub oil to top us up that's all."

"Here comes their cutter. Ask them if they're sending over a double line and if so, you will need the second adapter from them. Then find out their rate of discharge. Speaking from experience 2nd, it's one thing discharging from a tanker, and another taking it on board like this. I'll rustle up a makeshift one for you in the meantime, just in case." John concluded, leaving to sort out the contraption.

"Chief! They will be pumping on two lines but have only the one adapter. They said we should have been issued with them before we sailed, and suggest you get yourselves a pair from the naval base in Hong Kong, for the next time this happens. They will start pumping when I give them the signal. Should take us about 20 minutes." Rowlands said quickly, arriving at where John was working.

"Just as I thought! Here, give me a hand to tighten down this pipe on to the deck coupling." John replied, as he strained to put the article into position to get the fuel line connected up and ready.

They worked together for a few minutes until both were satisfied that it was the best they could do.

"Okay then ! You're in charge so take it away. I'll stay this side so that you can see me, and I you, just in case we get a breakaway hose. No sense wasting about 10 ton of good fuel as well." John directed.

"Fair enough Chief! Let's do it!" Rowlands responded, then blew his whistle and waved his arms as his signal to commence pumping.

John was able to give the tanker a good looking over whilst waiting for his order to drain down and disconnect, which did not take much longer than what he had anticipated.

"Disconnect starboard side and stand clear!" Rowlands ordered aloud, prompting John to act accordingly, hold his arm up to indicate he had completed his task.

The stokers had cleaned up the small spillage of fuel oil and cleared away their fire fighting equipment by the time the tanker started to turn and leave for its own destination.

John stood watching it sail away as did Rowlands, who came over and stood by him.

"That was a job well done Chief, now we can get a move on ourselves. Time for a snout first though." he breathed, as he offered John a cigarette.

"Yes, you've done a good job, well done! Don't forget to add those connectors onto your stores requirements into the office before we arrive. We never know when we will need the cavalry again, but I'll bet it will be a regular thing considering this ship is a special one that the navy has to keep their eye on." John responded evenly as he lit up their cigarettes.

"How are you settling down to your new duties? Perhaps the open decks are more your style than a dirty engine room? I was very happy on deck as an outside engineer, as I had the ship more or less to myself and was my own man, so to speak. Nothing like enjoying a cruise in weather like this, is it?" John asked soothingly.

"Yes Chief! I'm happy with my new duties for the moment. You certainly get to find the most odd sets of machinery, some of which would grace many a maritime museum at that, and especially on this ship. Once I've done my rounds and handed you my report, I'm off for the day, which I wasn't able to do before."

"So all in all, you're happy with things?"

"For the moment, as I've just say. Yes."

"That's good then! Maybe I can describe the situation best as trying to put square pegs into round holes. But now everybody is where they belong, the system is beginning to work well for us all. I'll say no more on that for now as it's a subject under re-scrutiny when we arrive in Hong Kong. One thing before I go, I only require one daily report from you now. I know where you're coming from, so try to use engineers technical jargon and terms of reference so as not to make it an omnibus edition if you like. I suggest you read it back to yourself to see if you could understand it at just a glance, then make it short, sweet, and to the point. Neither you want to spend your day doing paperwork nor do I want to spend all day reading it. However, you are still required to have it handed in to me at 1200 every day as normal. Okay with that?"

"That's fine by me!" Rowlands grunted, as he flicked his cigarette butt over the side.

"Well that settles that. Now then, even a Chief engineer has a job on board to see to. So it's my turn to get back on the job as I've got those infernal oil viscosity figures and the like to sort out.

See you later!" John said quietly then left Rowlands to his own devices.

'You certainly charmed the monkey out of that tree Cobber! As Aussie Clarke would have said.' John muttered quietly and made his way back down to his engine room office.

The South China Sea is the largest sea in the world, with a Jeckyll and Hyde character for most of its annual life. For it was only just over two days of glorious sunshine, millpond waters and man starting to relax on his raft of wood and steel, before it started to throw tantrums creating mayhem all over again. This time it was typhoon Hazel, who was turning out to be just as angry as her predecessor Gloria.

The *Tsun Wan* was a low profiled ship in that she sailed lower in the water than most ships, even within her size. This meant that any wave taller than her main deck was free to wash it as and when, and even try to seek out the weak spots so the water would cascade into her to make her sink. Many an ill prepared or such neglected ship was, and still is found wanting, unable to sustain the attentions of Mother Nature, so those ships flounder with disastrous results. But she was sturdily built and looked like a Horseshoe crab as she rammed and pushed her way through the countless milestones in the shape of the large rogue waves crunching up against her. During these times, absolutely nobody was allowed on the main deck, which meant life between decks was pretty hectic, stuffy and uncomfortable.

"Chief, message from the bridge! The Captain wants to see you on the bridge." the engine room messenger reported, placing the sound powered telephone back into its cradle.

John left the engine room knowing all was well there knowing Ho Ping had the watch, so he quickly complied with the message.

"You sent for me Captain?" John asked, holding on tightly to a stanchion on the bridge.

"We seem to have acquired a slight list to starboard Chief. The First Mate has looked into the for'ard hold and reports that part of the false decking has collapsed causing some of the cargo to come adrift, which has now settled in a big heap on that side. Can you alter the trim a tad so we can at least ride on a level keel?" Farquhar explained, pointing to the ship's inclinometer.

John looked at the indicator and remembered what Happy Day had told him on the *Brooklea* and saw that the list was not bad, but was enough to cause concern.

"This is an old Chinese ship built to run thousands of miles up and down a river, where oceanic conditions would never be met. To that end, I have no way of trimming the ship Captain, save for moving the cargo back and get it secured again. At a guess, the ammo is secure okay, so it must be some of the vehicles, which have come adrift somehow.

I would suggest that the army boys get down there and move their wagons back again, and the First Mate gets a team together to secure them down with double strength cordage. I'll get a welding team together and get more deck ringbolts down to help with the extra lashings. But we've got to bring some of the false decking from the after hold to re-in force the ones, which have given way, first. Maybe the army boys will lend a hand with that as well. Time is of the essence, I shouldn't wonder."

Farquhar nodded in agreement with all the suggestions, and then had the bridge messenger send for the First Mate and the army commander, who arrived together some minutes later.

Farquhar introduced Major Roy Brammel to John before telling what he intended to do and what was required from each officer.

"Sounds challenging, Captain! My men have been idle since we left, this will give them a few hours of exercise to make up for it. I'll get my men onto it right away." the major responded with a salute before leaving the bridge.

"I'll go with the First Mate, Captain! I want to check the for'ard hold for watertight integrity. But ask the messenger to get the outside engineer to report to me there, along with 3rd engineer Ottley." John said swiftly.

Farquhar issued the order to the messenger before concluding the gathering with his own orders.

"Chief, make sure your welders know there's a layer of ammo several feet thick underneath them, so be vigilant with their torches. First Mate, make certain that the chain locker is secure with no moving parts. If we can straighten her up, we can gain a few extra knots from her to add to the equatorial currents, which will make up our reduced speed. I hope to make the next set of islands before we finally sink." Farquhar commanded.

John went swiftly over to the navigation chart and looked at the almost empty sheet of paper, save for a few smudge looking marks on the end of a blue pencil line.

"How far to these islands Captain?" he demanded sharply, which raised an eyebrow from Farquhar, who, non-the-less answered directly.

"At this rate 6 hours. Why do you ask, given that we're about to enter yet another typhoon area and we're running on reduced power?"

John went over to the telephone connecting the bridge to the engine room, and shouted down it.

"Tell the 2nd to give us 20 more revs for 2 hours if you please. But watch out for any drop in lub oil pressure." he ordered sharply, before turning to Farquhar and explaining what he was doing.

Farquhar gave a big smile then dashed to his chart making adjustments to his calculations.

"That will suit me fine Chief! Must get there before the main event." Farquhar purred, as he noted the increase of speed on his ship's speed recorder machine, known as 'the log.'

"Now get below and sort those army wallahs out, if you please. I want my ship in full trim and streamlined again so all of us can sleep in our bunks again." he said, as he ushered them off his bridge.

"C'mon Andy! You and me have plenty to do down there, so hope you've got a good deputy to see that everything is lashed down tidy."

"Shades of the bloody *Repulse Bay*, John! But at least we're 'tween decks this time." Sinclair agreed as they hurried down through the maze of ladders and passageways until they reached the large watertight doors separating the cargo hold from the rest of the ship.

John operated the controls of the doors so it opened to let them into the cavernous hold area.

Fortunately for John, Sinclair stumbled backwards and grabbed hold of John to steady himself, which resulted in both of them falling in a heap on the deck.

"Oops a Daisy! Must be that last milestone she hit, John!" Sinclair chuckled, helping John onto his feet again.

"Actually dear friend! You saved us both from getting run down by a runaway jeep. Look here it comes again." John shouted over the noise, pointing to the loose vehicle rolling from one side of the ship to the other.

"Bloody hell! The army must be piss-poor in teaching their drivers. Look no hands! In fact no body!" Sinclair joked, but dodged out of the way as the offending vehicle shot past them again.

"We'd better get them roped down before they get too bashed up to drive." John opined, so both of them made a run for it managing to dodge the vehicle coming back again.

They were working fast and furiously trying to hold onto one vehicle whilst attempting to tie it to some immovable object, with little headway being gained. There was a racket with lots of swearing as the soldiers poured into the hold with large sheets of metal, then stacking them against a bulkhead, started to manhandle the vehicles as if they were mere toys.

Rowlands arrived with Ottley accompanied by a couple of welders, who commenced welding the re-inforcing partitions and the ring bolts onto the ribs of the cargo hold, whilst the soldiers and sailors got to grips with the vehicles tying them up one by one.

John saw they were winning the battle, so told Sinclair he was going to make his inspection and for him to come with him.

"Chief, that's my job!" Rowlands objected.

"Indeed it is! But on this occasion, I need you to take charge of the cargo hold and make sure there are a couple of suction pumps available in case we find a hole somewhere big enough to sink this vessel.

Once you've done that, tell the welders to stand by for a while, but the soldiers can return to their mess again. Thank them for their invaluable help before they scarper, and they have my permission to draw a few crates of beer from stores for their troubles. The purser will be fine with that, so no worries, to quote a well-known phrase. You will also need to start creating a small air pressure both here and the cordage locker in case we need extra buoyancy. Then get yourself aft and make a water-tight integrity inspection forward, until you meet up with me.

If you find any rivets under stress especially from the main deck upwards, then make a note of each one in situ. You will probably find that any leaks deemed a fluctuating trickle, in the main, will be coming from the upper deck area into the cargo hold. Those that squirt at you will come from the rivets that have been sprung. In which case, note the 'squirt' intervals, which should tally up with the movement of the ship. Just mark it down on a scale drawing so that we can deal with it later. Any other, shall we say, deemed as instant floods, which coincides with the ship's movement, then report it to me directly before you go back onto the bridge and warn the Captain. If you get my gist on that matter, which after all is only basic damage control anyway, then I need say no more." John concluded, but waited for Rowland's confirmation as to what he had said.

"Message understood Chief!" Rowlands avowed, as he left to do his instructions.

"Right then First Mate! Lets get moving, I'm sure Farquhar wants to know the score before the weather hits us again." John suggested.

"Just as well this tub is solidly built John, as I don't relish visiting Davey Jones's locker just yet."

"The only thing we've got to worry about Andy, is the main superstructure and the fact that we've got an open bridge. I mean, the heavy canvas awning over it is no protection to an oncoming wave. Just as well we decided to convert one of the cabins as a foul weather bridge."

"Yes, thanks for reminding me. I must get the lifeboat davits retracted, with all the boats turned inboard and lashed to the decks. Presumably we've got to shut down a few of the upper deck vent cowls as well?"

"Yes Andy, all main deck cowls except for the engine room ones, they can be turned round to face aft. Remind the Chief chef to sling his cooking pots too, just in case there's one big scalding accident or other, and that goes for the crews' galley aft too."

The two men conversed throughout, noting the jobs to be tackled once they had completed their all-important inspection.

"I've just seen the outside engineer who has given me his report. The soldiers have now returned and it looks as if there's nothing more I can do for the moment. How about you, are you satisfied enough to see Farquhar?"

"Yes, let's put him out of his misery." Sinclair agreed, as they made their way up to the now very draughty bridge.

Sinclair was first to make his report and receive instructions concerning the list of tasks he had made during his inspection. Once Sinclair was dispatched to do those tasks, John made his own, in similar manner.

"Okay then Chief! It appears that the work below has rectified the list, and we appear to be in good trim again. If you can spare me a couple more hours at this speed, we'll make those islands before we get hit again." Farquhar requested, as he pointed to the group of island that would be their next shelter.

"If the typhoon is coming from behind us, surely we can run with the weather? We're a sturdy ship from the keel to the main deck." John started to say before Farquhar stopped him.

"No Chief, we are obliged by maritime law to shelter as and

when the opportunity arises, no matter what quarter the weather is coming from. Our transit time and arrival in Hong Kong is somewhat way off the mark now, so it doesn't matter if we have to stay sheltered for another few days. The high command of both Singapore and Hong Kong know we're safe and continuing on our way. It appears I can operate independently from normal operational duties and most restrictions have been lifted so I can make my voyages virtually at will, but at the same time, in a covert manner, so as not to draw attention to ourselves."

"Is that why we're still dressed as a merchantman, albeit under the grey paint of the R.N, even though our Captain is Royal Navy? How can you explain the fact we're deemed to be a carrier of hazardous cargoes yet we've got 7 families living in the crews quarters aft?"

Farquhar looked at John for a moment as if to decide how to answer his direct questioning, but in the end decided not to.

"You have many questions which will be answered in the fullness of time Chief, but in the meantime we must be getting on with our allotted duties on board. Kindly send me the outside engineer when you get below Chief!" Farquhar concluded as he dismissed John from the bridge, just like John would do to anybody not required in his engine room.

John went out the back of the bridge and sought out Larter and his team, who were having a cuppa with Sinclair.

"Hello John! Must have smelt the pot boiling!" Larter joked, as he poured out a cup of coffee, giving it to him.

"We've got a problem with our emergency generator yet again, but this time we're out of fuel, John!" Penn announced.

"The only thing I can suggest is for you to use one of those old dynamo generators. Given that we'll have plenty of wind, it should give you enough juice to run your equipment, surely."

"We only transmit at set times now, but maintain a permanent listening watch. Our main problem will be to power the radar, even though it's only a navigational and weather radar." Larter informed.

"There you go Bruce! We know there's a typhoon on its way, and we're slap-bang in the middle of the ocean with the nearest land directly beneath us. Apart from being in the wrong ocean for some lumps of ice to gang up on us what more do you want to know?" John joked, to which Sinclair gave a broad grin, which induced a few smiles from the others.

"Yes Bruce! How's about that then?" Sinclair cheered.

"Some folk! You just can't take them anywhere!" Larter sighed.

"Sorry Inky, I've no petrol on board save for the supply in each motor lifeboats, and absolutely no diesel. But make sure you add it to the stores list for when we get along side again. Must go now and get my rabble roused, see you all later in the saloon." John concluded, leaving the cosy radio shack to brave the blustery wind of the boat deck.

CHAPTER XVII

Fu Ming

"Weigh anchor First Mate! Signalman, tell that freighter astern of us to pass to our port and give us plenty of leeway. Chief, give me your best rev speed and let's get out of here." Farquhar ordered.

"You can have revs for 14knots now Captain, but not a rev more." John instructed.

"That'll do me nicely Chief! The wind is on our stern quarter now, and with the 3knot current, we'll make Hong Kong in just under three days." Farquhar responded cheerfully, as John sauntered off the bridge and made his way to his cabin.

'*2 days to get our stores requirement made up. The way things are going, Bruce will have a limp wrist after sending this signal, for it's already 5 pages long and that's only from my department. Still, the army will be glad to get ashore.*' he muttered to himself.

"Chief can I have a word?" Ho Ping asked as he stood in the doorway of John's cabin.

"Certainly 2nd, what can I do for you?"

Ho Ping entered the cabin carrying two small sacks, which were bulging at the seams then holding them up for John to see.

"Chief! I found these sacks along with at least 300 more concealed in the spare prop shaft space. It is a well-known compartment but hardly anybody bothers with the space because all they would see is just enough room for the spare prop shaft to be housed. As we don't have a spare prop on board, I still had to open that compartment to see if I could find some extra storage space for my machinery spares. On having a closer look, I found it was packed full of different kinds of drugs. I am trying to find the culprit who stowed it for various reasons, but if customs come on board and find it then we're all in deep trouble." he declared.

John opened one bag, tipping its contents onto his desk.

"Doesn't smell like drugs to me, and the powder looks like foo foo*. Smells like Magnolia and other foo foos at that." he opined, then proceeded to open the second sack, dumping its contents on top of the other.

"This one smells of lotus blossom, this one of honeysuckle, another like magnolias. Maybe its some sort of foo foo making equipment?"

"No Chief! Look at these little brown packages. We've got all kinds of drugs here. This is opium, this is heroin, here's marijuana, and cannabis resin." Ho Ping said, pointing out the packages.

"Okay 2nd, so why the foo foo?"

"The opium dens and drug dealers in Hong Kong disguise their drugs to prevent the police drugs teams from finding it. Each person takes their dose by snorting smoke up their noses. The smoke comes from burning drugs on silver paper heated from underneath. This is called 'chasing the dragon', yet all anybody else will smell is perfume. The foo foo as you call it is the perfume, which could be smelled a long way off so it disguises the smell of the drugs."

John cast his mind back to the *Repulse Bay* and remembered Larter and Clarke coming off shore with such a load of trouble, and decided that from what he had seen from the outcome of sampling such drugs, he didn't want to get involved in any shape or form.

"So in other words when these sacks get used, am I right to assume they are what the locals might call perfumed dragons?"

"Yes Chief. I am afraid for us when we arrive alongside in Hong Kong, as there will be a certain welcome committee waiting for us when we step ashore. If they don't get their merchandise then nobody will be safe to walk the streets of Hong Kong, let alone Kowloon. Whoever is responsible for bringing it into the colony, will be in deep shit especially from the top mandarin of the drugs world

---

* Talcum powder.

called Mr Dung. He has influence and the reach to touch almost any person living there, including the local police commissioner."

"I am not one to stop the habits of any person whilst ashore, but I will not have my men taking drugs or even possessing drugs whilst on board. We need to find out who the person was to bring us into shame and how he was able to do it, but we only have until we reach the territorial water boundaries of Hong Kong to do so. So this is what we'll do 2nd!" John stated, then proceeded to put a plan together to catch this crewman who had put the entire crew into unknown jeopardy.

"You realise of course I will have to inform the Captain about this. But I will do so once we've found out who is. It will be the Captain's specific duty to punish this man and not by being lynched by the crew for not sharing it out to them. You have my full backing on your actions concerning this subject, as long as you stick to proper maritime, especially British law, which I will keep you informed of as and when you need it."

"Thank you Chief! I too am an honourable man, and have nothing to do with the dangerous world of drugs. I lost several of my family through Dung's gang warfare and other such dealings. If I can get back at him even just this once, then I will die a happy and proud man." Ho Ping averred, as they both gathered up the evidence, putting it all into a large brown paper bag.

"We'll put some of it back just to keep the smell, but stuff the bags with paper or kapok from the linings of sleeping bags, anything to make it look untouched. Tell 3rd Engineer Ottley I want to see him, and if you spot Rowlands tell him I want to see him too. In the meantime, set up a special watch over that area of the engine room, and note anybody who seems to have a particular interest in it. I'll see you later this afternoon." John directed, as Ho Ping quietly left the cabin.

John was in the middle of sorting out the intricate details of how to track this unknown drug trafficker when Ottley and Rowlands arrived into his cabin.

"You sent for us Chief?" Rowlands asked with much intrigue.

"Ah yes gentlemen, do come in and shut the door!" John invited, before he explained to them the reason for their special visit.

"Bloody hell Chief! I never spotted them whilst I had an occasion to inspect the area, no even yesterday." Ottley admitted, which was echoed by Rowlands.

"As far as I'm concerned that is not an issue, but what I need to do is to set up a surveillance system to help Ho Ping pin down the culprit, certainly before we reach port, most definitely before I inform the Captain of this. We must try to keep our department matters amongst ourselves, so don't start blabbing or hinting as to what is about to take place." John asserted, as he set about formulating a separate plan from the one he arranged with Ho Ping, yet without them knowing about it. He stated everything must be done covertly and each person would act independently so as not to tip off any suspect that they were on to him as a tour de force.

Once they agreed on a mutual plan of action, John concluded the meeting, to send the engineers away fully understanding what was required of them.

"Chief! I have had Chief Stoker Dave Banks brought in to help me. He has just informed me there is a stoker who is hovering around the target area. This stoker is acting strangely especially as his duties are confined to the engine room, not in the tiller flat or other such places." Ho Ping declared, as John arrived into the engine room.

"Good 2nd! Keep a close eye on him. In fact, pass the word round that we intend welding those deck plates down due to possible flooding from sea. I have 3rd engineer Ottley coming along this morning to weld those plates down as part of a set up to trap him. So if he starts to complain in the slightest way then inform me immediately. I will also have Rowlands to come down and pretend to do work in that area even though he cannot access the compartment. It should give the culprit the idea that if any combustible material stowed down there could be set alight, to set him off in a big panic. Again, let me know if he hangs around watching or gives any indication he has an interest. I have a strange idea we'll get him before the afternoon watch is over, if my name is Chief Engineer Grey." John declared, as Ho Ping nodded in compliance with John's directives.

"I shall be in my cabin if you need to see me 2nd! Be careful you don't let him see you watching him." John concluded, as he left the engine room.

'Must tell the Captain about this just in case there is some mishap or other. Clear my yardarm, as Aussie Clarke would have said.' John mused, making his way up onto the bridge.

"Chief! Glad you've arrived, as I was about to send for you. Come into my bridge cabin if you will, I have a particular problem which maybe you can solve for me." Farquhar insisted, leading the way into his cabin where he met the 3rd mate waiting for them.

"Chief, you know 3rd mate Hillman, but in fact he's really Major Ken Hillman from the Royal Navy's Special Forces Section. He'll brief you on what is what, as I haven't got a clue as to his operation. You know the army Major of course." Farquhar announced as an introduction, as the 3rd mate and the major nodded their recognition of John's arrival.

Hillman told John briefly about his covert operation and what was required of not only him but also of Farquhar and the ship.

John explained his own discovery and what he was trying to do, hence his reason to come up onto the bridge in the first place.

Hillman thanked John for his actions but told him call his men off and comply with a new set of actions, which all three started to thrash out.

"You have identified the main courier who I've been tracking some time now, as he's a cross between an eel, a chameleon and the ruddy Scarlet Pimpernel. Picking this ship for his largest shipment of drugs will be his biggest slip up and hopefully his last. As luck will have it, it happens we now have the means to crush this gang of murderous pirates who have been operating just out of our reach, as every time we get close they sneak back into the territorial waters of mainland China. They're what we call the untouchables, so perhaps now we have the table finally stacked in our favour for just this one time." Hillman asserted, explaining what he intended to do, and what needed to be done prior to arriving into port.

"Once we've got the gang, then we shall start making several arrests from a set of shall we say 'holier than thou' members of the establishment. But in the meantime, we must be extra careful we do things by operational codes as opposed to the gung-ho attitude which would be a natural thing to do given the same circumstances." Hillman concluded, folding up his maps and details of his operations.

John sat quietly for a moment before he spoke to give an observation only Farquhar could answer.

"In view of the circumstances Chief, I shall allow a fuel tank from one of the lifeboats to be used. No sense having a radar without being able to use it, now is there." Farquhar beamed, as the meeting broke up.

"I'll inform him right now Captain, I feel sure he will be pleased." John sighed, and left the confines of the cabin.

On his way out through the bridge, John met up with Sinclair, who was the officer on the bridge at the time.

"Andy, stand by for some cargo lifting and shifting. It appears your 3rd Mate is really an officer in the Special Commandos or something, who is about to get us involved with some armed junks which are China's answer to swashbuckling pirates of the Caribbean. It's a long story but basically we shall be slowing down to a crawling pace until we're looking like a tired old tramp ship but in fact more like a ruddy battleship. Tell Bruce he's got permission to use the petrol from the motor lifeboats, and get the radar lined up. Can't stop as I've got some very important items in the engine room to see to. See you later." John whispered, receiving a nod of recognition to what he had said.

"Well, shiver me timbers, and pieces of eight John me lad!" Sinclair mimicked in pirate fashion, as he swiped the helmsman with his hat, scolding him for not keeping on the ships course.

John went quickly down to the engine room and called Ho Ping to speak to him in the engine room office.

"2nd! Have you found the man we're looking for?"

"Yes Chief! The 3rd Engineer told me the only person showing signs of being distressed is stoker Fu Ming who seems to have an accomplice called Do Ping, both of whom have just gone off watch."

John told him what happened in the Captain's cabin and what the outcome was for them to abide by.

"But how does he signal to them, Chief?"

"It appears that some of that powder is a chemical agent which when burned, gives off coloured smoke. One colour to indicate all is well for the gang to come and get it. Another colour to tell them to collect it whilst in harbour, and so on."

"So we'll let him throw some of it into the furnace and wait for the gang to board us. My concern is for the women on board. These pirates always rape the women, kill most of the men and take the children away for hostage in case they get followed. So far they've been able to out-fox even the British efforts to punish them."

"On this occasion 2nd! These stokers joined us the night before we sailed, but doesn't know of our cargo, nor do they know they'd been followed on board by one of the deck officers, who is one of our special forces sent to deal with it. In the meantime, we shall be slowing right down to about 5knots for a while to get prepared for these cut-throats. Inform Ottley just to keep an eye on him, also when Rowlands arrives to tell him the same. Don't do anything except keep a discreet eye on our target. I have a long stores list to prepare for when we dock, and I dare say that I shall be required at some point to assist the Captain. So get your engineers on their toes and keep alert. I need you to be able to attend the engine room at any time from about the first dog onwards, so make certain that this so called Fu Ming and Do Ping or whatever their real names are, can be located at all times. You Chinese people are supposed to be the inscrutable type, so please don't let me down."

Ho Ping nodded his head in compliance with his orders before John finally left him and went back to see the 3rd mate, if not the Captain.

He arrived onto the bridge and discovered the 3rd mate was now the duty officer.

"3rd mate! It appears that our suspects are called Fu Ming and Do Ping, if that in fact are their real names." John said quietly and out of earshot of the Chinese helmsman.

"Yes that's him, he's a very dangerous man but have not come across Do Ping before. Probably he's Fu Ming's backup, in which case we'll nail the both of them in due course. Fu Ming belongs to the most powerful drugs baron in this part of China. If his henchmen don't retrieve their goods by the time the ship has docked, then you can bet your last penny serious trouble is not very far away. For when the shit hits the fan, then Dung will be found right in the middle of it. If we can put his fleet of pirates out of business then he'll be powerless to stop the challenges of the other drug barons snapping at his heels, who will make mincemeat of him. In short, Dung will be in the shit either way, just like his surname, if he doesn't come up with his side of the deal. Mind you though, there're a few colonials involved in all this. So when we do eventually tie up alongside and my back up team has arrived, all of them will be grabbed in a double sting operation. I can't tell you much about it as I really don't know, but there will be several senior well-to-do British people who will definitely be taking an early departure from the colony in the form of a prison ship already on its way." Hillman explained quietly.

"But this ship is under navy ownership, surely this gang has sufficient intelligence to let us pass knowing this. They wouldn't dare tackle a navy ship surely?"

"If you look around you Chief, you will see this ship looks like a typical tramp steamer. Look at the paintwork! It's been stripped down due to the foul weather. We've even got women on board who are parading on the after decks with their children. No Chief! We look and fit the disguise of a merchantman perfectly, especially when we look as if we're on full steam yet only doing about 8knots. In fact it really doesn't matter about our speed, as they have 3 very fast junks, which can outrun or outmanoeuvre most merchant ships let alone the British warships that steam into harbour. They've been clocked at being able to do a good 30 knots, and are able to operate in water of only 1 fathom. So no competition as far as they are concerned, when it comes to the navy's patrol boats. On top of that, they've got a harpoon cannon on their bows so they can send their grappling irons over to capture and stop any ship trying to escape, them along with a few heavy machine guns will induce any ships Captains to stop and give way."

"Well they've got a nice little surprise waiting for them 3rd! How many on their craft?"

"There are 3 fast junks with 15 men on each, but there is also a small flotilla of slower junks and sampans with lots more on each. I reckon on about 10 on each of the junks with roughly 200 of the bastards on board the others. They are the ones strip a ship bare then carry the loot and other confiscated items off the unlucky ship.

As I've said, once they've raped the women and girls, they kill most of the crew, saving the Captain to sail it to wherever he is able and virtually on his own. Sometimes they scuttle the ship near some rocks to make it look as if it floundered on them."

"You've been on their case for a while then?"

"I lost my best mate and a bloody good sergeant, John Gourdie along with his team of 6 men some 6 months ago to those butchers, because the lads were fingered by somebody in the local government. Their bodies were found mutilated and their craft sunk just off one of the outlying islands. I've been brought in from Singapore to smash their fleet and grab those bastards ashore who had my pal and his mates done in. They don't know me in any shape or form, but I have a team of 8 men already in Hong Kong that will do the business and redress the balance, so to speak." Hillman explained calmly.

"Well, you've got a ready made battleship under your feet, with several cannons perfect for the job and a good 200 soldiers to help you. No doubt the rest of us will be around to help you give these pirates their come-uppance that's for sure." John enthused, then left the bridge to attend his other work.

The ship slowed down to almost a walking pace, giving Farquhar the time to get his ship prepared. The crew and the soldiers worked well into the evening, slaving away to put into place their hidden surprises, so by dawn all looked peaceful and serene on board.

John was on the boat deck having an early morning cigarette when Penn walked slowly past him with a cuppa in his hand.

"Morning Sparks! Looks like good cruising weather. I see the radar is going hell for leather now." John observed

"Hello Chief! Yes, we've had it up and running for a while now, and it looks as if we've got company been following us for some hours now."

"Thanks for the tip, must get going!" John replied swiftly, as he went to look at the stovepipe, which was the ships funnel. It wasn't long before he noticed the smoke turn a yellow colour and that it smelled of perfume. He walked swiftly into the bridge reporting it to Farquhar who was sitting on a low stool that kept him almost hidden from view.

"Very well Chief! 2nd mate Luk Yu, take up your position as officer on the bridge. Helmsman, you will obey the 2nd mate's orders. Mr Soon, make sure you write down all that is said and all commands given. There're too many islands around to play dodgems, so I shall maintain a plot just in case we stray into forbidden waters. Major, have your men stood to and wait for my orders. They must remain hidden until they are ready to fire. 3rd mate get yourself aft to the poop deck and have your team stood to, but keep yourself well hidden.

Tell the women and kids to come onto the after deck. First Mate, you will get yourself onto the for'ard cargo deck. Any rapid closing from those junks on our bows make your signal. Chief, tell your men below to speed up a little bit and start to make smoke, as if we're going flat out. Get Ho Ping to make certain Fu Ming and his pal have a particular nasty job to do so that you can have a few others come to help them. Have them tied up good and proper then brought to the bridge via the accommodation passageways." Farquhar ordered in quick fire succession.

John looked at the little dots on the radar display screen and tried to look out to sea to see where or what they were, but he was not able to see anything due to a light mist, which seemed to shroud the ship.

Farquhar kept looking at the radar screen and spotted a quick movement of 3 dots that seemed to converge on their position.

"Here they come! There're two ahead at about 4000 yards and 0degrees on either side of the bow, with one dead astern about 3000 yards approaching fast. What is your visibility 2nd Mate?" Farquhar shouted.

"About 300 yards Captain, but can't see anything yet." Yu responded calmly.

"Chief, tell the engine room to speed up a little bit more, I want to be able to have all 3 within a 500 yard range of me." Farquhar ordered, which John did quietly.

"Range ahead is now 1000 yards matching the one astern. Signalman tell the Major, when I've shouted out the range of 400 yards, have his guns ready at that point, but still concealed. Once he's dropped his shields, he will fire a 3 round salvo of H.E and 2 of incendiary from each gun. Remember to take the roll of the ship into account. Fire on my signal! 2nd mate, make sure your helmsman keeps a steady course." Farquhar barked, to seal the final details of their plans.

With an eerie silence all 3 junks appeared out of the mist as if by magic, and fired several grappling hooks which snaked over the gap, snaring on various parts of the ship. A raucous voice was heard coming from a bullhorn telling the Captain to stop his ship or be riddled with machine gun fire.

Farquhar nodded to Luk Yu to comply with the order, whilst he calculated the range on the radar.

"Signalman, tell the Major to commence firing." Farquhar announced, as he stood up and looked over the parapet of the open bridge.

All three junks were hit simultaneously in such dramatic fashion that not only the pirates were surprised, but also the crewmen who were waiting for the would-be boarders. As the shells smashed into the wooden hulls of the junks, one of them tried to cut itself loose and make a run for it, but was hit by an incendiary shell making it blaze from stem to stern. Hillman came rushing onto the bridge to see the 3 junks were sinking, and demanded the survivors be brought on board for questioning.

"But who would you question Hillman?" Farquhar asked with puzzlement.

"Any one of them. You've just smashed the 'Chimes' prime ships, Captain. So called because the one on the junk with the red dragon on its sails is Ding, the one with the yellow is Dang, and the one in the green is called Dong. Ding, Dang, Dong, hence the nickname of 'Chimes'

"We will render them dead in the water first, then wait for their other vessels to catch up. We'll dispose of them in the same manner, as they wont know until too late it was their ships which got blown up not ours." Farquhar demanded.

"I want those three brought on board Captain, for only they know who the government informer is. This is my only chance." Hillman pleaded.

"Very well Hillman. But what about Fu Ming and his oppo?"

"Those pieces of trash? Have them hung from the highest yard-arm for them to see, otherwise they'll fight to the last man."

"Very well Hillman, this is your show, but I object to hanging a man without trial."

Hillman walked swiftly over to Farquhar and said.

"My pal and his team got no trial from these butchers, nor did the countless women they raped, or their men folk they butchered, have recourse for justice. If you won't hang him then I will!" he hissed.

"Very well 3rd mate! 2nd Mate have them hoisted above on the for'ard derrick if you please. Let's say I've just given them a suspended sentence." Farquhar requested calmly, watching the screaming, choking stokers finally hoisted aloft.

"There you are 3rd mate. What now?"

"Have a few cutters lowered over the side to pick up those men wearing their sail colours. They are the ones I want. Chop the others up so the sharks can get them. I want no trace of these scumbags, save those silk-cladded mannequins. I would also suggest that when the others arrive, you use machine guns on the sampans and the guns on the junks, for they too are loaded with weaponry."

Farquhar acquiesced to Hillman's requests and before long the Chimes gang-leaders were on board, lying on the bridge, all trussed up, and blood soaked, but shouting and screaming in their native tongue protesting their innocence and of the Captain's piracy attempt on them.

Hillman was not having any of their ranting, as he kicked each one of them in turn, and started to interrogate them. Soon translated what was said for the benefit of Farquhar or others standing around, but it was Hillman who spoke back to them in their own kind, thus tormenting them even further.

Despite Farquhar's words of caution on the Geneva Convention, Hillman kept up his savage interrogation techniques on them, but was interrupted by the announcement of a flotilla of junks rapidly closing on them.

"Here they come! Like bloody vultures!" Hillman snarled.

"Make sure you sink the bloody lot of them. But get some

pieces of real evidence they have sunk, or nobody will ever believe it. Especially the ever sceptical rivals these people seem to have." Hillman directed.

"Very good 3rd mate!" Farquhar cooed, then turning, shouted to Brammel to reload and sink all before them.

"Certainly Captain. Our guns are only 25pounders, but they are the finest anti-tank guns ever invented, which can blast a hole in any tank put against it, especially at this close a range. These bits of wood will be no match for them, you just watch. Thank you for the opportunity to get some good gunnery practice for my men." Brammel purred and soon had his guns pouring high explosives into the flotilla being smashed to drift wood.

The rattle of Bren guns were also heard, riddling the oncoming craft so full of holes they were sinking faster than the occupants could bale out from such a destructive force.

John looked at the bright red stains on the jade green coloured water; to note these pirates were finally getting what they deserved, and felt better at the sight. But what took his eye, was the dead body of his erstwhile stokers that were dangling and swinging in the breeze, when Sinclair finally arrived back onto the bridge.

"I'll bet he was fu-ming and his oppo a dope to be discovered, and to see all his mates sunk before their very eyes." Sinclair joked, as he offered John a cigarette.

"Let's hope none of his friends will be waiting for us when we dock. I fancy a good run ashore without it being spoilt by some crazy Chinese man tracking every move I make."

"Far from it John! Let's put it this way. We've just put the biggest drug baron in these parts right out of business. Whatever drugs have been confiscated by us is a big blow to the local demand, which is nothing compared to the dirty great big hole in the pecking order amongst the drug barons who are at hammer and tongs with each other to supply those drugs ashore.

Once the word gets out amongst the underworld community about all this, which will travel faster than a bush fire, then an almighty gang warfare will break out to see who will take over the mantle of 'top dog' if you like. I suspect if they eventually identify the ship and some of her crew, then they will be, shall we say, granted a few wishes, as their gratitude for bringing about this new order. Mind you, if we are approached and identified, the best thing to do is accept these gifts as complementary tickets or whatever and have a bloody good time in spending them. The other side of the coin comes from those whose business interests have been seriously curtailed, then that's the time to worry."

"No wonder the 3rd mate is keen to hang onto those pirates! The corruption in the local hierarchy must be rife for these pirates to get away with it for so long." John replied after much thought.

"Speaking of which, he needs help in collaring these faceless bastards. He's already asked me to help him and I told him my friends would also be there if he needed them. I told him you,

Bruce and Kim, and even Farquhar are all for it. Perhaps when we get together in the saloon tonight as customary, he will broach the subject. I should imagine he will, so we can be prepared for when we get boarded by the Customs & Excise brigade as we enter the local territorial waters."

"Sounds ominous to me Andy, but tell the man I'm with him on this. No sense chopping the tail off the tiger when he's still got teeth to chomp into you." John stated earnestly.

"That's a fact John. Anyway, must go and see to my troops even if you've finished for the day. See you in the saloon later, the skipper is opening the champagne this time round." Sinclair concluded as he sauntered off, leaving John to go on his own way.

It was the usual 'last night' on board whereby a party was given for the passengers to celebrate another safe journey, every officer was required to attend the bash in the saloon to fete the passengers. In an ordinary ship, there would probably be female company to grace an otherwise dour affair, but on this occasion it really was a 'men only' affair. In fact, there were women on board as crew members wives, who were too busy tending to their families to carouse the evening away.

"Captain!" Brammel said loudly to command the attention of the slightly noisy revellers in the saloon.

"I wish to offer you and your crew a toast, in recognition of the great honour you have bestowed upon my Battery as this engagement completes the circle. Our Regiment, the 49th Field Regiment of the Royal Artillery is based up in the New Territories of the Hong Kong colony, at a place called Sek Kong. But our Colonel would be more than happy for me to do the honours for him tonight. My Battery first won its spurs during the 55days siege at Peking, fighting a drugs war, and was given its name as the Dragon Battery. Since then our battery has served with distinction during the last war commencing with the defence of Dunkirk, Torbruk, El Alemein and Korea, but this single engagement has brought the battery right back to its roots, if you like. As previously mentioned, our guns are 25pounder anti-tank field guns, which are extremely mobile and are deadly accurate killers of anything that moves up to a good 2000yards away. Although I have to say it was not so much as an imbalance of weaponry, but by the very fact that we have fought against today's modern drugs overlords. Their successors to our original foes." the major announced, as his officers and men raised their glasses to Farquhar and any of the ships officers who were present.

Farquhar responded with equal diplomacy, as he thanked Brammel and his gunners, mentioning as he was a gunnery officer himself, he was able to appreciate and subsequently praise the very high standard of shooting the battery had shown him during their action.

But it was his quip of 'Barn doors, and his granny doing better', which drew a round of raspberries and some gentle banter from the army boys, which finally got the party started.

Hillman said a few words as did Soon, as the evening gave way to a more relaxed and a bonhomie attitude which was enjoyed right up to the last group leaving the saloon to sleep it off before the real world hit them again in the morning.

The ship skirted around several islands to make its approach from behind the main island of Hong Kong then line herself up to swim its way down through the narrow, winding channel known as the Lye Mun Pass. This is a stretch of water which is only five hundred feet wide and 40 feet deep, before it opens up into a large, much deeper sheltered harbour that can be favourably compared with the harbours of Rio, Sydney and San Francisco.

It has islands circling around it on the one side, some even larger than the island of Hong Kong, and the mainland on the other to make it almost land locked. It is teeming with vessels and craft of all sizes and shapes which brings its natural beauty alive.

Hong Kong as a Crown Colony, dates to the year when the Treaty of Nanking was signed in 1842. This agreement ceded the island of Hong Kong to Great Britain. However, in 1860 the convention of Peking added the tip of the Kowloon Peninsula and the small island known as Stonecutters. Then in 1898 the area was further extended by the lease for 99years of land known as the New Territories, which also included the rest of the Kowloon Peninsula, and about 250 smaller islands in adjacent waters. The entire area is some 400 square miles with several high peaks adding to its majesty with the tallest being Taimoshan, of some 3,500feet. It has 2 capitals, Victoria on the island of Hong Kong and Kowloon on the mainland. But so as not to confuse anybody, the entire colony was simply referred to as Hong Kong with Victoria as its administrative centre.

The colony lies just south of the Tropic of Cancer, which means it is milder with a less high humidity level but is still subject to monsoon weather to match Singapore.

The Japanese occupation of the colony saw the massive drop

in inhabitants, due to the atrocities as carried out by them. But shortly after the war, people started to come flooding in their thousands from all parts of China to escape communism. All of which greatly enhances such a thriving and dynamic community, of some 2 million souls, with probably a half a million more living afloat in Junks, Sampans or other water-craft.

The export trade is booming, but it still has its own heavy industry such as shipbuilding/ scrap/ repair yards, steel mills and the like. You are able to buy anything from a baby to a battleship, by virtue it is called a 'free port', and there are no restrictions on currency exchanges. No small wonder the colony has been dubbed and recognised as The Treasure Chest of the Orient.

This is John's next port of call and temporary home.

CHAPTER XVIII

Dung

"**C**hief, I'm finished with main engines, secure from sea." Farquhar informed John via the sound powered telephone.

John made his signals to the engine room crew to comply with the Captains orders, which was greeted with a loud cheer and sudden stampede up the vertical ladder, as the stokers rushed to sample the delights and attractions in abundance ashore.

"2^{nd,} we're alongside for two days before we move down to the repair yard. I understand that you are from these parts, so drop your reports and stores requisites off into my cabin before you shoot ashore. We shall be down somewhere in the Taikoo/Wanchai ship repair docks area, but it will be up to you to find us again. I need you to report back to me in 3 days, so you have my blessing and have a good time. Make sure you leave a contact number in case I need you before then." John directed, as he signed the engine room logbook.

"Yes I know where you will be, and thank you Chief! I go now." Ho Ping responded with a large smile, then left John to the now very empty, hot, but silent engine room.

'Now for the 3rd mate's sting, whatever that is. Oh well, last to leave gets to bring the cat in and put the milk bottles out.' John mused, as he switched on the extra cooling fan to reduce the temperature before he too left the engine room.

"Chief, I was just coming down to get you." the outside engineer said cheerfully.

"Rowlands? What is it you want off me now?"

"The ships shore supply umbilical cords have been installed. I have my last report and stores requirements ready to hand in. But I do believe we have some unfinished business to deal with, and I wish to have it dealt with now before I can shoot off ashore."

"Well, first off, you are required to assist the offloading of the cargo and the army, before you think of stepping over the gangway, but that is all down to the instructions of the 3rd mate. So don't ask me why. Secondly, as far as I'm concerned once you've done that you may get ashore, but keep yourself available for the move down to the repair yards. Last but by no means least, as far as your affairs on board are concerned, it will be dealt with but outside my own say so. So I suggest you take time out to reflect on what eventualities or outcomes this affair may produce, but be prepared none the less. Before you dash off, you'd better get Ottley to assist you in the discharge of the cargo, as he's the one with the drawings I gave him. Once he has done so, he is to report to me personally."

"I acknowledge your orders and will comply. But I have a good idea on the outcome, bearing in mind just whom my father and uncles are. All of which does not bode well on your behalf. For now here's my paper work, and I'll definitely see you on board as directed." Rowlands sneered, leaving John clutching his paperwork.

"We'll soon see just who is right" John shouted to the rapidly departing engineer.

'If he thinks that now he's alongside he's safe from maritime jurisdiction then that man has another shock in store for him, well placed relatives or not. Speaking of which, I'd better get a move on and see Farquhar and his 3rd Mate' John said softly, as he entered his cabin to change out of his overalls.

"Chief! You are required to meet in the saloon as of almost five minutes ago." the steward said alarmingly.

"Have the local 'Chain Gang', erm the local Hoi Polloi arrived on board yet?" John asked almost off handedly.

"No, not yet. Maybe that's why you as the Chief Engineer are requested to attend the gangway, if not the saloon as of right now." the steward replied, checking the time on his watch.

"In that case steward, you'd better help me get dressed into civvies. I believe there is some sort of a palaver going on that even I must take part in."

The steward rushed to help John change from uniform into civvies, and even gave him a brush down before John left his cabin.

"Thank you steward. Once you've finished here, I don't suppose I'll see you again for a while."

"You're wrong there Chief! I'm the Chief steward on board, which means I have a duty to see my officers are well cared for whilst on board. Having said, I do have certain interests ashore which will, shall we say, take up some of my spare time, if you get what I mean."

"You carry on steward, I hope you have a good time ashore. Just make certain I have, shall we say, a good supply of de luxe comforts to be able to host my guests."

"Why certainly Chief! You name it and it will be provided. Mind you though, you'd need to have this telephone number if you want bed warmers to help you sleep, if you know what I mean." the steward concluded with a wink and nod, as he gave John a grubby little card with all sorts of telephone numbers written upon it.

John looked at it trying to fathom out which number was which before the steward gave him a clean one with just one number on it, but also a written message as to what he could expect from the person on the other end.

"Thank you for these steward, but somehow there are other arrangements already made and unbeknown to me, which I would almost certainly be obliged to take up." John said apologetically, as he didn't fancy the inference these cards had projected into his mind.

"Well suit yourself Chief! But should you find yourself in trouble in one of the 'bucket' shops or even in a *Perfumed Dragon* establishment, then the big number is the one to call, sooner than later, if you get my meaning." the steward advised sternly.

John pooh-poohed the idea of such likelihood, but told him that his advice would be kept in mind all the time ashore.

The steward nodded in agreement, before John stepped out of

his cabin to make his way onto the upper deck for some fresh air and perhaps see some of the locality around where the ship was docked.

All seemed to be quite deserted and quiet where the ship was docked, which in stark contrast to the other ships' berths, were teeming with life and the usual hustle and bustle of a busy dock.

"Hello John! Waiting to greet the local 'Chain gang' or what?" Sinclair asked, offering John a cigarette.

"Hello Andy! Don't know about that, but thanks for the cigarette as I'm fresh out." John responded affably as he started to smoke the offered cigarette.

"The Captain is due to come down to the gangway very soon, to welcome the local V.I.P's. We, the senior officers have been requested to attend the gangway for them. The army has been discharged ashore now, so it's all down to Hillman and his gang who have just sneaked on board some minutes ago."

"Is this something to do with Hillman's third phase of his operation?"

"Something like that, John. I can feel something is about to happen, so just keep loose during this impromptu 'cock and arse' party and never mind the scantily clad females who come gagging for a bit of salty sailors. This is a part of the world where money is God, which uses drugs to create the climate in which it thrives. Powder and perfume are the catchwords, so be extra careful John, else you'll end up in some sleazy joint ashore with your bollocks cut off and rammed down your throat as you scream." Sinclair whispered sternly.

"Thanks for what you've just said, here's me thinking of a good run ashore Andy."

"Sorry to have put you off John, but this really is a paradise for doing just what you want to do, or even dream of. This is of course, providing you've got either the drugs or the dosh to do so. The best way to enjoy this paradise is to pretend you're one of the British troops on tour for a while. That way the locals will try and fleece you during your shopping trips, but leave you alone because it would be a lengthy jail sentence otherwise. Other than that, just keep yourself to yourself." Sinclair advised.

"In that case, I'll make sure you or Bruce, and even Kim is with me when I venture off this bloody ship." John moaned.

Sinclair laughed and slapped John's back gently as he told him he was just trying to wind him up, and that Hong Kong really was a paradise for all to enjoy, depending on what the individual wanted to enjoy in the first place.

Before John could reply, several sleek limousines pulled up alongside the gangway just as Farquhar arrived accompanied by Hillman, Look Yu, and Soon, all dressed in Merchant Navy officer's uniform.

As each person arrived on board Farquhar gave them a cordial greeting, then introduced them to his awaiting officers, before leading them along the deck and into the saloon where the customary reception was waiting for them.

Once everybody had arrived into the saloon they settled down making small talk.

Farquhar started the ball rolling by announcing that his ship was an old insignificant ship compared with all the big ocean liners and merchant-ships, which come and go. He was a bit shy but welcomed the visit of these high-powered dignitaries, also stating his uncertainty as to why they came.

A very large ginger bearded man who speaking with a Scottish accent stood up to speak about each ship getting a welcome as part of the good nature of the colony, and each Captain who offered his hospitality would have it returned several fold during his stay here.

Each self-important person stood up to give a small account of themselves thus to ensure the good will of the economy of the colony, hoping Farquhar and his crew would reciprocate the mood accordingly.

"In other words scratch my back, give me a nice full brown envelope and all will be well, Kim?" John asked aside in a whisper.

"It's what makes the world go round, John. I'm waiting for that well-groomed Chinese man to speak. I know him, so does Ho Ping, and so does the 3rd Mate, I suspect. If I'm not mistaken it's the baron himself, Mr Dung, with his bodyguards who are all dressed up as business colleagues. And by the way, once this is over I shall be ashore all the time with my relatives I haven't seen for many a year now. " Soon whispered back.

"I wish you a happy re-union Kim!." John started to ask but was discreetly shushed by Soon, who told John to be quiet and just listen to what was happening.

There were several short speeches made by these visitors which all boiled down to the fact that they were only on board to see that justice and fair play in the commercial world was adhered to. In doing so Farquhar and his officers were obliged to obey the golden rules of such a prosperous and generous nature of earning ones rice bowl.

The small Chinese man, identified as Dung, was the last to speak, but when he did all the other visitors looked almost in awe of him, listening to each word he spoke.

"Captain Farquhar! I am a very lenient person towards any man who can show initiative and the ingenuity to take from me what doesn't belong to them. For that they get to live, as long as they return whatever they took from me in the first place. To cut to the chase, I am here to collect my cargo, baggage, or belongings, whichever word you care to adopt.

So unless you, shall we say, render unto Caesar, within the hour then you and your officers will be part of the menu on the floating restaurants in the Aberdeen Harbour." Dung said icily, full of menace, backed by stares of intimidation from his henchmen.

Farquhar started to say he knew nothing of what Dung was talking about, when Dung cut him short.

"Commissioner Goulding! Be good enough to explain to this stupid man, we know he's got our luggage on board and know exactly where we would locate it on this miserable excuse for a ship." Dung snapped.

Goulding told Farquhar exactly where it would be found on the ship and how much was there, just in case Farquhar or his officers had other ideas of keeping some of it. All he had to do was just sit there and let his own men go to fetch the luggage.

During this time, Dung's henchmen and a couple of Goulding's men stood up moving threateningly towards Farquhar and his officers.

It was Hillman who stood up, challenging the authority of Goulding and his heavy mob about their allowing all this to happen, given that they were government officials and were supposed to prevent such underworld deals such as this which would undermine the financial stability of the colony.

One of Dung's thugs came over, pushing Hillman roughly back into his seat and telling him in Pidgin English to keep his mouth shut.

Hillman asked Dung a few more questions, which he took great delight in answering, suddenly realising he had everybody exactly where he wanted them.

Dung stood up telling Farquhar and his officers he can do exactly anything he wanted to do without punity and there was nobody in the Colony big enough to stop him, not even the might of the British Forces. Dung bragged on for several minutes whilst his cohorts brandished large machetes and guns that were held close to Farquhar and his officers.

John cleared his throat before he pushed away his 'minder' and stood up to face Dung.

"Okay Mr Shit, Crap, Dung or whatever your name is. How do you know you've got the right ship? I mean, just where in my coalbunkers would you expect to find your baggage? How did you get it smuggled into a part of the ship knowing full well everything in the bunkers eventually gets thrown into the boilers?" John snarled, which drew gasps from Goulding and the others.

"What's your name?" Dung snapped, but his name was whispered by one of the other local dignitaries.

"Ah yes, it's Engineer Grey! It appears you must be such, what you people call, an asshole, not to realise a coalbunker is the best place to put my luggage into without it being found. Before you meet your maker, you will take me down to your bunkers and personally dig it out for me with your bare hands." Dung screamed while two of his henchmen grabbed hold of John.

"It appears Mr Shit face, you're making one big mistake!" John started to say, before his captors dumped him bodily onto the deck.

"Yes Dung, you've definitely got the wrong ship. This is the *Tsun Wan* not her sister ship the *Tsun Wah*. Same type, same builder, but with the crucial difference in the spelling of their names." Soon provoking yet two more men mountains to move menacingly towards him.

"Mr Shit, before you and your men decide to take the law into your own hands, which is normally the case anyway, just where does Goulding, and the assistant harbourmaster come into all this?" Hillman demanded.

Dung turned round to Hillman telling him exactly what he wanted to hear, before he exposed a tape recorder he had hidden in his jacket.

"Now men!" Hillman shouted, as several armed men came barging into the saloon, shooting the men with the guns killing them outright. The others with machetes or other weapons simply threw down their weapons, meekly holding their arms up in surrender.

Dung made a dash for the exit but Hillman rugby tackled him and subdued him long enough for one of his men to tie him up. Hillman issued a string of orders, which involved Goudling, and the other so-called dignitaries tied up in a bundle.

Coming over to Goulding and the other British visitors, Hillman started to interrogate them in such a manner, any refusal to answer got a very painful reprisal. Dung started to prattle away in his own language, inducing Hillman to kick him in the groin stopping him in mid sentence.

When Dung finally came round, John gave him a glass of oil, which Dung had to drink, although he tried not to do so, he was finally forced to drink the entire contents.

"There Mr Crap! Wasn't that nice? That should give you an idea as to what is about to follow. Now lets take Mr Shit down to the engine room to see just how smart he thinks he really is." John snarled, as he signalled Sergeant Major Brannon, who was Hillman's 'right hand man' to help him drag the man away.

"Don't forget Goulding and company!" Farquhar suggested, which started a mass exodus from the saloon and down into the engine room.

When they got down into the engine room, Dung was untied then given a shovel and ordered to start digging out his so-called luggage from the coalbunker.

John stood in front of where the coalbunkers should have been and beckoned Dung to start digging. When Dung met a solid steel wall, John kicked the man's backside so hard he was lifted a foot up in the air.

"Now then you shit faced clever bastard, just show me where you've got your stuff stowed." John taunted, as Dung frantically searched for the telltale signs of coal, but found none.

"Okay Mr clever Crap with a capital K! Tell me just where am I supposed to put coal on an oil burning ship?" John tormented as Dung stood looking totally bewildered.

"But I don't understand! This is a coal burner. My No1 courier told me so."

"I told you about the difference in the *Tsun Wan* and the *Tsun Wah*, but oh no, you just didn't listen!" Soon sniped.

"If this is the work of your so called No 1, I should hate to be your no 10. You fuckin' stupid slant eyed bastard!" Hillman snarled.

"Just who is your No 1 Shit face?" Farquhar demanded, but only got a mumbled reply.

"You mean Fu Ming and his sidekick Do Ping? Well, fancy that, because we've already saved you the bother in correcting their incompetence. We gave them a bird's eye view of the destruction of your pirate fleet, but I dare say they were too stretched to say anything, considering they were hung from the for'ard derrick. Given a 'suspended sentence' as Captain Farquhar had decreed." Hillman said sarcastically to the now very nervous and seemingly frail man.

"Bring him back up into the saloon Sarn't as I have another surprise for him, let alone Goulding and his cronies." Hillman demanded.

Once they all arrived back into the saloon, Hillman had the 'Chimes' gang leaders brought out and thrown roughly onto the floor for Dung to see them.

Once they saw Dung they pleaded with him to get them freed, whilst Dung on his part, tried to deny their existence.

Hillman had the 3 pirates sit up in a row with Dung, Goulding and the others before going behind the bar to bring out some berets, shoulder insignias, identity necklaces and other items.

"These are what remains of my good friend Capt'n Gourdie formerly from the Para Regiment, Petty Officer Roy Sedgewick and his six man patrol. Goulding! You are the one who fingered them, and you Harbourmaster, are the one who let these pirates operate within the territorial waters. It is no good denying these charges as the Chimes gang will testify in any court, if only to save their yellow skins." Hillman stated, then went on to dictate what was going to happen to each of them.

Dung vowed that each officer and crewmen of the ship would be hunted down and killed. Goulding attempted to hide behind diplomatic immunity, as did his friends. The Harbourmaster appealed to the pirates to save him due to the several favours he had done for them.

Soon and Larter were taping and writing down all what was said, with Farquhar taking on the role of overseer, making sure that Hillman did not slightly overdo his Spanish Inquisition type of interrogation on the captors, to render them dead in the process.

It was several minutes before Hillman made his decision as to what would happen to Dung and his men, before turning his attention to Goulding and his cronies.

"Maybe the Colony can breathe more easily now that Dung and his gang have been sorted out, but I suspect Goulding and his partners in crime will be a much more difficult nut to crack. But having done so, each of them will swing just as well as Fu Ming and Do Ping." Farquhar stated.

"On the contrary! Mr Dung is a valuable member of the community, as are Goulding and the Harbourmaster. I suggest that you untie them and let them go if you know what's good for you!" a cultured voice commanded from the saloon doorway.

John and the others turned round to see a tall slender figure of a well-dressed man enter the saloon, flanked by several police officers.

"Stand fast you men! Staff Brennan! Get these men disarmed and tied up" Hillman shouted, somehow appearing from behind the new visitors.

"Well, if it isn't Deputy Dog Governor Jenkins and his poodles! It appears Captain Farquhar, that we've got a nap hand now. It had to be somebody higher and with a lot more going for him than that idiot Goulding, even though he is, or shall we say, will be the next ex Chief of Police. I mean he's too stupid to run such an organised crime and business with the likes of Dung. Come to see that your acolytes are safe and well, or have you come to deny your involvement with them, you fucking snake in the grass?" Hillman declared. Then held his pistol at the head of Jenkins, whilst his escorts were tied up and thrown unceremoniously onto the deck to accompany the others.

"Just who the hell are you and why are you threatening a member of Her Majesty's Government?" Jenkins blustered, flying into a rage over his undignified treatment.

Hillman started to pistol whip Jenkins into silence, quoting a man's name with each blow.

"3rd Mate, I suggest you control your temper else we'll have nobody to take to the gallows." Farquhar said anxiously, stopping Hillman from hitting the cowering Jenkins again.

Hillman who was breathing heavily, seemed to look blankly at Farquhar for a moment before he gathered his composure again.

"Jenkins is the ringleader on his side of the coin and in cahoots with Dung in this drug smuggling racket. He let my pal and Dung's pirates butcher his men, as payment for Dung hiding earlier discretions made by Jenkins. This particular man apparently likes small boys and big time gambling. These Police Officers are part of the so-called Vice Squad who take backhanders off the 'Chimes' gang. My O/C with a couple of agents from MI 5 and MI 6 plus a few of the top echelons from Interpol, including the Chief from the British Met Police are due any time now to take this bunch of filth back to Britain for processing through the criminal courts. Most of them will end up being hung for their involvement in the murder of my pal and his troop, let alone the murders or so called accidental deaths of other government investigators. Now that they have confessed quite openly tonight with their confessions taped and witnessed by you and your officers, I think we've done a good job." Hillman maintained.

"What's going to happen to Dung and co?" John asked

"Dung is totally finished. His power base has been destroyed, which means his opponents will take all his wealth and territory to share it amongst themselves. He will be discreetly handed over to his rival gangs in some sort of a trade off, who will give him a new cement overcoat to wear as he takes his last walk over a short pier. His pirates will be sent to the gallows, if only to save them from the attentions of the families of their victims." Hillman stated with satisfaction.

"In that case, we can have a peaceful run ashore without fear of some monkeys jumping out on us." John reflected.

"Something like that Chief! Sorry to spoil your entrance to this wonderful place. This dark side is not normally on view, nor is open for the general public to fret about. Hope you have a pleasant stay to make up for it." Hillman concluded, ordering his men to remove the prisoners from the ship.

"Stonecutters Island 3rd Mate?" Farquhar asked

"No, Stanley Fort! Our special unit there has the facility to entertain Jenkins and his lot, and in exactly the same manner as the Japs did to our troops not so very long ago."

"Oh well then, it appears I'm short of a good 3rd mate now. Glad your mission was a success and I'm glad to be of assistance to you." Farquhar said sombrely, shaking Hillman's hand in farewell.

"As it happens Captain, your ship is a very special ship which my controller no doubt will be needing from time to time. You will get a communication from him as and when we need your good help again. Until then Captain, it's goodbye! Sarn't take this load of shit away." Hillman stated, then left with his men.

The silence in the saloon was shattered by the voice of a steward announcing the mail had just been sorted out and everybody should come and collect it.

"Chief! I've got a few letters for you, two of them being registered letters. Sign here if you please." the steward stated, as he encountered John.

"Two registered letter for me? Who the devil would send me not one but one of those?" John asked taken aback with the news, signing for them to begin ripping open the first special envelope:

> *'Dear John Grey. I've only been in the colony a few days now but am in the Bowen Road hospital in Hong Kong suffering from an old complaint of Beriberi and of course a dose of dysentery. It will either do me in or render me impotent, but hopefully it's the last one as the correct answer. When you arrive we can meet up again, even though and ironically, I am shacked up above a local brothel in the Wanchai district of Hong Kong. If you have any further manuscripts or papers, which can be extracted for use from your ship, then please send me a copy.*

I'm now on my last tour of duty with HM Dockyards, Tamar being the easy one compared with Sembawang.

You should know, and unofficially, that you have already been shadowed by our lot, and like what we see. You have the job savvy but you need to be more Ruth than Less, for me to be able to get your promised seat with the college in Southampton. You must realise that whilst I can speak up for you, your friends will have to match you as per job on board, for them to follow you. In other words John, and to be perfectly honest, you might have to ditch your friends in order for you to progress upwards as you are destined to achieve. There is no room for the old School Tie connections, unless of course, they have proved themselves just as good as you in their own rights too. Having said that, they each have a strong case in their defence. I'll leave it there for you to draw your own conclusions on this matter, but you still have the unfinished business of the Balmoral Hotel presentation to honour, so please do not let your sponsor friends down, which includes Happy Day and Joe Tomlinson. Look forward to be hearing from you wherever you are. But don't forget to look out for me, by courtesy of my old friend Mr Ting who has a town house in Cameron Road Kowloon side, also a mansion up at a place called Sha Tin heights, I think. Failing that, Mr 'Peanut' the Dry Cleaners of Sembawang Road, Singapore.

I am also informing you of something that you should be aware of:-

Belverley, Trewarthy, Creswell and Co have all been sued for millions by the International Scientific Research Authority for attempting to patent your ideas on several items including your ICE DOCKING theory.

What they didn't have was the exact plans description and the actual mechanics on how to achieve the phenomena, which Professor Van Heyden produced on your behalf. Anyway, that will take a couple of years and several millions of the Triple Crown money to resolve. So be aware of that in case you get a few fat brown envelopes from them as sweeteners for you to side their cause. Hence the need for being hardened and to be the bastard needed to survive these things.

On that note, you might take them up on their decision to

retain your several thousand pounds reward money you should have received long before you decided to change shipping companies. I suggest you contact some Seaman or Docks Unions to take up your cause to claim it all back from them. We this end wait eagerly to see the outcome of that at least.

Take care my young friend, and look forward to seeing you again.

Fergus McPhee.'

"The old rascal must have flown up here to escape the typhoons. Must try to visit him after we dock in the morning. He obviously hasn't heard the latest concerning Andy, but I really must speak to them about all of this. I can feel some good runs ashore coming our way, so lets hope we can get a few of them under our belts before we sail into pirate waters again." John said quietly to himself, starting to open the second one but got interrupted by Sinclair.

"John! Guess what me old mate? Mitchell has certainly been successful in getting our lolly from the Triple Crown company, look!" he said breathlessly, showing John a large cheque stapled to a letter headed sheet of paper, with Mitchell's signature on the bottom.

"10,000 British smackers to do whatever I want. Never had so much as a bawbe to my name only a few years ago, now I'm rolling in it. Get yer glad rags on and let's hit the town." Sinclair whooped eagerly.

John opened his envelope, which matched Sinclairs, but his cheque was well over double of Sinclairs, who, managing to espy the amount, carped on about the unfairness of it all.

"You were only a Bosun then, Andy, whereas Bruce, Tansey Lee and I are Officers, so maybe the reason why it was shared out like this. Let's see how much Bruce got to confirm this." John said soothingly to his old friend.

"Aye, suppose you're right there John, but I'm an Officer now and almost ready to take up a Captaincy post." Sinclair agreed sullenly, as his euphoria suddenly evaporated into the afternoon heat.

The two friends sought out Larter who was in the saloon having a drink.

"Bruce, have you opened your registered letter yet?" Sinclair asked swiftly, whilst nodding to the others in greetings.

"Yes! I found it a big insult. I shall be contacting the Maritime Law Bureaux let alone Lloyds, about this. Look, what they paid me for my troubles, twelve lousy grand." Larter moaned.

"Think you got short changed Bruce, take a look at mine, and I was the one in charge of the expedition. Now show him yours John!" Sinclair said angrily.

John gave a quiet sigh, fished out the envelope and showed them the cheque confirming what he had said about officers and crewmen.

"Between us, we've been given around 42grand. I dare say Tansey Lee; Crabbe and the army officer each had around the same, pro rata that is. Even Crabbe admitted to a few grand, and he was only a 5th Deck Officer. As far as I'm concerned, all what we got would only represent around less than a 10% pay out of the amount awarded by Lloyds. I can guess just who pocketed the rest, the thieving bastards." Larter said bitterly as he downed his drink, then called the steward over for a refill.

"Not for long, by what McPhee has told me in his letter. Belverley and company are being sued for millions that apparently they don't have right now. Getting their just desserts, if you pardon my pun. So maybe we're lucky in getting this amount. At least we can put it to good use apart from a bloody good run ashore." John said cheerfully, managing to cheer up his two friends.

"Yes, I'll be able to put some of it away to get my Masters certificate. What about you Bruce?" Sinclair asked with renewed cheer.

"I've got plenty of plans lined up which will keep me here, as I see a good future for the country and I'll be in the right place at the right time if it all comes good for them. Maybe even get to retire to Oz land maybe to set up a radio station of my own." Larter replied hopefully, looking to John for his opinion.

John declined to offer his hopes and wishes, but told them that as he got the most, he would treat them to a bloody good run ashore once they'd secured alongside the ship repair yards at the other end of the harbour.

Larter's two sparkers cheered at the prospect of a free run ashore, and started to list all the things they could do whilst here.

"Hold on a minute you two! I'm only paying for one decent run, so if you'd like to contribute towards them, then I would be much obliged. Besides if what 3rd Mate Hillman has said stands true, then we'll be getting quite a few freebies and complimentary tickets to visit some of those places you mentioned. You can keep the dope houses though, as I've no intention of chasing any perfumed dragons, even though it's for free. Never know what or where you might end up, so stay away." John laughed, ordering his round of drink for them all.

The small party lasted well into the night, before everybody decided it was time to get turned in whilst they still had some shut-eye time left.

"Perhaps Fergus has something there about going it alone. If Bruce and Andy are serious, they have made it easier for me now. Maybe if I tell them about Fergus's letter they might change their minds." John whispered into his pillow, finally succumbing to visit the land of nod.

CHAPTER XIX

Lashed Up

The *Tsun Wan* had been alongside Holts Wharf on the Kowloon side of the harbour for a few days before they moved down to the Taikoo ship repair yard for two weeks, getting her engine fixed up again along with other modifications, which were needed. As there was no immediate prospect of getting ready to put to sea, apart from the odd day to sort out the technicalities on board, her officers were left alone to enjoy some valuable shore time.

"Okay, what's next on the list? Lets have a recap in case we've missed out on something." John asked in general.

"We've completed a good list that would do any tourist guide proud, including the under the counter stuff the local drug barons entertained us with. The Cable Car lift up the side of Victoria Peak; The floating restaurants in Aberdeen Harbour; Enjoyed a banyan on the beach of the real Repulse Bay; Visited the San Miguel Brewery out at the place where our ship got her name from; Watched the making of a Kung fu movie by a bloody good martial artist, erm Mr Lee or whomever: Saw the Hong Kong version of the Tiger Balm Gardens and the pagodas; Visited the walled village at Kam Tin; Had a bet down at the Happy valley Racecourse; All of that and more, yet as far as I'm concerned the best so far was sampling all the nightlife with willing girls munching our bunches under the tables whilst we slurped our drinks in those bucket shops. Mind you though, the floorshows were a bit tame in comparison with John's Taraniti experience. We've quaffed a few yards of ale in the China Fleet Club, and even visited your pal McPhee and his friend Mr Ting out at his fantastic mansion overlooking the bay. Not to put a finer point on it, we've been lashed up ever since we stepped ashore." Sinclair said, rattling off the long list.

"We mustn't forget our early morning hot buttered rolls full of decent gammon from Rikki's Restaurant, and of course our late night snacks of hairy pie from the Chanteclere. Don't forget my quick trip to Morse House, where I'm supposed to set up operations here." Larter said with a nod of his head.

"All that in 2 weeks and still we haven't spent more than about twenty quid each, or the equivalent of 300 Hong Kong dollars by my reckoning. Hillman wasn't wrong, when he told us by getting rid of Dung, the word would spread like wildfire and for the local druggies to show us their gratitude. Probably when we finally leave, should we return their gratitude will be long since forgotten, or at least used up after this time around." Larter added cynically whilst looking at the large street map of the colony.

"No matter Bruce! But it sure has been one hell of a run ashore so far which will take a lot of beating without exception." John added with satisfaction.

"So what do we do for an encore, any suggestions?" Sinclair asked offhandedly.

"What say we go to visit the Major and his lads. We could always phone them up and ask them to give us a tour of that part of the area we missed out. Maybe we could stay overnight in their Officers mess. Then of course we mustn't forget that we've been invited to the Whitfield Barracks officer's dinner bash at 1200. Also there's the freebie hour at the local massage parlour down the Chatham Road afterwards. We've been guaranteed there will be two of the lovelies for each of us to do the honours. Something to do with their natural lack of height I suppose." Larter offered.

"Where have your two fellows got to Bruce? We've seemed to have lost them almost from day two." John asked.

"They've got themselves shacked up with a couple of air stewardesses down at the Kai Tak flight terminals. Something to do with a friend of one of them having a sister working for one of the air lines that comes here quite frequently, Cathay Pacific, maybe the North West Orient, and a cousin on the British Overseas Airways Corporation (BOAC) who land here nearly every two weeks, I think he said."

"Well that's okay then. It's all down to us three now to fly the flag and all that." John responded, donning yet another freshly laundered shirt.

"Where did Farquhar get to? Haven't seen him since we arrived." Sinclair asked idly.

"I'd give you just the one guess. It starts with the letter R and ends with the letter N." Larter responded with a grin.

"Yes, there's definitely something cooking there. He's probably getting another trip organised for us, rather than having a good time ashore. I noticed the *Antares* and her escorts arrived earlier on today. Which means we'll probably be getting a visit from Hughes and some of his cronies." Sinclair groaned.

"In that case let's get lost ashore where he can't find us. We'll start off with the officer's bash, then our last freebie before we kip for the night. Bruce, kindly do the honours and phone the army boys at Sek Kong. Ask them if they'd be kind enough to give us a conducted tour of the place for a couple of days or so. If not, then we can come back to Kowloon and spend overnight there. By that time, with a bit of luck maybe the fleet will have sailed away again." John directed, which was agreed whole-heartedly by the other two.

John and his friends went to a 'Chinese area', which was out of bounds for the local based troops, but not to the sailors of the Merchant Marine.

The taxi arrived outside a brightly lit building whose neon sign read in large letters 'Me Fuk' bar, making John laugh when he realised the Chinese always use their last names first, therefore giving it the reverse quotation.

Entered the dimly lit bar they were met by what Bruce described as the 'Mamma San' who was in charge of the bar girls.

"English Sailor boys! You no 'cherry boys' so come in and sit over here!" she invited, showing them to an empty and secluded part of the bar. With a shout and a clap of her hands, summoning several young girls clad in highly decorated brocade

Cheung Sam's were buttoned up around their necks yet with a slit on each side of the skimpy skirt end of the garment which showed their legs almost up to their bums, and that every one of hem were knickerless.

Once the friends sat down, she asked them to pick one each, which they did.

"They first time girls! You pay them ten dollahs first." She demanded.

"What! We pay before we see merchandise?" Sinclair responded quickly.

"No ten dollah no first time girl." She rebuked, holding out her hand for the money.

Larter shook his head and told her the girls will get the money not her, who responded with a toothless smile and waved the girls to sit down by them.

They each had one girl sitting next to them asking if they'd buy them a 'green drink', which from John's experience in Singapore, meant that the girls were trying to earn their living by using the 'Green drink' or 'Gleen dlink' as they say, as the standard currency for them to pleasure their male guests. The more 'gleen dlinks' the more intimate or explicit acts of a sexual nature they performed.

"So what's the menu then Bruce?" John asked.

"Two green drinks and it's a hand job, three is a chest rub, four's a munch your bunch time under the table, all the way up to ten for an 'all nighter' in bed with them, but you'd only be allowed two visits on the nest, and even then you'd normally get thrown out after a couple of hours anyway. Each drink they have will cost you two dollars or half a crown if you like, on top of your own order but here's the so called menu if you don't believe me." Larter chuckled, handing the so-called 'menu' around for them all to take their pick.

Sinclair was quick to point out that 12 shillings and sixpence[*] was a decent offer for an 'all-nighter' but decided that the girls

---

[*] Or 63p today.

back in Sembawang were professionals, therefore much better value, and besides they were 'clean' compared with whatever these girls might be carrying or suffering from.

John opted for the four drinks to enjoy the personal attentions of his young hostess, who had already opened the top of her Cheung sam and exposed her tiny breasts for him.

"My name is Suzy Fong! Maybe you like to feel me?" she asked coyly, as she let him look at her small yet perfectly formed pair of breasts.

"You likee?" she asked taking hold of his hands, then placing them to cup her breasts for him to enjoy. Whilst he obliged her with gentle caresses so as not to hurt her, she opened his coppice and put her hand inside his pants then gently fondled him. He saw the others were being treated in the same way, so decided to enjoy the girl's attentions whilst he was still compis mentis, unlike some of the drug laden sailors sprawling around the in some of other cubicles, being systematically robbed by their erstwhile bar girls.

The music was from the latest chart hits from the likes of somebody called Elvis Presley, Fats Domino, Johnny Ray, Connie Francis, Bobby Darren and many others, blaring loudly from a juke box shining like beacon at the other end of the dimly lit room. The friends started their drinking session like there was going to be drought, which was a norm in the Colony at the best of times. All of which set the scene for the girls to 'drink under the table' which afterwards seemed to rejuvenate the men enough to look for another bar with yet another round of carousing.

"Bloody hell! They were no 'first timers' the way they performed on us. Our Singapore girls are real professionals, which means that these girls have a long way to catch up. My question is this. If they're supposed to be 'first timers', then how or where did they learn all what they did to us?" Larter asked.

"Maybe watching blue movies whilst slurping sticks of Blackpool rock, probably." Sinclair said knowingly, with a nod of his head.

"Well it's a good scam they're pulling anyway. But I think it's time for us to head back to Whitfield barracks for our transport out to Sek Kong" John replied, which concluded their session for them to leave.

They hailed a taxi, which took them back down onto the main Nathan Road to the gates of the barracks, but were stopped at the main gate by one of the guards.

"Engineer Grey and party?" the soldier asked politely.

"Yes, I am he. What is it you require of me?" John responded in like manner.

"There is a typhoon warning in force which means your trip out to Sek Kong has been cancelled due to all transport being stopped. If your ship is docked Hong Kong side then I suggest you catch the next Star Ferry over as it will be stopped for the duration." the soldier advised, looking at his watch.

"You have about one hour to do so gentlemen." he added abruptly.

John told the others the news, making them rush down the small slope leading them out from the barracks, and attract the attention of a passing taxi, it took them quickly past the Peninsular Hotel and the famous YMCA, then down by the big square that had the Kowloon Railway station, and to the concourse of the famous 'Star Ferry'. There was no such thing as orderly queues here as it was everybody for themselves, but they managed to barge their own way through the crowded ticket barrier to arrive on board and select their own little spot near the departure gangway as every row upon row of seats were already taken by earlier and quicker passengers.

The ferry seemed to skip through the increasingly choppy water slipped easily alongside its jetty where the mass of passengers poured off it and hurried away.

"Look over there lads! A cart full of Wanchai Burberrys! We'd need one of them when the ruddy monsoon rains start bucketing down on us. They stink of waxed paper and whatever chemicals to make them water proof, but although they're made from bamboo sticks they're much better than any western umbrollies so they are." Larter quipped as they ran over and bought their very fat, green and brown umbrellas, with Larter flicking one open and shut again just to see if it was okay.

"Okay then gentlemen, now what? Maybe purchase a souvenir Hong Kong Bible, or AFO's as we used to call them on board?" Sinclair asked.

"What's one of them, and I didn't know you could read Andy?" John quipped.

"It's a dirty book full of spelling mistakes John." Larter chuckled.

"Yeah! Fug me fug me she crid, as he fugged her on the soda!" Sinclair said aloud.

"So he fugged her on the soda then turned her over onto her hans and nees onto the flor and went bang for bang. He banged her twit as she banged her hed against the wall and fugged her long time again!" they both said in unison.

"Hey Bruce! That was in AFO No3, so you must have read the same one I did." Sinclair laughed.

"Yeah! Borrowed off you I did! No 5 is even better though!" Larter admitted, then they laughed even more at John's non-plussed expression.

"Never mind John, we'll get you one to see what we mean." Larter added, tousling John's hair for him.

The mood changed slowly from one of jollity, back to the here and now, as they realised they had to go back on board whether they liked it or not.

"According to ships orders, we're supposed to make our way back to the ship in case we're needed. So I guess we've got a day or so on board to while away." Larter stated, hailing another taxi for them.

"At least this time we're alongside the harbour wall. Maybe we can get a few services brought to us given we can't go for them ourselves. So why miss out, that's what I say." Sinclair said thoughtfully.

"Yes, what a good idea. Get on board then have our food, beer and bed-warmers come aboard when we need it." John agreed, as they instructed the taxi driver to take them down to the docks and to their ship.

John had a peculiar feeling as he tramped his way over the gangway, but dismissed it from his mind but put his goose bumps down to the rapid loss in temperature. He felt as if the magic bubble of well being in the company of his two best friends had been well and truly burst, and this typhoon to blow that magic away forever.

They arrived into the saloon to find a steward setting up the bar for business, and for them to be the first officers to arrive on board.

"Afternoon Chief! The galley will be flashed up soon to provide food for you if you need it. We've just loaded a supply of beer on board, so we might as well enjoy this typhoon in style." the steward informed him happily.

"That suits me fine steward! 3 rounds of the usual and kindly bring them over to our table" John responded tiredly.

The typhoon lasted for several days before the all clear was sounded and everybody could get back to normal again.

During that time, John was able to inspect the new repairs and other works which the ship needed doing despite the weather. His drawing of the new enclosed bridge was accepted by the ships management team, importantly to be fully endorsed by McPhee, who told John it would be sent as further evidence to support John's admittance to the ISDM college.

It was also the time for Farquhar to get his officers together and discuss their future, both for the ship and her crew, which unsettled a few of them.

"We can understand the logic of the ship's future, Captain, but as far as we officers are concerned, just how do you propose to keep a good cohesive team together in the circumstances you have described." Sinclair asked bluntly.

"Yes Captain, I am particularly concerned about all this, given this ship really belongs to me and my family. How would an RN officer fit into the overall scheme of things?" Soon asked, which started the ball rolling as some of the other officers asked direct and pertinent questions, but answers from Farquhar seemed either inadequate, or he simply either no clue how he to answer them.

Farquhar became extremely agitated over the cross questioning his officers gave him, admitting he had never experienced such questioning from his subordinates before. In the end, he blustered or bluffed his way out of the situation by telling them whilst he was the Captain of the ship, everybody had to abide by his sole authority of decision making on board. Any future insubordination by his Officers would result in dire consequences.

John stood up telling Farquhar in no uncertain terms the *Tsun Wan* was a merchant ship, owned by a family although temporarily under a shipping company's commercial agreement; As he was RN he was the odd one out amongst them, so should have the decency at least, to listen to his Merchant Marine Officers whose lifestyle he was trying to emulate, albeit on a temporary basis. He told him that under Merchant Navy law, he had no right to re-instate the outside engineer to his former job, which undermined John's remit as the Chief engineer. He also stated quite categorically, unless he conforms to mercantile marine laws and customs, he would be forced to sail the ship out on his own, to wit, without an officer let alone a crew. Just for good measures, John mentioned the word mutiny, which was a common thing in a civvy line, making Farquhar really sit up and take notice.

"If you wish to continue as the appointed Captain of this ship, then you had better stop thinking battleships and bullshit, but for once, start thinking about merchant ships to earn your money." Sinclair said icily, rising from his seat and left the saloon, followed shortly by the others.

"Bloody hell Bruce, talk about reading the riot act. Do you think Farquhar will heed what we say?" John asked with concern, as they shared a cigarette on the boat deck.

"He's in a no win situation at the moment, and in something of a cleft stick. On the one hand, the ship has been designated to the military, for transportation of munitions and weaponry between here, Borneo, Singapore and Malaya, which is the main reason why he is on board as the Captain. On the other hand, the management board is trying to off load it, as it's now becoming a high maintenance item for them to carry the costs. Kim's family has already taken legal steps to finally reclaim the ship, which will take effect from the end of the military contract. Once that happens, most of us will be shore bound until we get re-assigned." Larter declared.

"Any idea as to when that is likely to happen? Has Kim given out some hints about this? I mean, we've been away from home for some time now, and according to company rules, we're due for some UK shore leave. So what's the score on that Bruce?" John asked in rapid succession.

Bruce looked at John and started to smile.

"John you're incorrigible! Ever since we've known you, you've never asked just the one question, but a ruddy series of them. The only thing I can enlighten you on, is yes we're entitled to UK shore leave, but don't know when. One thing is for sure though, if they intend keeping us out here, then I for one will be asking for the shore leave UK side to sort out my things before locating here. And, I shall be demanding they pay for it all. "

"If there's one thing this company is good at, is looking after its officers. At least from my experience of being able to return home for my father's funeral. For they paid all my expenses including a donation to pay the undertaker and made sure I had enough in my pocket for travelling."

"There we are then John! All we've got to do now is keep our noses clean and out of Farquhar's way until he buggers off again. Speaking of which, it's time I did too. See you later!" Larter said amiably, as they left to go their own separate ways.

* * *

John was working with Ottley, when the heard an announcement, "Do you hear there, all officers are requested to meet in the saloon in 30 minutes," came the metallic voice over the ships tannoy system.

"Dave! You'll just have to complete this job without me after the meeting, as no doubt our Captain will have other things on his mind for me to do. C'mon, lets get cleaned up and mustered!" John urged.

"No problem Chief! I'll get a stoker to give me a hand if that's okay?" Ottley responded cheerfully.

"Better take Chief stoker Burgess, he's the best welder on board." John grunted, leaving to go to the declared meeting.

"Ah Chief! We have our first sailing instructions just came through, which will involve a longer return trip to Singapore than coming up here. Here is your engineering bumf to wade through." Farquhar greeted cordially, offloading a parcel from his own big pile to give to John.

"Thanks Captain, some light indicative reading no doubt. Glad to hear we're sailing again, as I was beginning to think we've been welded to the harbour wall."

"You and me both Chief! Now lets meet the rest of the gang to enlighten them, on what you civvies call a pre voyage meeting." Farquhar responded politely, then led the way into the saloon.

John put his pile of instructions down onto a table next to Farquhar, sitting in a seat, which was next to his.

"Good morning gentlemen! I have some good news and some bad news for you all. First the bad!" Farquhar announced breezily, then commenced to explain what the meeting was about and how it would affect all on board. He stopped from time to time to give anybody the chance to pose questions or observations, until he had completed his dialogue with his officers, which took nearly two hours.

Everybody gave Farquhar a polite ovation, which seemed to leave him non-plussed, until John whispered to him the officers were responding politely and with sincerity to their very first pre-voyage meeting from Farquhar. He also told him that since the air had been cleared between them for some days now, everybody was looking forward to a fresh start, and that he, Farquhar had certainly done that.

Once Farquhar got over his slight embarrassment, he thanked them for their response before announcing the meeting over with a final one tomorrow sometime once the cargo had been loaded and stored away.

"It seems Chief, now the ice has been broken, we can all relax for us to get on with our jobs on board. One thing though! I as Captain of this ship, reserve the right to do my duty as befitting any Captain no matter what type of ship he commands. Which means..." Farquhar said curtly but got cut short by John.

"Yes Captain, I understand exactly what it means, because it also applies to the position of Chief Engineer. He too has the same reserve when it comes to running his department." John said quickly.

"I'll agree to that! Just so long as you understand I'm the Captain and have the final say in all matters on board."

"In engineering terms I hold the same rank as you, but you are without question, the Captain of this vessel." John breathed and saw the recognition on Farquhar's face to what he said, for him to continue.

"Now that has been settled, I request you sign the outstanding warrant on 2nd Engineer Rowlands. He's a liability in the engine room, but wishes to remain on deck as the outside Engineer. I personally would much prefer he got transferred onto a more modern ship where he can extend his recent knowledge of a much more modern ship using modern engines. Having said that, steam is steam whether it's via a direct thrust through the engines such as ours or via kinetic power to provide indirect thrust from turbines, which is more prevalent in today's ships."

"Thankfully, the decision on that officer is now all down to you Chief! But if you had him transferred it would make me one officer short."

"As it happens, I've got a preponderance of manpower, blessed with an outstanding bunch of stokers, all of whom deserve their promotions. I intend keeping Ho Ping as the 2nd, and 3rd engineer Ottley as the outside engineer but to understudy Ho Ping. If you care to take a good look at the promotions listing, it will be in keeping with the company policy of integration.

You should also note the references to Chief stoker Banks, of the Asian members of my team, and other promising men right down the line to the lowest stoker. In short I've got a full crew of good quality engineer officers and men. Mind you though Captain, all are provisional until such times as each officer converts his promotion with the necessary trade papers, or leaves the ship. Ho Ping should be excluded from that, as he was, after all, the original Chief engineer of this vessel. On that score, he would be the natural successor to myself as I only hold the command due to, shall we say, British interests." John stated, handing over the proposed promotion listing.

Farquhar looked at the list, stroking his chin thoughtfully for a moment.

"Okay then, have it your way. But I'll need to speak to Rowlands in front of you first, before I sign his warrant. Have this list implemented before we sail tomorrow. Must dash now, I've got a pow-wow with the Navy boys in the dockyard within the hour." Farquhar conceded, leaving in a hurry.

'I can't believe that our few home truths have changed Farquhars attitude and demeanour. Maybe somebody in his lot has had a word in his shell like ear holes. Whoever it was, I'd like to buy him a few beers. It's early days yet, so let's wait and see.' John muttered to himself, rounding a corner in a passageway leading towards his cabin.

"Still muttering to yourself I hear, John!" Sinclair chuckled as the two men almost bumped into each other.

"Hello Andy! I'm suspicious of Farquhar. A leopard can't change his spots overnight, unless somebody shoved a double-barrelled shotgun up his arse pulling both triggers."

"Actually John, word has it that he's up for promotion if he can pull this stunt off we're about to do. So he needs us more than we need him, so to speak. Mind you though, his medals vouch for him being a very brave man. Maybe the news of this voyage has set him back into his old self again, but will be seen at the time. Anyway, I have it on good authority that once he's promoted, he's off this ship for good."

"Speaking of which Andy, Bruce has got something on that subject, if you care to visit him sometime. Shore leave has been cancelled for all officers, so must get these bloody papers sorted out before we secure for the day. See you in the saloon later Andy."

"Aye right you are John." Sinclair agreed, as they parted company.

"2nd Engineer Rowlands! It is the decision of the Chief Engineer your career would best be served on a more modern ship, so you could expand your knowledge to express your own ideas more fully. Your warrant has been duly signed and sanctioned by the management board, which means you will leave the SS *Tsun Wan* today. You will be joining your next ship as its 2nd Engineer, which is the modern freighter the *Yuen long*, due in at the end of the week.

You will be required to report to the shipping agents office on leaving this ship, where you will be able to collect your outstanding pay as a full 2$^{nd.}$

We hope you find this an amenable solution to your problem, for you to take this opportunity to get yourself back on your promotion track again. Have you any questions?" Farquhar stated firmly but diplomatically.

"Thank you for your consideration Captain, but there is no need for concern. I'm joining the *Fern Bank* from the Bank Line fleet, but as its Chief. A real Chief mind you, not a jumped up one like you Grey. I've already told you who I am and who my relatives are, and as far as you're concerned Grey, you'll end up demoted before you leave this lousy good for nothing scrap heap. Good day and good riddance to you all!" Rowlands snarled, picking up his case and stormed out of Farquhars' cabin.

Farquhar looked puzzled at what Rowlands had to say, asking John to explain, which he did in emphatic terms.

"It seems he is in for a bloody great shock soon, as his ship bounces off the bottom of the oggin. I feel sorry for all his future Captains already. Glad you decided on getting shot of him Chief, he's obviously a poser and a con artist. I have to admit on this occasion, I've had to use some of your own words on the report, as I've never had the experience in such matters, especially under civvy rules. Anyway, I've signed your promotion listing and am quite happy about it. I intend sailing early tomorrow morning at 0330 under the cover of darkness providing the weather forecast is correct, but I need to sail without smoke or soot billowing out of my funnel. Kindly see to that, also to make sure we've got the extra fuel and oil on board. I shall be ashore until around 0100, so if you need anything see the First Mate. My final briefing will take place at 0230. Incidentally, our sister ship the *Tsun Wah* will be alongside around the 2200 mark. I think that's all, any questions?"

"No Captain, I think we've covered everything, given the nature of things as they stand. Have a good run ashore." John replied earnestly.

"Thanks! Must go now, so see you at 0130." Farquhar concluded, ushering John to the cabin doorway.

"Oh! I've just remembered one thing Captain. My special report suggests certain provision for pyrotechnics which needs special deck space. Whilst I have no reservations as to its stowage, certainly under Ottley's management, given he is the one responsible for the trim of the ship; I would stress the need for extra life support systems which would ensure, shall we say, the life of the cargo."

Farquhar looked at John for a moment before flicking through some of his reams of paperwork until he found what he was looking for, and formulated his own reply.

"Ah yes! Article 10, section 45, paragraph 31, item 8.1." Farquhar stated, before he read the chapter and verse of his instructions.

"I agree with your argument. But what you don't know is some of the crew will not be making this particular trip. Sufficient to tell you, most of the crew have been under the influence of the dreaded perfumed dragons ever since we docked. Meaning, we've been compromised insofar as our imminent operations are concerned. However, we British people have a long running tradition of coming up with unexpected and downright simple plans which always seem to outwit our opponents, and always seem to work because they are so bizarre or downright outrageous. Happily for me I count myself as one of them; otherwise I would not have contemplated such a hair-brained scheme as the one we're about to embark upon. Where you come into the equation Chief is this! I need a fully competent team in the engine room for when I go into an action period, whereby I need the full engine room team to act accordingly. Needless to say, I need full control of the ships speed to counteract the natural nuances a ship could or would adopt in these waters. Then of course there is the need for a comprehensive damage control team to eliminate the threat of sinking, let alone getting caught up in somebody's fishing net."

"I can provide all power and resources into your hands Captain. But there is one thing I cannot do, and that is…" John started to say before Farquhar interrupted him.

"We have no choice in this matter Chief! You will do your utmost to support your Captain, albeit for better or for worse, in sickness and in health, blah blah, if you get my drift. Just give me your best shot on this and we'll come through with flying colours!" Farquhar stated in a chilling voice.

"You have my full support Captain, just as long as I don't end up with egg on my face afterwards, or be made to carry the can for some bodged hair brained plan you've involved all of us in."

"Trust me on this one!" Farquhar retorted.

John paused for a moment before acquiescing, then gave his answer slowly.

"Let's get down to it then Captain. The sooner we cast off the sooner we can tie up back alongside again."

"Well done Chief! Our, shall we say, passengers, will no doubt be grateful to find out that me and my crew are up for such an undertaking. Must go now, but see you as arranged." Farquhar said thankfully, then left swiftly for his appointment.

CHAPTER XX

Junks

"All systems checked and all readings logged, Chief!" Ho Ping reported, as John arrived down into the engine room. "Thank you 2nd! Just take it easy for the first few hours, as we've got a new prop and shaft fitted which will give us a few extra revs from the last lot. Just keep an eye out for the new 'wrong way round procedure' as it still has to be tested. I've got a new electrical testing unit installed, which will help to tell us when we've got an electrical problem as opposed to a mechanical one. Once we've got a few hours peace, I'll show you all about it. In the meantime 2nd, you've got the privilege of running the show until we get back into harbour again."

"But what will you be doing, I should know of in case of emergency?"

"I shall be monitoring you and all the rest who got promoted yesterday. I need to fill in certain documentation, which will substantiate or disprove each promotion I recommended. You will be the lucky one between us, as you've got a real live engine under your command, whereas I as Chief, will be condemned to pushing a bloody pen around, adding to the already overabundance of ruddy paper work a Chief has to do."

"You keep paperwork Chief, I'll see to the engines!" Ho Ping said with a big smile.

"Okay then 2nd! I'll watch from the observation platform to see your engine crew performs as normal. Any problems then try to deal with it yourself before you call upon me. Good luck!" John concluded, then climbed up into his engineering office out of Ho Ping's way.

"Chief! The Captain wishes to see you on the bridge!" a breathless messenger blurted out.

Putting his pen and notepaper down, John followed the messenger out of the engine room and up onto the bridge.

"Chief! We're going through the narrower channel taking us to port of Lantao Island. We've got plenty of water between our keel and the seabed, but just in case we should hit a high spot, we'd need some tricky seamanship to get us under way again. Here's where I suspect we'll meet, so here's what I intend to do." Farquhar said quietly, showing him several pencilled marks on his navigation chart, then explained what he intended.

John listened intently at all what was said, making suggestions or observations as to the practical or mechanical items Farquhar could make use of.

They discussed the points for a short while, while Farquhar checked his navigational position issuing orders on changes of course or speed as they went along.

"I'll get the 3rd Engineer to rig up a few portable pumps to assist the main ballast pump on a rapid change of weight, forward or aft thus to create a see-saw motion, as if to seemingly jump over the hurdles. You have a good solid ship under you, so we can scuff over a few sandbars and the like if you need to. And, if you need an extra turn of speed then I can deliver up to 18knots for you, but only in emergency and even then only for about an hour or so. You do realise of course, we've only got a 10foot draught, even though our water mark is altered to show around 14." John opined.

"Yes Chief! My draught is well noted, but thank you for the information. We've still got a cloudy sky, which will keep us cloaked until the morning, so I'm hoping we'll be well clear of the islands and the Colony by daybreak. Providing of course, we don't meet up with any more of those bloody pirates, then our get away will have been successful. Now we're at sea, I intend holding a brief meeting with the officers after breakfast, just to put you all in the 'Rembrandt', or picture, if you like."

"That shouldn't take you long Captain, given we're very thin on the ground, so to speak. Even thinner as far as the crew are concerned too."

Farquhar gave a little chuckle at John's revelation, telling him that as far as he was concerned, he had everybody on board he really needed, and it had to be this way for the voyage to succeed.

"In that case Captain, I think its' about time we speed up and clear away quicker than at present, so that the crew, and especially the passengers, can get some much needed sleep, Captains included."

Farquhar gave another little chuckle as he rapidly checked each prominent bearing to ensure he had a smooth passage though the shallows, which were in front of the ship.

"Once we're free and in open waters, then I'll need the full speed you were talking about. It will give us some distance between the ship and the last island on the route. When achieved, then perhaps I will get my head down too. Have Ottley to check the deadlights, as I hope to remain in 'darkened state' for as long as possible. Just one small light even a cigarette end showing, could be seen from miles away which would give us away." Farquhar explained.

"Very well. I'll inform my stokers not to smoke whilst on deck after dark. Do you need me any further?"

"No, that's all for now. See you at around 0630." Farquhar advised, as John took his leave from the bridge, but in doing so came across Sinclair.

"Hello John! Come to see the distant lights of Hong Kong?" Sinclair asked politely.

"The Captain sought the advice of an Engineer as to how you Sailors can get over the hurdles which seem to be in abundance around this part of the harbour." John said jokingly.

"Chance will be a fine thing John. Now let me tell you..." Sinclair started to say as he rose to John's bait.

"5 junks moving in vee formation dead ahead, range 8000 yards! 4 more on green 10, range 10,000yards. Probably a fishing fleet." came a whispered voice sounding from somebody not of the crew. John's looks of surprise made Sinclair chuckle softly.

"Brian Westwood from the Singapore Naval base whom you've already met, along with a Yank apparently his opposite number down from their Philippino base in Subic Bay, have fitted us up with special radars and electronic devices which our Yank cousins are testing before we drop them off in a couple of days time. In fact John we've got a whole parcel of them stowed on board in those crates you saw being loaded earlier, and a crate of our own boys in the after cargo bay. All cloak and dagger boys and armed to the teeth, so don't go upsetting any of them. By the by, our Major and his team are also on board to keep an eye on those crazy Yank buggers." Sinclair informed.

"Who me? No thanks Andy; I've got enough on my plate with my own department let alone trying to sort out theirs as well. But then, it's what you get for being the boss of your department. And before you say anything, I hope you become just that soon. I'd like to be around to see you as Captain with me your Engineer. What do you say?"

"Sound pretty good to me, but that seems a long way off at the moment. Anyway, must check these sightings. Catch you later!" Sinclair said softly, then rushed over to speak to the radar operator.

"Morning Chief! Time for breakfast and a briefing with the skipper." Thompson announced cheerfully.

"Morning Tommo! Any chance of a cuppa first?" John asked sleepily, climbing down from his bunk.

"One cuppa on the table even as we speak Chief!"

"Have you met any of our passengers yet?"

"Passengers? Oh you mean the gaggle of army officers in the cabins. Yes, some of them. Some of them sound bloody Yank to me, although I can't help wondering why we've got those cowboys on board a British ship. Any ideas Chief?"

"I've no idea steward. Maybe our Captain will put us in the 'Constable' during this meeting of ours. In the meantime, kindly get a message to the outside engineer for me. Tell him I need to speak to him rather urgently."

Thompson nodded his head, left to do John's bidding, then came back almost as quick with Ottley tagging along behind him.

"Morning Chief! Understand you want to see me?" Ottley asked swiftly.

"Morning Dave! Yes, we've got several crates of Yank army wallahs stowed in the for'ard cargo hold. Better get some life support systems up and running before they start flaking out on us. I'm due to see the Captain shortly, but will come to see how you're getting on. Any problems in getting this done, get a couple of off watch stokers to give you a hand."

"We've got some of our Special Forces boys on board but Yanks? Where the bloody hell did they come from? In fact what the hell are they doing on a British freighter and not on one of their super duper troop ships?" Ottley asked incredibly.

"Don't ask me Dave, I'm only the Chief Engineer. Leave all that to the Captain, just look after our own end and all will be well. Must go now, but get the job done as of last night so to speak, never mind your morning rounds."

"Fair enough! On my way now." Ottley responded and left as quickly as he arrived.

'Glad there are some good engineers up and coming, and Dave Ottley will do very nicely given the promotion breaks as I certainly have done.' John mused, leaving his cabin to see Farquhar.

"Morning Chief! You already know Hillman our ex 3rd Mate, this is his Sarn't Hoppy Hopkins and his section, but these are a few of their American counterparts who have hitched a ride with us. Meet their CO. US Marine Major Hal Haliday who will be requiring your services before long." Farquhar greeted, as John entered the saloon.

John looked at the large beefy man with an impressive chest full of medals before he greeted everybody with a nod and a smile, then sat down by Sinclair and Larter, at a table covered with a large pile of maps and pamphlets on it.

"More easy reading Captain?" John joked, giving a cursory glance over the table.

Farquhar conducted the meeting, telling everybody where the ship was going, why the soldiers were on board, and other general background information. There were several diagrams, maps, and information being displayed, with salient points discussed over by the officers.

John stifled several yawns as he found the proceedings boring, because he had no input to offer them, until Sinclair raised a technical problem which required his attention.

"The safe working load on the cargo booms can only be raised by a quarter even if both booms were lashed together to work as one, using both winches in tandem. From my limited knowledge of Sailor's terms, you'd have to reeve a second block 'n tackle to the main boom to take the extra strain. Again, as a booster, you could always harness up to use the capstan on the foc'sle help give him an extra lift, but you'd have to devise a series of rigging, blocks 'n tackles to do so. The alternative would be to go alongside somewhere where there's a dockside crane. Make a swift offload to get the ship away before somebody knows what's going on."

"Thank you Chief, glad to hear that you're still with us!" Farquhar said with a grin, before he took up John's suggestions.

Haliday mentioned there was time for one of their ship support vessels, which had the equipment on board to sail from their base at Subic Bay to r/v with them at some offshore island. But also stated should this ship be spotted then it could jeopardise their mission.

"Okay then gentlemen. We'll make for the island just off the coast of the Non Dang River as planned, jettison our cargo under cover of darkness, just as the Chief Engineer has described. We have 3 days to practice offloading by night, and for your support group ashore to get organised.

According to the chart, it looks like their territorial waters are all shore side of the 25fathom line, except around these islands, which are around the 5fathom mark. But as you are already aware, we can sail into shallower waters to within 2 fathoms off the mainland." Farquhar concluded before handing over to Hillman and Haliday.

"We intend for the ship to continue on her way south, then to pick us up one week from our landing zone. We will operate radio silence throughout, with the special ops frequency only used on an emergency basis, excluding the final get out phase and r/v pick up again. The electronics team headed by Brian Westwood will remain on the island, supported by one of our Subs out of Subic Bay." Haliday stated before Hillman finally concluded the meeting, and everybody left the saloon.

"Chief! When we're running 20 miles off the mainland coast during the day, I intend we steam at around 8knots. I will need you to make as much smoke as you can to make it look as if we're just a coastal tramp ship. But at night I shall be requiring full revs from you, around the 18knot mark if you can make it. If so, then we'll be able to make the r/v drop zone in good time, subject to weather conditions." Farquhar informed.

"12 hours at 8 knots and 12 at 18! Can make 12 at 14 but I don't know about the 12 at 18, given the fact we'll probably be pushing against the tidal currents. I can give you around 16knots for a little longer period if you need it, but no more."

Farquhar grabbed one of the coastal charts and studied it for a moment before responding.

"I'd have to go out some 200 miles or close to within 5 nautical miles of the shoreline to clear the tidal stream. I can't guarantee an overcast sky for our cover and we could be seen at any time, hence my 20 mile margin." Farquhar argued, mumbling a string of figures.

Sinclair came over to see what was going on, hearing Farquhar run through some mathematical hurdles.

John told him what Farquhar had requested off him and his answer, but gave a solution to the problem, asking Sinclair to tell him as he would listen to a Deck Officer before an Engineer.

"It appears Captain, that if the Chief can't give you the speed for the times you need, then all we've got to do is take a seaward dog-leg. If we go across the stream instead of full on, we could make full speed during all of that time. Our outward dogleg need only be 20 to 30miles off the coast, which would take us out of any possible radar range. We could maintain a constant 14knot speed for the entire transit, to arrive in almost half the time, or at least a good day earlier than planned. That saving might be taken up by the next typhoon, in which case it would only delay us about the same amount if we stayed as planned." Sinclair stated, pencilling a triangle onto the chart.

Farquhar looked at it for a moment and did some more mental arithmetic then turned and beamed to Sinclair.

"By the Lord Harry! That will work a treat First Mate, well done! I'll make a good navigator out of you yet. Work out the relevant courses and speed to offer me your recommendation as soon as you have done so, before we announce a change in the army wallahs plans. See Chief! It takes a decent 1st Mate to understand what a Captain has to do in these circumstances." Farquhar said elatedly, then rushed away.

"See what I mean Andy! He would only have rubbished it I had told him. I can give you a steady 16knots in these conditions, but you'd have to reduce it to around 10knots in heavy weather. Having said that, maybe you could trim the dogleg out to say 2 hours steaming in case the return leg takes much longer. Even a parabolic course would suit your needs."

"Hmmm! It sounds a better option. I'll make up the two recommendations to see what he says. You'll probably know the options he's taken via the engine room telegraphs. Your 2nd should be warned on what to expect though."

"Fair enough Andy. Must go now or we'll be having baked Yankpot for dinner. They've been put into the holds without proper ventilation and the like. See you at lunch then!" John concluded with a wave and left the saloon.

"Hey Limey! Call this a ship? It's nothing but a piece of shit floating around the place! When are you going to sort out our crap accommodation, 'cause it's like a fuckin' hot hole down there for my men." a soldier shouted into John's face, grabbing hold of him by his lapels.

He saw a group of soldiers lounging around the for'ard cargo deck, egging their companion on with their foul mouthing, using slang words that John had recognised from his trip across the States.

He looked at the irate soldier who was tall, very wide like a man mountain, and stood in his way blocking his movement. John merely sighed, then with one swift movement swung his heavy wheel spanner upwards in an arc to hit the soldier in the crutch so hard, the man gasped then fell down in a big heap at his feet. All the other soldiers went dead silent in disbelief.

John bent down grabbed the soldier by his lapels, dragged him a few feet before propping him up against a deck ventilation shaft.

"You might be able to gob off to your officers in your outfit pal but not whilst on board this vessel, especially to me, the Chief Engineer. I outrank your officers by a long chalk, so unless you start showing some respect around here, this particular Limey will see you and your men get diddley squat and fry for the rest of the voyage. Do I make myself clear sergeant?" John said calmly into the sergeant's ear, who was struggling to contain the sharp pain between his legs.

The sergeant nodded, gasping out his apologies through his pain whilst trying to stand up again.

"Just remember I'm the one who decides whether this piece of shit as you call it moves or not. If your mission is so important to your country, should it all go down the pan due to your bad mouthing, then it's your neck on the block not mine. Now get out of my way and let me get on with my work." John replied sharply, then left the hapless man to his friends to find Ottley.

"Hello Chief! Just putting the finishing touches to the a.c.u. To save time explaining, here's my drawing plan of action for you to read." Ottley greeted cheerfully, handing John his notes and sketches.

John read them through picking up on a couple of points before he handed them back.

"Seems fairly straight forward Dave! But I intend making a slight alteration to your work, which will involve a special piece of equipment. It is a certain piece of knowledge, which I picked up a while ago, and something you might appreciate when it's all finished. To give you a clue, it will, shall we say, cool things a tad for our American cousins." John said with a twinkle in his eye, leading Ottley down to the ships fridge space.

'I'm not one to bear a grudge, but that sergeant and his pals will soon learn not to trifle with an engineer on board a ship, especially not out at sea.' John muttered under his breath, getting Ottley to install the extra equipment.

"There you are Dave, an instant air-conditioned cargo hold! It would certainly grace any fruit carrier. Our passengers will be glad of a breather from the hot weather." John chirped, then turned the valve to start it up.

Ottley looked at the needle on the valve and at the temp gauge and then at John, before giving him a big grin.

"What a nice trick! Maybe our own lads in the aft cargo hold would appreciate some of it."

"Perhaps next time, as this is only on a trial period only for this part of the voyage. No need to upset our lads, now is there, besides, these Yanks are full of hot air anyway." John replied with an equally large grin.

"I would like to read the manual that gave these instructions though."

"Actually Dave, it's a special invention of my own which is being patented back home, as is the electric circuit tester I gave you. Just remember what you did but keep it to yourself as you might just need it someday."

"My lips are sealed Chief. Maybe it's time now to get some scran, as my belly feels as if my throat is cut."

"Fair enough Dave! You've done a good job to deserve your day off. Don't bother making your midday report as I've seen enough to satisfy myself. See you later." John concluded as both men left the cramped and freezing compartment.

***

"Chief, the Captain wishes to speak to you in his cabin. Something to do with our passengers in the for'ard cargo hold." Thompson said when arriving into John's cabin.

John stood up from his desk covered with neat piles of engineering manuals and drawings on it, stretching himself for a moment.

"Oh thanks Tommo! Glad you came in, as I was beginning to get stiff and bloody tired. Captains cabin did you say? I'm on my way, and thanks for your info. Never mind the table, just make sure I've got a clean overall for my next shift if you please. Oh, and do me a big favour! Get hold of Ottley and tell him to switch the trial nozzles off, as quickly as he can." John said tiredly, stifling a yawn and left his cabin.

"You wished to see me Captain?" John asked civilly, on entered Farquhar's bridge cabin.

"Sorry to get you out of bed so early Chief, but we've got a problem. The Major here will tell you what is what." Farquhar said quietly nodding to the American officer.

"Morning! What can I do for you?" John asked politely.

"Morning Chief! I have a complaint from my Top Sergeant Gleave who says he and his men are freezing in their accommodation. The temp gauge shows it's almost down to zero, so unless something is done, my men will end up looking like carcasses of meat in a deep freezer."

"Almost zero degrees? It can't be! Your sergeant and the rest of your men approached me yesterday, complaining it was too hot and over 30 degrees. Now he's complaining it's too cold?. The thing is, I had their temperature controlled so they could get used to the hot conditions for when they go ashore playing soldiers in the jungles. Your men have got the same life support systems as those billeted in the after cargo hold, but they've not complained to date. Maybe your sergeant is too touchy at the moment, considering the stress you will all be in this time tomorrow. " John replied, acting the 'all innocence'.

Haliday shook his head telling John he'd already been down to inspect the conditions himself, could vouch for his men's morale.

"The end game is we're not about to play around with snowmen or penguins, if you get my snowdrift, that is."

"Indeed not, because we're some 4,000 miles away from the nearest iceberg, but let's go down to see what we can do for your men". John replied swiftly then turned to Farquhar.

"Captain, ask the messenger to get me 3rd Engineer Ottley if you please. He conducted the work according to standard practice, whereas I checked it for safety and correctness. As I found all to be correct then I can only suggest one of your men must have altered the settings in an attempt to shut it down. If that's the case, then it's all down to your men, not my equipment nor my engineer officer." John said sharply, which made the major argue against the perceived odds.

When Ottley appeared, John told him of the complaint for one of the soldiers to tamper with the machinery making them into walking icicles. John gave Ottley a sly wink, which Ottley picked up on.

"I wonder what ham fisted soldier tweaked the wrong cock to make the drip react in reverse of the cross head valve which controls the brine. Instead of raising the temp control he lowered it to counteract the brine cross flow over the a.c.u. fans." Ottley said slowly with his eyes looking up to the deck-head as if to recall the equipment, but was in reality averting his eyes in case he started to laugh.

"Hmm! Yes, that sounds about right, 3rd! I'm going down to investigate the unit, but you get down to the plant to shut off the supply." John agreed readily, sending Ottley away before he gave the game away.

"Right then gentlemen, lets see what the sergeant is complaining about." John suggested and led the way down to the hold, where he met the sergeant and his men all huddled up in one big group.

"Playing good friends are we sergeant?" John asked sharply, looking at the temp gauge on the a.c.u.

"Major, why did you pick this goddamn piece of shit to use for this mission. First of all we're roasting like pigs, now we're turning into goddamn icebergs. Can't you do something?" the sergeant drawled as he came over to greet his officer.

John looked at the a.c.u. and discovered it had been almost wrecked with large dents into the side of the metal panelling.

"There's your problem Major. It appears either there are mice in the hold wearing steel clogs, or there is a wrecker amongst your men hell bent on freezing his mates in the process. Look at this unit! It cannot be repaired nor have I got a replacement." John stated diplomatically, showing the Major the damage.

Haliday turned to Gleave and tore him off a strip for allowing this to happen, then ordered the men out of the hold onto the main deck, when Farquhar arrived on the scene.

"Captain! Our men are forced to billet themselves up on deck for the rest of the voyage. At least they will not get roasted, or in this occasion frozen to death." Haliday said angrily, getting his men move out of the hold and onto the deck, carrying their bedding.

"There is no way you can do that Major as it will tip your hand to any passing ship who cares to eyeball us as they pass. Chief! What can you do to alleviate our passengers discomfort?" Farquhar asked quietly, standing between John and Haliday.

"Leave it to me Captain! I have the outside engineer onto it even as we speak. Give me about 1 hour to check the rest of the system just in case." John asserted, then grinned at the sergeant and his sidekicks on passing them by.

"Well of all the cock-a-mamie stunts to pull. You limey bastard!" he hissed.

"Told you sergeant! I'm the Chief around here so you and your men had better start to show us Limey jackpots as you call us, some respect." John responded with a smile before disappearing to the far corner of the hold to where his machinery was housed.

John came back within the hour to tell Haliday, who was still with his men that they could now return to their billets again.

"Thank you Chief! Come on men, get below again and leave the ship alone in future. That goes for you too sergeant." Haliday ordered, who was greeted with a muffled cheer from his men.

"It's an old ship Major, and very temperamental. But given a bit of care, she'd take you all the way up the big river you want to sneak up. And fetch you all back home again safely." John informed him, as Haliday started to leave with his men.

"Yes Chief! She's perfect for our mission without a doubt, but this is one hiccup in the proceedings my men could do well without."

"Better speak to your sergeant about that. Just ask him about wheel spanners, like the one I'm carrying right now and see what he says. Hope your men get rested now major. I'm off to the engine room for a spell. See you at breakfast." John concluded, showing the Major the heavy spanner with a hook on the end of it.

"Hello 2nd! How are you getting on with your new team?" John greeted, landing onto the observation platform next to Ho Ping.

"Okay Chief! Burgess is good, and deserves his promotion. Have a problem with the new prop shaft bearings. One of them must have been damaged when being put on, as it's crunching a bit. I've got a spare one of the old type but it could be fitted with an hour providing we can stop for that time." Ho Ping advised, showing John the replacement bearing.

"Yes, that'll do it. We'll be stopping at a couple of islands around this time tomorrow so just keep it well greased and cooled for now. Have you conducted your rounds yet?"

"All monitoring completed, log already signed Chief."

"Fair enough 2nd! On your way out, send me your 4th engineer. See you at breakfast, as I need to brief you on a certain matter." John said, dismissing the departing 2nd.

CHAPTER XXI

Hairy Moments

During the following day, whilst the ship was making her way inexorably towards their r/v point, the soldiers were testing their weapons and other equipment whilst the crew were preparing to off load their heavy items that were on board.

John was on deck talking to Sinclair discussing the problem of weight transfers and the technical merits of the existing lifting gear.

"You'll need a second stay line attached to the upright derrick to prevent it from snapping which will take care of that end. You've already shipped a double-reeved block 'n tackle, then lash the two booms together, so it's not a problem Andy. The way I see it, unless there is a loss of body weight of around a fifth, then you'll never get those items offloaded safely. But then who am I to tell what you already know Andy."

"Nae bother John, as it's exactly what I figured. You've obviously learned a lot from me that's a fact, John. It can be done, but if speed is of the essence then no way will it happen. Whoever thought this one through must have had a dockside crane in mind, not the derricks on this ship. I'll go and speak to Hillman and his oppos, see what they say, it's a British thing not Yank, if you get what I mean." Sinclair said with his usual broad Scottish accent.

"Indeed, but in the meantime, I'll get the power rating for the winches upgraded for the first test." John responded as they parted company.

John encountered the sergeant again, who was talking to his men, and politely interrupted his spiel.

"Oh it's you! What is it you want this time?" the sergeant asked in a surly manner.

"My apologies for interrupting you sergeant, but we have a weight problem with your craft which was not thought through during the planning stages of your operations. Come with me and show me the diagrams of them, or at least how you intend operating them, as we might just have to strip them down so we can offload them." John said as a matter of fact, as they walked over to the deck cargo.

Whilst they were making their way, John spoke about their previous encounter.

"I understand you've had a nasty accident by falling over some upright stanchion, sergeant. Sounded very nasty and debilitating. Hope you've recovered from it now, but remind me to tell the deck officer responsible to get it removed for you." John said softly, with a wink and a smile.

Gleave nodded in appreciation of John's diplomacy and grunted his approval, as John proceeded to show the sergeant the various parts and how they were used, until both were satisfied.

"A good piece of ingenuity has been used, look. The craft is in 2 parts. The lower half, which is the hull, is aluminium with a cladding of wood. Judging by its construction it would give you a decent armour protection up to deck level least. On top of that you've got a twin petrol engine and twin props and its own independent steering gear etc.

The top half is only plywood, which is slotted and clipped onto the hull. You have a false funnel and a steering wheel, all connected up to the rudder by a couple of bolts.

The front part of the craft has upright spars to hold up the canvas to form a sunshield, as has the stern section. I should imagine the plan is for it to look like some sort of local riverboat or fishing vessel when it's all put together. You have some false decking to stow your fuel and weapons under, as your main decks will have dummy equipment to make up the pretence. Which leads me to suspect the top half could be jettisoned at any stage in some sort of emergency for you to make a quick getaway. Do you agree with my findings?" John asked, completing his examining of the craft to show the sergeant the parts.

"Well hot diggity Limey! Goddam it man, you can strip it off quicker than you can a prostitutes drawers!" he exclaimed when he saw what John had shown him.

"I'm not one to apologise for my actions, but on this occasion Limey, you've certainly come up with the goods. I have to admit all this is new to me, but from what I've seen looks okay. Maybe that's what the backroom boys intended us to do in the first place but forgot to tell the major about it." the sergeant added, scratching his head, looked intently at the two halves of the craft.

"You seem to me a very brave, dedicated man, but you appear to be less informed than us, your British cousins, shall we say. If you want to live to an old age, then less of the Limey tag and you can forget the crackpot bit if you don't mind. My name is Chief Engineer Grey to you, or Chief if you prefer. But remember this for all times, we British people, unlike your lot, do things quietly, without fuss or overstating the obvious problems before us. We get around the problems as you've just witnessed just so that we can get on with our tasks, or in your language, the prime mission. This is a classic example of your top brass, so what do you think of what you, as a sergeant, has just discovered which could have jeopardised your prime mission had you not taken the time to investigate first?" John said with his soft County Down accent.

The sergeant looked at John then at the evidence before him before he gave his answer.

"I reserve the right to answer, erm Chief! My brief is to inform my Major on all things even though he knew about it in the first place. That way we both know of the ongoing development of our mission."

"Well said, as it's the very attitude I would expect from my engineers, and bearing in mind that we're only civilians after all. To change the subject and in direct line to the here and now, I suspect there're two craft like this one, with the fourth one which seems to be much bigger.

Mother hen and her 3 chicks if you like which you could confirm during your mission briefing as such. Lastly, it appears unless you've got a few friends ashore to help with your needs, and I'm talking fuel; I can supply you with a few extra gallons of petrol but not enough to go around. If your strategy is having a base camp, or an escape route placed on the landing zone, then I can have it dumped there with the rest of your stores, in case you need it to get out in a hurry. I suggest you select your fastest craft for that though, then pray we're waiting around for your return." John said casually but with a smile.

The sergeant was taken aback with this information.

"Thank you sir, erm Chief! Will report it to my commander, sir!" the sergeant said in military fashion, as he snapped to attention and saluted John.

John smiled, offering offered some sort of a salute to the sergeant by saying:

"I thank you for your address sergeant, but I'm no American Red Neck. So kindly keep all that crap for your own upper ranks, as I'm just a civilian engineer on board a ship doing my job to help you military men do yours. Maybe one day you'll reflect on my words, to realise just who your real friends are."

"As you say! Must go now and kick some ass to get things done around here." he responded, then gave him another robotic salute.

"Just so long as you don't kick mine on your way past sergeant." John quipped with a smile as the man mountain cast his huge shadow over the deck on his way towards his men.

John made his way to the saloon where he knew the army officers and their N.C.O's were holding mission briefings, and found Sinclair and the sergeant were each explaining the problem of offloading the heavy craft into the water.

He waited until they were finished before holding up the instruction pamphlets he had found and went through with the sergeant, explaining the weight problem had come about during an earlier discussion he had with the First Mate. These pamphlets told them exactly what needed to be done to overcome the difficulty.

Both Majors scanned through the pamphlets eagerly for

several moments then stated they realised what John said and had given them, was a missing factor in the final briefings they themselves had taken some weeks earlier.

"We had better start getting some practice in taking one of them apart and putting them back together again major." the sergeant prompted.

"Yes major. You've got about 2 hours daylight left to do so, before we darken ship again." Sinclair stated as he nodded his agreement to the sergeant.

"Right then, let's get on it right away. My men will muster the weapons and stores for you while you're doing it." Hillman suggested to Gleave.

"Okay Sergeant Gleave you heard the man! Have all the men mustered on deck, on the double!" Haliday ordered sharply, which dispersed all the soldiers, leaving John and Sinclair to themselves in the now very quiet saloon.

"Perhaps we can now get the other problems solved John." Sinclair stated, explaining what he needed to know.

"Quite simple Andy! As soon as you drop anchor, it's a simple case of co-ordination. Offload our boys first from aft, then have them moved forward to the middle of the ship. Then use the davits from the lifeboats as cranes to lower the stores and the like down to them. In the meantime, get the Yanks offloaded and their craft re-assembled. Once done so, they will float aft to receive their stores in the same manner. You are able to do this on both sides now, especially now as you can use just a single boom per craft. Just make sure you've got enough men with heaving lines to help load up, given speed is of the essence. For that, you could always suggest keeping half the soldiers on board to move the stores down, then on completion, they could disembark using a scramble net if you've got one. Failing that, a few stout lengths of rope for them to slide down." John explained.

Sinclair looked at John with amazement, asked.

"Are you after my job too? For you certainly know your stuff John. Where the blazes did you learn all this if it wasn't from me?"

"Tut-tut dear friend! Remember our collision encounter on the *Brooklea*? Well that was almost what Trewarthy did, only in reverse." John said quietly, as he finished drawing a sketch of the scene.

Sinclair sat for a moment to reminisce the occasion, then slapped John gently on the back.

"Yes by damn! That really was some hairy moment. He might have been a surly bastard, but he certainly knew how to handle his ship." he said, as it all started to flood back to his memory.

"Amen to all that Andy. Must go now to see to my own part of ship! We engineers are very busy people what with our engines and sorting out the sailors too." John chuckled, as he rose and left his friend pondering over the drawing John gave him.

"Oi watch it stokes! Your turn for the wets tonight." Sinclair said jokingly to his departing friend.

The ship finally arrived at the tiny group of islands off the mainland in the early hours of the following morning, and anchored in a sheltered cove to offload the small army which had the cream of the British and American Special Forces all in one special unit.

They were about to create mayhem in certain parts of Indo-China, as part of a political initiative sponsored by the countries of the Asian Treaty Organisation. Let alone the implementing schemes emanating from to the good old 'U.S of A, who seem to know better than anybody else on the planet.

Yet if Hillman's mission turned out to be a monumental disaster, the politicians would deny all knowledge of, or the existence of such a unit. Such are the perils of a cloak-and-dagger operation in another person's country.

Hillman made his goodbyes and thanked Farquhar for the excellent time made in offloading his team, as did Haliday. With a final check of the return trip they left the ship, taking their men to the black and empty island, which would be their temporary home.

"Okay men, you heard the man! It's time we slung our hooks and scarpered, First Mate. Chief, I need a good turn of speed to clear this area, so give me as much as you can." Farquhar ordered with satisfaction, as he had his ship sail from out of the blackness of the island and into the inky gloom of the vast open wastes of the South China Sea.

The quietness on board after the departure of the noisy soldiers was a welcome relief for the remainder of the ship's crew. Even the weather was kind to them during their transit to Singapore, and there was much relaxation for to be lazing in the sun, whilst the voyage lasted.

"Evening Bruce! Haven't seen you since we left HK, how have you been?" John asked amiably as Larter came over, sitting next to him in the saloon.

"Hello John! No, the Navy had kept us very busy up to now. We've still got a special radio listening watch to keep whilst we're at sea, in case our friends need us sooner than we think. I've managed to bum a spare radar set, and an electronic warfare set from the Yanks, which we'll need on our return trip. Thankfully they let me have one of their operators to man the bloody thing as I'm overworked in the radio shack as it is. " Larter said glumly, as John placed a drink in front of him.

"Well, never mind. According to my calculations, we should be docking sometime in the morning. As far as I'm concerned we deserve at least a few days off for our troubles, but I fear we might only get a day or so ashore with the girls. According to Andy, that is."

"Oh well, that is something at least. Here's to the girls, cheers!" Larter responded by downing half his pint in one go, before offering John one of his cigarettes.

"The ship seems like the Marie Celeste what with half of our crew missing and the ruddy noisy Yanks gone. Maybe if the company sees we can do without half the crew it could set a trend on future voyages. What would the Brethren make of that Bruce?

"Yes you're right there, the ship is lovely and quiet. But I somehow don't think our Brothers would wear the loss of jobs on board, let alone loss of face, unless of course there is a complete change in the way ships are built and run. More cargo space less crew, hence more profits for the company yet no increase in pay for those on board. I'm glad Macaroni has a decent flexible working policy whereby any sea-time is all down to the individual operator.

I've had nearly 25years of radio watch-keeping at sea, between the RN and the Merchant Navy, so if this company decides to do without my services on board then it's okay by me. Given the promise of a shore station would more than tip the balance in favour of shore time over sea time. But what about you John? Are you still on course with that college offer, or are you going to finish your time at sea as Chief of some big liner as you've been on about for some time now?"

"The college is still pie in the sky for me at the moment, Bruce. And as far as sea time is concerned, I need to reach the top of the ladder before I contemplate any future plans. Perhaps a couple of voyages as a full Chief might do the trick before deciding, who knows." John replied sombrely.

"I think Andy is in a similar position to you John. His rise from bosun to First Mate was certainly meteoric, even faster than your own promotions, but he needs to be the ships master before he starts to think Civvy Street. One thing is for sure dear friend, life is catching up with all of us fast, and now is a good time to start thinking of our after-life from the sea."

"Yes Bruce, it's been a good life so far despite our trials and tribulations on board let alone ashore. Still, wouldn't have it any other way! Anyway lets change the subject before we end up crying into our pints, as the beer is watered enough as it is." John said stoically, ordering another round for them.

John stood at the back of the bridge and watched Sinclair guide the ship up the twisting and turning shallow waters of the creek, which led them to the large naval base at Sembawang.

"Keep an eye on your bearings as you pass them First Mate as your speed will dictate your next bearing and course adjustment. You need to slow down when you pass certain places due to speed restrictions, even be prepared to go astern if you encounter a vessel negotiating the same bend or stretch of water. We've got a 10 foot draught, so watch the trace on your echo sounder in case you run out of water." Farquhar said quietly in a running commentary, as he coached Sinclair in the finer skills of river navigation.

The ship glided slowly over the still waters in the early morning, leaving a trail of black ribbon from its funnel and a phosphorescent trail as its wake. The early morning air was full of the heady scent given off by the waking flowers, heralding yet another tropical day for the rising inhabitants of the island.

The sun was emerging out of the dark green canopy of the thick jungle, casting millions of little rays of light over the land, which seemed to extinguish mans puny efforts with his electric lights.

John shivered slightly as the soft breeze fanned his cheeks and felt his skin roughen up under the rash of goose bumps suddenly appearing all over his body.

"This is part of the day that I like best Chief! Nobody about, all quiet, nice and cool, with a successful voyage just being completed." Farquhar said quietly, sitting in his chair, which raised him above anybody else on the bridge.

"Yes Captain, I always enjoy entering harbour, especially from the foc'sle. The special smell that comes from the land seems to lend a touch of magic to the proceedings."

"Indeed Chief! I'm of the same opinion, glad to hear it. Turn to port now First Mate, and enter the harbour. Prepare to put the brakes on but keep on your transit course." Farquhar replied, issuing Sinclair with further instructions.

The *Tsun Wan* steamed slowly past some sleeping warships making her way towards an empty berth where several people and vehicles were waiting to greet them.

"We're berthed just ahead of the minesweeper. As soon as the head rope are over and secured, tuck your stern in nicely before you get your stern ropes over." Farquhar advised, looking at the dockside through his binoculars.

Sinclair issued a string of orders, had the ship placed nice and neatly ready for the ship to be tied up alongside securely.

"Tell the engine room we're finished with main engines. Get the gangway over and connect up the ships shore supply. Secure from harbour duties." Sinclair ordered, as he came back from looking over the side of the ship.

"Bravo First Mate! That was a good show." Farquhar exclaimed, clapping his hands in appreciation.

"Thank you Captain. Maybe I can have a crack at taking her out as an encore?"

"Certainly First Mate. Mind you, you need one more return trip before I let you loose on your own.

In fact, you will have the opportunity to plan the next voyage, starting with the chart you used to get up here in the first place. Anyway, as to the here and now, get the ship cleaned up and re-stored with provisions. Chief, make sure we've got enough fuel to take us to Timbuktu if necessary. See it is done before anybody shoots ashore.

With regard to local leave, make sure everybody returns back on board by 0600 tomorrow, no excuses for being adrift. Chief, it would be prudent of you to keep an engine room watch on board, that also applies to you First Mate, so keep a deck watch on board at all times. I need to keep the ship ready for sailing at a moment's notice.

Right then gentlemen, must shoot ashore and meet our welcome party, but I will be found in the Joint Services Command HQ which is part of the Navy's Admiral's building. Just phone the dockyard telephone exchange and have them put you through. The thing is gentlemen we need to be alert to pick up our friends we left behind on those islands on time, before anything goes radically wrong with their departure. Remember to sound the ships horn as instructed First Mate. Anybody not on board when we sail will forfeit their job on board let alone any pay due to them. And that by the way gentlemen, was the fate of all those not on board when we left Hong Kong." Farquhar directed as he left the bridge.

CHAPTER XXII

Questions

"Okay First Mate! Even though it's 0300 in the morning and there's no vessel in the creek and again no disrespect intended, but I need a fast transit down the creek, so I'm afraid you'll have to wait until next time. Once we've reached the roads you can take the conn until we reach our r/v point from then on if you so wish. Chief, when we're out in open waters I need as much speed as you can muster." Farquhar informed them quietly.

Sinclair nodded his head and rushing out to the bridge wing to take charge of the deck crews fore and aft, had the ship cast off neatly for Farquhar to run his engines.

"Bosun! Tell the engine room to obey telegraphs. Starboard 20! Slow ahead." Farquhar ordered, as John left the bridge to go below to the engine room.

"Morning 2nd! Hope you managed to get some shore time in. We're in for a quick transit down the creek, so be on your toes, and make sure the messenger gets down all orders given. I shall be in the office if you need me." John greeted as he arrived next to Ho Ping.

"Morning Chief! I keep good watch! We've got 2 Engineers and 5 stokers missing from my muster list." Ho Ping replied cheerfully, handing John the list.

"Thanks 2nd! I'll sort out the watches accordingly. Once we're full away, you can revert to cruise watches. Make certain you can sustain revs for 16knots. If not then do your best but inform me otherwise. Come and see me when the Captain has us full away so we can discuss the watch rota system."

"Very good Chief! Must go now!" Ho Ping said hurriedly, rushing toward some gauges and monitoring gadgets John had placed around the engine room.

"Carry on 2nd! See you!" John said with a smile, leaving the very busy man to his work.

'Lucky man! This might be a museum piece of a ship let alone its engines, but it certainly adds a certain quality to the person who keeps it running as if it was brand new. That prick of a 2nd did not appreciate the fact these engines were in fact, and still are, the main bread and butter and the foundation of any decent marine engineer. Thankfully Ho Ping is one man I can't teach anything about the engines or all the machinery on board, which means I can concentrate on the finer points of being a Chief Engineer. Bloody paperwork and yet more paperwork.' John groaned inwardly, standing for a moment to watch Ho Ping in action, before he ensconced himself in the much quieter but stuffier engine room office.

"Chief! We're full away now, time for a watch change." Ho Ping announced on entering the office. John looked at the brass clock on the bulkhead, which told him it was only 0430, but he was finishing off his paperwork anyway.

"Thank you 2nd. Here, I've made out a duty list for you. Providing that the weather is good to us we can have one day at least in a relaxed state. You will notice I have given you a floater to keep your eye on things, but the rest will be 1 watch in 3 due to the shortage of personnel. I recommend you be present during the day watches but make sure you observe proper meal times, then be on standby only during the night watches. Once we're near our r/v point then we'll go into 1watch in 2, as per the second roster." John explained, showing Ho Ping the list.

Ho Ping read through the lists carefully, nodding his head from time to time.

"I get this onto the notice board Chief. Thank you for doing this for me. Only you know my engines as well as I do and know whom we can trust with them, so I am happy with my orders."

"That's the spirit 2nd! Now I dare say we've enough time to get ourselves out of here to attend the Captains emergency meeting in about 10 minutes from now. Have your relief settled and join me then." John said quietly, rising from his desk, he made his way up out of the noisy engine room.

John made his way along the main corridor of the ship and up to his cabin to where he met Ottley.

"Morning Dave! Looking for me or what?"

"Yes Chief! I've got to prepare part of the for'ard cargo space to accommodate frozen carcasses, yet according to the manifest, we've not got the excess to warrant it. Maybe you could enlighten me on some detail or another as to how I will manage it." Ottley said with tiredness in his voice.

"We've got a meeting with the Captain about now, so why don't you listen to what he's got to say. Maybe it might be something to do with bringing back a few dead soldiers, but all will be revealed."

"Sounds fair enough to me Chief! But what about the living bodies in the same compartment?" Ottley persisted.

John sighed but smiling at Ottley merely said the Captain would probably give him the low down and that John would assist him in his work.

"Cheers Chief! See you at this meeting!" Ottley said slowly.

"Once the meeting is over, get yourself turned in. I need a bright and bushy tailed outside engineer on board not a wet blanket around the place. Come to see me in my cabin at 0900 to kick things off if necessary." John concluded, to which Ottley nodded and left to go to his own cabin.

"Morning gentlemen! We have a couple of special passengers on board who will be co-ordinating the withdrawal of our boys from the Indo-Chinese mainland." Farquhar stated quietly then introduced the strangers before commencing his special meeting. The meeting ebbed and flowed as each facet of the planning was examined and sorted before everybody understood what each officer had to do.

"In the meantime gentlemen, and hopefully if the weather holds good, we've got a good 24hours to get ourselves rested and prepared. For when the shit hits the fan we'd all better be bright-eyed and bushy-tailed and on our toes to get our boys out in one piece. I shall call a special pre r/v meeting to check all has been done. Have a pleasant voyage gentlemen." Farquhar concluded quietly, as he left the saloon with the passengers.

"Bloody hell John! No wonder Farquhar was made skipper of this tub! We're only going to take our ship into a possible shooting match with the Indo-Chinese Navy! And here's me thinking that if I joined the Merchant Navy I'd get away from all that bloody hassle. I had enough from the last bloody lot to last me a lifetime." Sinclair growled.

"Me too Andy! Lets hope the company will give us danger money for all this. I don't mind a joke but sod a ruddy pantomime. But what I can't understand is why us? Why don't they send a submarine or something to pick them up?" " Larter added, as he too grimaced at the thought of what lay ahead of them.

"Perhaps it's got something to do with the ship looking like an ancient tramp ship, therefore a least likely suspect under the watchful eyes of whomever are after the boys. The yank major admitted that fact last time I spoke to him, so it's only my supposition. Anyway, I'm off to say hello to my bunk for a couple of hours. Maybe after breakfast we'll learn it's been some sort of a wind up for us." John said wearily.

"Aye! What a good idea! I've got the forenoon watch anyway." Sinclair agreed as they made their way to their respective cabins.

"Okay then Dave! Here's how you do it. So watch very carefully as I will only do it just the once." John instructed, as he showed Ottley the method of freezing a large area with just a puny device such as John had put together.

Within half an hour the compartment was showing signs of freezing fog as the temp gauge plummeted down to the zero mark.

"Bloody hell Chief! No wonder the poor Yanks were freezing their balls off! And you're the one who invented it?" Ottley said in amazement, starting to shiver in the enveloping freezing mist.

"All my own work Dave! The system works perfectly providing the equipment is spot on, so I'll switch it off for now. Ventilate the compartment to return it to normal then you can have a go. You must be able to do it in sequence the exact way I've shown you, else you'll blow the system "

"I've written it all down Chief, look!" Ottley said modestly.

John looked at the writing making a mental picture of what he read, before he handed it back.

"Just the one operational mistake. You make a quarter turn on the control valve, not a half. Then check the gauge needle shows the correct flow for 1 minute before you open it to the half turn where you leave it until the correct temp has been reached, before shutting it back down to the quarter again. The other thing is, you make a thorough check of the assorted equipment to see all is sound and usable before assembling it, especially the outflow connection from the main fridge. Use centigrade at all times Dave, other than that, its okay."

Ottley entered the corrections onto his notes and read it back for John to confirm it was now correct.

"That's it Dave! I must be off now, so unless you've got anything else to bring to my attention you can carry on with the rest of your work."

"No Chief! Nothing to report as all is under control." Ottley replied cheerfully.

"Good, that's what I like to hear. One thing I nearly forgot to tell you, is you've been included in with the engine room watches during the r/v and pick up. Short of decent engineer officers on this voyage I'm afraid." John conceded.

"Looking forward to it already! That's one strange set up down there most of us will probably not ever see again. Golden opportunities and all that Chief, that's my motto." Ottley said with a glint in his eye.

"Engineer Ottley, you'll make a damn fine Chief one day." John said with a smile then left the freezing compartment.

Somehow or other, methinks I was like him a very long time ago. No wonder Happy Day, Jim Gregson and even Tansey Lee gave me my rights of passage the way they did. Now it seems it's my turn to keep the tradition going.' John sighed as he arrived back into the warmth of the upper deck.

"Chief, the Captain wishes to see you on the bridge." The bridge messenger informed John who was taking his ease on the after cargo deck.

John followed the sailor up to the bridge to find Farquhar and 2 of the passengers were looking out to seaward through powerful binoculars.

"You wish to see me Captain?" John asked politely.

"Ah there you are! Commodore Morgan here wishes to know about the ship's performance, speeds, and turning distances and the like. Maybe if you write down a few details for him so that he can plot his way." Farquhar announced pleasantly, as the officer approached him.

"Morning Chief Engineer! I'm Commodore David Morgan U.S Navy in charge of this entire operation, and that officer over there is Colonel Len Woods from the U.S. Marine Corps, who between us have got a dicey problem, which will take a bit of working out to do. So maybe if we can find a quiet spot with these goddamn plots and plans to give me some idea what we're up to." Morgan drawled.

"Now then gentlemen, what is it you want to know about this ancient ship we're on?" John asked, as they gathered around a small table at the back of the bridge.

The 2 Americans put several questions and drew several diagrams for John to look at for him to reply. Once the problems had been sorted out and the plans altered according to John's facts and figures, even giving them a few ideas of his own to ponder over, the Americans thanked John for the valuable information.

"Captain, your Engineer seems to be a credit to you. He spotted a few items we seemed to have overlooked, which gives us a better plan to work on." Morgan said expansively as he pointed to the revised and re-worked plan for Farquhar to see. Farquhar muttered a few figures, having checked his sea chart with a few angles and distances before he gave his own opinion.

"Yes, it should work. Given that we can get inshore much further without running aground and at the speeds you want, seems feasible enough." Farquhar agreed with an approving nod.

"Providing that we make our run in under cover of darkness and we're down wind from the land." Sinclair added, as he came from the main navigation chart to check the ships head. (the course in which the ship was taking).

Morgan nodded to those statements and even added a few ponderable items of his own.

"It all boils down to the mobility of the men, sir! That is to say, how many can make it back and what motorboats are serviceable to get them off the beach. Plus of course the distance covered by the territorial water limitations."

"You forget gentlemen, we're an old ship chugging along the coast. Any prying eyes will not stay on us for long, as we'd not be worth looking at anyway. They'll be looking for a submarine on the surface, or even a warship of some description, in which case they'll have a few of their vessels hiding someplace ready to pounce should any such hostile vessel stray into their waters. All we've got to do is pick the men up then get the hell out of there into international waters before we're caught in theirs." Farquhar said slowly as he swept his binoculars over the empty horizon.

"Sounds a bit hairy to me Captain, but if that's the plan then it's up to us to make it work." Morgan stated sombrely.

John asked if he was required again before taking his leave, but was dismissed with thanks from the 2 Americans.

"2nd! I have a feeling we will need to provide an emergency turn of speed for about 1 hour or so. If we calibrate the sprayers and use finely filtered oil, plus ensuring plenty of lub oil is going around the system, we can give the Captain about 15knots. Then again, if we trimmed the stern down say about 4 feet we could muster a good 20-knot mark. Whilst I have a couple of ideas I would ask you as the original engineer of this ship, what would you use to provide this speed?" John asked Ho Ping, who was taking his ease in the saloon.

"The second option plus a higher boiler pressure, Chief!" Ho Ping replied after a moments thought.

"Yes, that's my favoured option. She is light overall, but if we load her down with seawater, and I mean aft only, we could give the propeller more bite which would give us a better optimum speed on full power. As we've got no trim system, we'll have to figure out which compartment we can safely flood by using the ballast pump. The way I see it, we need another 4 -5 foot of water to give us our optimum thrust, do you agree?"

"Yes Chief, my thoughts as well! In which case I would flood the spare prop shaft space, the engine room and after sanitary bilges, but would probably only give us around 30 tons."

"The prop would need more than that, if only to keep under the sea swell."

John scratched his head for a moment thinking hard on the problem before speaking again.

"We could get the bow anchor and chain moved aft, then have the outside engineer rig up the deck pools to give us more weight. We still have several empty fuel drums in the after cargo bay, we can have them filled up."

"That should just about do it Chief, although we may still be a few tons light. But it will have to do in the circumstances. I'll get the welder to secure the deck plates above the spare prop shaft space. In fact there's no reason why we can't flood the primary prop space either, and the engine room bilges too."

"That's it then 2nd! Let me put it to the Captain first, just in case he has other ideas. Once we've got the go ahead I'll get Ottley and a team of stokers to fill up those barrels and the swimming pools, you see to the rest. See you later." John said quickly as he realised that between the pair of them, they had improved an ancient engines performance way beyond what the manufacturer had intended.

John went swiftly up to the bridge to seek Farquhar, but was told by the 2nd Mate he was down in his day cabin with the 2 Americans. John thanked him and left the bridge as diverted.

"Captain, the 2nd Engineer and I have worked out an idea, which might help, even though it could alter the overall plan somewhat." John announced as he entered Farquhar's cabin.

Farquhar looked disdainfully at John but allowed him into his inner sanctum.

"What have you got that we haven't already gone through Chief?" Farquhar asked irritably.

John told them about his idea, showing them his theories and how he was able to give an extra few knots, which could somehow help the rescue pick-up of the men ashore.

The 2 Americans were enthused by John's idea, but Farquhar stopped any further discussions by revealing a special plan he had already hatched, even before leaving Singapore. He did however, acknowledge John's plan, which became the new emphasis of conversation.

"I have certain reservations to your plan, although I hasten to add it still has its own merits. Let's discuss it then gentlemen!" Farquhar stated, as the officers crowded around to see what John was so enthused about.

Farquhar started to dismiss John's theories one by one, as the answers to his question did not seem to satisfy him, but was cut short by Woods.

"In fairness to the Chief, this is a well thought out plan. The way I see it is we have to get in and out as fast as possible, if only to reduce the body count. If the Chief can produce the extra speed then I'm all for it." Woods stated as the officers continued to pour over the sea charts.

"Yes! I agree with certain aspects of the Chief's proposals, but we need to be as light as possible to get over the sand bars, even though the chart shows 3 to 5 fathoms. You forget this is the Non Dang River that has a tendency to silt up especially after monsoon rains, which they've had recently. We're already on the

2-fathom mark as it is, even before we enter the zone, so we'll be cutting it a bit fine. Besides, we're supposed to be going in as an innocent ship, so nobody will take a blind bit of notice to us. At least that is my own theory and what I'm banking on." Farquhar stated convincingly.

"The thing is Captain, we've got a high performance shaft and propeller fitted, which I can enhance with the graded oil and fuel on board. This means we can give you an emergency full ahead speed of around 22knots. Providing we could lower the stern part of the ship down a further 4feet or so as suggested. At present, the prop is thrashing the water when we seesaw through the ocean swells and high waves. An extra 4feet, will give that extra bite to the prop and maximise the engine speed." John explained.

Farquhar studied his charts for a while whilst mumbling several mathematical calculations.

"How much weight aft do we need to get the 4feet?" Morgan asked.

"It works out at 2 inch depth per 80 tons." John answered quickly

"What about in fresh water Chief?" Farquhar asked promptly.

"Given sea water is much denser, once we hit the river mouth the main fresh water outflow the ship would be lowered by another 2 feet. Irrespective of that, we would still need to lower the stern to give you the speeds you need." John responded quickly.

"Just as I thought Chief! Because we'll be entering a fresh water zone off the river mouth, as you will see from the chart. You can forget the drums, and the for'ard anchor as I have other plans for them, but how long will it take you to flood the rest?" Farquhar asked smoothly.

"If all is in readiness, about 15minutes, but I need a starting line to give you the exact time."

"That should make it about perfect Chief! Because once we've cleared the shallows on our way out, you can flood up and get us out of here as quick as you can. Whilst we're at it Chief, I would need a good 2hours at a decent speed in case we hit a spot of bother." Farquhar said glibly, as the 2 Americans looked at each other with great concern.

"What's a spot of bother between friends Captain? No worries on that score as a very good Aussie friend of mine would say. We can withstand a 20mil shell at a 1000yards Captain, or my name isn't Chief Engineer Grey. Just make sure we're well out of range when the big stuff starts raining on us. I look forward to your final battle plan meeting Captain, in the meantime, I'll get my department ready for your demands." John said nonchalantly, and left the others to their briefings.

CHAPTER XXIII

Fathoms

"We've got about 2 hours before we reach our first r/v point gentlemen, so lets take time out for our last minute checks." Farquhar announced as he went round each of his officers to ensure everybody was ready.

The two American officers had their own tasks to perform, which were eventually dovetailed into Farquhar's action plan, but Larter who suddenly appeared with his signal pad disturbed everybody.

"Captain! Just received a flash signal from our boys on the island." Larter announced, before handing it over for Farquhar to read.

Farquhar read it out in front of everybody, creating a stir among the American officers, but Farquhar made a calm reflection.

"Looks as if we've got to act fast gentlemen. We'll pick up the men and equipment from the island first, before we make our approach on the river mouth. It appears that Hillman with a section of his troop have gone upstream to rescue the Americans, and want us to be around when they come back.

We will be able to handle the river patrol boats, but the two coastal patrol frigates are a different matter. On top of that they seem to have a big brother prowling around somewhere, so we'll have to be on our toes, so to speak. Here's an update of plan Y, so listen up!" Farquhar said quietly, as he issued a fresh set of instructions.

"Any questions gentlemen?" Farquhar asked gruffly, but found none to answer.

"Sparks, I need you to make a special signal, so come with me and I'll write it out for you. Our timing really is of the essence now we've got the heavy mob about to breathe down our necks, so we'll need some extra, shall we say, insurance policy to get out in one piece. The last thing I need to mention is that we're still too smart to appear to be a worn out tramp steamer. Maybe a liberal dusting of soot rubbed into the upper deck to take the shine off things. The bow is still showing new paint especially on the embossed name of the ship. Get a few gallons of yellow and brown paint daubed over the hull to make it more of a rust bucket, despite the fact that all inside is immaculate enough to grace a posh liner." Farquhar ordered, as the rest of the officers left.

"2nd! Get all officers and men mustered in the engine room immediately, nobody excused. That will include you Dave, but I won't keep you for long!" John directed, as the 3 Engineers left the meeting.

"Looks as if we're in for a bit of excitement then Chief!" Ottley chirped.

"We might only be engineers Dave, but we've got one hell of a responsibility to make sure we can get away in one piece. Once I've finished the meeting, I need you to assist me on deck. All will be revealed later, and I'll happily answer any of your many questions later too." John added, which seemed to stemmed the rapid-fire questions Ottley was posing him.

John made an excursion to his cabin before going down into the engine room, where he found a sea of faces looking anxiously up at him, as he stood on the observation platform.

"Okay men, listen up as I won't have time to repeat myself. In about one hour from now, we'll be approaching the islands where we dropped off our boys. Most of them have gone onto the mainland to rescue the Yanks who have somehow bodged things up a bit. That means we will need to provide a first class get away for when we do pick them all up again. So here is what I intend doing." John announced, then ploughed into his own plan of action, until reaching the end when he asked for any questions or observations from his entire department.

Ho Ping asked a couple of questions as did the engine room 3rd. A couple of stokers spoke up giving John a point that he had not thought of. When he answered, he told them so, thanking them for their astuteness. He even gave them the specific task to do from what they had mentioned, raising a few jeers from their other mates.

"Okay then men, action stations in 1 hour. Suggest you get something to eat and prepare yourselves. Good luck to you all!" John concluded, climbing the ladder and out of the engine room, followed closely by Ottley.

"Right then Dave! Show me your preparations for'ard, and the racks aft." John ordered.

"Step right this way! I've had a word with the 3rd Mate regarding the construction aft as it will be him who will be using it." Ottley said, showing off his Heath Robinson affair with pride.

John gave the rack a thorough inspection, before he was satisfied.

"Don't forget to give me a copy of your drawings Dave! Those oil drums will roll off it sweet as a nut. Now lets see how you got on with the problem for'ard." John directed as they made their way for'ard.

John found nothing amiss with Ottley's work and commended him, before giving him another task to undertake.

"Ouch Chief! That was unexpected! Still, as long as I don't get into trouble removing parts of the ship when it's needed." Ottley quipped.

"You won't need it Dave, as I'm in charge of the Damage Control team. Just you make certain your team is on the job even as it happens. Now, get those portable pumps rigged up for fire fighting, but have 2 ready for the flooding operations. Incidentally, whilst we're picking up the lot from the island, have your men help the sailors with the winches. They need to do things quietly and speedily, which doesn't seem to be in their capability to do so, hence your extra duties on deck young man." John commented.

"If you say so! Let's hope we can get in and back out again before the slope heads catches on."

"Don't worry about that, if what the Captain has up his sleeve is anything to go by, we engineers are here to make sure the ship doesn't sink, that's all. Anyway, it's time we both got ready now. Keep in contact at all times Dave, and good luck." John concluded, leaving Ottley to make made his way onto the bridge.

"Chief! We're approaching the island now, thankfully under an overcast sky. The wind is blowing shoreward so I don't want any smoke coming from the funnel just yet. But when I do, suggest you set off a few smoke canisters to combine it with what you're already making. The older the sip we can make her appear the better their surprise will be when they finally find out what we're not." Farquhar advised with a grin.

"All under control Captain! My damage control team are getting set up, but I've got some stokers to operate the winches so as to keep things quiet." John replied, and got a nod from Farquhar.

"First Mate! Better get down onto the fore deck to take charge. I want no noise, nor even a light showing. I will not be dropping anchor, so be aware of the ships movement when you haul the shore party in." Farquhar ordered quietly.

The ship moved slowly and quietly to a stop almost within reach of the island, with Farquhar issuing orders to his deck officers, and helmsman.

John stood at the back of the bridge with Morgan and Woods, waiting for his orders to commence his own part of the action.

He looked out over the short distance of water between the ship and the shore with a borrowed pair of binoculars to see several small craft approaching it.

"Here they come, port side to! I count 5 craft." John said quietly.

Farquhar looked at the radar screen then out to where John had stated, before he went to one of the bridge windows and waved to Sinclair on the for'ard cargo deck.

The derrick booms swung out to raise the little craft out of the water one by one, whilst the occupants climbed swiftly up the scramble nets to arrive on board.

Within minutes, both craft and equipment had been stowed in the hold, for Sinclair to give his signal all was picked up and stowed out of sight.

One of the British officers arrived onto the bridge to give his report.

"The American team achieved their objective and have 3 parcels to bring back. Unfortunately they were sold out by one of the guides and have been mauled a bit, they are now holed up here." the officer stated, as he pointed to a place on the chart.

"About 2 hours ago Major Hillman took most of our troop upstream to rescue them. Instead of staying behind to look after the back door and prepare a rearguard action, he intends to create a diversion so the Americans can get away. The electronic surveillance team were able to pick up the hostile ships in the area, which we reported on earlier. Just before leaving, it appears 2 coastal frigates have just passed the area, one going east the other west. They meet up about 5 miles down the coast every 8 hours or so, but are due back in the vicinity around 0600.

According to our ships recognition booklet, they look like the *Tsingwah* class frigates, with 2 single gun mountings, one forward and one aft. Looks like 3.5 inchers to me. Plenty of 20 mm cannons though. They've got a big brother, snooping around here who looks like one of the old *Xiang* class medium cruisers, also mentioned in our booklet. There're 4 ancient inshore patrol boats that come out in pairs as far as the tidal mark of the river mouth before returning back up river again. They've only got a 20mm cannon for'ard, but can do a good 20 knots.

That's the local opposition mentioned, so better take charge of the booklet for your tactical information in case you need it. But in the meantime, whilst we were waiting for you to return we disguised ourselves as fishermen to do a marine survey for you from here to here.

There is a sand bar across the river, which is exposed during low tide, but covered by a good 4 to 6 fathoms of water at high tide. The river is tidal for about 8 miles upstream, but when the tide turns the outflow is around 6knots. There's also a rip tide going across the river mouth, which has made a 5-fathom channel shore side of the sand bar. Between these 2 islands there's narrow dog-leg passage about 3000yards long and around 50 yards wide between each side of the bend, with about 5 fathoms of water all the way through. It's like a funnel for the tidal surges that sweeps the beaches seaward side of the islands. In other words Captain, due to the sand bar you can't enter the river mouth unless you use the channels I've just marked. All around here it's less than 2 fathoms, even at high tide, which in itself is only about another fathom. The main central part of the river is pretty deep at around 6 fathoms up to the 8mile point where it branches off. The point where the Americans are is here, only 3 land miles away but all mangrove swamp and marshland something akin to the Norfolk Broads, therefore only suitable for our chariots and smaller river craft." he informed them quickly, pointing to various places on the chart.

The two Americans looked at the tracings the officer made on the chart and started to get agitated.

"Goddamn it man! Get this bucket up river and pick our men up before our parcels get destroyed along with the men."

"Easy does it gentlemen. We'll slip through that channel, then around the sandbar first before I drop anchor. It should take us about half an hour or so. Don't forget, we're a civilian ship on innocent business, so all we've got to do is sit there and catch our men as they come bowling out of the river like a bat out of hell." Farquhar said quietly.

"Thank you for your report Captain, it has given me an extra dimension to my plan. Have you got communication with your Major or what?"

"Yes Captain! Last update I have is Hillman was about to engage the large troop formation who manage to surround Haliday and his men. Their unit was only 1 platoon strength but they've got a body count of 6 so far, and intend bringing them all back."

The two Americans cursed and grumbled over Haliday's plight, demanding a place for the body bags to be stowed for taking back home again.

"Never mind the bodies gentlemen, let's talk about the living. Colonel, kindly arrange for armed men to take up firing positions but in places where the casual eye would not detect them. If we're still here by daylight for these frigates to start poking around, then we'll need all the help we can get."

"What do you mean, anchor off the river mouth Farquhar?" Woods demanded angrily.

"It's quite simple. I shall be dropping my surprise packages whilst I approach the left edge of the sand bar. Then as we swing on our anchor waiting for the high tide I shall drop some more on the right hand edge. I will make it look as if we've been run aground on the sandbank again trying to get ourselves free. All we'll do is wait for the incoming tide then slip over the bank to the deeper water of the river. Once we've picked the men up we'll go through this gap in the island again and drop the last of my surprise packages for them to unwrap, just wait and see." Farquhar growled, as he had his ship steer gently through the narrow dog-leg of a gap in the islands.

"Give me an echo sounder report for 10 minutes! Commodore Morgan! Mark off the depths on the course line I've pencilled in on the chart if you please." Farquhar demanded.

Morgan grunted, taken aback by the sudden demand especially from a junior officer. Never the less, he grabbed a pencil and did what was ordered.

"Depth as shown given a 5knot speed and at 1 cable length between each mark! 5 fathoms! 5 fathoms! 5 fathoms! 6fathoms! 6 fathoms! 5 fathoms! 4 fathoms! 4 fathoms! 7 fathoms! 7 fathoms, 7 fathoms," came Morgan's monologue.

"Ah! We've found the deep channel area. Keep it coming!" Farquhar exclaimed.

"Now let's see what water we've got up to the sand bank." Farquhar said with relief, as the ship cleared the narrow dogleg of a channel.

"5fathoms, 4, 4, 3, 3, 3 fathoms, 2 fathoms, 2 fathoms, 3 fathoms, 3 fathoms!"

"I'm taking her all the way round the bank until we get back to this course. Mark the chart well!" Farquhar declared, as the ship made a slow circle around the bank.

He had some of the oil barrels dropped off as he went around the left-hand side, then anchored off the bank when he got back round from the other side again.

"Now we wait. Any radio contact Commodore?" Farquhar asked Morgan who was listening intently to the radio he had set up at the back of the bridge.

"Not a tweet from them! I can't understand it! Their equipment is the latest in fast comms." He moaned.

"Just as well its overcast, and we're in darkened ship state. We can sit here for another 4 hours or so, until the hostile ships arrive that is." Farquhar grunted, as he kept a vigil on the surrounding area with his binoculars.

"2nd mate! Arrange an all round lookout watch to complement the anchor watch. Specifically a double lookout on top of the bridge, the bows, stern and each side midships. Then stand down 1 man in 3 until further orders. Chief! Your men can do the same." Farquhar ordered quietly.

John left the bridge and went down to the engine room.

"How are we doing 2nd? Okay men?" John asked quietly, getting a muffled cheer from his men.

John explained the situation to the men, telling them what to expect soon.

"In the meantime 2nd, we'll stand down half the engineers and the rest of the men. Watch on watch off until required again. I will take your watch, as I need you rested up. Port crew stand fast, Starboard crew will take 2 hours off. We're still at darkened ship state, so no smoking on deck nor naked lights nor any loud noises. The galley will be issuing food shortly so get fed and rested." John ordered, but reminded the men to keep quiet as they went about it.

John went on deck to see Ottley.

"Dave! Stand the men down until further notice. But remind them no smoking or loud noises. The galley is now open for visitors so get them and yourself fed and rested up. I'll be in the engine room for the next 2 hours if you need me." John ordered quietly.

"Cheers Chief! See you in about 4 hours then. By the way, our passengers are happy with their hotel suite. Let's hope the ruddy Yanks are just as appreciative." Ottley chirped.

"See you then Dave! Make mine a buttered roll while you're at it." John smiled, as he ushered his 3rd engineer away, returning to the hot and clammy engine room.

John climbed into his bunk feeling totally knackered yet knowing that Ho Ping was more than capable of handling anything during his absence, managed to switch off his overhead bunk light before falling fast asleep.

CHAPTER XXIV

Surprise Packages

The insistent rough handling by Thompson, telling him to get up rudely disturbed John.

"What? What's the mean pressure 2nd!" John mumbled disjointedly, focussing his eyes and brain on the person who was dragging him out of bed for nothing.

"Chief! You're required on the bridge. The Yanks are on their way, quick, you need to get up!" Thompson insisted.

John managed to get his faculties back in quick time and asked for a cuppa before he left the cabin.

The steward chuckled at John's request, handing him his cuppa as ordered.

"That was quick Tommo! Is this mine or are you giving me yours?" he asked politely.

"It's yours Chief! I've been a steward long enough to understand the subtle demands of my officers. Yours is the simple kind, so sup up and get up!" Thompson said firmly.

"On my way! What's the time anyway?"

"0430! The rest of the ships crew are already up and stood to."

"Oh well! The sooner I get up and out of here, the sooner I'm back again." John said with a yawn draining his cup, before slipping on his shoes and grabbing his hat.

"Once more into the breach Tommo! Let's show these bloody stupid Yanks how we Brits handle things." he sighed, then left the cosy confines of his cabin to face the big bad world again.

"Morning Chief! We've got a full pack of foxes chasing our little chicks, look!" Farquhar announced, handing John his powerful binoculars.

John took his time focussing them to see the progress of the Americans before he had a quick scan over the surrounding riverbanks

"I suggest we start making as much smoke as possible now, Captain. The wind appears to be heading shoreward, which means that we can give them a curtain to hide behind." John observed, but instead of responding, Farquhar issued several orders in quick succession.

"Commodore Morgan, get 2 oil barrels ready with a 10 minute timing then give them to the First Mate, as quick as you can. First Mate, get 2 lifeboats into the water as of 5 minutes ago, then put the Colonel's charges into them. Lash the steering wheels to their midships position and let them drift upstream with the incoming tide. Chief, flash up your smoke lockers, then tell the engine room to give me revs for slow astern. Colonel Woods! Get on deck and organise the recovery teams. 2nd mate, I shall be swinging around on the anchor chain, so get for'ard and prepare to slip it. You marine officers know what to do, so let's get to it." Farquhar snapped, sweeping the scene once more with his binoculars.

"Captain! Major Hillman has just signalled he's pulling out and will appear to our port side, giving his grid reference." Penn announced, as he entered the bridge.

"Very good Sparks! I need you to keep a close eye on the bridge radar screen, and report any rapid movement from seaward side of the islands."

"Several craft coming into sight starboard side." a lookout announced.

"They're being chased by 3 patrol boats, but looks like the Yanks are keeping them at bay." came another lookout report.

"Slip anchor! Bosun! Allow the ship to stream itself in the crosscurrent and maintain it's natural course. Slow ahead! Given the incoming tide is strong, we should be able to keep us stationary more or less on the spot." Farquhar ordered, positioning the ship across the river mouth.

"Sparks, tell the Yanks to come around us to be picked up starboard side, but steer clear of oncoming lifeboats. Messenger, tell Colonel Woods to stand by to receive our friend's starboard side, then tell the marines to open fire when the patrol boats come within range. Get those lifeboats away whilst under the smoke screen. The incoming tide will take them among the hostiles. Tell the Yanks to prepare their craft for scuttling, as we won't have time to recover them.

Tell Hillman to prepare to be picked up as we pass his position, in about 20 minutes." Farquhar commanded swiftly.

The sound of shots and shellfire was getting louder, with some incoming bullets rattling against the ships side. Occasionally one would ricochet with a pinging noise off the ship, but not enough for the crew to start ducking their heads. This went on for a few minutes until a large column of water appeared several yards on the port side.

"Where the bloody hell did that come from?" Farquhar asked with annoyance, looking to starboard.

"Fast moving contact bearing green 170 range 9,000yards." the radar operator announced.

"Bloody hell man, why didn't you tell me when the range was further out?" he snarled, as another shell whizzed over the ship to splash harmlessly away from the oncoming escapees.

Farquhar noted the fall of shots realising it was one of the frigates coming to make mischief on the escaping Yanks.

"Lookout, keep an eye on that frigate. Let me know when he approaches the end point of the sand bar. Somebody keep an eye out for the other bastard coming in from the other direction. Chief! Get ready to flood as soon as we pass over the sand bar. Sparks, tell Major Hillman there's a sudden change of plan! He is to make his way to the island side of the sandbar where I'll pick him up on my port side. He will have about 10 minutes to get there." Farquhar snapped, keeping his eye on the Americans who were almost alongside the ship.

A large boom was heard from within the smoke, followed by another, silencing the guns of the hostiles, which creating a rousing cheer from the boarding Americans.

Morgan waved his hand as his signal all the men were on board, prompting Farquhar to get his ship moving again.

"Starboard 20, half ahead! Stand by to pick up port side!" he ordered calmly, as two more twin columns of water appeared where the ship would have been.

"See Colonel Woods! Only now they have realised we're the real target." Farquhar said with relish.

As the ship slowed right down to pick up the others, there were two large muffled explosions followed by a large bang and a show of pyrotechnics being exploding.

"There you are Commodore! It appears some of my little surprise packages have just been opened. Those oil-drums were in fact Farquhar mark 4 mines named after the man who made them."

"Farquhar, meaning you of course Captain?" Morgan asked as he saw the hapless frigate forced upwards out of the water, before its magazine exploded, blowing the ship to smithereens.

"Something like that! One down and one to go! Now let's get out of here." Farquhar responded as the blast rolled over the *TsunWan* like thunder.

"2 slow moving ship contacts ahead bearing green 10 range 8,000 yards with a faster one astern of them bearing green 15 range 12,000 yards." the radar operator informed.

Farquhar looked through the swirling smoke to discover there were 2 small merchant ships approaching the deep-water channel. "Chief! Keep the smoke coming, as I need to somehow disappear through the channel between the islands. It might just obscure us visually, but won't fool their radar if they've got one." Farquhar purred.

"Commodore! Stand by to take some bearings down. Once we've got onto our reverse exit course, you can get down and see to your men, but have my First Mate come to the bridge." Farquhar added.

Before Farquhar could relay his set of bearings, they heard two explosions coming from the 2 small merchant ships.

"Oops! Sorry gentlemen! The rip tide must have carried a couple of my packages along the channel for you to meet them.

Let's hope the warship catches one as well." Farquhar muttered.
The signalman reported the two ships had blown up and sunk, creating a panic with the other oncoming frigate.

"Keep a close eye on him signalman. He might still be undecided as to who we are, given we're appearing to clear the area. They'll be thinking about submarines, not an unarmed merchantman." Farquhar said hopefully.

Morgan was now used to obeying orders from a very competent naval Captain to acknowledge his orders, promptly entering all the bearings that were given him. He advised on the changes of course to bring the ship onto its required transit, which Farquhar followed. Before long the ship was squeezing herself down the narrow channel again to make her escape..

"They've seen us and are turning to follow us!" the signalman reported.

"Slow ahead! Cox'n, keep us midstream all the way down. Stand by to drop a couple of packages when we've turned into the dogleg. They might be able to see us this side but not when we turn the corner."

Farquhar had the ship move slowly and safely through the narrow passage whilst the pursuing frigate raced to catch up.

The ship came serenely out of the channel between the islands to turn and make her way out to sea, whilst Farquhar kept a close watch of the pursuers.

An orange flash followed shortly by a large bang told Sinclair the second frigate had gone the same way as its friend.

"Scratch 2 frigates Commodore!" Farquhar shouted jubilantly.

"2 river patrol boats and 2 frigates are a good tally Captain, but look what's waiting for us on our starboard bow. Let's see you scratch that one." Morgan's stated petulantly.

"Large fast moving contact bearing Green 120, range 15,000 yards. Classify as a cruiser!" the radar operator reported with excitement.

Farquhar swivelled round to look at the bearing and saw it was the big brother to the 2 frigates.

"We'll keep it slow to try and bluff our way past them. Chief! Start flooding up and get your boilers up to full steam, but for now I only want revs for about 10 knots. Commodore! Take these bearings, then work out both theirs and our own position in relation to the territorial water zone!" Farquhar ordered, as he took some bearings which would work out just where the cruiser was in relation to themselves. Once he had done so he trained his binoculars onto the rapidly closing hostile, mumbling angles and distances.

"He's on the limit for his territorial waters, but we've still got about another 10,000 yards to get clear." Morgan reported.

"Thank you! We'll either get away with it or they'll start throwing lumps of metal at us. Our little spot of bother at the river mouth will seem like a Sunday afternoon picnic compared with the spot of bother we're about to receive." Farquhar said ominously.

"There you Brits go again, with your goddamn 'spots of bother'. If it were me, I'd scream rape and murder and have the big boys come to rescue us." Woods said with bitterness.

"We don't do that sort of thing in the British Navy. We try to sort our own mess out first, as you've already witnessed in the river mouth." Farquhar replied sharply.

"Hostile contact appears to be increasing their speed and running a parallel course to us. Suggest he is tracking us," the radar operator reported.

"Chief! Are we flooded up yet?" Farquhar asked hurriedly.

"Yes Captain, we'll be reaching full steam in about 10 minutes. You are advised it will take us a good 30minutes to build up the speed given we'll be fighting against the currents or sea swell." John reported quietly.

"Thank you Chief! Port 15! Steer 195." Farquhar started to say when they heard a low moan and a whistling sound before 4 large columns of water splashed across their bows.

"That means they've identified we're the culprit who blew their brothers into smithereens and the game is up." Farquhar stated calmly, as he had the ship turn directly towards the danger.

Within moments, several more splashes appeared very close to the ship which almost washed the ship from stem to stern.

"That is the polite way of telling us not to go any further, and to heave to." Farquhar said, as the ship reverberated to the exploding shells.

"Cox'n, er Bosun whatever!! I intend zig-zagging either side of the present base course. Use 15 degrees of port rudder then come back onto base course for 30 seconds, before using 15 degrees to starboard and back again. Do this for 5 minutes. Messenger, here's a stop watch! Tell the bosun on each 30 second marks. Chief! Are we on full steam now?"

"Almost ready Captain."

"That will do me! Give me all you've got Chief! Once we're out into international waters and beyond the range of their guns, we can go home."

"Hah! Do you seriously expect this rust bucket can outrun a cruiser let alone get from under her guns?" Woods scoffed.

"Colonel! You will be best served by bringing your 3 guests up onto the bridge to witness this one-sided combat, just in case we British get accused of not being able to deliver them in one piece. Leave the bridge if you please!" Farquhar ordered.

"Pah! Bloody Limey sailors! Once the cruiser catches up and board us, then the entire operation has been wasted, let alone the lives of several of our men." Woods said vehemently, leaving the bridge muttering obscenities to himself..

"We're not at full power Captain. Maybe a slight change of course to go across the current would help." John reported, to complete the bridge telephone link to the engine room.

Several more columns of water appeared even closer and all around the ship, making the ship rear and buck under the underwater explosions.

Woods arrived onto the bridge with the 3 'packages', who were briefly introduced to Farquhar.

Morgan told them of the dilemma they were in, which added yet more anxiety and distress between them. They told Farquhar they had to escape rather than be re-captured again, and it would be his fault if they were to fall into the hostile forces hands again. They started to issue orders to Farquhar demanding he do all sorts of things to escape.

"Gentlemen! You might be big nobs in your country, but as I'm the Captain in command of this vessel you will abide by my actions without interference. I asked Colonel Woods to bring you up to join your Operational commander Commodore Morgan here, merely to see what we're up against, before you both start making peace with your maker. Now please stand at the back of the bridge and just watch how we Brits do our work. If you don't like what you see, then clear the bridge right now. But remember, if it wasn't for Major Hillman and his men, let alone my actions at the river mouth, you three would be screaming in agony enduring yet another mundane day of torture." Farquhar snapped, as another salvo slammed all around them.

"Bloody hell, they really meant that. For God sake Captain do something!" one of them pleaded.

Farquhar chuckled as he looked at the cowering men, then turned his attention to the danger facing them.

"That was our final warning gentlemen. What is their range now?" Farquhar commanded.

"Range 9,500 yards! It looks as if they're trying to head us off."

"Now he tells me!" Farquhar said sarcastically, as another salvo screamed towards them, dropping into the very space the ship would have been only moments ago.

"Okay, we've got them plotting our main course and anticipating our zigzags. Starboard 15! Steer 200 for 1minute then reverse the helm to steer 170. We're closing at a rate of one cable in less than a minute, which will play havoc with their gunnery ranges. With luck we can duck under their big guns yet still be out of reach of their secondary armament." Farquhar ordered swiftly, while another salvo crashed into an empty space of water.

"Commodore Morgan, don't just stand there gawping! Get to the chart and give me an expected time of arrival at the 25 fathom line then a further 10,000 yards as a safety margin against their main armament. Given that we're increasing speed slowly up to 20 knots. Once I've found the gap in their gunnery ranges, we can sneak down that slot and get out to sea. Their main armament has the depressed angle range of about 9000 yards up to the maximum of about 14,000 yards, and their secondary of about 6,000. Monitor the ranges from the radar screen to work out the gap for me. If you can't do such a basic task of ranging then I suggest you wear your rank as an impostor." Farquhar snapped, which drew gasps from the 3 passengers.

Morgan knew yet again not to argue, but obeyed without hesitation, starting to make the calculations for Farquhar.

After a few minutes had elapsed and several more salvoes which were meant to blow the ship up, but thankfully missed them each time, Morgan told Farquhar they had about 10 minutes to go to reach the line. Farquhar acknowledged the information calmly as he had his eyes glued to his binoculars, issuing helm orders as each salvo literally engulfed the ship in water.

"Four fast moving ship contacts approaching in line formation bearing green 30, range 30,000 yards." the radar operator reported in a loud voice.

"Very good! Commodore you heard the report so get the hostile cruiser plotted. Make a comparison with the new contact and tell me the reciprocal bearing between them." Farquhar ordered sharply.

The next salvo must have had a stray shell, which struck the bow of the ship, destroying the upper deck of the foc'sle, shattering the for'ard derrick. The blow made the ship shudder for a moment, before it raced into the oncoming sea-swell.

John assessed the damage done then went down to take charge of the damage control team, where he met Ottley with the 3rd mate.

"Okay Dave! This is where I came in as a 4th, so to speak. Come with me and give me the benefit of your wisdom, to see if I agree with it. 3rd Mate! No offence but I would suggest you come with us to make your observations at the same time, just so you are able to make a report which covers your angle of the inspection."

"Thank you Chief, that is why I'm here in the first place." the 3rd Mate said curtly.

"In that case, step this way Chief! Mind your nut going through these small watertight hatches, as it hurts like mad if you forget to duck." Ottley advised cheerfully, and led the way.

"Quack!" John responded amiably, giving Ottley a playful tap on his shoulder.

He made a close inspection and an assessment of the damage but allowed Ottley to make the initial assessment.

"You've got the idea Dave, but here's what you need to do. Get into the anchor cable locker and shore up the bow, with 6x4 sheets of metal. Make sure they are welded correctly, then get some of the prefab sections from the cargo bay and have them tacked down over the existing upper deck. Get a compressor to provide a small pressure in the for'ard section, then shut down all watertight hatches right back to the soldiers citadel. Report back to me when done so Dave!" John commanded as yet another column of water cascaded over them.

"We've had a few popped rivets amidships Chief, but I've bunged them solid. The only snag now is we're out of wooden bungs. " Ottley reported, as he acknowledged his orders.

"Leave that to me Dave! Use half of your team to see to the bows then use the other half to go onto the decks. I need to keep that half of the team as a standby team for other such emergencies. Report to me as soon as you've completed the repairs, and good luck." John shouted over the noise of the explosions and splashing water.

John went back onto the bridge, reporting that whilst there was a hole in the prow of the ship and a hole in the foc'sle big enough to drive a double Decker bus through, the work was all in hand. "Due to the bow being raised out of the water caused by the trim down aft, we can still maintain full power, Captain."

"Thank you Chief! Just a lucky strike that's all. It must have come from their secondary armament otherwise had it have come from their main armament, we'd be sunk long before now." Farquhar said with a grin.

"Crossing the 25 fathom line now Captain!" Morgan informed loudly.

"Thank you! What news of the reported ship formation?" Farquhar asked calmly.

"They've changed course heading directly towards us in line abreast." the radar operator stated flatly, reporting yet another fast moving contact which had just appeared on their port quarter.

"Hmm! Keep an eye on that one for the moment to let me know their transit course and speed." Farquhar ordered quietly, scanning the horizon then back to the cruiser.

John looked out to seaward to see the hostile cruiser was getting steadily closer to them, when he noticed large flashes of light come from over the horizon, which startled him to make him report it.

Farquhar and others on the bridge trained their binoculars towards what John had reported, but nobody needed them, as they saw with their own eyes the hostile cruiser had been bracketed all around by several large columns of water.

"That gentlemen was the broadside calling card of Her Majesty's Ship *Antares*, and she's on time. It seems Hughes's gunnery is still just as good, even though he is a bit of a dodo!" Farquhar exclaimed.

The American officers with their 3 passengers looked out to see the cruiser was being drenched with the fallout of the salvoes, which were coming from some ship over the horizon, and started to cheer as each salvo arrived.

The hostile cruiser seemed to have slowed right down, starting to turn towards the unseen attacker when several shells splashed all around it once more.

"Steady on Hughes! Be careful you idiot! Careful of your broadsides! You're only supposed to frighten them off not ruddy well sink them!" Farquhar shouted, as another salvo actually smashed into the cruiser. That salvo destroyed most of the cruiser's guns, pulverising its superstructure into the bargain, all within a heartbeat.

The flashes where the shells hit were shortly followed by loud rumbling of explosions, just like thunder does after a flash of lightning, as it rolled over the *Tsun Wan*, making her tremble from stem to stern.

The cruiser appeared to stop dead in the water, with smoke pouring from all the shell holes made. The loud roaring, whistling sound announcing the arrival of another incoming salvo must have delivered the killer blow, as the ship simply disintegrated, disappearing in one big bang which scattered bits of debris over a large area around it.

The blast was so fierce that the resulting shock wave caused by the explosion forced the *Tsun Wan* to keel right over at a dangerous angle before it finally righted itself again.

Farquhar smiled broadly as he looked at the astonishment on the Americans faces.

"Oops! Sorry about this, and all that! Hard cheese, never mind! Oh well that's one spot of bother we're out of now, but it looks as if you Americans have the little task of talking your way out of its aftermath. Mind you though! This is a tactical lesson you lot should have learned from the Battle of the Little Big Horn:

One small unit drawing the whole enemy force into a trap by their main forces who were hiding who were waiting to pounce on them. Surrounded not by Indians this time, but by the shells of ten 14 inch calibre guns. Just like Custer, no contest!" Farquhar said philosophically, as the Americans stood looking at the space where their antagonist should have been.

"God damn it Farquhar! You bloody Limeys and your spots of bother always seem to grossly understate the truth of the situation! What in blue blazes are you trying to do, start Goddam

WW3? How the bloody hell are we going to explain the sinking of not one but three of their warships, let alone the sinking of two innocent merchant ships!" Morgan cursed loudly, while the 3 passengers started complaining bitterly and vociferously.

"Just remember, it was your bloody necks that were on the line not ours, so stop belly-aching and think yourselves lucky we Brits are around to get you out of yet another fine mess only you lot got yourselves into. To us it's just another day at the office that's all." Farquhar said evenly quite unconcerned, training his glasses towards the distant shapes of 4 British cruisers appearing over the horizon.

"Here she comes! Her consorts with her still have not come into range, but are not required until another hostile comes onto the scene. So scratch one cruiser and add it to your tally whilst you're at it. Once the news gets out about this, there'll be one almighty international argy bargy about it." Farquhar informed with satisfaction and a large grin on his face.

"How do you know that Farquhar? We've got a cruiser squadron based in Subic Bay, who have been reported to be on manoeuvres in these waters." Morgan asked in disbelief.

"In which case your navy boys will get the fault for all this. However, you seem to forget that first and foremost I'm a Royal Naval Gunnery Officer, with several years' war service, including ordnance and bomb disposal, so I know exactly what type and calibre shells destroyed that cruiser. They could only have come from the *Antaries* as she is the only 14inch heavy battle cruiser in this part of the world. Your battle cruisers only have 12inchers, and give off a different sound when their shells are in trajectory, let alone explosion sounds and other tell tale signs. Besides, this was part of my insurance policy I told you about and arranged even before we left Singapore. As stated, it's your men we've rescued, so it will take a team of your fast talking Diplomats, and a team of Philadelphia lawyers to get you out of this one." Farquhar countered.

The 3 passengers looked through borrowed binoculars,

witnessing the emergence from the horizon of an even larger cruiser escorted by 3 slightly smaller ones.

"What are these ships Captain?" one of them asked.

"The middle one you see is the *Antaries*, and each side of her are the 10 inch cruisers *Valour* and *Diomedes*. The one at the back is the 6 inch cruiser *Herald*. She's their shepherd who acts as their rearguard as she is the lightest of them and the fastest cruiser this side of the Pacific. What you see is the British 23rd Cruiser squadron whom nobody dares to tackle, not even your heavy mob in Honolulu. Incidentally the other hostile ship poking its nose in further down range, will soon be getting the same treatment from the *Herald*, so we can relax now." Farquhar said proudly.

"Well whoever they are they certainly took their time getting here." one of them said grudgingly.

"Nevertheless, maybe now you lot will understand how we British are used to winning our naval battles. It will now be up to your lot to sort out the diplomatic battles ahead of you."

"Point taken Farquhar! Now lets get out of here and back to civilisation again." Morgan grunted, as Woods and the 3 passengers filed off the bridge.

The ship swung onto its course to take it back to Singapore but were met and greeted briefly by their rescuers, who wished them a safe voyage back.

"Messenger, tell the ship's company to stand down and assume cruise watches. Chief, tell your men they did well today. Give me revs for 15knots as I intend arriving Singapore in about 2 days. Give me a full damage report as soon as you can. Stores requirements, dockyard assistance and all that you know of." Farquhar said with a smile, as the 2nd Mate came to take over the conn.

CHAPTER XXV

Nelson's Blood

During the next couple of days the ship sailed through untroubled seas. Hillman along with members of the ships crew were tending to his troops, and saw to Gleave and his men.

John came down to see the big US sergeant who had been badly wounded, laid up with several others of his men, yet the British casualties were smaller in numbers yet suffering relatively lighter wounds.

"Looks as if you've had a argument with a whole regiment, Sergeant Gleave. Maybe it won't hurt so much if you spend half an hour every now and then in the freezer we made for your body bags." John chirped, offering the man a cigarette.

"Now, he's only sending me to the mortuary along with the other poor stiffs! What's with you guys?" Gleave grumbled but started to enjoy the cigarette.

"You Limeys sure know how to mix it with those slope heads. Wish I had a few of your boys in my team. Your smokes aren't too bad either." he added after a few deep drags from his cigarette.

"Just you boys relax. We're British! Which means each one of your walking wounded gets a tot of Nelson's blood." John said condescendingly.

Gleave frowned for a moment then trying to rise from his stretcher, started to curse John.

"Don't tell me you're giving us blood to drink as well?" he shouted, until John passed the open rum bottle under his nose.

"Well in that case, make sure I get some of that!" he said quickly, relaxing back down onto his stretcher.

"Here you are soldier!" John said quietly but with a big grin gave the man a large glass of rum.

Gleave grabbed it and swigged it down in one.

"Goddamn it Chief! What the hell was that?" he gasped hoarsely, struggling to get air down into his lungs.

"It's what our sailors get weaned on from an early age. They get one of those each day, including Sundays whether they like it or not. Navy grog, or as a good friend of mine would insist, Pussers Rum." John said with a chuckle, seeing Gleave relax in himself.

"Maybe your men would like some too, only it's strictly one tot per man per day." John teased.

"Yeah well! Give me another one on account I'm the Master sergeant around here. And I'll have Scritzenheimers too on account he's teetotal and a bloody bible thumper." came the demand, but with a little smile which played on the man's lips.

"Certainly Master Sergeant! Maybe you'll be up and about soon to give us poor engineers more grief again before you disembark." John purred.

"Aw shucks Chief! T'was nothing intended if you know what I mean. You did a good job on our accommodation and I dare say our comrades in the body bags will last until they get home again." he said meekly.

"You're a professional soldier, just as I'm a professional marine engineer, but we've still got our tradition to maintain. You kicking arse wherever you go whilst I tend noisy machinery to make certain you get there to kick arse in the first place. Get well soldier, good luck to you and your men." John said softly, handed over another full glass of rum, then shook Gleave's hand who offered a silent thanks by the gasping man.

John left with sounds of gasps, coughing, and few curses thrown in as the sergeant felt the effects of the alcohol.

Later on when John was relaxing in the saloon with Sinclair, the 3 passengers walked in, flanked by Morgan and Woods. Hillman happened to come in behind them and made his way over to John's table.

"Those are three very senior diplomats from the American Senate, who were taken hostage over a month ago. We, my troop and I that is, were detailed off to assist their snatch squad to rescue the diplomats, but got themselves into deep trouble in the process. Thanks to us we're all here on board, but if you listen to them, they did it all single-handedly with every man jack of them an Audie Murphy or a John Wayne. Because of that we've been shunted sideways, out of the limelight in favour of Haliday and his men. The Yanks are all show yet not a brain amongst them when it comes down to the real nitty gritty stuff. So my troop will live on and perhaps get involved with other nefarious missions just like this one, whereas the Yanks will be welcomed home to get pensioned off as heroes." Hillman moaned, as he went on to explain the political set up and the American involvement.

"Let's hope they don't get into a punch up of their own or they'd bloody well lose. Unless of course we happen to hold their hand, just like we did at Normandy and the Korean job." Sinclair opined.

"Amen to that." Hillman said sourly.

"What will happen now, to you and your men major?" John asked politely.

"Some of my wounded men will be kept in BMH Singapore until they're fit to rejoin the regiment. The rest of us will be returning to H.K. on your next trip up there in about 10 days from now. But I'll say no more on that if you don't mind."

"Our lips are sealed major! Anyway, care for a decent wet or are you happy with a warm San Miguel beer?" Sinclair quipped, as he got up to fetch another round of drinks.

Sinclair had his chance to take the ship up the creek unassisted and docked it neatly alongside the jetty during the early hours of the morning when nobody was about.

The 3 passengers were swiftly ushered ashore by Morgan who left in a hurry in a sleek limousine, whilst Woods, Gleave and his men were bundled into a covered wagon and left also in a hurry. An unmarked lorry arrived to collect the body bags before quietly slipping away into the early hours of the morning.

Farquhar got his officers together then thanked them for their excellent work during that mission, but stressed they were not to speak about it until the official word got announced in the press.

"First Mate! No leave allowed just yet, so start a tropical routine to commence at 0700 today until further notice. Chief! Get in contact with the ship repair unit to see if we can speed up the reinstatement of our bows. I'm off ashore to see the Admiral if anybody wants me." Farquhar announced, leaving the saloon to his officers.

"Here's me hoping we could say hello to the girls." Larter groaned as he was handed a message from the signalman.

"Well, lucky me! I get to go and collect the mail from the post office. Seems that there's no peace for the wicked!" he sighed, reading the message then screwing it up, tossed it neatly into the nearest litterbin.

"I'd come with you Bruce, but I've got our illustrious 2nd Engineer to sort out." John said wearily, leaving the saloon to make his way to the engine room to speak to his officers and men.

"2nd! There's no general leave until this afternoon. Any man living local can shoot ashore but must be back on board by 0700. Get the rest of the men turned in, then have them mustered on the after cargo deck at 0800. If you need to shoot ashore make sure the log has been entered up and the appropriate safety checks observed before you do. Once the shore supply is connected up the electricians can secure too. See you at 0800." John informed.

"All logs and checks observed Chief! I go ashore in 1 hour, to see you at 0730." Ho Ping replied softly, wiping the oil from his face.

"In that case, have a nice shower 2nd, or your family won't recognise the black man turning up on their doorstep." John chuckled, taking a clean rag from his pocket and wiped the 2nd's forehead clean.

Ho Ping smiled at the gentle kindness John showed him, leaving with a wave of his arm.

CHAPTER XXVI

A Deal

It took a week to repair the ship and give it a new coat of paint, during which time John and his friends enjoyed the personal hospitality of the girls they had befriended.

"Let's hope this will last for a while as I don't fancy going to sea just yet." Sinclair said softly as all six of them relaxed at the side of the large open-air swimming pool.

"What? Not to get your navigation exams completed? And here's me thinking you're all for your masters certificate." John joked.

"Plenty of time for that if we're doing the ammo run back and fore to Hong Kong. Besides, I think we should be about due for some UK leave now. Must catch up with Kim to see how we stand." Larter offered, which made the girls look a little perturbed.

"Yea, maybe a month to sort out things before coming back. Just dandy that would be." Sinclair said quickly as he hugged his partner with re-assurance.

John stood up and went for a last cool swim for a while before returning to the group who decided it was time to get the girls back on duty again.

"I for one will be glad to take my girl out of there and make an honest woman of her. " Larter moaned, as they arrived back at the bar which was one of many in such a small village.

"Yes, who would miss 3 girls out of all the bars. What do you say John?" Sinclair asked offhandedly.

"You might just be right there Andy. Everything is just pie in the sky at the moment, until Parfitt and co, tells us otherwise." John replied without committing himself.

"Maybe we'll bump into Kim when we get back on board to tell us." Larter concluded, as the three friends walked through the large wrought iron gates of the base, making their way to the dockyard.

***

"Morning John! According to the notice board there's a special meeting for all officers at 1100. I've had a word with Kim, who tells me that Parfitt and Stafford are coming out of their ivory tower to come up and give us a talk." Larter stated, sitting next to John to take his breakfast.

John who had already eaten his breakfast, stayed to chat with Larter during his.

"We were only talking about this yesterday, so maybe we'll get something more tangible than just rumours Bruce."

"One thing is for sure, the ship can't just wait around doing nothing. She needs to be earning her expensive keep. Maybe they've got another cloak-and-dagger run for us, in which case my office will be overrun with electronic surveillance gear again, let alone the bodies who come to man them. Whatever happens we need some more sea time to boost our bank accounts, especially if we're in line for our UK leave."

"I try not to think of that as it will become a nice little surprise for me when we do get notified. Maybe we'll sail back this time Bruce, in which case Andy will call it the slow boat from China. Even though he's navigating it all the way home."

"Yes, I fancy a trip up the Suez for a change. But even then it would take us a good 5 weeks. By the time we got there it would be time to start rowing back again." Larter said with a grin.

"Perish the thought Bruce! Anyway, must go and sort out the troops. See you later." John chuckled, as he left the dining room.

John arrived into the saloon early with Sinclair, taking a seat whilst waiting for the meeting to start. The other officers started to arrive with Larter and his two radio officers coming in almost last, before Farquhar, Parfitt and Stafford sauntered in with their arms full of paper work.

"Morning gentlemen. Glad to see everybody fit and well after your last, shall we say, detour of a voyage." Stafford said loftily.

Farquhar started the meeting with a few announcements, before Parfitt and Stafford spoke in turn to tell the men what the next few months had in store for them, and the projected itinerary for the ship.

There were a few surprises in store which affected most of the officers, not least John and his 2 friends. Once the explanations were offered to each question posed by the officers, the meeting was drawn to a close.

"Thank you all for attending, if all goes well then each one of you will be rewarded by the end of this period. Chief! I would like a special word with you before I go, if you don't mind." Parfitt concluded, then left with Stafford and Farquhar.

John followed the 3 men to Farquhars cabin where they asked John to come in and shut the door.

"We propose to get your 2nd Engineer up to Chief Engineer standard during these next few return voyages, so when you're away on holidays, will be able to look after the ship for us. Here is the draft proposal and details which we would like you to take on board and try to accommodate us in this matter. You will note that even though you are still an acting Chief engineer, you will be accorded the salary of a full Chief." Stafford stated flatly, handing John some documents.

John scanned them quickly asking various questions until he was satisfied with what was asked of him.

"I have no objections in these proposals gentlemen, but it would mean jeopardising the ongoing and structured tutorials for the other junior officers. Could you not just get another Chief as my replacement?" John asked after a short while.

"We appear to be short on quality English speaking engineers above 3rd engineer. We appreciate the shortfall of those instructions, but we need Ho Ping more. Once he's got command of it all then we'll be able to begin the second phase of our development programme in integrating native officers to the running of our ships out in this part of the world. The thing is, Grey, every ship afloat listed in the Lloyds Register, is required to have at least 6 English speaking officers on board, whether they're British or not. That is to say, Captain plus one deck officer, with the Chief engineer plus one other, plus of course the Radio Officer and maybe the Purser or Doctor. With you leaving even for a few weeks, it puts our company out of compliance with those rules. To put it bluntly, stops us from sailing our ships." Parfitt explained anxiously.

"If I do what you ask, then once Ho Ping passes his exams he automatically becomes the Chief engineer of the ship anyway. Therefore, it would not matter if I have a few extra weeks off back home before you bring me back again. That is the condition gentlemen." John said with confidence.

Stafford gave Parfitt a startled look before they both nodded in agreement.

"Okay then Grey, you've got a deal. You've only got 4 return trips, mind you." Stafford said assertively as he held out his hand to shake on the deal.

"So be it. I will get him up to Chief standard but only as far as his trade is concerned. Unlike another certain 2nd Engineer who professes to know it all, you will need to get the necessary examination papers and the professional body of people to conduct it. Whilst I can help him in the basics of the language and the mathematics needed, you will also need to book him into some college to help him with his maths classes. Without that, he'll never pass in a month of Sundays. Anyway, it's all down to your end of the deal from what I've just read."

"Agreed, Grey. So there you have it Captain, both sides of your command in training, just as we had planned. The *Tsun Wan* is a special cargo ship but it is still a training ship of which you should be proud to be Captain." Parfitt said loftily.

Farquhar agreed that it was a privilege to sail with his present set of officers, but stated even he would be on the move soon, therefore it would be up to his relief to put up with the comings and goings of a ship without a regular crew on board.

"Merchant ships are always like that Captain. You left a few of the crew up in Hong Kong who need to be brought back here again before we can man another ship out of here. Anyway, it's going to be the new practice in a short while. More cargo less crew, that is, unlike a ship stuffed with sailors as your ships are. But that is another moot point I don't intend taking up just now." Stafford said haughtily and started to leave the cabin.

"Keep in touch via Mr Soon, Grey. You too Captain. Must be off now." Parfitt said pompously as they left.

John let out a sigh of relief and sat down on a vacant chair.

"What do you make of them two, Captain?" John asked, offering Farquhar a cigarette, which was declined.

"Oliver and Hardy springs to mind Chief. It seems as if both of us have our work cut out from now on. I for one will need these next few days prior to sailing, to get organised and fully squared away if we're going to play silly games on a ship full of high explosives. My navy boss is not too happy about that score, but needs must if only to keep the political balance between your navy and mine." Farquhar offered.

"Amen to that Captain. Before I go, you will know we're mechanically safe and sound and the ship has now got its seaworthiness certificate back again." John said, standing up, donning his cap to leave.

"Thanks Chief!" Farquhar called as John stepped out of Farquhar's cabin and left.

"Take her out First Mate, but don't forget to untie the ship from the jetty or we'll be towing half the dockyard away with us." Farquhar joked, as Sinclair responded to the order.

"Obey telegraphs! Chief! Tell your men to stop making smoke." Sinclair ordered.

John acknowledged the command then went down to his own world where he stood observing the engineers and stokers perform their tasks.

His eyes darting here there and everywhere whilst he conducted a few tests and monitored a couple of items to see all was well.

He stood on the observation platform with his arms folded, shouting a few orders at some of the stokers to keep them on their toes. Occasionally he referred to the 2nd, who merely grinned or waved in acknowledgement to the orders given.

The hectic hour, as John called it, was over as the ship got herself full and away.

John called the 2nd over and praised him for his professionalism, told him although the men were going into cruise watches, the officers were in fact required to do watch and watch about, as per his own pre-voyage meeting he'd had with them.

"Only for this return voyage 2nd! Then we'll split the officers into 2 teams, like we did on the last one. This will give you a chance to catch up on your maths and the like." John said in Ho Ping's ear, due to the noise of the engine.

The 2nd nodded, pointing to the engine room office led the way.

"I sleep here Chief! Get on with my drawings better." Ho Ping explained as they entered the compartment.

John shook his head slowly.

"We both know you don't need me to show you how to run the engines, boilers or any other machinery down here 2nd. Besides you need a quiet place to relax and think through all the mathematics, calculations, testing and diagnostics. I have got one of my engineering bibles which you'll need for a while, so once you've come off watch, come to see me in my cabin and get it. I have already given you your tutorial plan and instruction times, all you've got to do is fit it around your watches. Your duties have already been underlined 2nd, so don't worry about anything else except learning what I have shown you. I've got another engineer to see now, so see me later." John explained.

"Thank you Chief!" Ho Ping said with a beaming smile.

'Must be a happy little so and so, as he's always given me a big smile even though I shout at him at times. But there will only be one Happy Day as far as I'm concerned!' John mused, as he climbed the ladder and left the noisy engine room.

"Dave! You will do just the one round per day, as I need you down the engine room during instruction times. But if you have something of importance which needs fixing then it comes first. The inference I'm impressing upon you Dave, is I need you to get more time in down the engine room so you are fully conversant with the machinery down there."

"Fair enough! It's a cracking idea setting us into 2 crews. It means we can have more time off. Maybe even more time ashore too, I shouldn't wonder." Ottley replied cheerfully.

"Yes well, be that as it may. This ship may be a training ship, but she's only a rowing boat compared with some of the ships afloat. Which means she doesn't really warrant a full range of engineer officers on board. That goes for the deck officers too mind you. So what I'm trying to do is get you all as much experience as possible in case you're required to run the engine room on your own, so to speak. Having said that, most of the ships nowadays are steam turbine or diesel, so this ship would only serve for the purposes of understanding the principles of steam operated engines."

"I learned from my Uncle's steam operated combined harvester, especially from the railway engines down at the goods yard near by my Granny's house." Ottley volunteered.

"Good a place as any! All you've got to do now is get your maths and theoretical work mastered. I have just the book for that, so if you dovetail your instructions with the 2nd, I can take the both of you at once. My cabin is the instruction room and you have the times. See you later then." John concluded, as Ottley started to move away.

"Oh by the way! I noticed No 2A3 cargo segment for'ard has a ventilation problem. Have to see the skipper about it because there's some dodgy pyrotechnics in there."

"What do you mean by dodgy?" John asked quickly.

"Perhaps the Captain being dynamite with such things he'd know." Ottley said with a grin.

"You carry on with your instructions. I'll see the Captain." John ordered, and walked swiftly to the bridge.

"Captain?" John asked, arriving onto the bridge.

"He's in the bridge cabin Chief!" the duty officer informed him.

"Captain! The outside Engineer reports there's a vent problem in the for'ard cargo hold. If it's what I'm thinking then it will need your personal attention." John informed on entering Farquhar's cabin.

Farquhar was in the middle of explaining some navigational details with Sinclair, but stopped abruptly and demanded to know what exactly was the problem.

John repeated what Ottley had said, which made Farquhar move swiftly out of his cabin, ordering John to come with him, to show him.

"I see! What we need to do now Chief is get the temperature right down in this segment. In fact, we'd better freeze the entire hold. Time is of the essence or we'll blow like a bloody volcano. What about aft?"

"The torpedoes and mines aft are okay seeing as they're disabled."

"Okay then Chief! Get that temperature right down immediately. Let me know when you've fixed it." Farquhar ordered as both men left the confines of the hold.

John rushed to his spare equipment store and assembled the same equipment he used on the American soldiers. Within half an hour he managed to get the device working and a further half an hour later he was able to report the entire hold had its temperature reduced considerably.

"Good Chief! We'll freeze the lot and have it off-loaded as quickly as possible."

"Can't freeze it Captain, just down to single figures on the thermometer."

"Oh well, it's better than nowt! It just means the army boys had better be on their toes when taking it away, that's all. Now let's get back to something more mundane shall we." Farquhar said grimly, dismissing John with a nod of his head.

"Ships shore services connected up Chief! Men stood down and I'm off ashore now." the 2nd informed John.

"Thank you 2nd! Be back in the morning by 0800, as you've got a full day's instruction to go through." John replied, watching the 2nd hurry down the gangway and ashore.

"Hello John! We're at Holts wharf Kowloon side again. I know of an army transit camp nearby that has a decent bar there. Maybe we can get ashore soon and check it out." Sinclair said with a smile, pointing to the area he mentioned.

"We've still got the small matter of off-loading the dodgy ammo, Andy."

"Indeed John, the very reason why we're docked at this special wharf the army keeps for themselves. Never mind, the NAAFI's Tiger bar opens at 1100 anyway, so we'll be offloaded long before then."

"Gives me time to change and take a shower. Breakfast first though, as I'm ruddy starving."

"I've already had mine and I'm going right off scrambled egg now. Let's hope Kim gives us a better menu for the return trip."

"Why do you think I always have fresh buttered rolls with slices of bacon. Nothing to spoil yet all to enjoy" John chuckled, then left for the dining room.

The return trip was nearly as dull except for the tropical storm they had to endure before managing to hide behind one of the group of islands for shelter.

It was a welcome couple of days off for the engine room crew who managed to use the time in extra instructions, before the ship finally arrived back into Singapore.

"Finished with engines. Secure from docking, get the gangway over!" Sinclair ordered, as Farquhar sat in his high chair.

"Chief! You can shut down now for a couple of days."

Farquhar informed John who was standing at the back of the bridge.

"What about shore leave Captain?" John asked politely.

"Ah yes! Announce tropical routine as normal, First Mate." Farquhar said almost as an afterthought.

"Right then gentlemen, I'm off ashore. Next pre-voyage meeting is in 2 days at around 1000. Make a note on the board if you please, First Mate." Farquhar ordered, leaving the bridge to make his way ashore.

"Lucky for some. Just being able to swan off like that. I've still got the rest of my duties to perform." Sinclair moaned as he signed the bridge logbook.

"Same here Andy. My 2nd has just gone ashore and home, whereas I've got a full day's paper work to do. Maybe if you get time Andy, phone the girls to have them come aboard around 1900?"

"What a good idea John! See you later then." Sinclair said as they parted company.

CHAPTER XXVII

Decisions

John stood in the engine room briefing his entire department before they got ready to get the ship moving again.

"We officers are few in number, but we've got a full stoker crew, which is why I need you all when we sail. Each of you have had a specific job to do during normal times, but now I will be expecting all of you to be aware of each other to assist if you are able to do. Once the hectic hour is over and we're full away again, we can split down into modified cruise watches as I've already explained to you all. Engineer Ottley! You will be my relief, to be relieved by the 4th. You electricians will need to work watch and watch about as per my detailed instructions." John commanded, before he despatched them to their places and for him to act on the first telegraph order.

Soon the hectic hour had passed with much relief on the faces of the stokers, they sorted themselves out with who was on watch and who was to do what.

John took charge of the proceedings until he was happy with things before he left the engine room to Ottley.

"Any problems Dave, get a messenger to my cabin as quick as you can. Good luck!" John said, then looked around to see all was well before he left the engine room.

This was the first voyage with only 3 Engineer officers and 3 Deck officers on board, although with a full crew of men. It was also Sinclair's first full voyage as Captain, although Farquhar was on board to keep an eye on him.

"Engine room on cruise watch now Captain! All machinery in working order." John reported calmly on entering the bridge.

"Thank you Chief! I've got a load of trucks aft which might need extra venting due to them not being defuelled before loading." Sinclair advised.

"We have an extra vent already fitted down there for such

emergencies Captain. But I'll get the sprinkler system advanced in case." John replied, looking at the ship passing a line of others coming the other way.

"Looks like rush hour in the Straits today!" Farquhar opined, giving each passing ship the once over with his binoculars.

"Look First Mate! Each one is giving us a wide berth when they see our flag Bravo." Farquhar announced pointing to the ships, which suddenly seemed to find a curve in its course. Sinclair and John looked at the scene to make them chuckle.

"Tut tut! Ruddy cowards!" Sinclair said with mock disgust.

"Now you know what its like being a leper. Yet they wouldn't bat an eyelid when passing a warship, which is full of explosives at the best of times." Farquhar laughed, then reminded Sinclair to keep his eye on the bearings for him to change his course and speed.

John left the bridge and went to his cabin to get some rest before he was needed again.

Yet again the ship arrived back in Hong Kong for a few days before making her way homeward again. During the time whilst the ship was away Ho Ping was in Singapore attending a college, who would be required to take charge of the engine room for the next return trip, with John keeping an eye on him.

By the time the 4th return voyage was completed, every engineer or deck officer were much more learned and more capable of handling things than they would have been before.

"Right then Ho Ping! No shore leave for you today so lets get your task book seen to, for me to make my recommendations to the examination board." John advised, as they entered his cabin for John to make his assessments.

"All ready for you Chief! Here's your book back." Ho Ping said with his usual grin.

It took him a good hour whilst Ho Ping just sat there looking out the porthole watching the world go by in the dockyard.

"Right then Ho Ping! Get yourself changed into clean tropicals. The moderator of the examination board is an old friend of mine who's very strict on examinations. I'm coming with you so I'll meet you on the gangway in 20 minutes. We've got a tilley coming to pick us up, so don't forget to bring your drawings along with any other workbooks. Go now and put your best uniform on." John advised, ushering Ho Ping out of this cabin.

'*His practical is spot on, his drawings too. Shame about his calculus and maths though. Let's hope Fergus will pick up on the fact he was the original engineer on the ship in the first place.*' John whispered, as he too got himself all spick and span for the ordeal that lay before both engineers.

Arriving at the venue for the examination they found there were other officers nervously waiting for their exams too, although John and Ho Ping were the only engineer officers.

When it was Ho Ping's turn, John was required to accompany him, and whilst Ho Ping stood at a desk John went over to hand his recommendations to the presiding examiner.

"Morning Fergus! Glad you're back with us again." John greeted.

"Hello John! Yes, am back for my last look so to speak."

"Leaving us already then?"

"Flying back to Blighty in a week or so. Have a hand-over to get through though."

"Never mind. Hope to see you later today on board if you care to join us."

"Glad to John, now down to business. 2nd engineer Ho Ping!" McPhee said authoritatively, commencing to test the engineering knowledge of Ho Ping, who somehow still managed to keep his smile all the way through the difficult parts of the questions.

Finally after one hour of questions and answers Ho Ping was asked to leave the room for the deliberations. This was where John's personal eyewitness accounts were taken into consideration along with other background details, which could influence the decision-making.

John was asked to bring Ho Ping back in to the room.

"Engineer Ho Ping! It is the decision of this board you have done enough to prove you have the capabilities of a Chief Engineer in the tradition of British Engineers. On the other side of the coin, you will need to improve your theoretical skills. For that very reason we can only recommend you be promoted to acting Chief Engineer pending a further theoretical test in 6 months. If you pass this test then we will recommend you to become a full Chief Engineer.

As far as you're concerned acting Chief Engineer Grey, due to your work in getting Ho Ping to the standard which only a credited Chief could do, we will recommend you now have the full title of Chief Engineer as of today. Congratulations to you both on a splendid achievement."

McPhee stated pleasantly.

John looked at Ho Ping's ever-smiling face then to the now big smile on McPhee, before he too felt somehow elated, as he could feel the goose bumps forming on his arms and legs.

"Thank you gentlemen! I will go home a happy man now." Ho Ping said, turning to and shook John's hand.

"You helped me John Grey, and I you. Now we are both Chiefs!" Ho Ping said with gratitude and with a grin from ear to ear, left the room.

"That was a sneaky thing to do Fergus! Why didn't you tell me I was up for the turkey shoot too!"

"Now that would have been favouritism dear boy. You had to come in blind so to speak, for the rest of us to see if you really did provide us with another Chief Engineer. Besides, if you had known, you would not have prepared yourself as well as you did." McPhee said with a smile, as the other examination officers came and shook John's hand in congratulations.

John thanked everybody as he left, but confirmed with McPhee about the get together later.

"Shan't miss it for the world dear boy. See you later." McPhee promised, as John climbed back into his tilley to go back to his ship.

'That's my side of the deal completed. Now let's see Stafford come up with their end." John whispered to himself, walking across the gangway to meet up with Larter.

"How did it go John? Ho Ping got promoted?" Larter asked cheerfully.

"Yes, but only an acting Chief." John said glumly.

"But then I got promoted to a full Chief, and Fergus McPhee is coming over to celebrate with us later." he added happily.

"Congratulations John! You've finally made it then. Wait until Andy hears of this. Lets go get him and have a swift run ashore before McPhee calls." Larter said with jubilation, feeling very happy for John.

"What's all the commotion on the gangway then?" Sinclair demanded roughly.

"Andy! John's got promoted at last. His 2nd is now Acting Chief, but John is now the big white Chief, or in his case the small white Chief. Isn't that great!" Larter said with enthusiasm.

It was Sinclair's turn to congratulate John, and by putting one of his big arms round his shoulders gave him a playful hug.

"Well done John. Now you'll be able to go and tell Cresswell and co where to get off." Sinclair said with glee.

"Sod the duty work detail, this calls for a drink or three. C'mon lets get down to the Armada club to limber up before McPhee calls on us later." Larter suggested, which the others instantly accepted.

When they arrived at the seemingly always busy club, they managed to find an empty spot up on the veranda where they decided to have their drinks.

"So much for me getting Ho Ping promoted. They must have known all about it beforehand, as I certainly posed some very naughty questions just as Happy Day and the late Jim Gregson did to me. Perhaps its all politics I don't know, but at least Ho Ping really deserves his recognition." John stated emphatically.

"Well whatever! Time for a quiet hooley. Tiger tops as the chaser for a good tot of Nelson's blood." Sinclair suggested, as he went over to the beer washed bar and brought back a large tray of drinks.

All three of them enjoyed their time which seemed to steal away from them.

"Hey, it's time we went back on board to meet old misery guts McPhee." Sinclair announced with alarm when he looked at his watch.

"Yes! Mustn't keep our patron waiting on the gangway. Better get a bottle of Mr Dimple on the way out or he'll be even more a misery guts." John stated, as they got up and left the now even more crowded bar.

"Popular place that is, on account it overlooks the floodlit football ground. Many a ships' team have squared off on that field for whatever trophy is going, but at least everybody comes back here to either celebrate or drown their sorrows. All in good fun I might add too." Sinclair volunteered, just as the floodlights flickered into life.

The 3 friends scrambled back over the gangway and made their way into the saloon to settle themselves down before McPhee's visit.

John went over to speak to the steward, giving him a large bottle of Dimple whiskey and a crate of Tiger lager to serve them.

"Usual fee Chief?" the steward asked cheekily.

"Oh go on then. One double and 2 bottles. Mind you though, we'll want some scran later on. Maybe king prawns, egg fu yung dan, with the usual trimmings all round. See to it will you steward."

"Just give me the nod Chief and it will be on your lap in no time." the steward replied cheerfully.

John sat down with the tray of drinks to enjoy the company of his friends. The other officers knew not to interfere with their privacy, but envied them from their own little worlds.

"Chief engineer Grey! Stand up and meet your patron!" a booming Scottish voice said loudly, invading the hushed quietness of the saloon.

John turned round to see McPhee approach them looking magnificent in the full regalia of his Scottish ancestry.

McPhee turned all the heads as he breezed past them before stopping at the table, as John stood to greet him.

"Welcome aboard Fergus! You certainly look the business. Come, sit with us and enjoy a wee dram of your favourite tipple." John greeted, as he signalled over to the steward to provide for them.

"Chief Engineer John Grey! I have two boxes to give you, although one of them has Ho Ping's name on it. Due to the euphoria of the moment, the examination board forgot to give you and Ho Ping these." McPhee announced loftily, making all the other officers in the saloon take notice.

John took hold of the first parcel, which bore his name then carefully opened it in front of his friends.

It was a dark blue box with gold lettering on it, which stated John's name, his rank and the date. When he opened it he saw a solid silver wheel spanner painted white nestling next to a gold one. He took them both out and examined them slowly, before holding them up for everybody to see.

"Those are part of your badge of office John. The white one to match your new boiler suit, and the other one, solid gold, which I suggest you keep somewhere safe. The other box is for Ho Ping, which is a silver one denoting he's an acting Chief." McPhee advised.

John looked at them, mumbling that whilst he never got his silver one, never-the-less these would more than make up for it.

Sinclair started to sing and prompted the others in the saloon to sing 'for he's a jolly good fellow', before somebody asked John for a speech.

John made a short modest speech which made most of the listeners sit back to reflect on their own promotion efforts, before they all clapped heartily in response.

The small gathering progressed well into the evening before John nodded again to the steward to bring on the food.

"It seems as if the local nosh, makan, or scran whichever you care to name it, is just as tasty as you'd get anywhere around here. Glad we're here to enjoy it first hand." Sinclair mumbled with his face puffed out with the delicious food. The smell made the others in the saloon jealous for them to leave to go get their own.

During all this time McPhee was telling them about various news items concerning the shipping companies and what was happening in general in the shipping world.

"So at the end of the day, Parfitt and his sidekick Stafford knew of all this even before they stuck me with the last few months of sheer hell. The crafty bastards." John opined. Which was generally acknowledged as the truth.

"Still never mind John. You're taken off the *Tsun Wan's* list of crew and are just like me at the moment. Both without a billet, with about a week for me to get home for a long rest." McPhee declared.

John remembered the deal he made with Stafford and Parfitt and told the others about it, which was greeted cheerfully, yet somehow Larter and Sinclair seemed to be taken aback by the news considering they too were looking for their leave as well.

McPhee sensed the feeling of disappointment from Larter and Sinclair, and told them they too would be on their way home, just as soon as a relief was found. He even prodded their own pride by telling them they were too good to find an instant relief, which seemed to do the trick, although John knew deep inside him that was not really the case.

"Whatever the outcome, we'll all be home around the same time." John said cheerfully, managing to rally the party spirit again.

"Amen to all that! Maybe I'll get my golden sextant from Farquhar before I go, if there's such a thing." Sinclair said with renewed cheerfulness.

"Aye, and me a ruddy golden Morse key." Larter quipped.

"There you go. Must go now John, but contact me sometime in the next few days, as we'll have a 'farewell to Singapore' party before I fly home again. Incidentally and sorry I forgot, all 3 of your will be flying home very soon, although I don't know if all together. It all depends on the reliefs, given that John's already got his." McPhee announced, as he stood and weaved his way through the tables of the saloon. John went after him and accompanied him to the gangway.

"My tilley is waiting for me John. You get back in there and enjoy the rest of the evening. Never mind about your 2 friends, as I've already told you in Hong Kong. Must go now." McPhee said with a hiccup, and staggered over the gangway holding on to the ropes as he went.

John waved to him as he left in a cloud of dust, before returning to the saloon, and carried on where he left off.

"Isn't it about time we had the girls to call on us?" Sinclair asked, quaffing yet another pint in quick time.

"Judging by your intake Andy, you'd be in no fit state to answer to the demands of your girl." John sniggered.

"Dinna ye fash yersel on that score laddie!" Sinclair said in his broad Scottish accent, slumping down into his chair.

"It appears that McPhee's sporran or whatever has suddenly reminded Andy about his clan back home, let alone the clan he hopes to raise out here." Larter chuckled, as both he and John struggled to get Sinclair to his feet.

"Better we get him turned in first, before we get his girl on board. Imagine the surprise he'll have when he wakes up in the morning." John said with an impish grin on his face.

"Yeah! Let's do it. C'mon John, you get his feet and I'll get the rest." Larter agreed as they struggled to carry the big body of their friend out of the saloon and into his cabin.

"We'll wait until she arrives, to make sure all is well." Larter advised, as he used the cabin phone and dialled the bar.
Soon all 3 girls arrived for Sinclair's girl to settle down next to her sleeping giant.

"Leave by 6.30 or he'll be in trouble." John whispered, tiptoeing out of Sinclair's cabin and went to join the others.

"Sleeping beauty is okay, now lets get down to business again why don't we." John stated, as his girl sat gently on his lap.

CHAPTER XXVIII

Another Berth

"**J**ohn, I've just received confirmation of your UK leave and flight details. Come to my office after lunch and we'll get you sorted." Soon advised.

"What about Andy and Bruce? " John asked anxiously.

"They've been mentioned too, but I can't remember the exact details. Kindly inform them for me if you will. Must dash to get these things organised." Soon said with a nod.

"Thanks Kim! On my way." John replied gratefully, then carried on his way to the saloon.

"Bruce! I've just got word about our UK leave. If you see Andy before I do tell him about it, but be in Kim's office immediately after lunch. See you later!" John said, just as he met up with Larter.

"Why that's just great! On my way now dear Chief." Larter responded cheerfully.

John made his way towards the engine room to speak with Ho Ping, who was in the middle of an instructional period.

"Sorry to interrupt Chief, but I've got until 1600 to wind up our hand over. Not that it will take long, only it's something that has to be done and all by the book so to speak."

"I'll come to see you after lunch and before I shoot ashore, John." Ho Ping advised.

"Better make it around 1400, on account I've got to muster in the Pursers office before then."

"It sounds as if you've got your leave notice then John. Okay, I'll wait for you in the saloon." Ho Ping replied with his famous infectious smile.

"Cheers Chief!" John sighed as he left the engine room quickly in case some engineer collared him with a few inane questions.

John met his friends in the dining room and after their meal they trooped down to see Soon, who was waiting patiently for them.

"Come in gentlemen, glad you all arrived together as it makes my task much easier." Soon said amiably. After the friends sat down taking their ease, he explained the procedures giving details of their travel back to Britain.

"Can't you get us on the same plane, given there's only 2 days between the 3 of us?" John asked.

"Yes Kim. Can't you wangle it so we travel home together. I dare say John wouldn't mind waiting an extra day or so, would you John!" Sinclair asked.

"I don't mind waiting Kim, considering I'm supposed to be on leave anyway."

"It's not as simple as that. Once the time arrives for John to leave, after then he's not covered by our insurance. He would have to pay his own way home is yet another reason." Soon stressed.

"Kim, you've got our medical records there, are John's jabs in order or does he need a booster which takes two days to settle anyway?" Larter asked offhandedly.

"What about the fact John's already been home and as such he forfeits a day's leave anyway?" Sinclair asked cagily.

Soon looked at the 3 friends then shook his head slowly, looking through John's record.

"His medical records are in order, but I suppose we could drop a day from his wages and main leave. But then, he'd still fall foul of the accommodation let alone the company insurance factors. Sorry gentlemen, as much I'd love to, there's no possible way that I can swing this to help you. John would have to wait for you in England." Soon said apologetically.

"It's okay Kim, we understand. It just means we've got less time with the girls to say goodbye to them than we thought. Did you say that Mr McPhee will be on the same flight Kim?" John asked swiftly.

"Again I'm sorry I can't help you John, as I don't have the passenger flight information. All I can give you are your travel documents, your outstanding pay along with your leave pay. The other thing that I can tell you and its straight from Stafford, is that you will not be required to return to the *Tsun Wan* and that you will be re-allocated another berth somewhere else."

"That sounds about right Kim. You can't have 2 Chief Engineers on any ship let alone on a small one like the *Tsun Wan*. Oh well, looks as if I'd better get myself organised for my trip home now. When do you want me to sign for my travel warrant Kim!" John responded philosophically.

"Right now if you don't mind. Don't forget your plane is due to leave Changi airport around 1100 tomorrow. I'll see you have transport to take you there in good time. In the meantime I suggest you get ashore and say your farewells. Just sign this paper and take this envelope." Soon said sadly.

"I've got enough money to travel with Kim, but I'll take the travel documents. Kindly arrange a banker's draft for me and send it to my home address, in case I lose it. Can't be too careful these days." John sighed as he signed the piece of paper and got his package.

"I'll get it done this afternoon John. Have a good run ashore now and I'll see you around 0830 in the morning." Soon concluded as he rose from his table and shook Johns' hand.

"You're a good man Kim Soon." John stated, as he returned the handshake and left with his 2 pals.

"There you are John! Kim's as good as told your future, so don't be sad about it. Anyway, lets get ashore and paint the town any damn colour you choose." Sinclair said cheerfully.

"Got to see Ho Ping and Ottley first before I go anywhere, so lets make it around 1600. Bruce would you be kind enough to phone McPhee's office and find out if he's on this plane too?"

"Certainly John. Let you know later." Larter stated as the 3 friends left Soon's office and made their separate ways.

The friends piled into a taxi which took them out of the dockyard and into the village of Sembawang then to the last bar in the block of several, where they were to meet up with their girl friends.

"I'm not looking forward to this bit as it's going to be a very sad time for the girls, even though they already know this day was coming." John said bitterly.

"They all knew from the be ginning what the score was, but you're the only one that's not committed yourself to your girl, as we are. Both of us have the same intention on remaining out here, or at least return soonest, and with Kim Soon make honest women of them. So we don't envy you on that one iota John." Larter replied softly.

When they arrived t their usual 'reserved' seats, the girls came over with the drinks and sat beside their partner to chat.

"We weren't expecting you boys until tomorrow, maybe your ship came in early?" one of the girls asked.

"Something like that!" Sinclair said quietly, which made the girls sense there was something wrong for the boys to look so glum. John's girl looked into his face for a moment

"What's the matter with my John? Why so sad?" she asked quietly.

John cleared his throat and told them of his unexpectedly early departure in the morning.

This news stunned the girls into silence for a moment until the girls started to weep into their hands, and for the friends to put a comforting arm around their respective partner. The Proprietor of the bar and Kim Soon's partner came over to see what was the matter for her friends to weep. When they were told, the Proprietor told Kim Soon's partner to take a bottle of whiskey from the store and give it the friends, telling them it was a parting gift from him.

Larter thanked the man but told him it was John going this time, with them next but didn't know when.

"Okay! You have been my best customers for a long time now and I'll give another bottle then." He replied, sitting down at an adjoining table to serve them their drinks.

"But you can't go home just yet John, your tour of duty isn't over yet." She whispered, with tears rolling down her cheeks.

"Maybe not for the Royal Navy boys, but we're Merchant

sailors doing a different job to theirs. You should know that and for you to know that this would happen one day." He said softly, holding her close and comforting her as best he could.

"That's not fair! I was hoping to have another little while with you so I can prepare myself." She said, wiping her face dry in a fresh serviette.

"The girls can have the rest of the day off to be with you, but they must return for opening time in the morning." The Proprietor announced, removing the empty whiskey bottle then gently ushering them out of the bar.

Kim Soon's partner and the Proprietor waved to them as they left in a speeding taxi towards the bright lights of Singapore city. It was a night for them all to remember, yet just one more memory in John's mind to be stored and treasured despite the sad farewell and parting with his Singapore Girl.

"Well here we are John! Have a good flight, and remember what we talked about. Keep in touch." Sinclair said glumly, as did Larter.

"Yes John, don't worry about your girlfriend. She's my girl's sister and I'll see she doesn't come to any harm. Maybe you'll come back from your college days to join the rest of us, but she'll be far too busy here to be able to get over you. Take care and drop us a line some time, care of the *Tsun Wan*!" Soon said gently as they all shook John's hand in farewell.

"Look here's your old friend McPhee to keep you company. No doubt Mr Dimple will accompany you most of the way as well. And do us a favour John, if you get on the *Duke of Lancaster* ferry from Heysham go tell the bosun he couldn't sail a wee..." Sinclair said with jollity.

"Boat in a bath tub!" John and Larter said in unison.

John picked up his heavy suitcase and waved to goodbye to his friends as he walked across the tarmac alongside McPhee.

"Oh well, 1 down 2 to go!" Larter said stoically, watching the plane lift up into the cloudless sky and disappear into the sunlight.

"Unfasten your seatbelts. Drinks will be served shortly." came the plummy voice as John kept looking down at the world speeding past him.

'I wonder what's going to happen to the Tsun Wan and the crew.' He muttered, but got a surprised look from McPhee.

"Still talking to yourself John! Once you start answering back then they'll be taking you away to the funny farm." McPhee said with a grin, offering John a full glass of whiskey.

"Here's to the *Tsun Wan* and all who won't be sailing on her." McPhee added, clinking their glasses gently before downing their drink in one go.

"Yes, Fergus, meant to ask you about that." John asked with intrigue, starting a long and meaningful conversation that seemed to last all the way back to Britain.

John watched McPhee's lips move and hearing his voice but his mind was with his Singapore girl, the life he left behind with his two friends now far away, and at the prospect of his happy homecoming once more.

'I wonder what's going to happen during my leave this time?' he thought, stepping off the plane and onto the soil of the 'Sceptred Islands' of Great Britain.

Perfumed Dragons is the eighth book within the epic *Adventures of John Grey* series, which comprises of:

A Fatal Encounter
The Black Rose
The Lost Legion
Fresh Water
A Beach Party
Ice Mountains
The Repulse Bay
Perfumed Dragons
Silver Oak Leaves
Future Homes

Also by the same author
Moreland and Other Stories

All published by Guaranteed Books, an imprint of
www.theguaranteedpartnership.com